ASCENT

The Inferno Trilogy
Book Three

ASCENT

A. R. Nicole

Published by

PINECONE PUBLISHING
PineConePublishing.com
ARNicole.com
AR@ARNicole.com
Follow on Twitter @ARNicoleBooks, Pinterest, and Facebook

Cover and Interior Design: Nick Zelinger, NZGraphics.com
Editor: Barb Wilson, EditPartner.com
Book Shepherd: Judith Briles, TheBookShepherd.com

ISBN: 978-1-7320699-4-7 (print)
ISBN: 978-1-7320699-5-4 (e-book)
Library of Congress Control Number: 2019932328

First Edition

Printed in the United States of America

For My Grandfather:
You loved me,
You worried about me,
You cared for me as only a grandfather can.

I miss you, Grandpa Eugene.
I wish you could have been here to see this.

Books by A. R. Nicole

The Inferno Trilogy
Book One: Descent (2018)
Book Two: Torment (Spring 2019)
Book Three: Ascent (Summer 2019)

**Watch for The Aftershock Series
Coming in 2020**

BOOK THREE

ASCENT

PROLOGUE

I held her in my arms that night, that night when I brought her here. She won't stay long. She can't. We can't. It's the safest place for now. Besides, I can't really have her. Not yet. But soon…

They'll try to find her. I know they will. It won't take them long to know she's missing. But they won't find her. No one will find her. She's mine. She's finally mine.

They will not take her from me.

In the darkness, Dante ran his fingers through his beloved's hair. He smiled. It felt like silk.

Soon, she'll dress in nothing else…if I let her wear anything at all.

1

LOGAN CHUCKLED TO himself in the backseat of the SUV. Thank God Blake was driving. They'd be dead by now if Gabriel had managed to get behind the wheel. They were headed south, the front fender pointing toward a now very familiar neighborhood.

Weren't we just here?, he mused sarcastically.

He and Blake had been able to hold Ryder captive at his desk until just after four o'clock in the afternoon. The young detective had been more than his usual pain-in-the-ass self, agitated and in a blatantly foul mood. He'd also spent the vast majority of the day staring at his cell phone, at one point begging the thing to chirp before he'd hurled it into the wall.

Nolan had taken it away from him, for the safety of the poor battered machine. Logan could see Gabriel staring at the bulge in Nolan's right pocket, actively devising a plan to get it back before they got to their destination.

"Would you stop staring at his pants, Ryder? It's getting a little awkward back here," Logan said with a chuckle.

"If he'd give me the damned phone back, I wouldn't have to," came the mumbled reply.

"Gabe, we're partners, but we're not that close. I know you're impressed, buddy, but stop staring," Nolan said, elbowing him in the ribs across the center console.

"Give me my fucking phone, Blake."

"When we stop."

"Fuck you."

Nolan shrugged and threw the right blinker on as they neared the traffic light. Gabriel sulked in the passenger seat until they pulled up outside the bungalow. Logan sighed and grabbed each of them by the shoulder.

"All right you two, kiss and make up. I don't need you trying to kill each other in there while lover-boy is trying to make nice."

Gabriel glared at him through the rearview mirror but kept quiet. Instead, he held his hand out for his phone, which Nolan palmed him without another word. Gabriel and Blake followed him up the front steps, each perching on the porch railing as Logan rang the doorbell.

Instantly there was movement behind it. Frantic movement. When the door creaked open, instead of the guilty blue eyes the trio expected to find, Noah Mason's worried face appeared. The deep lines in the young man's forehead instantly softened, and he let out a long breath he hadn't realized he'd been holding.

"Oh, thank God. You must have heard. Come in, come in," he said, ushering them inside.

Um, what?

What the hell does that mean?

What's wrong with him?

The three detectives glanced back and forth among themselves, each wondering what kind of news could possibly have Noah so agitated in the middle of the afternoon. They shuffled into the living room without a word.

Within seconds of the door closing, Barbara Parker came sprinting out of the kitchen, hot tea in hand, looking equally haggard.

Gabriel's blood froze. Something was very wrong here.

Where is Grayson?

Noah and Barbara sat huddled together on the couch, looking at the trio expectantly. Several awkward moments of silence passed with shoes scuffing nervously across the wooden floor and hands shoved deeply inside coat pockets. No one wanted to speak first. It didn't take long for Noah to decide he'd finally had enough and break the silence.

"Well?" he asked in an agitated tone. "Have you heard from her?"

The three detectives again looked looked at each other, confused.

Logan spoke first. "Have we heard from who, Mason?"

"So, you haven't heard from her either?"

Noah looked directly at Gabriel. The detective's face was like stone. No expression. No hint of life in his eyes. It was like he'd already disappeared inside his own head.

"From who?" Logan repeated.

"From Grayson, of course!" Babs shouted. "She didn't come home. She's not at work. Where is she?"

"She didn't come home?" Gabriel asked flatly.

Noah shivered at the blackness creeping into the young man's eyes.

"No, she didn't, genius," Barbara spat back. "No one's seen her since yesterday."

Noah laid a hand on her arm and tried desperately to keep the fear out of his own voice. "She didn't come home. She's not at work. Never showed up for rounds with her juniors or for the OR today. I parked next to her 4Runner this morning in the parking deck. We were holding out hope that she was with the three of you at the department somehow. We…we were trying to not panic…"

"Her car's in the deck? At the hospital?" Blake asked, eyebrows raised.

"Yeah. I checked on her badge with security. Gave them a song and dance about how she lost it and was too busy to come down and ask herself. It was last used to access the main building offices after midnight, then nothing."

"You haven't heard from her at all today?" Logan asked.

"No. And she's not picking up her phone. It goes straight to voicemail, like it's turned off. Have you?" Noah responded.

The three detectives shook their heads.

"Did you call the station?" Logan pressed.

"No," Noah said, shaking his head dejectedly. "She'd told me that she was going down to see you gents last night. I...I just figured she was with you and so I didn't worry. Seems rather stupid now..." He drifted off.

Gabriel took out his phone and looked at the screen again. No messages. No missed calls. Nothing.

"Something's wrong, guys," Blake whispered to the wall.

"Yeah, no shit," Logan said.

Gabriel walked to the front window, leaning against the frame for support. Four sets of worried eyes followed him. He didn't speak. He stayed silent.

"Try her again," Logan said, nodding at the pair on the couch.

Noah took out his cell phone and dialed. He lowered it a few seconds later, shaking his head.

"Nothing. It goes straight to voicemail."

"She's not going to answer," Gabriel mumbled. "He has her."

"What? Who has her?" Blake asked, craning his head around to look at this partner.

"Cain. He took her."

"Took her? Like, kidnapped her?"

He nodded.

"Aw, goddamn it, girlie," Blake groaned, pulling out his cell phone and stepping over to the door. He put the phone up to his ear and waited.

"Hey, captain? It's Nolan. Yeah, we've got a problem here. Grayson Carter is missing... That's right. We need to put a BOLO out on a guy named Douglas Cain and his car."

Harrison grabbed the phone from him. "And add on a search warrant for this piece of shit's apartment or wherever he lives... Yeah. Yes, captain, it's Logan... No, we're sure. She didn't show up this morning but her car is at the hospital...Sure, yeah, a warrant for the office would help, too. Thanks."

Harrison eyed Gabriel as he handed the phone back to Nolan. "Captain's getting us warrants for the house, the car, his office, and whatever we want. It's just going to take time."

"We don't have time," Ryder spat back, spinning away from the window and stalking toward the staircase. "He's taken her, and he's already at least a half day ahead of us."

He stormed up the stairs and to her room, nearly forcing the door off its hinges. It smelled of her. He could see her sleeping on her bed, curled up underneath her comforter. He closed his eyes. This was not supposed to happen.

What was she thinking? I should've gone after her last night. I knew I should have gone after her. I should have called this morning to make sure she'd stay at home.

He desperately looked around the room for any real sign of her. There wasn't one.

Goddamn it, Grayson...

The sound of a throat clearing by the door snapped him back into reality. Ryder found himself standing over her bed, her sheets fisted in his hands.

Noah Mason was leaning against the door jamb, looking at him. "You know, as sick as he is, Cain is right about one thing. She is precious, detective."

"I know."

"No, I don't think you do," he countered, pushing off the wall and walking into the room. "You've known her, what, maybe two months? You have no idea. You know nothing about her. You've seen her beaten up and pushed around and stalked like an animal. You've seen her weak."

"Weak? Are you fucking kidding me?" *I'm not in the mood for this, Mason.*

"No, I'm not. You have no..."

"Enough!" Ryder's eyes blazed. "It doesn't matter how I've seen her. It doesn't matter what or how much I know about her. Weak or not, that son of a bitch has her. I'm bringing her back. And for the fucking record, Grayson weak can put most men on their knees."

Noah nodded, stepping up to the bed beside him. "She's the best thing to come into my life, Ryder, and she's not here. She's got to be fecking scared out of her bloody mind."

Gabriel clenched and unclenched his fists in the fabric. He didn't respond.

Noah glanced out the window at the afternoon sky. "Find her, detective. You find her, and you bring her back to us. And then, when she's safe, you bring Cain to me."

Gabriel quirked his eye at the man to his left and chuckled. "What the hell for?"

"I'm going to kill him," Noah said bitterly.

There was no hint of mirth in the young doctor's eyes. Ryder could see that much. Mason had every intention of killing the man, and from the look on his face, he already knew exactly how he was going to do it.

Forget it, kid. You're not going to get the chance.

"No," Gabriel responded coolly.

"No what?"

"No, I'm not bringing Cain to you," he replied. "I'm going to kill the son of a bitch the second I lay eyes on him. Myself."

"Nobody's fucking killing anybody!" Blake hissed from the doorway. "I don't need my partner in fucking prison and Mason, you wouldn't last five minutes. Now, both of you get your asses downstairs. Noah, stay here in case she calls. Keep trying her cell. Gabriel. Car. Now."

Blake grabbed his partner by the collar and shoved him downstairs, not waiting for either of them to reply.

2

THE GRAY HAZE faded in and out, darker and lighter, deeper and shallower.

No matter how much she struggled against it, she kept slipping back into the darkness, then bubbling back up into the light. This wasn't like before, like the fog in the hospital after Greg Harlan had attacked her. She felt seasick, tossed about and manipulated by the new cocktail of drugs slinking through her veins. There was too much, then too little, then too much again. She desperately needed something to hold onto.

Grayson forced herself back up toward the waiting light. She was so close this time. She could feel the edges of the haze. They were just a fingerbreadth away.

Closer, closer…

She felt the weight of her head loll back onto something scratchy. Her eyelids each felt as if they weighed a hundred pounds, but she forced them open. The brightness of the overhead lights was blinding and painful, and she slammed them shut in protest. Then, hating the darkness even more, she forced them back open, focusing on whatever was directly on top of her.

Gray popcorn ceiling tiles met her gaze. She swung her head to the right. The scratchy thing grated against her cheek. Gray walls, the same color as the ceiling. She swung to the left. More gray walls, with gray pipes coming from the ceiling and passing uninterrupted into the floor. She pushed herself up as much as she could manage, which wasn't much, and looked forward.

More gray walls. And a gray door without windows, only a peephole. She tried to sit up, but something clamped down around her, stopping her.

Wait, why can't I sit up?

Grayson looked toward her right wrist, and her eyes widened. Her blood turned to ice. The hair on the back of her neck screamed as it shot straight on end in panic.

Beige fabric was wrapped around her wrist and lower forearm. It disappeared off the top corner of a rather small bed frame. She tugged gently and felt the sharp endpoint.

Restraints.

She twisted her head around to look at her left wrist. Same thing.

She strained as much as she could to get a look at her feet. Ditto and ditto. Same beige straps, each one snaking off the end of the well-worn mattress.

Her head swam as she dropped back on the scratchy pillow. Her eyes focused on her right arm. A line of bruises and small black circles tracked up her pale skin, all neatly in a row.

Track marks.

Holy shit, I'm strapped down in four-point restraints. Oh my God, oh my God...I've been drugged and restrained!

Her heart was racing up in her throat. She felt the thundering of blood in her ears and slammed her eyes closed again. A new wave of nausea roiled up in her stomach. She could taste the sour bile in the back of her throat.

It all came flooding back. The back stairway. The low voice. Something over her mouth. That voice...

Snap out of it!

Her own voice screamed inside her head, straining desperately to be heard over the roar of the blood rushing to her ears.

If you don't stay calm, you're never getting out of here! Now breathe...focus...

She complied, one long shaky breath in and out, eyes closed.

Again. Breathe.

One more long shaky breath, in and out.

Grayson forced her eyes to open, then calmly and systematically took in her surroundings again. Four gray walls, one with piping. A ceiling with individual popcorn tiles, no air ducts. Two sets of power outlets that she could see. Desk lamps set on the floor with high wattage light bulbs. Cement floors. One door directly in front of her, another one directly behind her if she craned her head back far enough. No windows.

Okay, now me...

The restraints were obvious. She was still in her clothes from the day before. Her coat was gone. A blanket was draped haphazardly over her lower body. She looked over to the corner and noticed two stacks of fabric, one white and the other vaguely green.

Scrubs? And towels?

Her badge had disappeared from her hip, and she couldn't feel her cell phone in her back pocket.

Shit, shit! Where is it? Even if I figure out where the hell I am, I can't call for help...

The sound of keys jingling at the door lock in front of her snapped her out of her own head. Grayson craned her neck up as much as her positioning would allow and watched the door open.

Douglas Cain smiled down at her as he sauntered through the doorway, a tray full of food in his hands. He slid up to the side of the twin bed and set it down onto a small black card table in the corner, just out of his captive's peripheral vision. He looked her over from head to toe, drinking her in, and then sat down on the edge of the bed.

Grayson's abdominal muscles instantly clenched, desperate to keep away from his lecherous eyes.

"Well, well, my Beatrice, you're awake. How wonderful."

Cain casually started undoing her restraints, one at a time. The instant her right arm was free, Grayson swung at him, but she was too weak, too drugged, and at a suboptimal angle. The moment she pushed herself up, her head spun from the ether.

Cain caught her wrist in his hand to keep her from scraping against the wall and held onto it. She tried to pull away, but it took all of her strength just to keep her eyes open.

"Tsk, tsk," he scolded, looking down on her with a fire brewing in his eyes. "That's not very nice. You shouldn't do such nasty things. Keep that up, and I'll have to put these straps back on."

Grayson instantly stopped struggling against him. Being alone in a room with Douglas Cain was one thing. Being alone in a room with him while strapped down and helpless was much, much worse.

He waited a moment, poised over her cowering frame, watching her panicked face. She watched the confident smirk wash over his face when the fight left her straining muscles. He seemed to know that he had her exactly where he wanted her.

Cain let go of her wrist and turned on the bed, undoing the remaining restraints around her ankles. The sound of the Velcro ripping apart was the only sound in the room. When he was finished, Grayson instantly scooted away from him on the bed, rubbing her wrists while eyeing him warily.

Cain just sat patiently, staring at her like a starving man.

When she hit a particularly sore spot on her wrist, she

glanced down, gasping at the needle marks she found near her veins.

No wonder my head feels horrible. How many times did he shoot me up with something? And with what...?

"What...what do you want with me?" she squeaked out.

"I want to keep you safe." He shrugged. "Would you like something to eat? You must be hungry."

He stood and pulled the small card table over to the bed. Grayson immediately recognized the scuffed-up tray and the black foam plates from the hospital cafeteria. A small wave of curious relief washed over her face.

Wait, am I still at St. Joe's?

Still, she eyed the tray's contents suspiciously.

"Oh, come now, I know what you like. It's perfectly safe. You have to be hungry," he encouraged.

Grayson didn't move.

"All right, I understand. The food will keep," he said, smiling warmly at her. "I know these accommodations are not ideal, but it's necessary for now."

"Necessary? Why?" she croaked. Her voice was dry and weak.

"You are precious, my Beatrice. I must keep my precious things safe."

"Let me go, Dr. Cain."

He leaned over her and brushed the back of his hand on her cheek. Grayson tried desperately to move away from him, but her head smacked back against concrete wall. She was at the edge of the bed and backed into the far wall. There was nowhere else to go.

"I just can't do that, Beatrice. Now, eat. The washroom is behind you. Get yourself cleaned up after you've eaten. There are clothes in the corner."

With that, he was gone, swiftly opening and closing the door behind him without a backward glance. She heard the deadbolt lock turn and the sound of his shoes retreating on concrete floors.

Grayson continued to rub the sore skin around her wrists as she shakily got up on her feet. She scowled at the tray in front or her. Eating was the last thing on her mind.

When she couldn't hear his footsteps any longer, she went to the door and tried the handle. It was locked, of course, but she twisted and pulled desperately, just to be sure. The view through the peephole was black. He'd put something over it.

She shuffled across the small room to the other door, which opened into a small washroom complete with stall shower, toilet, and vanity mirror. She wrinkled her nose.

What the hell? A prison cell with a halfway respectable on-call bathroom? What the hell is this place?

It was stocked with soap and shampoo and, sure enough, the two piles of fabric she'd seen before were bathroom towels and spare scrubs in her size. The edge of a small black form poking out from underneath the clean scrubs caught Grayson's attention, and she grabbed for it.

"Oh my God, it's my cell phone," she whispered.

She instantly turned it on and hit number one on speed dial, thrusting the box up to her ear. All she heard was light static. She looked at the screen and immediately saw why.

No signal. Not even a roaming signal.

Damn it!

She ended the call and looked at her battery. It still had more than an eighty-percent charge, but she knew it wouldn't last long if it kept searching for a cell signal. There was no Wi-Fi signal in range, either. She sighed heavily and quickly shut it off. She'd save the battery just in case she ever got out of here...wherever here was.

Grayson stripped out of her clothes and steamed up the little bathroom with hot water from the shower. Naked and trembling, she stared into the fogged-up mirror.

I've been kidnapped. I have no idea where I am in the hospital. I can't call for help. I'm at the mercy of a delusional serial killer. What in the hell am I going to do?

She slid down the wall onto the unforgiving concrete floor, curled up by the side of the shower, and cried.

3

THE SNOW WAS steadily falling outside, each individual flake glittering under the streetlights. No one was outside. It was too late and too cold for Cherry Creek socialites to be out slipping and sliding around in their Blahniks. They were all inside, behind closed doors, sipping on expensive wine and eyeing up each other's diamonds.

The cars parked outside on the street were starting to accumulate a soft white haze on their windshields. The outside of the condo complex was quiet. Graceful silhouettes passed silently in front of stylishly draped windows.

Some might have called the wintery scene beautiful, maybe even peaceful.

Ryder cocked his gun.

Logan motioned to the leader of the tactical squad lined up behind them. Eight cops in riot gear with automatic weapons, all ready to jump, nodded their readiness.

Now that's a beautiful sight.

The team silently entered into the lobby of the upscale building, motioning for the doorman to stay quiet and call for the elevator. The old man pressed a button on his console with a shaking index finger, then backed away toward the wall with his hands up. They all piled into the elevator, minus Nolan, who stayed behind to cover the doorman and the emergency exit at the end of the stairwell.

The squad fanned out on the fourteenth floor and lined the hallway. Ryder and Logan strode up the middle of the line to the door marked 1408, guns leveled. They each took a side of the door, leaning in to try to hear any movement behind it.

Nothing.

Harrison nodded briskly and Ryder reared back, splintering through the door with a single kick. The tactical team swarmed in around them, fanning out with guns drawn.

"Douglas Cain, Denver Police! Come out with your hands up!" he shouted, keeping his gun held high and trained in front of him.

The apartment was eerily silent. Nothing moved. Not even the air. The place was like a tomb.

The tactical unit started systematically working its way through the apartment, calling out "Clear!" when each room had been thoroughly searched. Harrison groped on the wall for a light switch. It took a few tries, but he found one and flipped it. Dim light from a chandelier floated down from the ceiling, and he pushed a button to increase it further.

"All right, this guy needs a different decorator…" he scoffed, his forehead wrinkling in disgust.

Gabriel spun around in a circle, taking in the full view of the great room. The room was beyond overdone. It was almost painful to look at. It was full of ornate tapestries, leather wingback chairs, and crystal chandeliers. A baby grand piano with a candelabra sat off to one side. A Botticelli reprint hung above an ornately decorated fireplace. Heavy drapes hung closed across the windows, obscuring the ambient light.

Judging from the dust accumulation on the piano, either the place hadn't been cleaned in a few days or no one had been home to play it.

"Is this guy serious?" Harrison asked, eyebrows raised as he fingered some of the tapestries hung on the wall. "What is all this shit?"

"It's an acquired taste," Ryder replied.

"Please tell me you don't share it."

"Only the piano," he replied, smirking. "Minus the candelabra."

"You would. I'm sure you play beautifully," Harrison shot back sarcastically. "Let's go back to the bedroom."

Gabriel nodded, following his former partner down the hallway toward the back room. The tactical team leader stood off to one side halfway down, gun lowered.

"All rooms are clear, sir. There's no one here."

Harrison nodded at him. Both men holstered their weapons and continued on toward the bedroom.

"Start checking walls, floors, pull up carpets. Look for any kind of hidden entryway," Ryder said.

The squad leader raised his eyebrows in protest.

"Just do it, Alan," Harrison muttered, nodding in agreement. "This fucker's weird enough to have a hidden room behind a bookcase or some shit like that."

The man nodded and made a circular motion above his head, signaling for his team to search the apartment again.

Ryder followed Harrison into the back bedroom and instantly felt his stomach heave. The four-poster bed, wall sconces, and Renaissance Italian artwork were a carbon copy of the main living room. The bed was sharply made. There wasn't a rug corner or a votive candle out of place. And there was a thin layer of dust on the overly elaborate dresser.

"He's not here," Ryder mumbled, walking slowly through the room. "He didn't bring her here."

"You're sure?"

He nodded. "He would've kept her in here. In this room. He would have lit the candles. He would have played the piano. It would've been a way to impress her."

"It's creepy."

"Not to him. This is how he sees himself. How he lives. This was all done to impress someone," Ryder said, running his hand along one of the bedposts. "Now we know who the someone was."

"And that?" Logan asked, pointing toward a large painting opposite the bed.

"It's a reproduction," Gabriel mumbled, not even bothering to look up from the floor.

"Even I know that, you ass," Harrison said, rolling his eyes. "I was talking about the resemblance."

Ryder raised his eyes and walked over toward where Logan was standing in front of a rather large reproduction of a non-Renaissance-era painting.

"Dante and Beatrice, 1884, Henry Holiday, London." Logan read the inscription from the small brass plate at the bottom of the frame. He shot a worried look at his partner, whose face was white and drawn.

The painting depicted a group of three young women toward the right, one dressed in red, one in blue, and one in yellow. The focus of the painting was clearly the young woman in the yellow dress. She was staring intently away from the fourth person in the painting, a middle-aged man leaning against the wall of a small bridge. He happened to be gazing right at her.

"Well, at least we know we have the right apartment."

Gabriel braced himself against the ornate fireplace mantel and swore under his breath. "He's been searching for her."

"Who's been searching for who?" Blake asked, walking through the bedroom door mid-conversation.

"Cain." Ryder scowled. "He's been searching for his Beatrice for years. That explains his personnel file. Find a candidate, find something unappealing or unacceptable, and dump her. But Grayson's perfect to him. Hence the escalation to murder."

"Oh. Oh…shit…" Nolan's eyes went wide when he followed Logan's gaze to the painting.

"If that's the case," Harrison interjected, "then he won't hurt her. He wants to keep her for himself, not kill her. It gives us time."

"Why wouldn't he just bring her here?" Nolan asked.

"I…I don't…" Ryder stalled, staring at the painting. "The last circle."

"Huh?"

"The last circle of hell. The ninth body. He hasn't killed enough people yet." Gabriel shook his head and leaned farther forward, his arms straining against his own dead weight. "He can't bring her here until he's killed the last one."

"Shit, this asshole's a piece of fucking work." Logan slammed his hand on the mantel, his frustration finally bubbling over.

Ryder winced. Logan never got upset unless things were desperate. Whether Cain intended to harm Grayson or not, they were running out of time.

"Blake, was there anything in the study?"

"I didn't see anything. No lists. No names. Nothing that would tell us who the next target is."

"Fuck." Harrison looked over at his former partner and shrugged. "I guess we'll bag and tag anything we find in there that pops out, replace the door, and keep a squad car on the apartment. If he comes back, we'll know."

Gabriel dejectedly shook his head. "He won't come back here until he's finished."

"Humor me then, okay? We've searched everywhere else we know to look. She's not here. We turned the goddamned hospital upside down. She's not there either. Where else would you have us watch?"

"A church."

Nolan threw his hands up in the air. "All right, Gabe, enough. It's too late at night for this two-word cloak-and-dagger bullshit. What is going on?"

But his partner was already halfway out the door.

"Apparently, we need to round up a list of churches." Harrison shrugged. "C'mon, bud, let's go or we're gonna get left behind. Wonder Boy is on a roll."

"Let's hope it lasts," Blake mumbled as he walked out of the bedroom. "Or we're not going to find her in time."

"Yeah, no shit," Logan replied, smirking. "Better hide the scotch."

4

TIME STARTED TO shift in the little gray room.

There was no clock on the wall, no alarm clock by the bed. She did have her cell phone, but she wasn't about to risk losing battery life by habitually turning the thing on and off every half hour to check the time. She'd turned it off at 3:18 p.m. on Thursday and had kept it off since then.

Grayson honestly wondered if Cain knew he'd left it out in the open. He hadn't taken her ID badge either. She'd found it covered in a thin layer of dust underneath her bed. She had a sneaking suspicion he knew she had them, which meant he knew how utterly useless they were to her. Still, it felt good to know both were tucked away, hidden inside the crappy little mattress, courtesy of a small rip that she'd made in between the squeaking springs.

Grayson kept herself as busy as she could, which involved pacing back and forth inside the small gray box, doing sit-ups on the concrete floor until her muscles screamed in protest, and lying face up on the uncomfortable mattress counting the pieces of popcorn on the ceiling. She stretched, tried to do yoga, and sang into the hazy darkness when she couldn't bear the silence a moment longer.

She'd finally given in and eaten a small bit of the food Cain had left behind for her. It had been cold and stale and mildly unpleasant, but it had been enough to keep her stomach under control. The bottled water he'd left behind had soothed her aching throat.

She sat dejectedly on the edge of the bed and wearily took the last few sips out of the bottle. There was part of her that immediately wanted more. The other part of her knew that the only way to get more was through *him*. The thought of drinking anything that came out of the black mold-lined faucet in the bathroom made her stomach lurch. She threw the bottle into the trash can.

Without warning, Cain abruptly burst into the room, carrying another tray of food and a pile of something under one arm. Grayson scooted back on the bed, her hands crossed in front of her and in plain sight. He seemed to brighten up at her submissive posture, the wildfire behind his eyes settling down to a faint glow. He set the tray down on the small table and set the pile down next to it. Grayson eyed it warily as he sat down next to her on the bed.

"A true change of clothes, my dear," he said, nodding in the direction of the pile, "and dinner."

"Thank you," she said quietly.

"Of course, my Beatrice." He nodded in reply.

"What time is it?"

"It's dinnertime."

"I know that. But what's the actual time?"

He looked quickly at his watch. "It's after eight o'clock."

"Okay. Why did you bring me clothes?"

"You need them."

"I have scrubs," she said, picking at the scrub pants she'd put on after her shower.

"Those are not clothes," he replied, wrinkling his nose in disgust. "And certainly not ones you should be wearing."

"I'm fine with these."

"Don't deny me, Beatrice," he warned gently, shaking his head.

The tone in his voice made Grayson close her mouth and swallow her sarcasm. It wasn't vicious, but it was demanding in the worst possible way. It was definitely a threat. She gently nodded instead.

And just like that, Cain was gone again.

It became a pattern. Twice a day, he opened the door, a tray of food and a change of clothes in tow. He would stay for a few minutes, taking in the confinements of the small cell while staring at her.

He tried to get her to eat in front of him. She always refused.

Each visit, she tried to coax something out of him. Where she was. What she was doing there. Why she couldn't see daylight. Why she couldn't have a clock in the room.

During one particular visit, she'd asked how long he was planning on keeping her locked up like an animal. It had provoked a reaction.

"You should not speak like that. It doesn't suit you."

"I'm asking you a question. You have me locked down here in a dungeon without sunlight or even a clock on the wall. I feel like a caged animal. I'm asking how long you plan on keeping me chained up like this."

He'd turned on her instantly, grabbing hold of her wrist to the point of searing pain. The bruises from the restraints were still fresh. She'd whimpered, trying in vain to rip herself out of his grasp.

"I am not treating you like an animal," he'd hissed forcefully. "I am keeping you safe. I cannot take you away, to where you truly belong, until things are done."

Grayson had fought back the urge to try to fight, knowing it would only provoke him even more, and instead kept a steady gaze on him.

"Why are things not safe for me? I don't understand." She'd looked down slowly at her wrist, keeping it still in his grasp. "You're hurting me."

Cain had instantly withdrawn his hand from her wrist and crossed the room to the small card table, putting as much distance between them as possible. He'd dumped out some ice into a cloth napkin and brought the compress back to her, placing it delicately on top of her already darkening skin without saying a word.

"Thank you."

He'd nodded at her and sighed. "Trust me, my Beatrice. Things are not safe for you now. But they will be. Soon. And then we can be together as we should be."

"But I don't..."

He'd held up a hand in front of her face, effectively silencing her. "There is nothing else to say on the matter. If you keep this up, I will have to pay a visit to Dr. Mason and young Miss Parker."

Grayson's breath had caught in her throat, her face instantly white. "You wouldn't," she'd whispered.

"Are you certain of that?"

She didn't answer. That meant no. That was the answer he'd wanted.

As he always did, Cain had removed the tray from earlier with him as he'd left the room.

By her piecemeal timekeeping, Cain had just left her the Friday night dinner tray. She could have guessed without a clock, actually. He'd brought fish. The hospital always served fish on Friday nights, a leftover tradition from the Catholic nuns that used to run the place.

Grayson slid off of the bed and walked over to the small table, sitting down in the lone folding chair. She felt guilty about even contemplating eating the food he had brought her, but she had completely refused her breakfast. Now, she was ravenous.

She opened up the plastic sleeve containing the utensils and took them out one at a time. Knife, fork, spoon, knife…

…wait, knife?

She drew the second knife out of the small package and eyed it warily, then quickly slipped it inside the long sleeve of her gray sweatshirt, hiding it from view. Her heart thundered in her chest. She was alone in the room, but maybe Cain had cameras on her. She couldn't be sure. She felt the smooth plastic against the skin of her forearm and swallowed nervously.

He counted. Every tray, he counted the silverware to be sure she wasn't keeping any of it. The black yoga pants and gray sweatshirt he brought her every day had no pockets, no place to hide anything. No bra. No panties. Nowhere to keep anything from him.

But she had her hiding place, underneath the mattress.

It had her cell phone, her ID…and now, a knife.

5

CAPTAIN M^CCALLISTER WATCHED his young detective pace up and down the length of his office, shirt undone at the collar and rolled up at the sleeves, tie askew, hair out of place. Gabriel Ryder looked like a complete mess. It was a once-in-a-lifetime train wreck the captain couldn't help but gawk at from behind his desk.

"All right, detective," he said in an authoritative but calming voice. "That's enough."

Ryder stopped walking and looked sideways toward his captain.

"Just start again from the beginning so I can keep up here. Dr. Carter went missing on…"

"Wednesday night…technically early Thursday morning."

"She was here?"

"Yes. She left the precinct sometime after midnight and before three a.m."

"And she went to the hospital to…"

"…try to somehow pin down who Cain's next victim is going to be. She…she feels like it's her fault. That people are dying because of her. She…feels responsible."

"And she tried to break into his office?"

"Her ID badge was last used to get into the main hospital office block. There were scratch marks on Cain's office door, like someone had tried using a credit card to jimmy the lock."

"I can't say I'd peg the young doctor for being a very good cat burglar," McCallister replied, smiling.

His detective smiled slightly in return. "Yeah. Me neither."

"So, she left the department office and then what?"

"Security cameras tracked her walking back into the main inpatient building, then veering into a back stairwell. She never exits."

"No cameras inside?"

Ryder shook his head. "No. There are cameras on the doors that open onto patient floors, but not on the maintenance floors. Most of them don't work anyway. It's an older part of the hospital, well overdue for an upgrade. He could have taken her out on almost any floor without being recorded. The hospital would have been nearly deserted at that time of night. He could have taken her anywhere."

"You believe this Douglas Cain is responsible."

"Without a doubt." He nodded.

"So he snatched her in the stairwell and just…disappeared?"

"That's what it looks like. We've spent hours looking over the footage. We can't find her. Or him."

"And the search of the hospital?"

"Nothing. He's not keeping her there." Gabriel grimaced against his impending migraine.

"You're certain?" McCallister pressed.

"We searched the place a couple of times, Captain," Blake interrupted, walking into the office with Logan on his heels. "She's nowhere on campus."

McCallister rubbed his eyes. "So, where is he keeping her?"

"We don't know," Blake replied.

"There was nothing at his apartment? Or in his office?"

"Not a thing, Cap," Logan chimed in, shaking his head. "The office was clean. Medical journals and books with titles I can't pronounce. The apartment was ridiculous."

"Ridiculous how?"

"It was like walking into a museum. All look and no touch."

"And gaudy," Blake added, nodding.

"Ryder?" the captain asked.

"It was appropriate for him," Gabe agreed. "The entire apartment is ornate and overdone, but appropriate for the time period he's trying to recreate."

"Gabe likes his piano," Logan joked.

"Can it, asshole," Blake hissed.

"Enough!" McCallister waved his hand at his detectives, effectively silencing the lot of them. Now was not the time for *The Three Stooges.* "Do you think she's still alive?"

The room went quiet. Logan and Blake looked at each other nervously, then over at Ryder. After a minute, he nodded slowly. "For now, yes."

"For now," the captain parroted back.

"He took her for a reason. But Gray...I mean, she was right. He has one more person left on his list. He won't do anything to her until after that last kill."

"Why not?"

"I don't know. It all revolves around Cain's fascination with the relationship between Dante Alighieri and Beatrice Portinari. But what he gets by killing one person for each level of hell, how that gives him the green light for what he wants in real life...I...I don't know."

He started pacing again. "Dante and Beatrice never had a true relationship, and there isn't a romantic one to speak of in the Cantos either. I just...I don't know where this fits in. He could be planning to kill her and then himself at the end of all this. He could be planning to marry her and live happily ever after. I...I just don't know."

McCallister rubbed his eyes again and leaned back in his desk chair. "So, what do we do?"

Ryder's eyes popped up. "Sir?"

"Well, Dr. Carter is alive, according to you, and we have until 12:01 Sunday morning to find her. So, detective, explain to me how we're going to find her if she's not at Cain's apartment and not at the hospital."

A heavy pause hung in the air.

"The church," Ryder finally answered.

McCallister squinted his eyes and sighed. "Explain, please."

Blake stepped up to the captain's desk with a piece of notebook paper in his right hand. He handed it over and started talking.

"We find her by finding him, Captain. We can't search the whole city room by room, so Cain has to lead us to her. If we catch him at the last church and tail him, he'll probably lead us straight to her."

"How can you be sure he'll go to her?"

Ryder spoke up. "He's been working toward this for months," he said softly. "Once he's finished his last kill, there's nowhere else he's going to go but to her. He's been patient for too long."

"Okay. So…this is it? Holy Ghost Catholic Church?"

"We think so," Blake replied. "It's one of the only catholic churches in the area that hasn't been hit and it's, um, appropriate."

"Appropriate how, detective?"

"It's big, beautiful, and perfect for a last hurrah," Logan interjected. "Go big or go home."

"You're sure?" McCallister asked, looking over the list again. "You're only going to get one shot at this, detective."

"I'm sure, Captain," Ryder said. "That's the church."

McCallister nodded in agreement. "Well, I'll post detectives at the others on this list just to be safe, but the three of you take Holy Ghost. Just take it easy and radio in if Cain shows up. Do not engage him without backup. Dismissed."

Logan and Blake nodded, filing out of the captain's office without a word.

"Ryder, hold on a sec." The captain motioned him back into the room.

Ryder screwed his eyes closed and brought his hand up to the bridge of his nose. *Now what?*

"Yes, Captain?"

"Can I trust you with this?"

"Is there a reason you think you can't?" he bit back, suddenly more than a little irritated that his own captain was getting in his way.

"You're close to her, detective," McCallister said, leaning back in his chair again. "I need you to bring Cain in. Alive and talking. Not in a body bag."

"I'll be fine."

"I have my doubts about that."

"I don't," he countered.

"Don't make me regret this, Ryder. I could let Logan and Nolan handle it and keep you here."

"I wouldn't stay here and you know that," he hissed.

"I do. Which is why you're going to put that mind of yours to work on finding the young doctor and not on how to sneak out of the office. Just don't let it go into overdrive. Use your gun only if necessary."

"I don't need a lecture, Captain."

McCallister narrowed his eyes and pointed a finger at him over his desk. "Ryder, just don't make me regret sending you. Or I will have your fucking badge."

"Yes, sir."

Gabriel walked briskly from the captain's office and to his desk where Nolan and Harrison were waiting.

"Get a scolding from dear old dad?" Logan grinned at him.

"Shove it," he growled, grabbing his coat off the back of his chair. "Get in the car."

"Oh, hell no," Blake said, grabbing the keys from his partner's hand. "I'll agree to you riding shotgun, but there's no way in hell you're driving."

6

HE WAS LATE. She couldn't say exactly how late, but he was late.

Grayson paced nervously back and forth along the four stride-lengths of her gray cell. How could it possibly send more shivers down her spine when he wasn't in the room than when he was sitting next to her, his fingers clearly itching to touch her?

She had ideas, of course. He was killing someone. He was planning to kill someone. He was planning to kill her. He was watching her through some hidden camera. He was writing a sonnet where he played Dante to her Beatrice. Each thought was fouler than the last.

Ick. I need to stop thinking.

She clasped her arms across her chest and ran her hands up and down over the fabric in an attempt to keep keep warm, but she couldn't keep herself from shivering. The gray sweatshirt and black yoga pants weren't cutting it tonight. It was definitely getting colder.

She turned her musings to the weather to try to force the more malevolent train of thought from her mind. Was it colder in here because it was colder outside? Was it snowing? Maybe there was a full moon out tonight. According to a quick on-off of her cell phone (46% battery life remaining), it was Saturday night. She'd been down here for three, nearly four days.

Wherever here was.

That first day, she'd sat smugly on the little bed for hours on end, legs crossed, convinced that at any moment someone would come bursting through the door to rescue her. Someone would notice she'd gone missing. Gabriel would come after her. He would find her, wherever she was, and take her away.

In one of her daydreams, they'd gone for hot chocolate afterward. But as the hours and then days had worn on, that confidence had been replaced by overwhelming fear. She couldn't hide it from herself anymore. She started pacing.

Grayson knew she was in the hospital somewhere. She could feel it. There was too much that looked like the hospital to make it some warehouse in the middle of nowhere. The bed, the linens, even the trays for the food. She'd seen them every day for almost five years. But she also knew that the hospital was the first place that anyone would have thought to look for her, especially with her SUV in the parking lot. They would have sent search teams through every hallway, every stairwell. Someone would have watched all of the footage from the security cameras. That meant only one of two things: either no one realized she was gone or worse, they knew she was missing, they'd already searched the hospital, and they hadn't found her.

That realization had dumped a lump of coal in the pit of her stomach that refused to go away. If they'd already come and gone, it meant Cain was in the clear. He didn't have to worry about anyone finding her, which meant she couldn't hope for a white knight to break down her door and carry her off to safety.

She couldn't hope for Gabriel.

She stopped pacing in the middle of the room as the realization hit her again. She took a deep, shaking breath.

He's not coming. Nobody's coming. I'm on my own.

She had very little time left. Saturday night would turn into Sunday morning, and Grayson was all too aware of what happened when you mixed Douglas Cain with Sunday mornings.

The sound of a key in the door lock made her jump. Grayson scurried to sit down onto the bed just as it opened. Cain entered as he usually did, quickly and efficiently, carrying his usual tray in one hand and a change of clothes for her in the other. But he didn't look the same, and it didn't take Grayson long to realize the sickening reason why.

He was dressed head to toe in black. Black turtleneck, pants, boots, skull cap, everything. Even more disturbing was the change in the energy that surrounded him. He was usually calm and reserved when he first arrived, the only sign of emotion the sickening lust blazing behind his eyes. Tonight, he was excited. Giddy, even.

He sauntered over to the table to put down the tray, which she realized held much more food than usual. And two sets of flatware. Real metal forks and knives.

She turned her eyes to the clothes that he carried under his other arm. It wasn't the usual sweatshirt and sweatpants combination. Everything was black.

Is that silk?

"Good evening, my Beatrice," he said, turning to face her and flashing a megawatt smile.

The sight of his happy face made Grayson sick to her stomach. She met his gaze but did not respond. She never responded to the name if she could help it. She never called Cain by his first name. And she definitely didn't call him Dante. She fought against the bile steadily rising in her throat and swallowed hard.

"Now, now, don't be cross with me," he said, shaking his head and setting the new clothes down on the end of the bed.

"Tonight is a special night. I apologize for being late. Certain elements were out of my control. But I have brought dinner for you and for myself. We shall eat together tonight."

He motioned toward the tray on the card table, then pulled it over toward the bed. Grayson scuttled out of the way so she wouldn't get hit in the knees. Cain briefly opened the main door, reached out, and brought a folding chair into the room before shutting and locking the door again. He placed the chair on the opposite end of the table from her and sat down, still beaming with pride.

She eyed the covered plates warily.

"Tonight, I have decided on something quite decadent for us. I hope you are in the mood for seafood."

She wasn't.

He lifted the lids off of two covered plates—ceramic, not foam—with a flourish. On each of their plates were oysters, mussels, some kind of small balled-up pasta she didn't recognize, and asparagus.

Subtle, Cain.

She watched warily as he poured out sparkling water from a bottle of San Pellegrino into two plastic cups. Grayson wrinkled her nose in disgust at the whole display, which Cain mistook as disapproval at the cups.

"I had a choice between the beverage and what it was to be served in," he said by way of explanation. "I thought the beverage itself would be more important."

He took a long drink from his glass. Grayson nodded curtly and took a drink. If he drank from the same bottle, then he hadn't tampered with it.

Too late she wondered if he'd tampered with the cup instead, lacing it with sedatives or worse, but the sparkling liquid was already down her throat. He hadn't put anything in her food before. Why would he now?

Oh wait, because it's Saturday night now, almost Sunday. Idiot.

"Eat, Beatrice. You have not eaten much since we have been together. You must keep up your strength." He picked up an oyster shell, tipped his head back, and swallowed the contents whole.

"You're keeping track of what I eat?" she asked, not bothering to hide the shock or the disapproval in her voice.

"Of course." He nodded. "I must see to it that you are taken care of."

"The last I knew that didn't involve policing my diet, Dr. Cain."

He arched his eyebrows at her. "Does it offend you?"

"Yes."

"Then I will stop," he shrugged, tipping back another oyster.

"Just like that?" Her voice betrayed her incredulity.

"Just like that," he replied. "I'm not going to make it a habit to make you uncomfortable or upset. I was merely keeping track to be sure you were adequately nourished and hydrated. If you feel that that is an intrusion, then I will stop, provided you make a promise to me that you will maintain those aspects of your well-being."

"Frankly, I consider all of this to be an intrusion on my well-being, Dr. Cain, but we've been over that before."

She picked up her fork and stabbed one of the pasta balls. "What is this?"

"Gnocchi. You'll like them. But traditionally one starts with the seafood."

"I'm not in the mood for oysters."

"Oh, really? That's too bad. They won't keep for long off the ice. I wish you would try one."

"Maybe later." *Or never.*

"Very well."

The two ate in silence for a few minutes. Grayson gnawed on her bottom lip until she couldn't stand it any longer. She slammed her fork down onto the table, as forcefully as one can slam anything onto a rickety card table, and looked her captor directly in the eyes.

"All right, enough. What is this?"

"What is what, my dear?" Cain looked across the table at her like they were having a perfectly normal discussion over dinner at home. Like there was nothing abnormal about eating a plate full of known aphrodisiacs in the middle of a cramped, gray prison cell.

"This. Dinner. You and me. Having it together." She gestured across the table. "You're usually in and out of here in ten minutes, if that. This is different. You're different. Explain to me what's going on."

"Why would you think something is going on?" he asked smoothly, resting his chin on interlaced fingers.

"Different clothes for you. Different clothes for me. All the foods are aphrodisiacs. Don't think I missed the chocolate poking out of your coat pocket." She motioned toward the side of his chair where his overcoat had been deposited.

"Is it so odd to think I would want to share a meal with my beautiful Beatrice?" he asked innocently.

"Stop calling me that! And a meal with me should be done in a restaurant. Above ground. With people around. Not in a dungeon."

She almost slipped and said 'a dungeon inside St. Joseph Hospital,' but Grayson caught herself in time. The less he knew that she knew, the better.

"Soon enough, my dear. Soon enough. But tonight is special. A momentous occasion. It is only right we should celebrate together."

"So then tell me," she said calmly, leaning back on her arms and eyeing him warily, "what are we celebrating?"

"You will know soon enough," he replied evasively.

For the first time since he'd taken her hostage, Douglas Cain looked uncomfortable. He shifted awkwardly on the rickety folding chair.

Okay, maybe I can work with this.

"I want to know now," she purred back. "If such an occasion merits oysters and expensive chocolate, the least we should do is have a toast."

She grabbed her plastic cup, still half full of fizzing sparkling water, and held it a few inches off of the table. He paused for a moment, then nodded and grabbed his own in a similar fashion.

"*Ad postremum amisso portas redemptionis peccator et exspectent ultimum.*"

"Translation?"

"To the loss of the last sinner and the gates of redemption that await."

Cain touched his glass to hers then tipped it back, draining it. Grayson took a shaky sip herself.

"Is something wrong?" he asked, noticing her tremor.

"So you are going to do it? You are going to kill another person tonight."

His face fell slightly. "I wish you didn't have to know such things."

"Tell me who," she demanded.

"There is no reason for you to know that. He is poisonous and shall be dealt with," Cain spat.

"I want to know who you're going after."

"That does not make a difference to me."

"It does to me," she persisted.

"He will shortly be inconsequential."

"No human being that is killed in my name is inconsequential," Grayson hissed, more forcefully than she meant to. "If someone is going to die because of me, I have a damned right to know who and why. You denied telling me for all the rest. I had to figure it out for myself. The least you could do is give me the common courtesy of an explanation for this one."

Grayson watched his face carefully as she spoke. Cain hid it well, but she could see the shock in his eyes. She smirked inwardly.

Yeah, buddy, I'm not stupid. I know what you're up to. Kind of.

"You…you understand why…"

She cut him off. "No, I figured out the pattern. I don't understand what you get out of it, but I know the last one on your list is considered a traitor. Now I want an answer. Who is going to end up in the city morgue tomorrow because of you?"

Cain stood and turned his back to her. Grayson scooted toward the far side of the bed, just in case she had gone too far. She wanted a fighting chance if he lunged at her. He didn't move. Instead, he spoke, very softly.

"The Ninth Level is reserved for the worst of sinners, the traitors. For the Devil himself. There are so many, my dear, but the one dangerous to you is of sound mind and body. A member of your family. Someone close."

Grayson's blood turned to ice. She couldn't force enough air through her vocal cords to ask the question she desperately wanted an answer to.

"Do not fret, my Beatrice. I will not harm your precious Dr. Mason. Or Miss Parker."

Grayson released a long breath. A silent tear dropped from her eye. *Oh, thank God for that.* "Tell me who," she whispered shakily.

"Traitors come in all forms, my dear. This one attacked his own family at a time of great sorrow. A brother. And he has attacked you, my love, a member of a different family. I know the trouble he has caused you. I know of the pain you have suffered. And it ends tonight. He will no longer have power over you."

Grayson wracked her brain. Who the hell was he talking about? She was completely lost inside her own head, trapped in her whirling thoughts. Before she had a chance to even fully process the words, Cain was on top of her, pressing her down into the bed with the force of his hips.

"My Beatrice," he whispered into her ear. "So soft, so smooth. You will be mine soon."

He leaned down and placed a kiss onto her mouth. Grayson pressed her lips together as tightly as she possibly could and slammed her eyes closed in protest. The feel of his tongue prodding against her seal, begging for entrance to her mouth, made her stomach twist and lurch in disgust.

Her eyes opened wide when she heard the sound of ripping Velcro and felt fabric wrapping tightly around her wrists. She watched helplessly as Cain continued to kiss her, his eyes closed, blindly binding her wrists in the restraints with ease. She felt the bile well up in the back of her throat.

He's practiced this. He's practiced kissing me while tying me up in restraints.

Grayson was frozen in place, consumed by overwhelming terror.

Cain opened his eyes, smiled down at her, and then carefully moved to the end of the bed. He tied up her legs, one at a time, then kissed the inside of her ankles. Grayson fought back the impulse to buck herself off of the bed and hit him. She hissed at the feel of his rough tongue against her skin.

"Rest now, my lovely one. I will be back for you in due time. Then we shall change you into some more becoming clothes. Satins and silks and lace from now on." He nodded at the new pile of all-black clothes.

Cain cleaned up their dinner and folded up the chair he'd been sitting on. He opened the outside door wide, briefly giving Grayson a glimpse of what was outside her cell, far more than he ever had before. What did he have to fear? She was tied up to the bed. There wasn't anything she could do.

Grayson saw piping running along the higher ceilings. She could hear the familiar low hum of an elevator in the distance. But most important of all, there was a red stripe painted along the ceiling. She bit the inside of her lip to keep the relief off of her face.

The basement. I'm somewhere in the old hospital basement.

She kept her face expressionless as she craned her neck up from the bed. Cain thought she was looking at him. In fact, she was looking behind him.

"Don't worry, Beatrice. We can be together soon."

This time, he turned off the lights as he shut the door. "Rest now," he murmured just before the door latched and the lock clicked into place.

The room plunged into inky darkness. Grayson kept her eyes shut and willed her breathing to even out, her heart to slow down, her anxiety to quiet itself. She was still deathly afraid of the dark. It was getting harder to breathe.

In, one two three four. Out, one two three four. Repeat.

She opened her eyes and let them adjust to the darkness. It took a few moments, but slowly, with help from the thin strip of light coming from under the main door, she was able to make out her surroundings again.

When her breathing was steady and her mind was clear, she began to work.

7

THE STREET OUTSIDE of Holy Ghost Catholic Church was quiet and peaceful.

Clouds had rolled in off the mountains after dinnertime, and a soft snow was once again falling on the city. The streetlights cast gentle pools of yellow light onto the whitewashed sidewalks. Every so often, a bird or a squirrel would scamper across, leaving small trails across the snow. The spiraling majesty of the gothic cathedral contrasted against the new snow and the contemporary skyscrapers of downtown, could have easily made the cover of *Architect's Digest*. It really was a beautiful night.

Of course, his cranky partner riding shotgun wasn't doing anything to make this a pleasant experience for anybody.

Nolan rolled his eyes over at Ryder as he reached for his coffee in the center console. His partner was huddled in the passenger seat, his coat collar pulled up around his ears, eyes fixated on the front of the church down the street. Harrison was in another unmarked car around the corner, covering the back and side entrances to the church.

Too bad. He'd know how to break the silence better.

Nolan took a long drink of coffee, shook the remaining contents back and forth in the travel mug, then reached back into the backseat for the thermos. He poured himself a full new cup, then nodded toward his partner's.

"You need a refill yet, Ryder?"

Gabriel shook himself back into consciousness. "Uh, no. No, I'm okay. Thanks."

"All right."

He put the thermos back as his partner picked up his own mug.

"Thanks for bringing the coffee, Nolan."

"No problem. It's not Belgian press, but it's warm," he replied.

"It's called French press."

"Whatever press," Nolan mocked, rolling his eyes. "I still don't get you sometimes."

"Meaning?"

"Meaning I don't get you. When I first met you, I thought you were the most stuck-up, arrogant prick I'd ever met. You had your fancy coffee and your fancy suits and that goddamned car. You were a piece of work. I didn't think I'd last a month with you."

"It's been almost four years, Nolan. You could've walked any time."

"Yeah, I know. I got to know you."

"I'm still an arrogant prick." Gabe chuckled into his coffee.

"Yeah, when you have to be. But then I see you pull something like Thanksgiving. Or the hospital a few weeks ago. Don't get me wrong, you've been a complete asshole this week. But you're doing it for her. So I get it."

Gabriel swirled the contents of his cup around in circles. "What the fuck is wrong with me, Blake?"

"Not a damned thing and you know it. Finally somebody's more important than your car. You need me to spell this out for you?"

"We have to find her."

"We will. Just be patient."

"I hate waiting."

"I've noticed, buddy."

The radio at the base of the center console scratched to life, interrupting their conversation.

"Hey, ladies. Coming your way. Dark sedan, parking just off the corner."

Nolan smiled at Ryder. It was after midnight. "Wait's over."

Gabriel nodded and turned his attention to the street. There it was, a dark sedan pulling over by the side of the church. The lights shut off, the driver door opened, and a tall man exited, dressed all in black. He crossed quickly to the rear passenger door and opened it, dragging a large bundle out of the back seat. He slung it over his shoulder and kicked the door closed, turning toward the side door. Ryder picked up the radio link.

"Logan, he's headed back toward you. Let him go."

"Let him go? Are you fucking nuts?"

"Just do it."

"If that vic is still alive, we have to…"

"He's not. Cain's carrying him like a sack of fucking potatoes. Let him go."

"You know it's a him because…"

"Size, body habitus, method of carry, take your damned pick. Get off the radio."

"He's getting feisty, isn't he, Blake?" came the chuckling reply.

"Shut the fuck up, Harrison!" he repeated.

"Okay, okay. He's headed up the side stairs now."

The radio crackled again and then went quiet. Blake and Ryder remained completely silent, watching the snow continue to fall. After several minutes, the subtle glow of a soft light began to filter out of the windows of the church.

"He turned on the lights?" Blake whispered.

"Candlelight. Around the body," Ryder replied.

"Creepy."

"Indeed."

The silence continued. Blake sipped at his coffee. Ryder's went cold, neglected in the center console. Ten minutes went by without any sign of movement.

"What the hell is he doing in there?" Blake whispered.

"Be patient," came the mocking reply from his partner in the passenger seat.

"Asshole."

"Hey you two. Shut up. He's coming out." Harrison's voice hissed softly over the radio.

Sure enough, the same tall figure dressed in black came around the corner, without his previous bundle in tow. The detectives watched Cain slide into the driver's seat, turn the lights on, and pull out into the snow-covered street.

"Shit, shit, get down!" Blake hissed.

Nolan and Ryder sunk down into their chairs as the car drove past, its headlights shining into the windshield.

Once the lights had passed, Harrison's voice scratched out over the radio.

"Now what, ladies?"

"Follow him," came the cool reply from the passenger seat. "Lights off. Don't lose him."

"Ten-four."

Blake waited until Logan drove past them to turn the engine over and make a U-turn to follow him. They kept far enough back to give Cain room, but never let him get through a light without one of their two cars on his tail. The snowfall intensified and the wind picked up as they drove east.

"Goddamn it, I can't keep up with him," Blake grimaced, leaning forward and squinting his eyes against the developing whiteout. "If I get any closer, he's gonna know he's got a tail."

"Stay with him," Ryder hissed, squinting into the windshield himself.

"Will you two stop arguing like a fucking married couple? I'm trying to drive here!" came the crackling voice over the radio.

"Shut up and turn right, Logan," Ryder hissed back.

They turned the corner, one after another, right then left, and tailed Cain to the back entrance of the old St. Joseph Hospital building. He slid into a parking spot on the edge of the street and got out of the driver's seat, smiling to himself as he walked into the building through an unmarked steel door.

"Follow him," Ryder said coolly into the handset before opening the car door and stepping out into the snow.

"Here we go," Blake mumbled.

Logan met them at the door, his right hand on his hip, fingering his gun. "Bastard went through and to the left."

"Keep low. Guns out."

They slipped into the back door quietly and followed Cain through the bowels of the old hospital tower. When he turned right, so did they. When he slipped gracefully into a stairwell, they followed. When he got ahead of them in the basement, they lost him.

"Goddamn it! Where the fuck is he?" Nolan hissed.

"Logan, right. Nolan, left."

Ryder pulled his gun out from the holster underneath his arm and cocked it, pushing between his partners down the center hallway. They obeyed his command and separated down the other passageways.

Gabriel slowly and methodically made his way down the hallway. The only sound in his ears was his own ragged breathing.

He's here somewhere. She's here somewhere. Come on, baby, tell me where you are.

A shriek echoed off the walls from the far end of the hallway.

Ryder felt a cold sweat break out onto his forehead as he accelerated toward the source. He sprinted his way down and around the sharp curves of the basement hallways, following the continuous, echoing screams. He rounded a right turn and skidded to a stop, raising his gun. He could hear Blake on the radio behind him, calling for backup.

Douglas Cain was standing in the middle of the hallway, his hands pressed against the sides of his face, howling in pain. Streaks of blood tracked along both cheeks and down his neck. Rivulets trickled down his forearms, dripping drop by drop onto the concrete floor from the tips of his elbows.

Grayson was standing in front of him, dressed in black and barefoot, her fingers dripping blood.

8

GRAYSON SWORE UNDER her breath. The harsh Velcro from the restraints was digging into her wrists. Her raw skin was screaming in pain. She strained, fumbling with numb fingers against the clasps.

She was running out of time. She could feel it. He'd be back any minute. For her.

Her heart jumped into her throat as an image of Cain standing in the doorway, bloody and smiling at her, flashed behind her eyes. She twisted and bucked against the specter, fighting the urge to scream. The fingers of her right hand brushed against plastic and she blindly pinched as hard as she possibly could.

Please, please, please, please…

Click.

Grayson craned her neck sideways and looked at her right wrist. The restraint was loose. A little more twisting and turning, the swift crackling of Velcro, and she slid out of the fabric. She pulled her right hand over toward the left and ripped off the binding, then went to work on the ones at her feet. She scampered off of the bed and ran to the door, pulling on it to try the lock. As always, it was solid.

Damn it!

Grayson slammed her fist against the door, then turned around and sagged against it. This was it. Whatever crusade Cain had been on was going to end tonight, and he had plans for her. Whatever they were, she wanted nothing to do with them. If she didn't get out of here tonight, she wouldn't get out. Nobody was coming. She had to figure something out.

She looked frantically around the dark room. The only difference tonight was the clothes. She turned on the floor lamp, unfolded them and laid them on the bed. A black silk camisole, black pants, and a long-sleeved cashmere sweater. They were lovely, but it made her shake to think about where they'd come from. She hesitated at the thought of putting them on, but Cain had touched her in the clothes she currently wore, and she felt dirty. The new clothes were the lesser of two evils.

She peeled out of her sweatshirt and pulled on the camisole, then the sweater. She was halfway through pulling on the black pants when the idea struck. It was stupid and wasn't going to work, but it was all she had. She had to try something. She couldn't just let herself sit quietly on the bed and wait for him to come back like a sick little puppy dog waiting for a beating.

Grayson turned her mattress over and found her hideaway, pulling out the ID card and cell phone. She placed them both in her back pocket. She slipped the extra plastic knife into the sleeve of the sweater, running her fingers over the serrated edge. She hastily stuffed her dirty clothes with the towels from the bathroom, then shoved that underneath the blanket on her bed, spreading it out until it vaguely resembled someone sleeping in restraints. She shut off the lights and hid in the dark corner beside the door. And waited.

It didn't take long for the familiar tap-tap-tap of his shoes to start echoing down the hallway.

Her heart rate skyrocketed. Her breathing shallowed.

Grayson closed her eyes against the darkness and exhaled.

A key turned in the lock. She looked straight ahead into the pitch-black room and let the plastic knife slide into her right hand. Her fingers went white around it.

The door slid open, and light poured into the room.

Cain's shadow stretched out across the bed.

"Oh, my Beatrice," he whispered as he stepped forward. He was completely focused on what was in front of him, utterly blind to his surroundings.

She waited, one step, then another.

The moment he was beyond the threshold, Grayson leaped from her hiding spot in the corner and took off past him out the door.

The concrete floor was hard and icy cold beneath her bare feet, but she didn't care. Her heart was beating hard in her chest. All she registered of her surroundings was a hallway that looked vaguely familiar and the sound of Cain's voice calling her name.

The adrenaline thundered in her ears as she rounded the first turn. The walls were familiar. The hum from the elevator was growing stronger. She knew where she was.

I'm going to make it!

A strong hand clamped down on her arm and pulled her backward before she passed the second turn. She cried out as she slammed against the wall and her head smacked back against the tile. Her vision blurred for a moment, but she quickly recovered.

Grayson screamed.

Cain was leering over her, his eyes wickedly bright, pinning her to the wall with a hand on each side of her body.

She stared at him, frozen. He smiled at her. A knowing, confident, completely inappropriate smile. Grayson dropped her eyes. Her hair fell across her face.

Tick, tick, tick, tick....

She lunged, slicing the left side of his face with the knife. Cain yelped and staggered back, the playful gleam in his eyes quickly changing to fire. His hand shot out and twisted her right wrist, forcing Grayson to drop the pathetic piece of plastic. It clattered to the floor.

She didn't care. All she knew was that Cain still had his hand on her, and it was all she could do to focus on getting it off.

Grayson lunged again and brought her nails up to his face, dragging them from his temple to his neck. Cain howled and loosened his grip. She twisted loose and stumbled backward several feet. She watched the blood run down the sides of his face, then turned, ready to run.

"Cain! Get your hands up! Now!"

Grayson whipped around to see Gabriel steadily approaching, his gun drawn and pointed at the man howling beside her. She unconsciously registered Nolan and Harrison coming in behind him, their own guns trained down on Douglas Cain.

Ryder's eyes were focused on the bleeding, hateful mess standing in between him and Grayson. He trained his barrel on Cain's chest. "I said get your fucking hands up!" he repeated, slowly stalking further toward the pair. He hesitated, shooting a glance at Grayson. She looked all right. Frightened and surviving on adrenaline, but alive and in one piece. He had to get her away from Cain, immediately.

Grayson stood stock-still, well aware that her kidnapper was exceptionally close to snapping, capable of doing anything at any moment. She could feel the evil pulsating off of him in waves. The more blood pooled beneath his arms on the concrete floor, the thicker the evil became.

The thought frightened her more than anything had before.

"*You*," Cain hissed in a deep, slow voice. "You are here to take her away from me." He turned his still-bleeding face toward Grayson and glared at her. "You will not go with them. You belong to me. You are mine."

Cain moved toward her, extending his hand for hers.

Grayson backed up against the wall.

Gabriel cocked his gun.

Cain's eyes widened.

Everything happened in an instant.

He lunged for Grayson, grabbing her left arm and twisting it behind her back. She yelped in pain, her back forcefully pressed against his chest. Cain leered at her as he pulled her up against him and smelled her neck.

"I love the smell of you, Beatrice."

Grayson sobbed and looked up across the room, completely helpless.

Gabriel brought his gun up and opened his mouth to give Cain a final warning.

Instead, his eyes opened wide in shock as a thin metal blade pressed against her neck. Cain had a knife leveled against her windpipe.

Blood dripped down the side of Grayson's neck and onto her chest.

It wasn't hers.

"You...you used this," she whispered.

"As Brutus killed Caesar," Cain nodded, gently kissing her cheek. "I thought you might like to see the blade used to destroy the final barrier between us."

"Get away from her," Gabriel hissed, edging closer.

Cain pressed the knife harder into her neck, forcing her to double over in pain and whimper. "Stay away from her," he countered. "Beatrice is mine. No one else will have her."

"Cain, put the knife down and let her go. Now."

Logan edged in closer, his gun leveled. Blake followed suit.

Cain twisted from left to right, keeping track of each of the three detectives while keeping his hold tight on the woman in his arms.

She was coming with him. They would not take her away from him. Ever.

He angled the knife blade and pressed down, relishing in her whimper and the startled eyes of the detectives in front of him.

"Set the guns down, detectives," he cooed, angling Grayson as a human shield. "We don't want any harm to come to my Beatrice's lovely neck."

He twisted his neck down and licked the skin next to the knife. Gabriel bristled and took aim.

Cain pressed the knife in deep enough to draw blood. Grayson screamed.

"Now, now, detective," he purred. "You're hurting her."

He smiled wickedly as the young detective faltered, the gun lowering ever so slightly toward the floor. "Well done. Now, be a good boy and kick it over to me."

Ryder sighed and looked at Grayson, seemingly focused on the small trail of bright red blood trailing down her neck, slowly soaking the black fabric beneath it.

"Gabriel...don't..." Grayson whimpered, twisting and struggling to get the knife away from her skin. She pleaded with her eyes for him to raise his gun, to put a bullet in Cain's head and get him off of her.

Instead, Ryder placed his gun on the floor and kicked it across the room. Cain smiled, the malice oozing from his eyes like black oil. He pulled on her wrist, forcing Grayson to bend forward with him.

When they reached the floor, he pulled the knife away from her neck and grabbed the gun. He kept hold of her as he stood and cocked it.

"Now you two." He nodded at Nolan and Harrison.

They looked at each other and then leveled their weapons at his head.

"Not on your life, buddy," Nolan sneered. "Let her go."

"None of you will have her. None of you," Cain spat, twisting Grayson's wrist tighter, forcing her to scream in pain.

He brought the gun up and pressed it into the small of her back.

"Now, if you please, back away. Arms up. No tricks."

Gabriel could see Grayson shaking from across the room. Cain was ready to snap. He knew it, she knew it, and they were both terrified.

Gabriel held his hands up at his sides and stepped back. He watched the blood drain from her face and saw the silent tears escape down her cheeks.

Oh no, she thinks…Grayson, I'm not leaving. I can't let that bastard kill you. Stop crying.

Ryder glanced from Grayson's face to her captor's. He saw Cain's eyes gleam. The bastard knew what he was doing. Gabriel's eyes narrowed.

Son of a bitch.

Cain seemed to catch the change in Gabriel's eyes.

"Now, now, my dear detective. No need for anger," he mocked. "It's unbecoming."

Beside him, Nolan opened his mouth to shut the prick up. The slight glint off the gun went unnoticed until it was too late.

Cain shifted the gun out from behind Grayson's back and raised it.

"Ryder! Gun!" he hollered.

It was too late. The muzzle flashed twice, and the walls echoed with the blasts. The bullets connected, and Gabriel fell backward onto the concrete floor.

Grayson watched helplessly, tethered, her breath caught in her throat.

No. No, no, no. Not another one. Gabriel!

She let out a strangled cry and sagged forward, letting all of her weight fall into her captor's arm. Another one. Cain had killed another person, all because of her.

She'd gotten out, finally gotten out, only to watch her captor kill another person in cold blood. Someone she cared about.

Someone I...

Grayson couldn't finish the thought. Tears ran down her face. She didn't stop them. It was all she could do to keep from collapsing onto the floor.

Then she heard it. Through her shaking breaths and soul-wracking sobs, she heard it. Laughter. Cain was *LAUGHING*.

Grayson looked up across the hallway. Gabriel's limp body was lying in a pool of blood before her. Her breathing stopped. The room went white.

In that moment, something snapped.

Grayson spun around in Cain's arms. She raised her arm as she twisted, forcing all of her pain and rage and power into her swing. Her elbow connected with his jaw, the sick crack of breaking bones echoing against the wall as loudly as the gunshots.

She screamed just to hear the power in her own voice.

The searing pain in his face forced Cain to immediately drop her wrist and bring his right hand up to his shattered face.

Grayson shot her left arm out and used all her strength to force the gun out of his hand. Cain was so stunned by the force of the blow to his face that he offered no resistance. The weapon dropped to the floor, and Grayson kicked it wildly toward the back wall.

She ducked under Cain's left arm, pulled it straight, and plowed through his elbow with the palm of her hand. He howled in pain as the bones in his forearm snapped and his elbow bent backward. He dropped to the floor.

Grayson stood over him, still hanging onto his left wrist, panting and completely disoriented.

What the hell did I just do?

She struggled to bring her breathing under control. Her vision slowly came back into focus.

Nolan's voice shattered any ounce of calm she managed to get back. "Grayson! Get over here! He's been shot!"

She snapped her eyes up and registered Blake kneeling down by his partner, Gabriel's head in his lap and his hands pressed over a dark stain on his partner's shirt.

Logan yanked Cain's wrist out of her grasp and pushed her forward. "Snap out of it! Go!" he commanded.

Harrison used his free hand to train his 9mm on the back of Cain's head. His voice dropped low as Grayson sprinted across the hall. "You move one inch, you son of a bitch, I will put two in your skull without thinking twice."

Cain couldn't begin to manage a reply.

Grayson slid to the floor next to Blake. Gabriel's eyes were clenched closed, his breathing was shallow, and he was losing a lot of blood. A dark stain covered his torso and another was forming over his right thigh. She grabbed either side of his face and called his name.

"Gabriel? Gabriel! Come on, damn it, look at me!"

His eyes weakly fluttered open, and he forced himself to focus on her grief-stricken face. "G...Gray..."

He didn't have the strength to even say her name.

"Shhh. Shut up. Don't talk. Just stay with me. Stay with me!"

He managed a meager smile before a surge of pain wracked his system and he groaned, throwing his head back into Nolan's lap.

"What do we do?"

Blake was clearly panicked; his partner was dying before his eyes and he was helpless. Grayson looked at him, a strange but welcome calm on her face. "Where are we?" she asked quickly.

"Main hospital, old tower."

"How many stories down are we?"

"Three from the floor we entered on."

"You came down the main stairs?"

"The back stairs."

Grayson shot up to her feet and looked around wildly. She took off around the corner. Nolan called after her. He looked across helplessly at Logan who was still standing over Cain. He shrugged his shoulders.

Suddenly, the PA system screeched to life overhead, and Grayson's voice echoed throughout the hallway.

"Code Blue. Code Silver. Basement Annex One. Officer Down. Trauma Activation Level One. Code Blue. Code Silver. Basement Annex One. Officer Down. Trauma Activation Level One."

Nolan heard her feet against the concrete, then felt her sit back down next to him. He moved over slightly so she could hold Gabriel's head in her lap. He slammed both of his hands over the chest wound and pushed, blood squishing in between his fingers and onto his shirtsleeves.

Grayson leaned close to Gabriel, running her fingers through his hair and whispering in his ear. Nolan could just barely understand her.

"They're coming, Gabriel. You promised you wouldn't leave. Just hold on. They're coming."

9

OF ALL THE parts of his job that he hated, sitting in the waiting room of a hospital after one of his detectives had been shot was by far the worst.

Carrick McCallister stood silently, white foam cup of coffee in his hand, attempting to find something interesting about the sub-par landscape painting in front of him.

He'd gotten the call from Harrison at home. His wife had rolled over in bed and handed him his cell phone, already open with Logan's voice faintly drifting out into the darkened room. Thank goodness for that woman. He always slept through his phone's ringtone, but she never did.

The moment he'd heard the words *Ryder's been shot*, he'd jolted wide awake. Melanie had slipped out of bed while he was still on the phone, and as he was grabbing his keys by the garage door, she'd put a travel mug of coffee and his phone charger into his free hand.

Now here he was, in jeans and a damned T-shirt, just waiting. Like the rest of them.

He turned and glanced around the room, taking a sip of his coffee. The hospital security guards and in-area Denver PD cops who weren't actively out on a call were filing into the waiting room two and three at a time. The usual low buzz of cop-talk over coffee was well established. Someone had already gone down to the cafeteria for doughnuts.

Blake Nolan was occupying the chair closest to the secure doors leading to the operating rooms. It was as close as he could possibly get to his partner at the moment. McCallister smiled. His detective looked a little ridiculous.

His clothes had been covered in blood when he'd come up from the basement. Thankfully, one of the surgical residents had taken pity on him and brought him a pair of clean scrubs. They were a tad big, and the colors were mismatched, but they were clean and dry. The blood-soaked boots, however, were a dead giveaway to the events that had happened just a few floors down.

Logan Harrison wasn't too far away from Nolan, finishing up his statement with one of the uniformed officers. From what McCallister had been able to overhear, his detectives had done everything right. Douglas Cain had been just a little too quick.

He watched the uniformed officer stand and nod, shake Harrison's hand, then head off out of the waiting room. McCallister took over his seat.

"Logan." He nodded by way of greeting.

"Captain."

The poor man looked exhausted.

"Thanks for the phone call."

"I figured you'd want to know when your best detective's been shot."

"Usually, yes," he replied, sitting foreword, his forearms on his knees. "How're you holding up?"

"I'm fine. This isn't the first time I've been here early in the morning waiting on news. I lost my first partner in narcotics to a tweaked out dealer with a semi-automatic. But I don't know how he's doing."

Logan motioned with his head toward Nolan, who was anxiously glancing between the locked double doors and the clock above them.

"That's what happens when your partner gets shot. You worry he's not going to come back out."

"I know that. You think I'm not worried?"

"Of course not. But Blake's never been through this. You have. You know there's nothing to do but wait."

Harrison just nodded and leaned back in his chair.

"Have they said anything, Logan? About how he's doing?"

"No. That basement exploded with doctors. Whatever it was she called over the loudspeaker, it got everyone's attention. They bundled him up and brought him straight up here. No one's said anything. I guess that's a good thing."

"Usually means they're still working, so yes."

McCallister paused, then asked the question he didn't particularly want an answer to.

"And Cain?"

"In the room next door to Ryder. Apparently, he might be in worse shape than Wonder Boy."

The captain's eyebrows raised up at that. "How do they figure that? You said none of you shot him."

Logan smiled. "Yeah, but you should've seen what *she* did to him."

The captain waited for him to continue. "I don't follow, Logan."

"I don't know what kind of self-defense training she's had— if any—but something kicked in and kicked in hard when Ryder got shot. Girlie got him in the face, got the gun out of his hand and kicked it clear like she was on autopilot. And then she just slammed her hand into his elbow and..." he closed his eyes for a second, remembering, "...let's just say I didn't really need to keep a watch on the prick. He couldn't have moved if he'd wanted to. His bones were sticking out through his skin. His arm looked like a fucking flamingo leg."

"That nice young woman did that? The same one I met a month ago in the department?"

Harrison nodded. McCallister nodded his approval. "Atta girl."

"Yeah, no shit."

Logan kept quiet about the incident at the Petal Club. The captain didn't need details like that. At least, not now.

There was a sudden bustle of activity by the waiting room entrance. Barbara Parker charged through the gathered crowd, beelining directly for Nolan and Harrison. Noah was following behind her, several duffel bags thrown haphazardly over his shoulders. They both looked exhausted, like they hadn't slept well in days.

McCallister felt a pang of guilt in his chest when he saw the disheveled look of the two new arrivals. He didn't know who they were, but they obviously knew his detectives and were intimately connected to Grayson Carter. He stood up to greet the advancing pair.

"Where is she?" Babs asked in a strained voice.

Logan stood up and started to hold out his hand to motion for her to calm down. She smacked it away.

"I don't want to hear any of your 'stay calm, ma'am' bullshit. Where is she?"

Noah stepped up behind her, dropped his bags, and wrapped an arm around her shoulder. Barbara instantly burst into tears and flung herself into his arms. She wailed into his shoulder and sagged against him.

"It's been a long few days, detective," Noah said softly, patting the back of Barbara's head softly. "Is Grayson okay?" he asked.

Harrison nodded.

"She's all right. Probably a bit shaken up still, but physically just fine. One of the surgeons checked her out earlier."

"Which one?"

"McMasters…McMartin…something like that."

"McWilliams?"

"Yeah, that's it."

Relief washed over the young doctor's face.

"That means something to you?" McCallister asked.

"He's one of our best trauma surgeons. She's in good hands." Noah eyed the older man in the jeans and T-shirt warily. "And you are?"

"Captain Carrick McCallister, Head of Major Crimes," he replied, holding out his hand.

Noah shifted Babs awkwardly in his arms and shook the man's hand. "Sorry. A bit wary of new faces, all thing considered."

"I don't blame you, son."

Barbara calmed herself down enough over the next several minutes to let Noah ease her into a chair. He took the seat next to her and handed her a tissue to dry her eyes. Then he noticed Nolan.

"What's going on?" he asked, pointing toward the haggard-looking detective in scrubs.

"Ryder's in surgery," Harrison replied gravely.

"Any word?"

Both men shook their heads.

"Sometimes that's a good sign," he said, hoping his voice sounded as optimistic as he'd meant it to.

"We hope so."

Noah scanned the waiting room. Lots of cops. Several surgeons and residents. No Grayson. "Where is she?" he asked quietly.

"Probably still getting checked out." Harrison shrugged. "Haven't seen her since they hauled Ryder and Cain up here. I followed the gurneys. She was behind us."

"She was here the whole time? In the hospital?"

"Seems that way." McCallister nodded.

"Shite. How did I miss her? I looked everywhere!" Noah flung himself back into his chair, swearing.

. "We all did. We conducted sweeps through that part of the basement and nothing. I'm going to go back through the files. Something got missed. Hopefully the crime scene guys come up with a reason why. Some of our best guys went through this damned place. We even sent the dogs down."

The captain shook his head. It was true. They had missed her completely. If Ryder hadn't been right about the church, they might never have found her. At least, not alive.

"Where is Gray?" Barbara's pathetic voice drifted up from Noah's shoulder.

"She's getting checked out, Babs. She'll be around soon. Just be patient," Noah said softly into her ear.

The last thing they needed right now was Barbara Parker flying off the handle.

The four sat together for a long time, eventually moving down to sit beside Blake and offer him some kind of support. Babs dried her eyes, and she and Noah listened closely to Logan's recount of the events in the basement.

The coffee cups got refilled. Noah and Logan made a trip to the cafeteria. They were passing out pastries when the PA system beeped softly overhead.

"Team two. Orthopedics. OR Eight. Team two. Orthopedics. OR Eight."

Captain McCallister noticed young Dr. Mason's forehead wrinkle in confusion. Not fear. Confusion.

"What does that mean?" the captain asked him.

Without answering, Noah walked up to the surgery desk, flashed his ID, and asked the older woman behind the glass several questions. She seemed to know him, and her smile said to everyone else that she liked him. He appeared to get the answers he wanted and walked calmly back to the group, all of whom were waiting on him expectantly.

Babs linked her arm with his after he sat down. There was even more confusion etched on his face.

"That doesn't make sense," he mumbled under his breath.

"What doesn't make sense?" Nolan asked anxiously.

"That page. It was for Ryder's room. But there isn't a second ortho team."

"Explain," Logan demanded, instantly on edge.

"There's only one orthopedic trauma attending here on the weekends, the call guy. I only know that because Gray complains about it when the busy summer months kick in and they're short on weekends. Dr. Allen's the attending, and he's already in OR nine with Cain. They're calling for a second team that doesn't exist."

Noah's confusion made everyone uneasy. Five pairs of eyes looked expectantly at the large set of locked double doors looming before them, anticipating someone to walk through them with news. Instead, a side door clicked open by the lobby entrance and several figures in scrubs walked into the waiting room.

"Grayson!"

Barbara's squealing caught the attention of the entire room. Everyone fell silent and turned toward the two figures in green scrubs that had emerged.

Grayson was just putting the finishing touches on tucking her hair underneath her surgical cap. It was her lucky one, Noah knew: black and white with old-school anatomic drawings of bones with a white ribbon in the back.

Babs jumped up from her chair and headed straight for her. Noah rose much more slowly and eyed her warily.

Why is she putting that blasted thing on? And why in the bloody hell is she in scrubs?

Her surgical glasses were in her right hand. Dr. McWilliams was standing beside her, tying his wedding ring onto his scrub pants and looking slightly unsettled.

Noah started pushing himself up from his chair but froze halfway up.

No. Oh bloody hell, no. Absolutely not!

He hustled over toward them. Barbara had already made it across the room and had flung herself at her roommate. Grayson stumbled back as she was enveloped in a crushing hug and a wave of blonde hair.

"Ooof! Hi, Babs," she said, trying to get her balance.

Noah pulled the blonde off of her and stepped between them.

"Just what do you think you're doing?" he asked, glaring at Grayson.

"Nice to see you too, Noah," she said hesitantly, placing the surgical glasses on top of her head.

"Answer the bloody question, Gray. What. The Hell. Do You Think. You're Doing?"

Grayson stood silent and still, not answering him. Barbara had stopped glaring at Noah for breaking her hug and was now nervously eyeing her roommate from toes to nose.

"Gray? What's happening? What's he talking about?"

"Can we please talk about this later?" she asked softly, shifting her shoulders to move around them both.

Noah's hands shot out and grabbed her instead. "No. We're going to talk now."

Grayson whipped her shoulders back and out of his grasp, stepping several feet away and glaring at him. "Don't push me, Mason. I asked nicely once. I won't do it again."

He opened his mouth to respond, but Babs grabbed his arm and pulled him back.

"Not now. Please," she whispered in his ear. "Don't fight. We just got her back."

Noah's eyes instantly cooled and his posture softened. *Shite.*

Grayson and Dr. McWilliams moved past them toward the main entrance to the OR. Logan and Captain McCallister were on their feet. Nolan was still staring anxiously at the double doors.

Grayson stopped right in front of him. She blocked his view, hoping the move would force the trembling man to look up at her. When he didn't, she sunk down in front of him and put a hand on his knee.

"He's doing okay, Blake. He's gonna make it." She said the words softly and sincerely. And she smiled.

Looking back, Nolan couldn't remember another day, short of when his girls were born, when he'd heard better news. He launched forward and hugged her.

McCallister grinned. It was the first real sign of life from his detective in several hours.

"You did good," she said as she pulled away from him and stood up, turning her attention to the captain.

"Dr. Carter." He nodded, smiling.

"Captain McCallister," she said, mimicking the gesture. "I need to know who has emergency medical power of attorney for Gabriel."

"Why?" Harrison asked, stepping up closer to her.

Grayson took a deep breath.

"Dr. McWilliams has looked into the more life-threatening of his injuries. He was shot in the chest, but the bullet missed virtually everything. The shot was wild. It broke a few ribs and tore through some muscle but it didn't cause any severe damage. The second bullet hit him in the left thigh."

"It's broken?"

, She nodded. "The wound needs to be cleaned and the fracture needs fixed. A rod on the inside of the bone, through the knee, and screws proximally and distally is what I'd recommend. And I need to get the bullet out."

"It's still in there?" Babs whispered.

She and Noah had walked up behind the group.

"Normally it's not required to remove it, but it is evidence in a police shooting, and I'm worried about how close it is to the profunda on the angiogram. I don't want it eroding into the artery over time."

"It can do that?"

She shrugged. "Stranger things have happened in medicine. There are more than a few case reports of metal ending up in bad places."

"So, Dr. Allen's going to fix it?" came Noah's voice from over her left shoulder. He emphasized the attending's name.

Grayson shook her head. "Dr. Allen is...busy."

McWilliams chuckled to himself. "That's putting it mildly, I think. Dr. Allen's trying to save Dougie's arm."

Noah and Babs looked at each other, both confused. McCallister shook his head, also in confusion. Harrison beamed. Blake's eyes went wide.

"Excuse me?" he balked.

"Young Dr. Carter here did enough damage to break the bones in his forearm, dislocate the elbow joint, and lacerate the major arterial system to the lower arm. One of my partners, a vascular surgeon, is scrambling to reattach everything while Allen's stabilizing the bones. They're a bit busy. Oh, and after that, someone will be reconstructing his broken face."

"But there's no second ortho on call, Gray, so who's going to fix the leg?" Noah knew the answer even before the question was out of his mouth. He still wanted to hear her say it.

"I am."

"By yourself?" Barbara asked quietly.

Grayson nodded. "Of course by myself. But I need permission. This isn't a hundred percent legal, but it needs to be done. So I need to talk to his medical power of attorney. Any idea who that is?"

The group fell silent for a moment. The captain was about to open his mouth and say that he had no idea who Ryder had selected when Harrison stepped forward.

"I'm the P.O.A.," he said.

Blake's eyebrows raised in shock. So did the captain's. "Really, detective?"

"Yeah. He asked me to be when he transferred units. I accepted."

He grabbed Grayson by the upper arm and gestured for her to move off into a vacant corner. "You and I need to have a talk."

She nodded and obediently walked where he steered her.

Grayson settled against the wall and looked up at Logan, expecting fire behind his eyes and a significant scowl. She did a double-take.

No wonder he wanted to move away from the crowd.

There were tears in his eyes. He was silent, but the strong, stoic detective was crying. She waited patiently for him to speak. It wasn't her place to push him now, especially since she was hoping to get his signature on a consent form.

Logan took a few shaky breaths, forced the water from his eyes, and then looked directly at her. All business.

"All right, girlie. You know I like you, but I don't know a damn thing about how you are with a knife. You've just been through something I wouldn't wish on my worst enemy and now you're asking to cut open a man I consider family. He's like a brother to me, do you get that? He's blood."

Grayson nodded and stayed quiet. He kept talking. "So you answer me straight. Right now. Can you really do this? And not half-ass it, but do it like the best of the best do it?"

She nodded again.

"Can you cut on someone you care about?"

She hesitated, then nodded.

"Hold your hands out."

She did. Palms down, fingers spread. They were still and steady. Logan looked into her eyes, his own on the verge of breaking again.

"You promise me you can do this?" he asked quietly.

She grabbed one of his hands in hers and looked right back at him. "I can do this, Logan."

Her voice was soft and steady. Her eyes didn't waver. She was sure, and he could feel it.

He nodded slowly. "You have my permission. Do whatever you need to do. I'll sign."

Grayson squeezed his hand gently, then let go and walked past him. She nodded at Dr. McWilliams, who pulled a surgical mask out of his back pocket and started placing it on his face.

"Be back soon," she said to the group as she followed him, disappearing behind the set of double doors that led into the OR suites.

The group of five stood still, separated, staring after her for a moment as the waiting room resumed its former low hum of chatter. Logan sat down next to Blake, who put a hand on the older detective's shoulder as he dropped his head into his hands.

"What the fuck did I just do, Nolan?"

"Having second thoughts?"

"Wouldn't you?"

"You're doing what's right. Don't worry."

"I just put Gabe's life in the hands of a kidnapping victim."

"Who happens to be the only one here who can help him. It'll be okay."

Logan glanced sideways at him. "You're calm all of a sudden."

"Someone has to be," Blake shrugged. "My partner's alive, Logan. Right now, that's all I really need to know."

McCallister sat down next to them with fresh cups of coffee. "Personally," he began, passing them around, "if Ryder's got a chance, I think that young woman is going to be the one to give it to him."

He raised his foam cup slightly as if to toast, then took a sip. Logan and Blake both picked up on the double meaning.

"At least their coffee is better than down at the office."

Blake smiled and shook his head. Logan chuckled slightly.

"Excuse me. Detectives?"

An unfamiliar voice floated over the group. Nolan looked up to see a middle-aged man in well-worn red scrubs standing nervously in front of them. His badge read *Evan Kramer, RN.*

"Can I help you?" McCallister asked.

"Um, Dr. Carter sent me out to see if anyone would be interested in watching Mr. Ryder's surgery. OR eight has an observation deck. She said you're welcome to come and watch what's going on if you'd like."

The captain looked hesitantly over at his detectives, one of whom was already on his feet. Nolan pushed through the group and stepped up to the man.

"I don't know about them, but I'm coming. Lead the way."

"Nolan..." the captain called gently.

"Captain, that's my partner in there. If I can be there, I'm going to be there. Period."

Harrison sighed from his chair and pushed himself to standing. "All right, you hard-ass, point taken. We're coming. Move it along."

10

ONE BY ONE, they filed into the observation deck above the operating room.

It was simple and utilitarian, with several rows of stadium-style seats and glass walls on three sides. It offered a direct view down into the operating room where a naked body was laid out on the operating table. Multiple figures in green scrubs were running back and forth.

A large machine with a C-looking extension was pushed off into one corner. Tables covered in blue surgical drapes lined the wall next to it. Several machines were at the top of the bed, along with a short, portly man wearing a cap and mask who was fiddling with the controls in time with the beeping machine.

Blake stepped up to the main glass wall and put a hand on it to steady himself.

"Um, Mason?"

"Yeah?"

"Can you…um…uh…explain this to me? I, um, I don't know what's going on."

The young man nodded and walked up next to him. Logan and McCallister joined him.

Barbara stayed back, curled up in one of the chairs. She couldn't bear to see any of it.

"That's Ryder on the table. The guy at the head of the bed is one of our anesthesiologists. He manages the ventilator, his heart rate and blood pressure, and keeps him comfortable. All those blue tables have the equipment Grayson needs. And those silver boxes, too. That monstrosity of a machine is the C-arm. It takes x-rays during the case."

He pointed off to one side of the room. "There's Grayson and Dr. McWilliams. Looks like they're almost ready to go."

"What are they wearing?"

"Lead aprons. It protects against the radiation exposure."

"Oh."

The four men watched as the pair exited the room, then re-entered, arms dripping wet and held at arm's length. They dressed in blue gowns and thrust their hands into latex gloves, then covered Ryder's left leg in blue surgical drapes. One of the many people in the room walked over to the C-arm and began pushing it toward the bed.

"What's happening now?"

"This is where my knowledge of the operating room and orthopedics ends, Blake," Noah shook his head apologetically. "Somehow, using all of that, she's going to fix his femur. We just have to watch."

"Can we hear them?"

Noah pushed a button on the wall and the clatter of the operating room poured in, echoing off the glass walls. The only person talking was Grayson.

"All right. We've got our length. The reduction looks reasonable. Let's get going. Knife."

Another person dressed in a blue gown and gloves handed over a silver-colored knife blade, which she took and used to cut into the skin near the knee. She took a large drill and something that looked like a long drill bit and placed it into the incision.

"Okay. AP of the knee, please. Shot."

The C-arm beeped in response and an x-ray shot onto the screen above the bed.

"Roll through to a lateral."

The C extension sunk below the operating bed and became a U, then beeped. Another picture shot up onto the screen. The sound of the drill firing screeched across the speakers.

"Shot there."

Beep.

"AP."

The U came back to a C. *Beep.*

"Entry reamer."

Another drill with a larger attachment was passed across to her and placed over the first piece, which had been left in place. The sound of the drill and grinding bone came across the speaker, then stopped as she withdrew the whole apparatus.

"Guide wire."

A long, thin wire with a small silver tip was passed over and placed into the same spot.

"AP." Pause. "Lateral."

Beep. Swung through to the U. *Beep.*

"Follow me up to the fracture site on AP."

The machine moved up toward Ryder's head and chirped again.

Ryder's broken femur bone flashed onto the screen. It looked somewhat straight. The bullet was visible as one dark mass.

Grayson reached forward and repositioned something below the leg. The bottom part of the leg moved while the top portion remained still. Blake felt sick to his stomach.

"Shot." *Beep.* "Much better."

The wire was through to the other side of the bone, and it looked much straighter.

"All right, up to the hip. AP and then a lateral."

Up in the observation deck, Blake was leaning up against the glass wall and breathing steadily.

Her voice was calm. Precise. When she asked for something, she got it. Immediately. There was no panic. No falter in her voice or her movements. She was fluid. He could tell this was her element. Her version of the interrogation room. When she was here, everything fell into place.

He leaned back slightly and tapped Mason on the shoulder. "Holy shit, Noah. She's awesome."

"Yeah..." the young man sighed into the glass. "I've never seen her operate. I mean, not alone like this. And not for a few years now."

"This is different?"

"She was a new second-year, working with a difficult attending. She was hesitant and nervous and he wasn't helping," he said wistfully. "This is totally different." He put a hand up to the glass, almost in apology. "She's so steady. I had no idea. Where the hell did this come from?"

"That isn't normal?" Captain McCallister asked, surprised.

Chuckling filtered down from the back row of seats. "No, for a chief resident, that's definitely not normal."

The group turned around to see a middle-aged man leaning back comfortably in one of the chairs, his legs kicked up on the row in front of him. He was wearing scrubs and a proud, fatherly grin, shooting glances over them into the operating room.

"Dr. Allen? What are you doing here? Aren't you busy in nine?" Noah asked.

"The vascular guys are going whole-hog on Cain's arm. I took a break to come watch."

"You're not going down there to help her?" he asked, startled.

Allen shrugged. "Does it look like she needs help, Mason?"

Noah looked back into the operating room, where Grayson was placing a long metal rod hooked onto a jig into the femur bone and pounding it into place with a large hammer. McWilliams was moving around on her command, assisting as best he could.

Noah looked back, shaking his head. "No, it doesn't."

"That's right. So sit back and let the young doctor do her job. If she gets into trouble—which I doubt—I'll go down there."

McCallister turned to fully face the attending surgeon. "Are you in the habit of letting your residents operate unsupervised, Dr. Allen?"

The man just smiled back. "Oh, good God, no. But every so often in your career, you make exceptions." He pointed out the window. "Grayson Carter is a big exception. Not that I'd ever tell her that." He stood up and walked down the short flight of steps to stand by the glass wall.

Barbara finally let her curiosity get the best of her and shuffled forward to get a good look. Noah hooked his arm around her waist, just in case she decided to black out at the sight of blood and try to take a header through the window.

"Look, I'll assume that young man on the table down there means something to all of you. So let me cut to the chase here. If I had a bullet shatter my femur, there's only one damn person I'd want putting me back together, and it sure as shit isn't one of my partners. And they do this shit often. I'd want her. Clear enough for you?"

The group stayed silent, turning back en masse to focus on the scene below. They watched Grayson run the room with precision. She placed screws through the long rod in the femur, by the knee first and then up by the hip. She cleaned out the bullet wound and fished out the bullet. A police officer dressed in a sterile white space suit took it for processing. She stitched up the wounds, placed several small dressings, and like that, she was done.

Beside them, Dr. Allen pulled up the final x-rays she had shot on a TV screen mounted on the wall. Harrison saw him shake his head.

"What?" he asked, on edge.

Allen looked over his shoulder. "I don't think there's a damn thing I can teach her anymore. This is as close to perfect as you can get." Allen walked over to the speaker by the wall and pushed a button.

"Carter!"

His voice boomed into the operating room, startling everyone but the young woman filling out paperwork in the corner. She simply craned her hear upward and looked at the observation deck, pulling off her surgical mask.

"Yes, Dr. Allen?"

"If I ever get shot, you're nailing my fucking femur, got it?"

"Yes, sir." She beamed.

"Good."

"Do you need help in nine?"

It took the occupants of the observation deck a second, but it clicked. Was she really asking to go help with Cain's case? Mouths agape, they all stared at each other. She had to be kidding.

One look at her face, however, told all of them that she wasn't.

Always the chief resident first, Noah thought to himself. *The job comes first.*

Blake opened his mouth to protest, but Allen waved him off. "Christ, no. Don't even think about it. I'm going to get my ass chewed for this as it is," he replied, smiling. "Just go with him to the unit, Carter."

Grayson nodded, standing up with the chart and placing it on top of the gurney. The nurses had moved Gabriel onto his hospital bed and were ready to wheel him directly up to the ICU. She grabbed onto one of the side rails and pushed, guiding the bed out of the operating room and out of sight.

"If you all want to follow me, I'll take you up to the unit before I get back into nine," Dr. Allen said, motioning for them to come along behind him.

He didn't get an argument. Five obedient followers filed behind him, one by one, out the door and toward the surgical intensive care unit.

11

CAIN HAD THE gun pressed to her back.

A small trickle of bright red blood ran down her neck from the spot where he'd pressed the dirty knife into the skin. He was twisting her wrist behind her back. The harder he twisted, the more her face contorted in pain. He could see the panic in her eyes. The fear. And the shock that he was stepping away from her with his hands raised.

He saw the winning smirk flash across her captor's face. Triumph. His body tensed, and the room exploded in deafening chaos. He felt the pain rip through his chest, then his leg, and he felt himself hitting the floor. The pain in his side grew, and he struggled to keep himself conscious. His body jolted, spasmed, and the world shifted.

The lights were blinding, and Gabriel squeezed his eyes shut against them.

He heard machinery, moving air, and dulled voices. He grimaced against the searing pain in his left side that came with each breath and focused on the voices. They were male, both of them. Across the room, maybe, but dulled by something. Everything was dull. And pounding. And throbbing. Then sharp again as he took a deep breath.

The lights were blinding, but they were getting hazy. He was caught in the haze. It was everywhere, and it was making everything but the light dull. There were the voices again. He strained to focus on them.

Someone was sick. Something had happened.

Nolan.

One of the voices was his partner's. He was sure of it. He concentrated on the second. It was deeper, harsher. It laughed.

Logan.

The other voice was Logan's.

Gabriel opened his eyes and tried to move, but the pain returned and forced him backward. The voices got louder. They were calling for someone. Not him. Someone else. He felt fluid snake into his veins and the haze increased, pushing the pain back down to a low hum. His face relaxed as he felt the warmth spread up from his belly. He fell back into the darkness...and there was Cain, with the gun pressed against her back.

He floated above himself, watching the same scene unfold again. Cain forced Grayson to drop to the ground with him, the knife pressed against the side of her neck. He grabbed the gun in his left hand and pressed it to her back as they stood up. He twisted her wrist and she grimaced. He spoke in her ear. She sobbed when he twisted again. And then Gabriel was forced to watch her face as he watched himself back away, hands raised.

Grayson...Grayson!

The scene went black. The light was back.

Her name kept echoing in his head. He'd heard Logan. He'd heard Blake.

But not Grayson. Never Grayson. Where was Grayson?

He felt the pain roaring back in his chest. And now in his thigh. It didn't matter. The pain didn't matter. Why couldn't he hear her? What happened?

Where was she? Was she all right?

Where is Grayson?

The noise in the background was escalating, higher pitched beeping and louder voices flooded his ears. He swam up from the haze and tried to break into the light.

He heard Logan's raised voice. It called his name, then someone else's. Gabriel opened his mouth, and all that came out was a low moan.

He struggled to sit up, and strong hands wrapped around his arms and legs. He fought against them, but the pain was too much.

The hands overpowered him. The pain overpowered him.

He tried to call out, and a harsh, guttural groan echoed across the room. They kept holding him down.

The fluid rushed through his veins again. Everything went black.

When the shadows receded and the haze began to clear, Ryder began to fight, desperate to break free. He couldn't hear the voices anymore. They were gone. But he was determined to fight. Against the hands, against the pain. Against anything that kept him in the dark.

Instead of the strong hands pushing him back onto the bed, he felt soft fingers wrap around his bicep. Something cool rested on his forehead. The touch was familiar, but Gabriel couldn't place it. His mind was too slow.

He fought against the haze again, and felt a soft hand trace down his cheek.

He stilled instantly. He knew that hand now. He knew that touch. *Her* touch.

"Gabriel. Gabriel, it's okay."

He forced his eyelids to open.

Grayson was curled up on the bed next to him, her blue eyes filled with worry. She ran her fingers along his jaw and drew a few wayward strands of hair away from his face.

Everything else faded into the background. The alarms, the machines, the hospital room, all of it. He reached up, wrapping his fingers around hers. They were warm and supple and soft. She was real.

She's okay.

Gabriel closed his eyes and faded into blackness.

12

THE HAZE RELINQUISHED its hold, and Gabriel violently swam up to the surface, opening his eyes in the dim light. He blinked and tried to clear the cobwebs he felt lingering around in his peripheral vision.

The offending bright light was gone, replaced with a dull blue haze from several monitors around the room. He was lying flat, on something only marginally comfortable, and his right arm was cold, except for one distinct spot. Half his forearm was warm and covered in something soft. He turned his head sideways, curious in spite of the morphine.

Grayson was passed out, dead asleep, her upper body folded over the side of his hospital bed. Her hand was wrapped around his right forearm. Her head was resting just next to it, her hair falling down around her shoulders.

He tried to move his arm. Her grip tightened. She was holding onto him.

He smiled. Pain seared into his side as he lifted his other arm and ran his fingers through her hair. It felt the same as it had before. She wasn't a dream. She was real. She was safe.

Thank God.

The feel of his fingers running through her hair woke her up. Grayson stirred only slightly at the first and second passes. At the third, she shook herself awake.

She wearily raised her eyes up from the mattress and looked up into the face of a very awake but morphine-loaded Gabriel Ryder. She propped herself up on her elbows and brought a hand around to his face, running it down the length of his jaw. He stared down at her, and she returned his gaze.

"Hi," he whispered in a scratchy voice.

"Hi," she whispered back.

"What are you doing?"

"Keeping you company."

She smiled when his eyes narrowed. He had questions. He just couldn't find the words to ask them.

"You do better when I stay here," she elaborated. *You don't fight.*

"Okay." He let his eyes close briefly. Her hand ran down his cheek again.

"Are you hurting?"

"No," he responded.

Grayson pressed a red button on the side of his bed.

"Dr. Carter?" a voice crackled into the room.

"We need some pain meds in here, please," she replied into the speaker above the bed.

"Give me a minute. I'll be right there."

A minute later, an elderly woman came into the room and smiled warmly as she put a syringe into the IV taped to his arm. Gabriel felt the warmth spread into his belly. The pain in his side transformed from a lightning storm into a dull rumble.

"Better?" she asked softly, running her fingers through his hair.

He nodded.

"Good."

He rested back against the pillows, completely content to let her do whatever she wanted to him.

"You came to get me," she said quietly.

He nodded. "Yeah, I did. I tried to find you."

The pain in his side flared.

Why the fuck does my side hurt so badly?

"Shh. You found me. It's okay."

"Grayson…" He struggled to move against the throbbing hum at his side, twisting one way and then another in a desperate attempt to sit up in bed.

"Stop moving. You're going to make the pain worse." She pulled the blanket up around his chest and pinned him in place with minimal pressure.

"Just rest."

She watched as Gabriel fought the haze of the medication. He ran his hand around the left side of his chest. His fingers bumped against bandages, and his eyes widened in surprise.

"Hey, get away from that," she chided, grabbing his hand away from his surgical dressing.

He wrestled out of her grasp and flung the side of the blanket off, exposing his left leg. He balked at the bandages at his knee and haphazardly felt the ones near his hip.

"Gabriel, stop," she scolded, grabbing his hand away and standing up.

Grayson grabbed the blanket and drew it back over him. When she tried to sit back down in her chair, Gabriel yanked her off balance, and she landed awkwardly on the bed next to him.

"Ooof! Hey!"

Grayson scrambled to back away from him, more than a little concerned that she'd hurt him, but Gabriel insistently pulled her closer instead. They fought for control until he tried to restrain her with his left arm. The surge of lightning through his side knocked him down. It was enough for Grayson to gain the upper hand. She settled back against the headboard, and he dropped his head to rest on her chest.

"What happened? What is this?" he asked, motioning wildly to his left side.

She ran her fingers through his hair and sighed. *How can I explain this without telling him everything?*

Grayson decided that being direct was just going to have to do. "Cain got two shots off with your gun. They both hit."

He nodded. "Where?"

"Your thigh and your chest," she replied softly.

"My chest?"

"It missed everything important. You're lucky he was a bad shot."

"And my leg?"

"It's been fixed."

"It's broken?" The growing agitation was evident in his voice.

She gently shushed him by stroking his hair. "It was," she soothed. "There's a rod down the middle of the bone now. The bullet's out. You're going to be just fine."

"Who did it?"

"Who did what?"

"The surgery."

"Someone I know." *Technically, that's not a lie.*

"It's okay?"

"Yes."

"Okay. What about Cain?"

Gabriel felt Grayson shudder against his side, and he instantly regretted asking the question. Nolan or Logan could have given him the answer just as easily.

Fucking idiot.

"Never mind. I didn't mean to..."

"Shh." She ran a hand down his cheek to quiet him. "It's okay. The last I checked, he's still in the operating room."

He opened his eyes and looked up at her, curious. "The operating room? He got shot?"

Grayson cracked a smile. "Not quite."

Gabriel looked up at her expectantly, trying to stay awake through the drug-fueled haze. She closed her eyes and sighed.

"After he shot you, I kind of lost it," she said sheepishly. "I broke his face and his arm. Apparently I lacerated an artery. He might lose his arm, even if they are able to repair everything."

"You broke his arm?"

She nodded.

"You got the gun away?"

She nodded again.

"That's my girl." He took a deep breath as pain shot through his left side again. Gabriel reached over and clutched it in agony. But the agony was getting better. The medication was finally winning.

Thank God. No wonder people get addicted to this shit.

"Go back to sleep, Gabriel."

"But..."

"I will be here when you wake up. I'm not leaving."

"I don't want you to go."

"I'm not going anywhere. Go back to sleep."

Grayson watched as Gabriel lay back onto the pillow and closed his eyes. The meds took over quickly, and his breathing leveled out. His heart rate slowed down. His blood pressure came down. The monitor stopped chirping. He was asleep and comfortable within a few minutes.

Gabriel collapsed back into the drug's haze, his dreams full of gray hallways and guns and the feel of Grayson's fingers running through his hair.

13

PHYSICAL THERAPISTS ARE sadists. They should all be shot.

That was the thought repeatedly running through Ryder's head as he limped down the hallway. Zach was a nice enough guy. He was bald and carried a few extra pounds around his midsection, but he wore his khakis and navy polo shirt well enough to hide most of it. In another place and another time, Gabriel probably would have liked the guy.

But the fact that he was standing at the end of the hallway, cheering him on like a puppy in obedience training, was just humiliating. The more he grimaced at the pain, the bigger the therapist's smile became. At one point, he'd thought that maybe he was reading too much into it.

Nope, there it is again.

The pain in his ribcage and his leg was improving, but it still surged up violently and without warning.

Like now. Goddamned physical therapists.

Thankfully, after one lap around the intensive care unit this afternoon, they decided to pile him into a wheelchair and taken him down to the main physical therapy unit. He could've walked it. He'd done three laps around the ICU this morning on his own, even before therapy, much to his nurse's glowering stares.

But apparently there was some order in the computer that said he had to take the wheelchair, and there were no exceptions. At least they'd let him change into the workout gear that Nolan had brought from home. It was bad enough having to be squeezed into one of those rolling health hazards like a ninety-year-old invalid. Doing it in an open-backed hospital gown just wasn't an option.

While Zach wheeled Gabriel down the hallway to therapy, Blake stayed close. He chattered on about the NFL playoffs and recent news headlines like his partner had been in a coma for the last month. He looked to be in desperate need of a nap. Ryder had suggested he go home and rest, but Blake had given him some vague excuse and played it off. He'd never been out of his partner's sight.

The main physical therapy unit was an impressive place. It looked more like a new-age gym than the sadist's playground Gabriel had expected. Floor-to-ceiling mirrors lined three of the four walls. The fourth was home to every type of band, ball, weight, and piece of balancing equipment known to man. It was definitely a therapist's dream come true.

Zach parked the wheelchair in the corner, and Gabriel shakily pushed himself out of it as best he could. Blake held out a set of crutches for him, which he waved off like he had been doing all day. Ryder knew he had medical permission to put his whole body weight on his leg if he wanted to, so that's exactly what he was going to do.

In fact, his leg felt pretty good. A little pain in the knee now and again, but nothing terrible. It was his chest that presented the bigger problem. He silently followed Zach back to a line of flat, padded exam tables and pushed himself up onto one of them.

"On your back, head up that way," Zach motioned.

"Go get some coffee or something, Nolan," Ryder said as he leaned backward on his elbows.

"Not a chance. Logan wants pictures."

"Put the fucking phone away," he spat as he lay down as instructed.

"All the way on your back," Zach said, stepping up to the side of the table. "This is going to be the easy part today. Just range of motion. Let me have the weight of your leg and only help when I tell you to."

Gabriel nodded and rested his head back, letting the therapist bend and straighten his knee and then his hip back and forth. The ceiling was thankfully painted white. Gray would have triggered another flashback to the damned basement, and he'd had enough of those dreams over the past night to last a lifetime.

And they weren't done. They were tucked down in the shadows of his mind, just waiting for sundown and a heavy dose of narcotics to rear their monstrous heads.

"Well, well, how's Wonder Boy this afternoon?"

Gabriel rolled his head toward the side of the table. Logan was staring down at him, just behind Zach, hands stuffed into his jean pockets and grinning like a cat.

"Good morning to you, too, asshole," he snarled, grimacing against the pain.

"So, that mood of yours hasn't improved, I see." Logan chuckled back.

"Where've you been?"

"Guard duty on one of your ICU neighbors."

Gabriel's eyes snapped open. "Oh." *Cain.*

"Besides, mother hen here has it all under control, don't you?" Logan asked, lifting his chin in Nolan's direction.

Blake glared at him over the therapist's shoulder. Before he could think of something smart to say back, another body joined their group.

"Well, how's the patient this morning?"

Dr. Allen stood at the bottom of the table, his white coat slightly wrinkled and glasses pushed back on his head. Gabriel pushed up onto his forearms and nodded hello.

"He's doing well," Zach said, stopping the exercises for a moment. "Full range of motion already, virtually painless. And he's walking."

"With crutches, I hope?"

"I don't need them," Gabriel replied.

The rest of the group shook their heads. Dr. Allen gave Zach a skeptical look, but didn't say anything. Instead, he took a few pieces of paper out of his back pocket and handed them over to Gabriel.

"Thought you might want these. Printouts of your x-rays. I'd show you on a computer, but there isn't one down here that's hooked up to the system."

Gabriel looked over the pieces one by one. The first were clearly the injury x-rays. It made him a bit sick to think that the twisted bone in the picture had actually been his leg.

The second set was from after the surgery. A long metal rod filled up the entire inside length of the bone, two screws up by his hip and three down by his knee. Harrison and Nolan took the photos and looked them over after Ryder was finished.

"Call me crazy, doc, but these look pretty damned good," Logan said, switching back and forth between the before and after pictures.

"I would agree with that, detective." Dr. Allen chuckled, putting his hands back inside his coat pockets. "With the exception of a little knee pain every now and again, you should get back to normal very quickly, Detective Ryder. We'll need to check on you in about two weeks, then another six or so after that."

Gabriel sat up and swung his legs over to the side of the table. He waited a second for the pain in his chest to die down, then reached out and shook the doctor's hand.

"Thanks for fixing me up, Dr. Allen."

The doctor scoffed and shook his head. "I had very little to do with it, actually."

The confusion was immediate and plain as day on Ryder's face. "I thought you…"

Allen waved him off, laughing. "I was in the next room over, trying to put Doug's arm back together with the vascular surgeons."

"Well, then who should I be thanking?"

Gabriel looked from Dr. Allen to Logan and finally to Blake, who coughed and sheepishly pointed toward the entrance to the therapy unit.

Ryder followed his partner's line of sight to the door, and for a minute he completely forgot what he'd been asking about.

Grayson was standing in the doorway, dressed in black jeans, boots, and an ivory sweater. She was clearly looking for someone, but halfway through the search, one of the other therapists walked up to her and started asking questions about something on a clipboard. The intrusion gave Ryder enough of a jolt to refocus, and when he looked at the expression on Blake's face, it hit him.

"She…she did this?" Gabriel looked back at the x-rays, then down at his left leg like it was a foreign object.

"Technically, I'm the physician of record." Allen nodded. "But she's responsible for the surgery going as well as it did. I just watched at the end. If there's anybody to thank for putting you back together, it's Carter."

Logan laid a gentle hand on Ryder's shoulder. "I gave her permission. You should've seen it, buddy. She was pretty badass."

Ryder quirked an eyebrow up. Logan smiled. "I'm not kidding. If I ever get shot, she's fixing my leg."

He looked back down at his leg. *What in the hell am I supposed to say to that?*

Dr. Allen nonchalantly buttoned his white coat and cleared his throat. "All right, Zach. Get back to it. I'll catch up with you all later." He turned and walked out of the therapy unit.

By the time Ryder thought to raise his head, Allen was already out the door.

And Grayson was gone.

14

SEVERAL HOURS LATER, the trio was back in the ICU.

Logan's relief unit was still watching over Cain, so he was taking the extra time to lean back in one of the uncomfortable plastic chairs and watch TV. Blake was attempting to play solitaire. A clever ruse, since he too was watching the B-list reality show.

"How can you two watch that?" Ryder groaned.

He'd refused to get back into bed after they'd wheeled him back from therapy. With a little charm, he'd been able to get a reasonably comfortable chair moved in from the waiting room. It wasn't great, but it was better than what Logan and Blake had to deal with.

"Let me guess. You'd prefer the History Channel? National Geographic?" Logan smirked.

"Anything is better than this."

"Good God, you're even a TV snob. Unbelievable."

Two sets of eyes rolled.

"Give him the remote, Logan," Blake interjected.

"Don't tell me you're in on this!"

"No, but he did get shot. We should let him watch what he wants," Nolan replied.

"Awww, hell, rub it in. Whaddaya want to watch there, Wonder Boy?"

"Just pick something that doesn't have housewives in the title, Harrison."

The older detective started flipping through channels, mumbling something under his breath. A brief knock rapped on the glass door, and a young nurse walked in.

"Mr. Ryder, time for your medications."

She started walking toward him with a syringe. Ryder instantly held up his hand to stop her. "What is it?"

"Morphine. For the pain."

He shook his head. "I don't need it."

"You don't want the pain to get out of control," she chided, taking the cap off of the needle.

"The pain's fine. I don't need that. It knocks me out." *And the nightmares come back.*

He hid his right arm behind his back so she couldn't get to the IV port. The nurse frowned and put the cap back on the needle.

"Okay. I need to make a call to Dr. Allen." She walked out of the room and shut the door.

"Ooooo, somebody's in trouble!" Logan smirked.

Ryder chucked a water cup at him.

"Hey!"

"Asshole."

"Quit it, both of you," Nolan whined. "I think I found the Nature Channel."

Several minutes passed before there was another knock at the door. Gabriel rolled his eyes, mentally steeling himself for another fight about narcotic pain medications.

Instead, he was pleasantly surprised to find Grayson leaning up against the doorjamb, arms folded. She was shaking her head at him.

"Do you have to be so stubborn?" she scolded.

"You've met him, right?" Blake piped up from the corner.

Grayson crossed the room and held out a small plastic cup. There were two white pills inside. Gabriel eyed them, then looked up at her suspiciously.

"You keep refusing morphine, and I can see from the hallway that you're hurting. Try these."

He vehemently shook his head. "I'm not taking narcotics." *I can't see you dying in Cain's arms in the daytime.*

She rolled her eyes at him. "No kidding. This is tramadol. It's milder and shouldn't knock you out."

He hesitated, then kicked his head back and downed the pills dry. "Happy?" he growled.

Grayson's eyebrows shot up. "Wow. They weren't kidding. You are in a bad mood today."

Shit.

Gabriel scolded himself and hung his head. "Sorry."

When she didn't reply, he opened his eyes. He registered the click of her boots on the tile floor, heading for the door, and he snapped his head up from the pale green tile. She was out the door before he could tell her to stop. Logan registered the fear in his eyes.

"Relax, buddy. She's coming back."

He was right. Less than thirty seconds later, Grayson walked back in the room with Dr. Allen in tow. She stayed on the far side of the room, away from him. Gabriel frowned at her. She didn't, wouldn't, couldn't look at him.

"Well, detective, I've got good news and bad news," Dr. Allen began.

"The good news?"

"Dr. McWilliams from trauma has cleared you to go home."

"And the bad news?"

"*I* haven't cleared you to go home."

Ryder's frown deepened into a scowl. "Why not?"

"I watched your second round of therapy today, and I agree with Zach. You're still weak and unsteady on your feet. The pain in your side isn't helping any. And you're still requiring IV narcotics for pain control."

"I just refused them."

"But you took them four hours ago before therapy," Allen countered, shrugging his shoulders. "It's the rules. You're weak, on drugs, and you live alone. That's a recipe for disaster. I can't discharge you."

"Then I'll just leave."

The tension in the room was mounting, and both Blake and Logan were becoming uncomfortable.

"That's your choice, detective, but you would do so against medical advice and at your own risk. I would sincerely recommend that you stay with us, at least for another night."

"I'd rather not," he sing-songed sarcastically.

"Gabe, it's not the end of the world to stay another night here," Harrison said calmly.

"I'm not staying here," he spat. Gabriel focused on the man in the white coat standing in front of him. "With all due respect, Dr. Allen, I appreciate everything that you've done for me, but right now, all I want is a real shower and to sleep in my own bed. And I can't do either of those things here. I'm going home."

"Look," Harrison said, butting into the conversation, "what if one of us stays with him?"

Dr. Allen shook his head. "I'm sorry, but it's not that easy. With the medications on board and the chest wall injury, he has to have a medical professional look after him. Someone with training in case something should go wrong at home. That means a nurse or higher."

"Shit."

The room was quiet. Ryder continued to face off with Dr. Allen from across the room, both men clearly unwilling to yield.

"What if I stay with him?"

Gabriel turned his eyes up to look at Grayson, who was in turn looking straight at him.

Really?

Really?

Really?

"Really?" Allen asked, eyebrows raised.

She shrugged. "I'm off of work for a while. I don't have anything better to do. And I have the initials behind my name to help him get out of here without signing out AMA. But it's up to him."

Gabriel hesitated, mulling over his options. He could still leave, go home, and get what he wanted. Logan and Blake would force themselves onto his couch, no doubt, so he wouldn't be by himself. But the second option, Grayson taking care of him…that had potential…to be wonderful or be an incredible disaster. Hell, he'd just snapped at her a minute ago for no good reason except that she'd wanted to keep him comfortable. Of the two possibilities, he was banking on the incredible disaster.

"I need an answer, detective. Are you staying or going?" Allen's voice echoed across the room.

"Going."

Dr. Allen nodded. "I figured. Now, do I need to get the AMA paperwork?"

After a beat on the clock, Gabriel shook his head.

Allen smiled to himself and turned to face Grayson. "You know what to watch for. Anything looks off, you haul his ass back in here. Give him a head injury if you have to. I'll go tell the nurses to get him out of here."

Dr. Allen walked out of the room, followed closely by Logan and Blake, who made some excuse of trying to find the car.

Gabriel kept his head down and concentrated on the floor, even when her boots came to rest in his field of view. Grayson crouched down in front of him and craned her neck around to try to look him in the eye.

Gabriel felt guilty and raised his eyes up to hers so she wouldn't throw out her neck. She smiled and laid a hand on his thigh.

"You just have to be stubborn, don't you?" she said softly.

"I'm sorry."

"Don't be," she murmured with a smile. "But don't think I'm going to put up with any of it once you get out of here."

That earned her a small chuckle.

"Don't be too hard on me, doctor."

"Back at you, detective. Now, come on, get up. Let's get you out of here."

Gabriel stood up and started limping toward the door.

"Where do you think you're going?"

"I'm leaving."

"Not like that, you're not."

He turned around to see her stepping behind the wheelchair. He frowned and shook his head.

"Absolutely not." *There's no way in hell she's going to push me around in that thing like I'm a fucking invalid.*

Grayson scowled. "Gabriel, sit down."

"No."

"Then you're not leaving."

"You're not pushing me around in that thing. I can walk."

"I know you can walk. But if you fall before I get you off of hospital property, it's a lawsuit. You want to get out of here? These are the rules. Get in." She pointed emphatically toward the wheelchair.

"You can't make an exception?"

"Dr. Allen's already making an exception letting you out of here with me playing nursemaid. Don't push it. Please."

At the last word, Gabriel stopped fighting. She was right. He eased himself down into the floppy leather seat, and Grayson helped him kick his feet up onto the footrests.

"Ready?"

He nodded. As she walked around to the back of the chair, he reached out across his body and grabbed her arm. She glanced down in surprise, expecting to see him looking up at her. But he kept his eyes locked on the floor in front of his feet.

"Don't let me be cruel to you, Grayson. Don't let me hurt you."

She frowned in confusion. "Why would you do something like that?"

He shook his head. "Just don't let me, all right?"

She placed a hand over the one grabbing her arm. "I'll be just fine."

Gabriel released her. She pushed the wheelchair through the door and down the hallway toward the elevators.

I hope so.

15

IT WAS AFTER five p.m. when Logan turned the key in the lock and opened Gabriel's front door. He made sure everything was well out of the way—which of course it was since the damned place was spotless—and then opened it wide.

Gabriel limped into his entryway, clearly still favoring his left leg and bordering on exhaustion. Once he was in range, he clutched onto the countertop for extra support. There was a small voice in the back of his head saying "I told you so, idiot" for not bringing the crutches home from the hospital. It was getting harder and harder to ignore it.

Grayson followed, a small bag of groceries in her right hand and an overnight bag slung over her left arm. They'd made a bit of a detour and stopped by her house, just long enough for her to pack some clothes and grab a few things from the cupboard.

Logan had been keenly aware that there usually wasn't much food at Gabriel's apartment, and he had been determined to ensure that Grayson didn't go hungry during her stint at the apartment. Gabriel lived off of scotch; there was no reason she had to for days on end.

Blake was out picking up the dinner that he'd called in on the way back toward downtown. They all needed to eat, and Gabriel seemed to be woefully sick of hospital food.

Grayson was the last to step into the vast apartment. Logan noticed his former partner's eyes didn't stray from her body as she made her way, slack-jawed, into the entryway.

That's new. Never seen him do that before.

Logan kept one eye on Gabriel and the other on Grayson. He didn't need to take in the apartment. He'd been there enough already to know the place by heart.

A two-story entryway opened up onto a massive floor plan. A gourmet kitchen and bar sat off to the right. The living room was down several steps to the left, and a long hallway, which led back to bedrooms and bathrooms, curved off to the right behind the dining room. The furniture was a cozy combination of rustic and contemporary, and each piece looked more expensive than all the furniture in her house put together.

Even to Logan, it was obvious Grayson was too afraid to touch anything.

She set the groceries down on the bar and her bag on the carpet by the door. She kicked off her shoes and walked over to the tall windows that looked out over the mountains. It was still just light enough to see the outlines of the peaks against the darkening violet sky.

"This is beautiful," she said.

Gabriel stayed rooted to the floor by the bar, keeping track of every place Grayson stepped, everything she touched. And Logan kept track of him. The longer he watched, the deeper the lines in his forehead became, until his worried interest in his former partner hit a boiling point.

Jesus, he's stalking her through his own living room. He's gotta cut this shit out.

"All right, I'm gonna get this one into the shower. Blake should be up in a bit with the food."

He hustled Gabriel down the hallway toward his bedroom without another word.

Once he heard Grayson start unloading the groceries onto the granite, he slammed the door shut behind him and crossed his arms, glaring at his former partner.

"What the hell, Logan?" Ryder asked, unsteady on his feet as he pulled his T-shirt over his head.

"You in the habit of stalking people in your own house, or is this something new?"

"What?"

"You heard me. I could've easily replaced you with Douglas Cain, plopped her in his apartment instead of yours, and gotten the same damned creepy feeling."

"Bullshit."

Logan shoved Gabriel back against the granite countertop and shoved a finger in his face. "You said once you and Cain wanted the same thing. Don't start acting like the fucker. I worry about you enough. I don't need to worry about that shit, too. Now get your ass in the shower. I'm tired of smelling antiseptic."

"Get the fuck out."

Logan was only too happy to comply. He stormed down the hallway and into the kitchen where he found Grayson putting the few meager items she'd brought from the bungalow into the refrigerator. He took a deep breath to steady himself.

"Kinda bare, huh?"

"You're not kidding." She nodded. "He doesn't eat here much, does he?"

"If he does, it's usually from a takeout box."

Grayson just nodded again in reply and shut the door, shaking her head.

"You want a drink?" he asked.

"I think we could all use one," she replied.

"Beer?"

She nodded. He grabbed two bottles from the six-pack she'd brought on the counter, popped the caps, and handed one over to her. The faint sound of the shower turning on filtered down the hallway.

"Cheers."

Logan clinked his bottle against hers, took a long swig, and motioned toward the windows.

"C'mon."

Grayson took a more modest sip from the longneck and followed him into the living room. They each took a club chair by the fireplace and looked out over the quickly fading outline of the western mountains.

"You care about him a lot, don't you?" she said after a long moment of silence. "Gabriel, I mean."

"Heh. Yeah. But don't tell anybody. It could ruin my image."

She smiled. "I get the feeling Blake does, too."

"I think his partner getting shot in the line of duty has brought out his mothering side."

Grayson giggled. "That's not a bad thing, you know."

"If he starts knitting, I'm going to have him committed."

She laughed into her beer. "You're not serious."

"Try me, sweetheart." He grinned. "I'm this close to calling the guys with the straitjackets on both of them."

Grayson shook her head at him and took another drink. They sat in amicable silence for a while, just enjoying the calm serenity of the silent apartment. Logan turned on the gas fireplace when a chill crept into the air.

"Doc, I've got a confession to make."

"Oh?"

"Gabe knows about the surgery. He knows you were the one to fix him up."

This was news. Grayson's face fell, and she got very quiet. Suddenly the fraying corner of the label on her beer bottle was fascinating. She picked at it incessantly.

"I…I didn't realize he knew. I didn't tell him."

"Dr. Allen did. It just kind of came up out of nowhere. I thought you should know."

She kept picking. "I didn't want him to know."

Logan raised his eyebrows, clearly surprised. "Why not?"

"I…I don't…it's difficult to explain. I mean, really, he should've been fixed by an attending. The only reason I did it was because Allen was held up. Gabriel was on the table; there weren't any other options. But…I…uh…I don't know, it just feels strange. To look at him and say, 'hi, I'm a resident in training. You're responsible for saving my life from a delusional psychopath, and they just threw my butt in there to fix you because I was the last option.'"

"From what Dr. Allen said, you did a great job. We watched. I'm no expert, but it looked good to me."

She shrugged. "And he told me as much. I went over the case with him after Gabriel got settled in the ICU. His leg is about as close to perfect as it was before he got shot. But it's like operating on family. It's just something that always leaves a bit of a sinking feeling in your stomach. Like maybe someone else could've done better."

"According to Allen, nobody could have. He said he'd have you do his leg."

"He was kidding, Logan," she replied, rolling her eyes over the rim of the bottle.

"Didn't seem like it to me."

Grayson shrugged and took another drink. "I don't want Gabriel to think he got second-rate care to a serial killer."

Harrison leaned across to put a hand on her forearm. "If he's stupid enough to think that, I'll beat him up myself."

Grayson smiled at him, just in time to hear a loud thud and the sound of crashing glass echo down the hallway. Her eyes widened, panicked.

Without saying a word, she sprung up from her chair and sprinted down the hallway. She followed the intermittent swearing to Gabriel's bedroom door and shoved it open. She looked wildly around the room, not seeing Gabriel or anything out of place.

Another muttered curse came from an opening in the wall to the right, which she followed to the en suite master bathroom.

Ryder was sprawled across the floor, dressed only in a pair of well-worn sweat pants, attempting to push himself up on the palms of his hands. The rug at the bottom of the vanity was askew, and several glass bottles from the countertop had fallen to the floor and shattered. The shards were dangerously close to his hands.

"Gabriel, don't move! You're going to cut yourself," she yelped as she hurried into the room.

He startled at her voice. From the blank look on his face, he was confused, not only as to why she was in his apartment but why in the hell she was worried about him in the first place.

Grayson crouched down beside him and instantly started looking him over. "What happened?"

He shook the fog from his eyes and seemingly reset in a nanosecond.

"Nothing," he snapped.

"You're on the floor and surrounded by broken glass. I'm not an idiot. Try again," she huffed.

Gabriel growled in frustration, but she kept her gaze steadily on him.

"I fell."

"That's better. Can you stand?"

"That's what I was trying to do when you barged in here," he barked.

"Careful, detective. I might just leave you here," she scolded.

The combination of the words *leave* and *you* snapped Ryder out of his mood. "I'd rather you didn't," he said softly.

"Yeah. Me, too. Now..." she replied, grabbing his right arm and looping it over her shoulder, "put your weight on your right leg and push up."

He did as he was told and stood up. Grayson steadied him and guided him over to the counter.

"Hold on to this," she said, tapping the countertop.

"Why?"

"Because I have to check your incisions, and I don't need you falling on top of me with the floor already covered in glass."

"They're fine."

She looked up at him and scowled.

"You came home with the understanding that I was to look after you. I can easily haul you back to the hospital and have you admitted again. Now, you can cooperate with me for two minutes and then go back to being a complete jackass, or you can limp back down to the car. Or I can make a really big scene and call an ambulance. What's it going to be?"

Grayson folded her arms in front of her chest and waited. The fire burning behind her blue eyes was more than enough to shut Ryder up. He nodded his consent, and she started to look him over. She ran her fingers over the wounds on his chest first.

"These look okay, but they need a new bandage. Where did you put the stuff they sent home with you?"

He pointed toward the side of a large bathtub. The supplies were sitting on the marble ledge. Grayson ripped open one of the packages and started methodically dressing the wounds.

"Now, let me see your leg."

Ryder sat up on the countertop and pulled his pant leg up, exposing his knee. After moving him around a bit, she placed several small dressings to cover the incision on his knee and the small poke holes she'd used for the screws.

"Okay, now the hip."

"It's fine."

"Jump down, Gabriel, and stop talking," she said, rolling her eyes at him.

He did as she asked, sliding down from the counter and pulling down the side of his waistband. Grayson tried her best to focus and stay clinical, but despite her best efforts, she lingered on the cut of his lower abs just a few beats too long.

Gabriel noticed and smirked. The fact that her fingers were tracing themselves absently over the skin of his upper thigh while she was momentarily distracted was stimulating in its own right.

"Is something wrong?" he asked smoothly.

She blushed and shook her head, hastily applying the last small dressing. "I should get something to clean this up," she muttered, and made a move to retreat as fast and as far as she could from the bathroom.

"Forget about it," he said softly and grabbed her arm.

She looked up hesitantly at him.

"You promised to not let me be cruel to you."

"I know," she nodded. "But why do it in the first place? All I want to do is help you."

"I'm not used to needing help. Or asking for it. This is new to me."

"Try to wrap your mind around it."

"I should be taking care of you."

"Don't be silly, I'm fine," she said hastily, tugging gently on his hand to get him moving. "Let's find you a shirt. Dinner should be here soon."

16

DINNER WAS LIVELY. Harrison and Nolan tossed back beers and told stories from their respective early days partnered with Ryder.

Grayson doubled over laughing as Logan described their first scene together, an odd couple in an Armani three-piece suit and a leather biker jacket. Blake followed up with stories of driving down one-way streets downtown, yelling case details out the window of his Subaru while Ryder was out on a run.

Gabriel sat on the couch, propped up on pillows with ice draped across his knee and a beer within arm's reach, smiling. It had been a long time since he'd been able to just sit in his damned apartment, have a drink, and not worry about serial killers or rapists or child molesters.

He knew he'd have to worry about Cain at some point. There would be a trial with evidence logs and arraignments and testimony to deal with. That was for later. Tonight, he didn't want to think about it. He just wanted to listen to everyone laugh and tell stories and watch Grayson smile.

Eventually, it was time to call it a night. His three guests hastily cleaned up while he sat helplessly nursing a drink on the couch. Logan and Blake said goodnight and headed back to their own homes and their own beds. Gabriel sat waiting while clacking and clambering echoed out from his kitchen. After the cacophony calmed down, Grayson came back into the living room, a bottle of cold beer in each hand.

"This is your last one," she said, handing one over to him.

Gabriel nodded and took a long drink.

She wandered over to the club chairs and sat down, pulling her legs up underneath her and staring out at the mountains. Even from here, the twinkling lights from the small mountain towns were still just barely visible against the black night. Grayson leaned back against the chair and sighed, taking a small sip from her beer and holding it in between her two hands.

Gabriel watched her from his vantage point on the couch. She looked tired. The way her body was molded into the chair, the way her head lolled off to one side as she looked out the window…she was dangerously close to falling asleep sitting up.

What in the hell is she doing here?

On a basic level, he understood. She had made a promise to her attending to look after him. After the way he'd treated her earlier today, on top of everything she'd been through in the last week, she should have been running the other way.

Back home. Back to Noah and Barbara and everything that had been neat and normal two months ago. But she hadn't. He'd snapped at her; she'd smiled back at him like it didn't matter. He'd pushed her away; she'd waited patiently until he'd come back licking his wounds.

Goddamn it, she shouldn't be taking care of me. I should be taking care of her.

And instead, here he was, an invalid stuck on the couch with a beer limit. He was a burden to her.

Grayson curled deeper into her chair and kept her eyes on the twinkling stars. When she didn't hear anything from the couch for quite a long time, she twisted around and looked back.

The darkness she saw in Gabriel's eyes immediately had her on guard. He was staring in her direction, but not seeing her. He was looking through her again.

She felt a shiver run down her spine. She still didn't know what to do when he looked like that. She set her beer down on the side table and draped her forearms over the back of the chair.

"Hey," she said softly, trying to get his attention. "Gabriel? Are you okay?"

He kept staring at her. Or beyond her. Wherever he was looking. He sighed and dropped his head.

Grayson frowned, got up from her chair, and softly padded over to him. She eased herself down onto the floor beside the couch, positioning herself directly next to him. She craned her neck up to get a look at his face. His breathing was ragged. He was fighting with himself.

What's wrong with him?

She gently laid her hand on his forearm. "Gabriel?" she asked softly.

He jumped at her touch and blinked rapidly, turning to look at her. She watched his pulse thunder to life, the beat visible in the veins straining against his clenched jawline. Grayson didn't move. She didn't dare to. She sat perfectly still, waiting for the hidden storm waging behind his dark eyes to calm. Waiting for him to give her an in.

She never got one.

Without warning, Gabriel sprung up from the couch. He immediately grimaced in pain, doubling over the arm.

Grayson pushed up onto her heels in an attempt to get up and steady him. He thrust his hand out to stop her and spun around, hastily moving down the hallway as fast as his injured leg would carry him.

"Gabriel!"

Grayson jumped up and ran behind him, catching up with him at the edge of the kitchen. She scampered in front of him and blocked his path, placing her hands onto his chest gently to make him stop.

He bristled at her touch. "Grayson, move."

"Talk to me. Please," she pleaded.

What the hell just happened? What's wrong with him?

He shook his head. "Just move."

He took her hands off of his chest, placed them at her sides, and then moved around her.

Grayson watched him limp down the hallway toward his bedroom, speechless. He opened the door, and promptly slammed it behind him. She stood stock-still in the hallway, looking after him. Whatever he had been thinking, it had upset him. Fast and hard.

She shook her head and walked back into the living room. She cleaned up the remaining plates and beer bottles, put the ice pack in the sink, and turned off the lights. She grabbed her overnight bag from the floor and carried it with her down the hallway toward the guest room.

Logan had pointed it out to her midway through the evening. It was spacious and clean, Spartan and cold. She smirked as she opened the door.

How appropriate.

17

GRAYSON DIDN'T RUSH unpacking her overnight bag. She tucked her two sets of clothes for the upcoming days away into a dresser at the far end of the room. She took her toiletries into the en suite bathroom and unpacked them one at a time.

Thankfully, she'd remembered everything, right down to her usual perfume. She put her hair up and turned the shower on, waiting until the floor-to-ceiling glass doors were fogged up and steamy before stepping into the warm spray.

She took her time, and when she stepped out of the shower, she was pruney and warm and completely sated. She slathered on lotion and the usual moisturizer to her face, then scampered out into the cold bedroom, grabbed her pajamas, and quickly ran back into the warmth of the bathroom.

She looked over them happily. They were new. A set of pants and a long-sleeved button-up shirt, both made of dark navy silk. There was a light gray lace tank top as well, to go under the sleep shirt. She pulled them on, then brushed out her hair. She checked the clock as she sauntered back into the bedroom. It was after ten o'clock.

He'd had enough time.

Grayson gingerly opened her bedroom door and walked down the hallway. She paused outside of the master suite. For a moment, she wondered if he was already asleep. She couldn't hear any noise, but there was soft light filtering out underneath the doorjamb.

She knocked twice, and waited. She didn't get a response.

She sucked in a shaky breath, turned the door handle, and pushed.

Gabriel was sitting in bed, a book in his lap and a dimmed reading light turned on by the side of the bed. He looked up when she walked through the door, startled to see her, but Grayson didn't notice. She was too busy taking in the bedroom, something she'd missed when she'd sprinted through it a few hours earlier.

The bed was modern and simple. The leather headboard and footboard were well-worn and likely incredibly soft to the touch. Her fingertips itched to run across them.

There were dressers on either wall, their dark wood slightly roughened but polished to a shine. The fireplace across the room was blazing, the licking flames throwing dancing shadows across the walls. There were floor-to-ceiling windows on the far wall that looked out over the mountains.

A single wingback chair stood over a fur rug near the fireplace. It looked comfortable. And it was a safe distance away from him, just in case she ended up being unwelcome.

While she crossed the room, she felt Gabriel drink her in. Her skin was pink and still flushed from the heat of the water. It only got hotter under his gaze. She saw his fingers twitch involuntarily out of the corner of her eye. It was as if he was desperate to touch her, to feel the silk of her pajamas thread through his fingertips.

Grayson navigated her way around the bed and sat down in the wingback chair. The crimson suede was warm from the fireplace. She folded her legs up, one underneath her and one bent in front of her chest. She wrapped her arms around her bent leg and looked across the short gap to the bed.

Gabriel had put his book aside and was looking at her

intently. She stared back at him for a moment, waiting for him to speak. He didn't. So she did.

"Are you feeling better?" she asked softly.

He sighed and nodded. "I'm sorry."

"What happened?"

He closed his eyes and rested his head back against the headboard. "Do you have to ask questions about everything?"

"You know my answer to that question already," she replied quietly.

"I'm just...I...you're taking care of me." He sounded dejected. Completely worn out. And embarrassed.

Grayson wrinkled her forehead. "So?"

"You figured it out."

"What? I figured what out?"

"Cain. You put the pieces together."

"It wasn't hard to figure out once he started persistently stalking me around the hospital."

"But you got out. You got yourself out."

Grayson wrinkled her forehead.

What is he talking about? He's all over the place tonight.

"What?"

"You didn't need me. You got out. I didn't save you."

Grayson's face fell and she bit her lip. "Didn't save me?"

"You got out yourself. I didn't find you."

"Gabriel, what the hell are you talking about? Of course you found me. You were down in the basement."

"You got out. Without me."

"Barely. Why does that even matter?"

"It just does. To me, it does."

"It shouldn't. It doesn't to me. Gabriel, you got shot trying to save me. Twice! You could have died."

"He had you. For four days. I didn't find you."

Grayson watched helplessly as Gabriel disappeared inside his head again. She saw his face go blank and his shoulders sag. He was looking past her again, into the fire.

She knew she had to get to him quickly, but she stayed rooted to the wingback chair. She was too afraid to move any closer. She didn't trust herself.

"Who said you were supposed to be the one to find me?"

"Me. I was supposed to save you from him."

"You did."

"I didn't take him down. You did."

"So?"

"You broke his face. You broke his arm."

"And?"

"I should have taken him down. Gotten him away from you. Instead, he played me. He knew I'd give up my gun."

Grayson scowled and shook her head. "Gabriel. Look at me. You. Got. Shot. Saving me. You need to stop this."

He shook his head and refused to look at her. She sat back and watched him for a few minutes. He was hurting. She could see it. He was starting to splint against the pain in his left chest wall. He wasn't taking a full breath.

Enough.

Grayson stood up and walked out of the bedroom to the kitchen, found the prescription bottle on the counter, and grabbed a glass of water. She headed back into the bedroom, startling at the doorway when she found him frantically scrambling to get out of bed to come after her. When Gabriel saw her at the door, wide-eyed, he sagged forward onto the edge of the mattress, relieved.

Wait, is he actually worried that I'm leaving?

She pushed the door closed and walked softly over to his side of the bed. Gabriel shifted to give her enough room to sit down. She held up her hand over his, and he opened his palm. When she dropped the two small white pills into his hand, he looked up like he was going to argue.

She shook her head right back at him. "Don't. Just take them."

Her voice didn't hold the conviction she had hoped it would. It sounded soft and shaky. She was pleading with him.

Gabriel took the water out of her hand and knocked the pills back without a word.

Grayson took the glass back and set it down on a small silver tray on top of the night table. She fished the book out of the twisted bed sheets, creased the page to mark his spot, and closed it.

She rescued his dark-rimmed glasses next. Grayson leaned over, grabbed them off of the comforter, and placed them on top of the book. She twisted the small knob at the base of the bedside lamp, and the room plunged deeper into darkness. The fireplace provided the only light, apart from what little filtered up from the street below.

"Time for bed. Get some sleep." She stood up from the bed and started toward the door.

"Grayson."

He called her name so softly she almost missed it. She turned around at the edge of the fireplace. "Hmm?"

"Will you stay?"

"I am staying. I'll be right next door in the guest room."

"No. Here."

His voice was low and slow and slightly slurred. The drugs were starting to take effect. She'd given him something much stronger than tramadol.

"I don't think that's such a good idea right now."

Grayson felt like such a hypocrite. How many times had he stayed with her? Held her when she was scared and crying? And truthfully, a large part of her wanted to do exactly that. Climb into the other side of his bed and hold him until he fell asleep.

But something was whispering in the back of her mind to stay in the guest room. So she backed away and shut the door softly behind her.

Gabriel didn't call after her. He was already asleep.

18

A GUTTURAL, TORTURED scream echoed down the hallway.

Grayson shot up in bed and forced her eyes to adjust to the darkness. She slowed her breathing down and strained to listen in the dark. Nothing. The apartment was quiet.

It must have been a dream.

She shook her head and lay back down on her side. Her eyes were almost closed when she heard the sound again. It was low, strained, and could only have come from someone in incredible pain. And there was only one other living soul in the apartment.

Grayson jumped out of bed and sprinted to the end of the hallway. She heard the sound a third time, coming from behind Gabriel's bedroom door. She slammed her shoulder into the heavy door, forcing it open, and stumbled headfirst into the room.

The fireplace was still on. Grayson rubbed her eyes and tried to focus on the bed in the dim light.

Gabriel was moaning and thrashing around on the mattress. The sheets hung off to one side. The comforter was nearly on the floor. He was shirtless. A sheen of cold sweat sparkled across his chest and stomach. His hair was plastered to his forehead.

He was having a nightmare.

Grayson ran over to him and knelt down by the side of the bed. She reached out, a half-hearted attempt to wake him up, but he violently thrashed forward and pushed her away. She didn't try to get close to him again. But he was talking in his sleep. He was bargaining with someone. Grayson leaned in as close as she could to try to hear him.

"No...no...let her go...Cain, let her go...put the gun down...don't touch her...don't fucking touch her...put it down...no...no, no, no...no, Grayson, no!"

His back arched off the bed as a scream escaped his lips again.

Grayson ducked underneath a flailing arm, then sat up and settled onto the side of the bed. Slowly and steadily, she started saying his name. Over and over again.

It didn't take long for something inside of Gabriel to register her presence. Minute by minute, he calmed down. The thrashing stopped. His breathing settled. But he kept talking in his sleep, mumbling over and over again, her name mixed with Cain's and "put the gun down" and "let her go."

When she was certain he wouldn't try to strike her, Grayson finally plucked up the courage to reach out and touch his forehead. It was slick with sweat and far too warm.

Shit. He's given himself a fever.

She bolted into the bathroom and grabbed a washcloth, ran it underneath the cold tap, and took it back into the bedroom. She ran the cool cloth over his forehead, then brought it down along his neck and chest. By the time she was done, his breathing had fully evened out. Low and steady.

She placed it on the small tray by the empty water glass, immediately forgotten, and ran her hand lightly across his jawline. The whispering and pleading started again. Whatever nightmare Gabriel had suffered a moment before, it was coming back.

I have to wake him up.

"Gabriel..." she whispered. "Gabriel, wake up. You're having a nightmare. Wake up."

His eyes fluttered open on command. He was awake, but not fully conscious. He was looking through her, still trapped halfway between his nightmare and the real world.

She tried again. "Gabriel, look at me. You're okay."

It seemed to take all the strength he had left in his body to turn his head to look at her.

Grayson's heart twisted in her chest. The look on his face, the relief in his eyes, was almost too painful to bear.

"Grayson..." he whispered in awe.

She knew that tone.

He's still half-asleep. He doesn't think I'm real.

He reached up and ran a hand across her cheek. She gently nuzzled into his palm.

"Hi," she squeaked.

"You're...you're alive."

The statement caught her off guard, but she tried to hide her surprise. "Of course I am. Why wouldn't I be?"

"You're alive. You're alive. You're alive." He kept repeating it, staring off over her shoulder at the fire.

"Gabriel, look at me," she coaxed softly.

The fog in his eyes kept clearing. He was still waking up. She curled her legs up on the bed beside him.

"Why wouldn't I be alive?"

"He had you. He had my gun."

"Who did?"

"Cain. He put the gun to your head. He pulled the trigger. I wasn't fast enough."

Oh.

A cold chill ran down her spine. Suddenly, Grayson desperately wanted a sweater to throw over the thin lace camisole she was wearing. She wrapped her arms around her waist and shivered.

"He…killed me? In your dream."

Gabriel nodded. "I didn't save you."

She ran her fingers through his hair. "But you saved me in real life. That's what matters."

He looked up at her and fully focused on her eyes. The firelight was reflecting off of her blue irises. He couldn't look away. "I almost lost you," he whispered.

She looked back at him, her bottom lip trapped between her teeth.

"Almost."

There was a beat of silence, and then, without warning, Gabriel launched himself off of the mattress, wrapped his hand around the back of her head, and pressed his lips to hers. Hard.

Grayson froze. His lips were warm and soft and salty with sweat. They were demanding, and she didn't have the strength to fight him. Without hesitation, her eyes closed and she gave in to him. She relaxed against him and tightened her fingers in his hair. He groaned softly and twisted her hair in his fingers, holding her steadily to him. Grayson felt herself going lightheaded. Her body needed oxygen. She didn't care if she died here and now. Air be damned.

Gabriel pulled back, just enough to breathe and look into her eyes again. Grayson felt her entire body flush as she took in the look on his face. Every ounce of heat and power that he possessed was concentrated on drinking in every inch of her, memorizing every breath she took. She stopped breathing. Her lips parted. Her heart stopped.

"Stay."

His voice was low, husky, and the sexiest thing she'd ever heard. It wasn't a request.

Grayson nodded, her heart thundering in her chest.

Gabriel relaxed back down onto the mattress and pulled her down with him. She curled into his right side. He wrapped an arm around her shoulders, his hand resting possessively on her hip.

She reciprocated, resting a hand gently on his chest and stroking along his ribcage.

Gabriel let himself revel in the overwhelming sensation of the pads of her fingers tracing patterns onto such sensitive skin. He allowed a few passes before the sensation nearly overwhelmed his self-control. He brought his left hand up to still hers and rested it back on his chest, held still by his own. Eventually, he pulled the comforter back over their bodies to ward off the cold.

Grayson was asleep within minutes. So was he.

19

GRAYSON WOKE UP feeling a little too warm and a little too confined. There was something wrapped around her waist, pinning her in place. Something else strong and firm was resting between her neck and the pillows behind her head. It was warm and surprisingly soft.

She stirred and tried to shuffle backward. She promptly ran into a hard slab of warm muscle, and that hard slab was definitely not wearing a shirt.

She opened her eyes and took in a strangely familiar room. She couldn't recall the floor-to-ceiling windows or the wingback chair directly, but they were familiar.

And she wasn't scared. Wherever she was, she knew she was safe.

The shifting of the warm muscle behind her and the soft groan coming from it caused Grayson to shift onto her side. She turned face-first into the rock-hard chest of Gabriel Ryder, who himself was desperately trying to get closer to her in his sleep. His arms wrapped around the small of her back and pulled her in closer to him. She giggled. His eyes were closed; his face was relaxed. He was still dreaming, and thankfully it wasn't a nightmare.

Grayson reached up and ran her fingers along his jawline. He was starting to get a decent five o'clock shadow.

He looks good with stubble.

On her third pass along his cheek, he stirred and pressed his cheek into her palm. Grayson brushed her thumb against the soft skin by the corner of his eye and back along the fine lines to his temple. He moaned and pulled her against him. She grinned and lay back, patiently waiting for him to wake up.

———

It didn't take long. The feel of her hand on his face had done enough to force his brain to swim toward consciousness.

Gabriel slowly opened his eyes, thankful for the lack of light coming in from his bedroom windows.

The first thing he registered was the time. The sky was completely dark. It was well before morning. The second thing was the warm, soft body that was bundled up in his arms. He looked down and was met by a pair of bright, sparkling blue eyes.

"Good morning," Ryder said softly, leaning down and placing a soft kiss on Grayson's lips.

He felt her sigh, close her eyes, and lean in against him. Her physical surrender pushed every one of his buttons. Gabriel pulled back and ran his fingers through her hair, pushing a few strands out of her eyes. Those eyes had the same warm, glazed-over look they'd had by firelight hours ago. Her lips were pink. Her face was flushed. He knew he'd never get tired of that look.

"Hi," she said shyly.

He took in the sight of her bare shoulders, licking his lips at the thought of tasting her skin, then dutifully reached over and pulled the comforter up over them. She snuggled down underneath it and sighed. He held her a little tighter.

God, why does this feel so damned good?

He'd woken up to a woman in his bed before, more than once, and every time he'd been agitated until said woman had stumbled out of his apartment and into the early morning. But now? He wanted Grayson here. He would give anything he owned, a pound of his own flesh, to keep her here.

To see her tomorrow. To wake up to her tomorrow. To kiss her tomorrow. And the day after that. And the day after that.

What the fuck is wrong with me?

She mumbled something into his chest that he couldn't hear. "What?"

She tipped her head back slightly. "What time is it?" she asked, yawning.

He twisted around, never loosening his grip on her, and looked at the clock on the nightstand behind him. "Four-thirty."

"Mmm. Too early," she grumbled.

"Yes, it is. Go back to sleep."

"How do you feel?"

He kissed the top of her head and smelled her hair. "I feel fine."

"Okay." Her voice was soft and fading fast. She was quickly falling back asleep.

Ryder gathered her up in his arms and pulled the comforter higher around her shoulders. "Go to sleep, Grayson."

He watched the sky pink up over the mountains as he stroked her hair and kept her warm. She occasionally stirred and mumbled in her sleep.

He couldn't make out anything she said, except once. One single time.

She said his name.

20

HOURS LATER, GABRIEL startled awake. He threw his gaze up to the windows and was met with the sight of heavy white clouds rolling in over the city from the already obscured mountaintops.

Well, in Denver, if you don't like the weather now…

He rolled over onto his back and put his left hand behind his head. His chest wall throbbed in protest. His other arm was pinned down beneath a full head of mussed-up hair and pretty pink lips.

Grayson was curled up on her right side, facing the windows, her head resting on his completely numb arm. Her hand was wrapped possessively around his forearm. Her tank top had ridden up overnight, and if he craned his neck just right, he could see the top edge of her silk pajama pants resting low on the curve of her hips. His fingers desperately wanted to feel her exposed skin.

Gabriel thought better of his current position and rolled back onto his side, ignoring the sharp pain in his ribcage, and rested his free hand on her hip. The feel of the silk on top of her skin was something he could definitely get used to waking up to. He brushed the hair out of her eyes and kissed the spot where her ear met her neck. Grayson immediately stirred and turned into him, nuzzling his chest. Her eyes fluttered open, and she looked up at him with sleep-heavy baby blues.

"Good morning, gorgeous," he said, pushing the hair out of her face.

Grayson stared up at Gabriel for a few seconds, wide-eyed, the sleep clearing from behind her eyes. Without hesitating, she pushed up and kissed him gently on the mouth. Her fingers walked up the back of his neck and threaded into his hair. She pressed up against him, insistent, and he dropped onto his back. Her hair fell around his face, brushing against his chest and his neck. The silk of her pajama pants brushed up against his torso, and his abdomen tightened reflexively.

They were going to have to have a serious talk about this sleeping-in-silk business. It needed to continue.

Grayson pulled back, breathing heavily, and looked down at him. "Good morning, handsome."

Her voice was low and sultry. She was loving being on top. Gabriel could feel the last tendrils of his control rapidly slipping away. She leaned down and softly kissed him again. He wrapped his fingers around her hair, twisting it into a knot at the nape of her neck. She was pinned against him.

"That was a nice way to wake up," she whispered.

He smirked up at her. "Yes, it was."

She turned to look out the window at the advancing snow-storm. "That looks nasty," she mused.

"It's going to snow. All day."

"Mmmm. It's a good day to stay in bed and do nothing," she murmured, lying down to look at the window and watch the storm.

Gabriel slid up behind her and rested his left arm over hers, linking their fingers. He dropped a quick kiss to the edge of her collarbone.

"Do you know how long I've wanted you to do that?" she asked quietly.

"Do what?"

"Kiss me. Like that. Like you did last night," she whispered back.

He smiled into her neck and kissed the fluttering pulse he found there. "Really?"

She nodded shyly.

"Well then. I'll have to do it again sometime," he chuckled, squeezing her tightly to him and kissing the top of her head. "Do you really want to stay in bed all day?"

She shook her head. "No. I try sometimes but I never make it. I won't get past 9 a.m."

"So what would you like to do?"

"*I'm* supposed to be taking care of *you*, remember?"

"And I'm fine."

"Gabriel..."

"I. Am. Fine."

"And I am still supposed to take care of you." She twisted around in his arms. "So what do you want for breakfast?"

"I'll take care of it."

She rolled her eyes at him. "Is it too much to ask to have control over one meal?"

He chuckled. "One meal?"

"One meal."

"Okay, one meal. What do you want?"

"I'm supposed to ask you that."

"I don't care."

"All right, fine."

Grayson winked at him and flipped the covers back, darting out of bed before Gabriel had a chance to react. He got out of bed as best he could and stumbled out into his living room just in time to see her throw her coat on and head out the door. He rubbed the lingering sleep out of his eyes and walked to the window. He didn't see her.

She must have headed east.

He did a lap around the apartment, attempting to work the stiffness out of his left knee and stretch out his ribcage. He walked back to his bedroom and noted the damp washcloth on the side of the bed. He remembered something cool on his skin from one of his nightmares. He fingered it briefly, then threw it in the laundry hamper and grabbed his book off the nightstand.

He made his way into the living room, turned on the fireplace, and sank down into one of the club chairs. The warmth of the fire filled the living room as snow gently started to fall outside the window.

Forty-five minutes later, Grayson still hadn't returned, and he was starting to worry. The book had long been discarded on the side table, unopened.

Where the hell is she?

He had just picked up his phone when there was a soft knock at the door. He rushed to open it. There she was, grocery bags in both arms and balancing two cups of coffee.

"Move it or lose it!" she giggled, shuffling around him and hastily placing the coffee cups on the kitchen counter before they dropped on the floor.

"What did you do?" he asked, chuckling under his breath.

"Um, I might've gone a bit overboard." She shrugged, opening the refrigerator door and unloading the bags.

Gabriel looked over the contents and raised his eyebrows slightly. "I think you might have."

"Hey, I didn't know what you had here. I guessed."

She pointed at one of the coffee cups.

"That's yours. Oh! And this." She rifled through one of the large brown bags and pulled out a smaller white one.

Gabriel sat down on one of the bar stools, his left knee aching in protest. "What's this?"

"Breakfast," she smiled as she put away the rest of the groceries.

He opened the bag. The glorious combination of sugar and butter and something dipped in chocolate enveloped him.

"Croissants?"

"I walked by the bakery on the corner and they smelled amazing. I couldn't help myself," she replied. "But if you don't like them, I bought bacon and eggs and can make some pancakes as long as you have baking soda somewhere around here."

Grayson walked around the counter and shrugged out of her coat, hanging it on the rack by the door. When she passed by him again, Gabriel grabbed her around the waist and pulled her to him. She yelped in surprise and steadied herself by grabbing onto his shoulder.

When her hand made contact with bare skin, her eyes grew wide and she looked down. No shirt, no socks, just a thin pair of pajama pants that hung rather low on his hips. Unconsciously, she pulled her lower lip between her teeth. Gabriel chuckled. She worked her bottom lip harder. All the chuckling did was make his abs tighten.

Is it getting hot in here? Why the hell doesn't he have his shirt on?

"Grayson?"

"Hmm?" she replied absently. Her eyes were still fixated on his torso.

"What's wrong?"

It took several beats, but finally she looked up at him. She felt him watch as the blush spread from her cheeks to her neck and down her chest.

"Um, uh, you're…you're not wearing a shirt."

"No, no I'm not," he countered, laughing. "Would you like me to?"

She shook her head violently. "No. No…no? No."

"Okay then. Shall we have breakfast?"

She nodded. Gabriel reached over her shoulder, grabbing the two cups of coffee and taking them into the kitchen. He pulled two large white cups out of the cupboard followed by two small white plates. Grayson started to protest, but the look in his eyes made her shut her mouth.

"Let me do this."

She didn't argue. Grayson kicked off her shoes and claimed one of the chairs by the fireplace. Several minutes later, Gabriel set a tray down beside her. There were the two white plates, each with a warm croissant, and two large cups of coffee, one with cream and one without. She picked up the cup meant for her and held it softly in between her hands.

Gabriel sat down next to her and did the same, his coffee in one hand and *The Wall Street Journal* in the other.

"You read the paper?" Grayson asked, quirking up an eyebrow.

"Of course." He nodded.

"I don't think I know of anyone except my program director who reads the paper anymore. And he's in his mid-sixties."

"So I'm old and stuffy, am I? Thanks for that," he said, glancing at her.

"Oh, I didn't mean…shit. That came out badly, didn't it?" She stared down into her coffee and became very quiet.

"It doesn't bother me."

"It bothers me," she replied, taking a sip of the coffee. "I shouldn't say something like that."

"It's not like I'm in my sixties, Grayson."

"How old are you?"

"Thirty-four."

"Oh."

"Does that bother you?"

"Of course not."

"All right then."

They fell into a comfortable silence. Gabriel focused on the headlines, and Grayson intermittently munched on her croissant. Soon, she got tired of sitting still and started walking around the living room, coffee still in hand.

Gabriel watched her out of the corner of his eye, curious.

She stopped at one of his bookshelves and scanned the titles. Lots of history, even more classics. Hardy, Faulkner, Stevenson, Hemingway, Stoker, Emerson. It was a reading list of the top one hundred classic novels. And many more she didn't recognize.

She ran her fingers over several volumes with well-worn bindings. They looked expensive, maybe even first editions. There was another whole bookcase on the other side of the television, filled with much of the same.

"You like to read," she said matter-of-factly.

"Yes."

"You've read all of these?"

"At least once."

"That's impressive. But don't you ever just read for fun?"

"Those are for fun," he said, setting down his paper.

"I mean something that didn't make the Nobel Prize list. Like *Harry Potter*. Or *Fifty Shades of Grey*."

"No, I can't say either one of those has made my list to date. They've made yours?"

"Maybe." She nodded, continuing on with her perusal of the shelves.

Gabriel remained quiet, watching her. She was hung up somewhere around Bronte.

"Can I read one? I mean, while I'm here?"

His eyes narrowed, only for a moment. He looked surprised that she'd shown the slightest bit of interest at what was on the shelves.

"Of course."

She took her time looking over the titles, at long last pulling one off the shelf. She grabbed a cashmere blanket off of the end armrest of the couch. She pulled the blanket over her legs as she sat back down in her chosen chair.

Gabriel glanced over at the cover. "*Pride and Prejudice*?"

She nodded.

"That's ambitious."

"I don't plan on finishing it in a day."

Grayson ran her fingertips over the well-worn cover. She opened to the first page and was instantly surprised by the presence of underlining and notes in the margins.

"Are these yours?" she asked, pointing to the ink.

Gabriel nodded.

"You've read this?"

"Several times."

"Really?"

"Yes. You don't believe me?" he asked, eyeing her over the edge of his paper.

"No. It's just, I don't know many men who voluntarily read Jane Austen novels."

He smiled. She had a point. "There was a reading class at Harvard that counted toward my major. The professor had a good reputation."

She put the book down and looked over at him. "You went to Harvard?"

He nodded.

"And majored in…?"

He smirked. "History."

She raised her eyebrows. *Seriously…history?*

"Yes."

"And you did well?"

"Summa cum laude."

"So, how did you transition from Harvard history star to Denver super detective?"

Gabriel shrugged and kept staring into his paper. "I wanted to do something useful with my life. I didn't want to stay on the East Coast, for several reasons. So, I got drunk my senior year, threw a dart at a map of the United States, and it landed somewhat close to Denver. I packed up and left. And that's it."

Grayson immediately regretted asking. Gabriel was suddenly sitting ramrod straight in his chair. He was going to rip his paper to shreds if he tightened his hold on the pages any further.

His past was clearly a touchy subject, and of course she'd plowed right into it like a bull in a china shop.

Idiot. Stupid, idiot girl.

She threw the blanket off her legs, took two soft steps, and sat down at his feet.

Gabriel saw her get up and assumed she was heading to the kitchen for a refill on her coffee. When she didn't pass onto the other side of his paper, he folded the pages down. He startled when he found her sitting at his feet, looking upset.

He threw his paper aside, scowling. "What's wrong?"

"I'm sorry," she said, picking at the expensive Iberian rug she was sitting on. "I know I ask too many questions. I shouldn't have asked about such personal things."

He bent down and grabbed her chin, forcing her to look up at him. "Anything you just asked me could've been found with a simple internet search, Grayson. I haven't talked about my personal life for a long time. I don't like it. It's not something I do well."

"It's none of my business."

"I disagree," he said as he pulled her to her feet.

She stood in between his legs, his head level with her abdomen. He pulled her closer. She steadied herself on his shoulders.

"Just go slowly," he pleaded.

"Okay," she said softly.

Gabriel leaned forward and rested his head against her stomach. Grayson stiffened, only for a second, then brought her hands up to run her fingers through his hair. They stayed like that for some time, one leaning against the other.

Gabriel rested his hands on the sides of her hips, his fingers absently sliding along the thin rim of exposed skin between the top of her pajama pants and her sweatshirt. Grayson kept one hand in his hair and ran the other along the straining muscles of his shoulders. She felt him relax underneath her care, losing control.

He reluctantly pulled back from her. "Are you done with breakfast?"

She nodded.

"I...I think I should get cleaned up," she murmured.

"Okay."

———

Damn it.

Gabriel regretfully watched her disengage from him and walk back toward the guest room. He kept his eyes on her until she disappeared around the corner, and he stayed rooted in his chair until he heard the shower turn on. Only then did he let out a long sigh and drop his forearms onto his knees.

What was he doing? Trying to seduce a young woman who had just been abducted? God, this was a new low. But another side of his mind flared in anger at the thought.

You're not abusing her, it screamed. *Just admit it. You've wanted her for a long time. But how far will you go, Gabriel? Are you really prepared to drag her down the rabbit hole with you?*

He tried to silence both voices by draining the last of his coffee and clearing the plates. His leg was feeling steadier. His side was throbbing less. He put the dishes into the sink and leaned against the countertop.

He was feeling more like himself, which meant he was dangerously close to being able to act on the thoughts running wild in his mind. He glanced down the hallway to where the sound of running water was echoing off of the walls. He'd kissed her. He had shared a bed with her. He'd begged her to stay. She had.

He wanted her, plain and simple.

Shit.

He shook his head again. Things were getting out of control.

21

THEY SPENT THE rest of the day in the apartment. Gabriel showered after Grayson, and she changed his bandages again. The wounds were already starting to show signs of healing. He'd barely have scars when all was said and done.

"You probably won't need these after today," she mumbled, pressing the tape down onto his skin.

"They look all right?" he asked hesitantly.

She nodded, trying her very best to keep her eyes off of his waist.

Goddamned six-pack abs.

They alternated between the couch and the club chairs, talking and reading. At one point toward afternoon, Gabriel started talking to himself in a language that Grayson didn't recognize. When he caught her looking at him, completely confused and trying to hide a smile, he raised his eyebrow at her. She blushed and asked what he was doing.

"I'm speaking in Italian."

She rolled her eyes at him. "Of course you are."

"It bothers you?"

"No, it's beautiful. I just can't understand it."

"Would you like to?"

Grayson bit down on her lip. "Don't tell me the Harvard graduate can teach me an entire foreign language in a day."

"No. But listening to the language in context can help build fluency quickly."

"So, what, you have *Rosetta Stone* lying around here somewhere?"

He laughed and shook his head. "No. Not quite."

"Well...what then?" she asked, looking over at him expectantly.

Gabriel stood up from his chair, walked over to the far bookcase and scanned the titles. He grabbed the book he was searching for and placed it gently in her lap before sitting back down himself and picking up his paper.

Grayson ran her fingers over the raised font on the front cover. The gold lettering stood out against the green fabric binding. *Another old book*, she mused.

The title was written in Italian. She couldn't read it. She opened the book to a random page. Exactly the same. All Italian, or something that looked like it.

"What is this?" she asked.

"It's a book of the *Grimm's Fairy Tales*. Translated into Italian, of course."

Grayson struggled to contain the smile on her face. The old fairy tales were some of her favorite things. She'd read them over and over as a little girl.

"So, you're going to teach me by reading me fairy tales? In Italian?"

He smiled at her from over the top of his folded newspaper, his eyes glinting behind his dark rimmed glasses. "If you'd like."

She nodded excitedly and jumped to her feet, handing him the book.

Gabriel set his paper down on the side table and led her by the hand to the couch. He pulled a small ottoman up to her feet, draped a warm blanket across her shoulders, and sat down on her left side.

"What would you like to hear?"

"There's a story called *Thousandfurs*. It's an early take on Cinderella, I think."

Gabriel raised his eyebrows in surprise. "Very good. You've read it before?"

"In English. I loved reading these stories when I was little. I'd fall asleep with my head face-first in the book. I never could finish it."

"We'll finish it." He opened the book to the proper page and began reading aloud.

Grayson tried following along, but after a while she simply rested her head against his shoulder and closed her eyes. His voice was captivating on a regular day, but Gabriel speaking in Italian was a whole new thing entirely. It was melodic, the way his voice rose and fell with the punctuation. He could have been speaking complete nonsense and it would have still been beautiful.

The light outside dimmed and gradually turned to purple, inky darkness. By the time everyone had lived happily ever after, the sky was black and the only snowflakes visible were the ones that happened to fall right outside the window. Otherwise, they were lost to the night and the whipping wind.

Gabriel closed the book and placed it beside him on the couch. "Did you enjoy that?" he asked softly.

He wasn't entirely sure Grayson was still awake. She nodded against him and purred contentedly, stretching underneath the blanket. He pulled it up tighter around her shoulders, brushing the hair lightly out of her face as he did so. "Good," he mumbled into her ear before kissing the tip lightly.

"Mmmm, what time is it?" She yawned.

"It's after five."

"What?" She startled and sat up abruptly, searching the wall for a clock. He was right. It was after five.

"Shit," she mumbled under her breath.

"What's wrong?"

"Oh, nothing, I...I was going to cook dinner, but I was supposed to start around three to get everything done in time."

"Three? In the afternoon? What on earth were you planning to cook?"

She sighed, defeated. "I guess it doesn't matter, does it? Even if I start now, I won't be done before eight."

"Grayson," he chided, pulling the blanket back up over her shoulders, "Why were you going to slave away in my kitchen for hours on end?"

Her shoulders were hunched over and she was staring straight at the floor. He kept his voice low and calm. He didn't want to frighten her.

"I...I wanted to cook a nice dinner," she answered meekly.

"So, we'll still cook a nice dinner. Something easy for tonight. Okay?"

"Okay."

She still sounded disappointed.

"We'll do complicated another time," he soothed, grabbing her chin and turning her face to look at him. "Don't be disappointed. I'm not."

She nodded slightly. He leaned forward and kissed the top of her hair. He stood up gracefully and pulled her to her feet. "Come on. My kitchen hasn't been properly used in quite a while. I hope the stove still works."

"It's an eight-burner Viking range, Gabriel," she said, rolling her eyes. "Chances are, one of them will light."

22

DINNER WAS READY in short order. Instead of the long, complicated meal she had originally planned on, Grayson started whipping together a quick pasta alla carbonara while Gabriel went into some hidden part of his apartment to pick out a bottle of wine.

The kitchen was like something out of a magazine: a Viking range, full prep station, not to mention Gabriel's collection of cutlery and top-of-the-line pots and pans. For a man who hadn't used his kitchen in a while, he certainly had kept it stocked with anything and everything he might need if he suddenly had an inkling to try.

Grayson pulled a tart pan out of one of the top cabinets. Truthfully, she didn't even own one of these herself. She always had to borrow Noah's, and his was on its very last leg. She followed the recipe from memory, mixing together chocolate, eggs, butter, sugar, and a rather expensive dark rum into a thick batter, pouring it into the buttered pan, and popping it into the oven. Forty minutes went onto the timer, and she turned her attention back to the pasta.

The pancetta, eggs, cheese, and spices all mixed together to form one surprisingly decadent dish without trying terribly hard. As she poured in the last of her ingredients and stirred the pasta, a cork popped behind her. She jumped and found Gabriel smirking at her as he poured red wine into two long-stemmed glasses.

"Find something you like?" she asked, turning back around to keep her eyes on the pan in front of her.

Grayson didn't hear him reply, but she did feel him step up behind her, not touching her, but very, very nearly. The feeling of being pinned against the counter without him even touching her was electric. She bit down on her lower lip and tried to focus on the food.

When he swept her hair away and planted a kiss on the base of her neck, she nearly had a seizure. It was rapidly becoming more and more difficult to stay standing upright in his presence.

"I did, yes."

She shivered at the feeling of his hot breath on her ear.

Gabriel slid away from her and opened a drawer next to the sink. He pulled out two sets of silverware and two dark blue linen napkins. He placed them on the counter, next to two stark white dinner plates. He leaned back against the counter for a moment and watched her work, then swept in from the side and stole the wooden spoon from her hand.

"Hey!"

He promptly ushered her out of the kitchen and over to the bar that overlooked it.

"Give that back," she protested, making a grab for the spoon over the countertop. "Dinner's not done."

"You've done enough," he scolded. "Sit down and drink your wine. You can direct me."

"What happened to me taking care of you?"

"I've told you, I'm fine. And you got your one meal at breakfast. Sit."

Grayson diligently sat on one of the barstools and watched Gabriel move about his kitchen. He was practiced, and he knew damned well what he was doing.

Never uses the kitchen, my ass.

He finished off the carbonara with ease. She didn't have to say a word. He dished out their meals from a white serving platter and sat down beside her.

"To you."

Gabriel raised his glass to hers. Grayson clicked hers against his. Together, they raised them to their lips. The wine was bold and heavy without a biting aftertaste. She looked at the bottle. It was the same wine he'd brought to her house on Thanksgiving.

Gabriel noticed the spark of recognition in her eyes. "You recognize it?"

She nodded.

"You still like it?"

"Of course. But I've never heard of it."

He artfully twirled his pasta around his fork. "Not many have. I brought it back from Italy."

"Of course you did," Grayson replied sarcastically, rolling her eyes at him and digging into her own dinner.

When he didn't respond, she glanced over at him and bit her lip.

"You went wine shopping…in Italy…"

He shrugged and nodded.

Grayson put her fork down and turned to fully face him on her barstool. "All right, that's it. What is going on here?"

"Excuse me?"

"This!" She motioned widely with her arm around the apartment. "All of this. The incredible apartment, the two-hundred-thousand-dollar Audi, the wine… there isn't a cop in this country that makes the kind of money it takes to live like this. Hell, most people in this country don't make that kind of money. At least, not legally."

"Are you accusing me of something?" he bristled.

That caught Grayson off guard. Her fork clattered noisily onto the counter, forgotten. "What? No! But you have to admit, it raises a few questions."

"As usual. So ask them. Get it over with." He set his fork down and stared off into the kitchen.

Grayson was startled by the complete change in demeanor, and she hesitated. This was clearly more than a slightly touchy subject for him.

Gabriel sighed, clearly annoyed.

"All of this, it's yours?"

"You mean did I buy it myself? Yes."

"Not with your police salary."

"No."

"Then with what?"

Gabriel grimaced. "Well-placed investments."

Grayson folded her arms across her chest and waited. He was avoiding answering her, intentionally. She could see the gears turning behind his eyes, desperately searching for a way to avoid answering her without upsetting her.

I can wait all night, buddy.

She didn't have to wait long. His sigh broke the silence. He grabbed the wine bottle, poured another glass, and without a word retreated to the living room.

Grayson waited a beat, then followed.

She found him leaning up against one of the windows, the muscles in his back flexed and tense. She could see them through his blue oxford button-down.

She sat down in one of the club chairs and curled her legs underneath herself, still waiting patiently, watching him calm down. He didn't turn around to face her, but he did eventually start talking.

"I'm the third child of Niles and Vivian Ryder. My father started a management firm in his early twenties, and by 1980 it was one of the premier high-stakes acquisition firms in the country. He worked hard, played hard, and made a ridiculous amount of money off of people who didn't know any better. My two older brothers were groomed from birth to take over the family business. Elite prep schools, Ivy League business schools. Their lives were planned out from infancy and financed well."

He paused to take a long drink from his wine glass.

"I was a mistake. My parents had made up after a scandalous affair on my father's part, and I was the result. It wasn't his last, but it did spark my mother's first. I grew up with an expense account, but I didn't have parents. They resented me; so did my brothers. But I had as much of a claim to the family business as they did, so I dutifully started on the same path. Four prep schools later, my father paid off someone important enough to get me accepted into Harvard, no questions asked. He couldn't hide my police record, but he could fork over enough money to make them ignore it."

"Police record? For what?"

"Fighting. Vandalism. Gambling. And worse. It took less than six months for me to decide I couldn't go through with it. I dropped business, which infuriated my father, but he kept paying my way. As long as I was at school, I wasn't at home to get in the way of his affairs or pilfer my mother's supply of vodka. When I graduated, I told him I didn't want anything to do with running the family firm. I'd watched him turn into an emaciated alcoholic, run around on my mother, and strong-arm my brothers into doing the same. He didn't care. He died a few years later."

"I'm sorry," she whispered.

Gabriel waved her off and finished his glass.

"What about your mother? Your brothers?"

"My mother spends most of her time shopping or out of the country. We don't talk often. And my brothers are like-minded with my father. We don't speak at all."

"Gabriel…" *He doesn't need to tell me all this.*

He barreled on. "Two weeks after my graduation ceremony, my brothers paid me a visit. They offered to buy me out of my portion of the family firm. I agreed. They wanted to pay in cash. I refused. I took the payout in stock instead, which carries a substantial dividend. The money I make off of their work more than pays for all of this. They offered to take it off my hands about two years ago, secretly hoping to use it to pay off some personal debts. I told them to go to hell and put in an order to buy up any stock that comes onto the market instead."

"You have them over a barrel then, don't you?" she asked calmly.

Gabriel grinned at her over his shoulder. "In a manner of speaking. I didn't go to business school, but I paid attention at the dinner table when I was young."

Grayson took a sip of her wine. "So, that explains the Armani suits and the Audi."

"Anything else?" he asked, turning to face her, his arms crossed over his chest.

She nodded. "The night Noah and Barbara took me out, to the Petal Club…a white box showed up at my house with the dress I wore. And the shoes and the jewelry."

She felt Gabriel's eyes on her, watching her closely. Her own were fixated on her lap, so she missed his fingers balling up into fists, the knuckles white against the pressure.

She kept talking. "I confronted both of them. Neither of them can afford something like that, and I know neither of them could get us into Gustavo's or the Petal Club. They hinted that maybe..." She looked up at him beneath long lashes. "Did you have anything to do with it?"

———

The last question had more fear in it than he had been expecting. Grayson's hands were visibly shaking in her lap.

Why is she afraid all of a sudden?

Then it clicked. If he wasn't the source, then Douglas Cain was the only other option. And if that monster had been behind such a wonderful night...

Gabriel's face softened as he looked Grayson over. She was clutching onto her wine glass like it was a life preserver.

"Of course I did."

Her head snapped up and she searched his face, looking for any sign that he was lying. When she didn't find one, Grayson set her wine down and launched herself at him. Gabriel barely had time to lift his own glass out of the way as she wrapped her arms around his torso. He set the glass down on the mantel behind him and wrapped both arms around her.

"Thank God," she murmured into his chest.

He smiled and stroked her hair. "I spoke to Noah that night we talked on your porch. Before I came to see you. I took care of the reservations," he said gently. "When he said you had nothing to wear, I took care of that, too."

"You picked out that dress?"

He nodded.

"It cost a small fortune, Gabriel."

"I can afford it." He smiled broadly. "Besides, it was well worth seeing you in it."

Grayson blushed crimson against his shirt.

"What on earth possessed you to do all that for me? You barely knew me."

He rested his chin on her head. "I'd barged into your home and accused you of murder, Grayson. I saw the tears in your eyes. I didn't know what else to do to try to make it right. I wanted to see you happy."

"So you bought me a dress and a pretty pair of shoes?"

He shrugged. "It was a start."

Grayson picked at the buttons on his shirt.

"Gabriel, what were you really doing at the Petal Club that night?"

He didn't hesitate. "Keeping an eye on you."

She wrinkled her forehead. "What for?"

"I didn't trust Noah or Barbara. I was worried something would happen to you. And I was right."

She looked up at him quizzically.

"The man at the bar," he reminded her gently.

"I took care of myself," she countered.

"Yes, yes you did. Another time I didn't move fast enough." His expression darkened. Grayson watched helplessly as the blackness took over his eyes.

"Stop it. He wasn't worth the effort of you standing up from the barstool."

"And he never should have gotten close enough to touch you," Gabriel barked.

"Shhh," she soothed, running her hands up and down his back.

His muscles relaxed at her touch, and he gently kissed the top of her head.

Grayson decided to change topics. "You danced quite well."

He shrugged. "A consequence of prep school and cotillions. I had to know how to waltz by the time I was eight."

"You don't enjoy it," she mumbled sadly.

"Of course I do, when it's with the right partner."

The chime from the kitchen broke the moment. Grayson pulled back from him and shrugged.

"Dessert." She walked off, leaving him alone in the living room.

He let out a breath he hadn't realized he'd been holding. *Jesus Christ, did I just tell her all of that?*

Gabriel grabbed his wine from the ledge and downed what was left before following her. She was cutting into something that smelled decadent and spooning vanilla ice cream on top of it. He waited for her by the bar, opening another bottle of wine on autopilot.

She walked past him holding two plates, and he followed without a word. He filled their two glasses and sat down next to her on the couch.

The chocolate torte was delicious, but completely lost on him. He was focused on the quiet woman beside him. Grayson was poking around at the food on her plate, lost inside her head. It was unsettling.

"What are you thinking?"

"I'm wondering…" She hesitated. Gabriel kept quiet. "I'm wondering…why on earth you're wasting time with me?"

He nearly choked. "What?" *Not this again.*

"Honestly. Why mess around with the person at the center of a serial killing spree?"

"Grayson…" he growled.

"With all this, well…and you…" She motioned around the apartment, then up and down his body with her hand. "It's not like you couldn't have your pick. You can certainly do better than a poor resident. What are you doing slumming with me?"

"Enough!" he hissed. Gabriel narrowed his eyes at her. "What in the fucking hell did you just say?"

Grayson squared her shoulders. She didn't really seem eager to hear the answer to the question she'd asked, but he knew she was too curious to leave it go. "I asked what you're doing slumming with me."

"Slumming." The word rolled of his tongue like poison. She nodded at the floor. "Explain to me just who I should be spending my time with instead of you."

She shrugged, trying to be nonchalant. Her voice shook too much to pull it off. "Someone tall, blonde, and dressed in Armani comes to mind."

"Vapid, self-obsessed, and narrow-minded. No, thank you."

"There are blondes in this city who can speak in complete sentences, Gabriel."

"I've been through my fair share of them," he countered. "Anyone at the precinct can tell you that. Hell, Logan can tell you that."

Grayson took a deep breath. She tried to cover up her disappointment with sarcasm. "Relationships that aren't really relationships. Easy and uncomplicated. Why stop?"

Ryder didn't hesitate. "Because a beautiful five-foot-six brunette fell into my arms in a conference room in October and turned my fucking life upside down. How's that?" He abruptly stood up from the couch and started pacing.

Grayson sat still, stunned, not knowing what to say. She'd expected a flippant answer, something ripped from one of the novels lining his living room walls. In no way was that even close to the answer she'd anticipated.

166 | A. R. Nicole

Gabriel didn't notice her stunned face. He just kept talking.

"I've done nothing but worry about you and spend my days and nights trying to track down the son of a bitch that was stalking you. The last thing on my mind since I met you has been finding something easy and uncomplicated."

"I've told you. I'm just a case, Gabriel. It's done now. You'll be healed soon. I'll just fade away."

"You're not just a case, Grayson. And you're not fucking going anywhere." His voice had dropped, the tone harsh and strained. He was losing control.

"You deserve so much better than me," she whispered, more to herself than to him. She dropped her gaze into her lap and started wringing her hands.

Gabriel had had enough. He dropped to the floor in front of her and grabbed her chin, roughly forcing her face to look at him. He registered the shine in her eyes. She was close to tears. He yanked her lower lip out from between her teeth and traced along the bruised skin with the pad of his thumb.

"Fuck what I deserve. I want you."

Grayson mewled softly, melting at the intensity of his voice.

Gabriel lunged forward, steadying her head with one hand at the back of her neck as he brought his lips crashing down on hers. She immediately went limp in his arms and leaned back against the cushions.

Gabriel levered up, one bent knee pressed against the bottom cushion of the couch, forcing her head back into his hand. She moaned into his mouth, and his tongue darted into hers. Her hands shot into his hair, pulling him closer to her. Gabriel balanced himself against the couch, nipping and sucking persistently on her lower lip. He reluctantly broke away.

Grayson was shaking beneath him, quietly. He leaned forward and kissed her forehead. Whatever asshole had damaged her self-esteem in the past, Gabriel made a mental note to track the son of a bitch down and kill him. That was next on his to-do list after personally ensuring that Cain got the death penalty.

He rested his forehead against hers and tried to calm his breathing. "I don't ever want to hear anything like that again. Do you hear me?"

Grayson nodded, barely.

He spoke softly, calmly, and with every ounce of control he had left. "From the moment you walked into that office, I haven't been able to get you out of my head. I have every intention of keeping you for as long as I can have you." He kissed her forehead again.

"But how do you know…we…I mean, we haven't…"

Grayson shook her head slightly, her eyes still closed. She couldn't look at him and still get this out.

Ryder knew from the hesitation in her voice what she meant. "We haven't what? Slept together?"

She nodded, red from the embarrassment.

He chuckled softly into her hair. "Yes, as a matter of fact, we have. Last night. But if you're worried about sex, don't. It doesn't matter."

A sarcastic huff escaped her lips.

Gabriel ran his thumb across her right temple until her eyes fluttered open. "I'm not joking, Grayson. I. Don't. Care."

"You'd be the first man in history," she scoffed shakily.

"Then so be it," he said, still running his fingers over her cheek. "I've thought about it, trust me. I'm a man, in the presence of a beautiful, intelligent woman. But I'm not going to force myself on you like some kind of wild animal."

He sat down beside her and pulled her into his side. "You've been through two months of absolute hell, culminating in your kidnapping and a firefight in the hospital basement. I'm not keen on taking advantage of you three days after you've regained your freedom."

"You wouldn't be taking advantage. I'd…I'd let you," she said softly.

"I know. And I would enjoy every moment of it, then wallow in a bottle of scotch the next day and never forgive myself."

She quirked her eyes up at him.

"The Ryder family way of dealing with guilt. Just trust me."

"Okay."

"Enough for tonight. It's late. Time for bed." Gabriel stood up from the couch.

Grayson didn't move. She just looked up at him, eyes wide, biting her bottom lip. It didn't take long for him to grow impatient. He swooped down and in one swift movement picked her up from the couch.

"Gabriel, don't! Your leg!" she protested, squirming to get out of his arms.

"I'm fine."

"Put me down!"

Now was not the time to argue. He set her down gently onto her feet. "I'll understand if you want to stay in the guest room tonight," he said quietly.

Grayson nodded and turned away from him. His heart sank until he felt her press something into his chest. He looked down.

The green book of Grimm's fairytales.

"Choose a good one," she whispered, before walking off down the hallway.

He turned out the lights in the living room and shut off the fireplace. He wasn't far behind her.

23

BY THE END of the week, Grayson was back at her own home and Gabriel was back to taking care of himself. He hardly noticed the sting in his chest wall anymore, and his limp only returned at the end of the day when he was fatigued. He wouldn't run with any consistency for the next month or so, but he was at least back to some basic forms of physical activity.

The apartment had become increasingly quiet and stuffy since Grayson's departure on Wednesday evening. Gabriel found himself drinking scotch by the living room window often, wishing she was curled up in one of the chairs behind him. Easy and uncomplicated would have provided a quick distraction without lasting consequences, but for the first time in his life, the thought was unwelcome.

By Friday morning, he'd had enough. He needed a distraction that didn't result in a hangover. He woke up early, showered, dressed in one of his best suits, and drove to the precinct. He got a few raised eyebrows as he walked through the main lobby and took the elevators up to Major Crimes. He sat down at his desk, coffee in hand, and waited. It didn't take long for his name to echo loudly across the room.

"Ryder!"

Captain McCallister stood in the doorway to his office, hands on his hips, scowling at the young detective. "Get in here. Now."

Gabriel stood up and walked steadily into his captain's office, coffee in tow. McCallister motioned for him to sit down, which he readily did. He didn't want his knee flaring up so early in the day. The captain was shaking his head, hands now folded in front of his chest.

"What the hell are you doing here, Ryder?"

"I dropped by for a visit," he replied nonchalantly.

"Don't be a jackass. I haven't had enough coffee for that yet. You're not supposed to be back until you're cleared for full duty."

"I don't have any intention of going out in a blue and white, captain. I'm just here to check in on the case."

"You realize I have major reservations about keeping you involved with this."

Gabriel startled forward in his chair, instantly on edge. "What? Why?"

"Ryder, Douglas Cain drew you and your partners into a firefight in the basement of the hospital. He shot you; you could have easily bled out down there. Oh, and by the way, it's now painfully obvious that you've grown attached to the young woman he was after. Your involvement with her muddies the waters considerably."

"Captain, Cain is dangerous. The case against him has to be airtight. He's not going to talk to just anyone."

"Well, you're right about that one." McCallister shook his head wearily and dropped down in his desk chair.

"Sir?"

"The bastard got transferred from the hospital to solitary yesterday. It's the only place he can stay locked up, supervised, and under medical control without stealing a hospital bed from someone who really needs it. Only problem is, he won't talk."

"What?"

"He hasn't said a word. To anybody. His guards, the nurses, the guy who brings his lunch, nobody. He's clammed up."

"Has he used his phone call yet?" Gabriel scoffed.

"No."

That gave him pause. "He didn't call his lawyer?"

"No. And he hasn't asked for one. We can't figure him out."

Gabriel cursed under his breath. "Let me talk to him."

McCallister shook his finger. "Oh no, absolutely not. If that asshole tries to jump across an interrogation table, you're in no shape to put him in his place."

"Then put someone else in the room with me."

"Even if I would okay that, detective—which I won't—you know Cain won't talk with two people in the room if he hasn't opened his mouth to one."

Ryder nodded. The captain was right. He couldn't argue with that. A knock at the door broke up the conversation.

"Enter," McCallister bellowed.

Blake poked his head through the door. "Hey, captain, Cain's still not talking and…holy shit, Ryder!" A smile beamed across Nolan's face as he flung the door open, crossed the room, and slapped his partner on the shoulder. "How the hell are ya?"

"Fine, thanks," Gabriel sputtered, trying to recover from the shooting pain in his side.

Blake swore under his breath when he noticed his partner grimace. "Fuck. I keep forgetting you're on the injured list. What the hell are you doing here? They said you were on leave."

"He *is* on leave, Nolan," the captain said forcefully.

"I'm technically not here." Ryder smiled.

"All right, what drugs are you on? I haven't seen you smile like that since I brought you that really nice bottle of scotch last Christmas."

"I'm not on anything, damn it," he shot back.

Blake laughed and slapped him on the shoulder again. "Still can't take a joke though. How's the doc?"

"She's all right," he said calmly.

"She do okay holed up in your man cave for a few days?"

"You would have to ask her."

McCallister leaned over the top of his desk. "Has she said anything to you, detective? About her abduction?"

Gabriel silently shook his head. He'd tried several times to get Grayson to talk about what had happened to her, but she'd quickly grown agitated and asked to change the subject each time.

He'd pushed her once, and she'd ended up curled under a comforter in the guest room for several hours, sobbing. He'd dropped the subject completely after that and had spent the better part of Tuesday afternoon trying to get her to smile again. Something about her time with Cain had her deeply disturbed, and she wouldn't say two words about it.

"She hasn't said a word," he said dejectedly. "I've tried. She won't say anything."

"Are you worried?" the captain asked.

"Yes, I am," he admitted. "She closed down whenever I tried to bring it up. She won't talk about any of it."

"Do you think she remembers it? Maybe the stress knocked it out of her system. What do they call that? Amnesia?" Blake asked from his place resting against a bookcase.

Ryder shook his head, his voice dropping low. "She remembers."

"How do you know for sure?"

"It's the physical response she has. She can't hide it. She gets quiet. She shakes. Her heart rate picks up and her breathing shallows."

"So?"

"Those are survival signs. The fight-or-flight response. Her sympathetic nervous system kicks in at the thought of Cain or that gray room."

"So, what now?" Blake asked.

"I…I don't know."

"How about the shrink?" he suggested.

"It sounds like she needs help, detective," the captain agreed. "Maybe she should talk to the staff psychiatrist."

"If I could get her to even recognize that she was actually abducted, maybe. But she won't acknowledge it even happened. I doubt she'll listen to me long enough to agree to go."

"Well, shit. Isn't that nice of her," Nolan huffed sarcastically.

"Shut up, you asshole, she's scared," Gabriel hissed. "She didn't have time to be scared when she broke free and fought him off. And she's spent the last few days avoiding it by taking care of me. Now that there's nothing else to distract her, it'll come full force. I'm worried she won't handle it well."

"Is there a good way to handle being kidnapped by a serial killer, detective?" the captain asked.

"Of course not."

"So, talk to her. Convince her to come in. I'll talk to Dr. Shin. I'm sure he'll see her," McCallister said, bringing the phone up to his ear and waving them out.

Ryder and Nolan walked out of the office, each taking their respective seats at their desks.

"Where's Harrison?"

"Interrogation. He's the latest one to have a shot at Cain."

"He really won't talk to anyone?"

Blake shook his head. "Can you get me time with him?"

"Don't even think about it. No. I'm not giving him the opportunity to break your other damned leg."

"C'mon, Blake," he pressed.

"No." The response wasn't forceful, but the tone told Ryder to drop it. He wasn't getting anywhere with his partner. They sat in silence while Blake worked on the paperwork in front of him.

"She's really not talking? Even to you?" he asked quietly.

"No, she's not," Ryder replied.

"Gabe, I don't want to be the one to bring this up, but did he…do you think he, you know, forced her to…um…?"

Ryder's head snapped up. *Christ, oh please God, no….*

"I…I don't know."

"Did the hospital do a rape kit?"

"I don't know."

"I'll look into it. Don't worry about it."

Ryder nodded blankly.

"Gabe." Nolan waved his hand in his partner's face to get his attention.

"What?"

"She really needs to come in."

"I know," he said. "I'm worried about her."

"Yeah, me too, buddy."

24

IT WAS CLOSE to ten o'clock at night when her cell phone rang. Grayson looked up from her book and over at the caller ID. "Logan Harrison" flashed on the screen.

Oh no.

She immediately turned the book over onto the bed to save her place and reached out to answer it.

Gabriel had insisted she take his copy of *Pride and Prejudice* home with her. At the time, she'd argued with him, insisting she could get her own copy at the local bookstore for $5.99. For heaven's sake, she could have download the book onto her iPad for less than that. But he'd insisted, muttering something about the feel of a real book and reading a classic novel under his breath.

Of course, he'd been right. And the fact that his notes from college were scribbled all over the margins in what looked like fountain pen made it feel just a little like he was sitting in a club chair next to her, instead of in an apartment halfway across the city.

Snap out of it, you lovesick puppy, she screamed at herself as she put the phone up to her ear.

"Grayson Carter."

"Hey doc, it's me."

"Logan, it's after ten on a Saturday night. What's wrong?"

"Nothing's wrong."

"Is Gabriel all right?"

A light chuckle echoed through the receiver. "My God, you two won't shut up about each other."

Grayson's heart fluttered in her chest and her face flushed. "Is he…you know, all right?" she pressed.

"He's fine, sweetheart. Don't worry. Blake's got him locked up in his apartment."

"So why the late call? I thought this was prime hunting time for you at the local bar."

Logan smirked on the other end of the line. "You know me too well already, girlie. It usually is. I'm still at the precinct."

"This late? Why?"

There was a long pause.

"Logan, what is it?" she pressed again.

"I just got done trying to take a shot at Douglas Cain."

"With a nine-millimeter pistol?"

The deep voice chuckled over the speaker. "No, but good thought."

"Did he spill his guts?"

"No, that's the problem. He won't talk."

"Don't worry," she said, trying to be supportive. "He'll crack eventually." Grayson furiously clenched the fingers of her free hand in her quilt and drew her knees to her chest.

I really don't want to talk about Douglas Cain right now.

"No, you don't understand. He. Won't. Talk. At all."

"To anybody?"

"To anybody. Except for ten minutes ago."

"He talked to you?"

"Kind of. He made a request."

The hesitancy in his voice sent a chill down her spine. "A request?"

"Yeah. To talk to you."

Her mouth went dry. She struggled to swallow.

No, oh God, no, no, no.

"M...Me?"

"You. Alone."

Grayson felt her heart rate kick up to a gallop. She could barely breathe. "Wh...what does he want with me?" she whimpered.

"He wouldn't say."

Logan waited for her to say something, drumming his fingers nervously on his desk. When he was met with nothing but shallow breathing and an otherwise eerie silence, he cleared his throat.

"Grayson? Doc, you there?"

"Yeah," she said weakly. "I'm here."

"I'm calling to see if you'll do it."

"What?" Her world started to spin. Was Logan crazy? The mere thought of that man made her skin crawl and her stomach heave. He'd kidnapped her. He'd nearly killed her. He'd touched her.

"Logan, I...I really don't...don't think I can do that," she stammered. Her hands were shaking so badly she could hardly keep ahold of her phone.

"Grayson, I wouldn't ask if I thought there was any other way. But we've been working this guy since before he left the hospital. He won't budge. He wants to talk to you. And just you."

"What did Gabriel say?" she asked hesitantly.

"He didn't. He doesn't know I'm talking to you."

"You sent Blake over as a distraction, didn't you?" *At least one thing makes sense.*

"You know my game already. I'm gonna have to keep my eyes on you." Grayson was convinced she could actually hear him grinning at her through the phone.

"Be serious. I can't be alone in a room with that man."

"You won't be. Not really. The captain and I will be right behind the two-way mirror."

"But I'll be alone in a room with him. Logan, I don't know, I…"

"At least think about it. Please. This may be our one shot with this guy. If we don't get some kind of confession out of him, this could all fall apart."

"Are you kidding me?" *He has to be kidding.*

"No, I'm not. We can get him for kidnapping you, and maybe for shooting Gabe, but unless he starts talking, we don't have enough to pin the nine murders on him. The fucker covered his tracks. There's stuff, just not enough of it to take to court."

"Logan…" she whined.

"I know, I know. Don't shoot the messenger. Cain's smart. He's got a clean record. He's a young, smart doctor. The right defense attorney will have a jury believing Gabriel was too aggressive, that he didn't declare himself or some bullshit. They'll let him walk, on all of it, and have the department pay out a settlement on top of it."

Grayson sighed, leaned back and landed on her pillows. She really, really did not want to do this. Her nightmares were getting worse all on their own. She didn't have to see Cain again to speed that hideous cycle along. She kept having one where Gabriel backed away and turned his back on her, leaving her alone with Cain's knife pressed into her neck. Waking up in a cold sweat was becoming a frequent occurrence.

And she was tired. So tired. The nightmares hadn't been so bad when she'd been with Gabriel. She'd give anything to have him with her right now.

"What time?" Her voice was weak and shaking.

"Seven. I'll pick you up and drive you down here at seven. Interview begins at eight."

"What do you want me to get out of him?"

"Whatever you can."

She hesitated. "Okay. I...I'll do it."

"You will?" He didn't sound like he believed her.

"Don't question it, Logan. I might change my mind."

"I'll see you at seven."

"Goodnight."

She hung up her phone and stared at the now-black screen. She reached over and turned off her bedside lamp. Darkness enveloped her room. She turned onto her side and huddled underneath her comforter.

What in God's name did I just agree to?

She tossed and turned all night. When she did manage to doze off, all she saw was Cain's vicious smile and his hateful, sparkling eyes.

25

TRUE TO HIS word, Logan was on time. He pulled the black department-issued SUV up outside of her bungalow at exactly seven a.m.

Grayson immediately scampered out onto the porch and down the icy stairs. She slid into the car without a word, and he drove off into the gloom of the gray winter morning.

"That coffee in the console's for you," he said, motioning to the to-go cup on her side of the center unit.

"Thanks," she said, picking it up and holding it in between her shaking hands.

"You can always back out of this, doc," he said softly.

"You should've told me that last night," she replied, just as quietly.

"I'm serious. I feel bad. I feel like I pressured you into this."

"You did," she scowled, only half-seriously.

"Sorry."

"Don't worry about it."

They drove in silence for a while. Grayson kept flicking her eyes in between her coffee and the passing cityscape.

"How does he look?"

"Who?"

"Cain."

"Why do you want to know that?"

"I want to know what I'm walking into," she murmured dejectedly.

Logan nodded as he turned east. "Fair enough. He looks beat to shit, but he's the same smug bastard. He thinks he's invincible."

"And he's only spoken once?"

"Just once. To ask for you."

They rode the elevators up to Major Crimes enveloped in a tense silence. Grayson couldn't get warm. The chill she felt went all the way down to her bones. She just couldn't shake the feeling that this was going to be a major mistake.

The pair walked out into a deserted squad room. Logan pressed gently on the small of her back and guided her around the maze of desks to the back hallway. She didn't need the direction. She remembered the way.

She recognized Captain McCallister waiting in the doorway of his office. She tried to manage a smile and failed.

"Captain." She nodded.

"Dr. Carter."

"Grayson, please."

"Grayson then." The older man smiled at her as best he could. She didn't bother trying to hide the fear etched on her face. She knew he could see it. And from the look he shot over her shoulder to Logan, he was already starting to think this visit wasn't a very good idea.

"I know Detective Harrison has told you what Douglas Cain requested, but understand that you are under no obligation to…"

She held up a hand to cut him off. "That son of a bitch has screwed up my life and put me through hell, captain. Not to mention he killed nine people in my name. If I'm the only one he'll talk to, then I'm the only shot anyone has of putting his ass in the electric chair. I have to be here."

The captain smiled at her. "Well, all righty then. This way."

He led the way down the back hall, with Grayson behind him and Harrison bringing up the rear. He steered her into a dim shoe-box-sized brick room. There was light filtering in from a large window, which—too late—she recognized as a one-way mirror.

Sitting on the other side, calm and smiling in a white jumpsuit, was Douglas Cain.

She froze at the sight of him. If she hadn't seen the handcuffs herself, she would've sworn he was standing in the middle of a group of residents on rounds, sneering at them as they stammered and shrunk in his presence.

"He can't see you in here," the captain assured her. "Or us."

"Does he know I'm coming?"

"No," Harrison said, "but he's hopeful. We've brought him here at the same time the last few days. As far as he knows, he's just here for another round with me."

"I get the feeling he knows I'm here," she said, wrapping her arms around her waist protectively.

"And if he does? Who cares?" he replied. "Knock 'em dead, sweetheart."

"You're...you're going to stay the whole time, right?" she asked softly.

"Of course. If anything happens, we're less than five seconds away."

She took a deep breath. *It's those five seconds I'm afraid of.*

"Okay. Here I go." She smiled hesitantly at the two men, then walked out of the small observation room and around to the gray door.

Gray.

Her spine stiffened. She knew the walls of the interrogation rooms were beige, not gray. It didn't matter. The second she walked into that room, they would turn gray all on their own.

She nodded to the two uniformed cops that were guarding the door, pushed on the handle, and walked into the room.

Cain twisted his neck to the door, and his face immediately broke out into a smile. "My Beatrice," he breathed.

The shock of hearing that name again triggered something deep inside of her. Grayson paused in the threshold. She'd had every intention of strolling into the room and calling him a murderer. A liar. A stalker. A psychopath. But that's what everyone else had been doing. It wasn't working. What if she played things differently?

She steeled herself against her churning stomach and forced a smile. "My Dante," she said smoothly, sitting in the chair directly across from him.

His smile grew wider.

Grayson eyed his restraints. Even with the splint encasing his left arm, he still had cuffs on both of his wrists and ankles. The chains on his wrists were bound to a belt around his waist, and the wrist and ankle chains were locked into the table and cement floor respectively. He only had a foot of movement, at most, in any direction.

As long as she sat straight-backed in her chair, he couldn't reach over far enough to touch her. Grayson relaxed into the chair and looked him over.

He was bruised. His face was a purple and yellow mess. Someone had tried to re-set his nose, but even under bandages it was clear he would never look the same. The fingers poking out the end of his splint were bloated and swollen.

She smiled inwardly. If she had to, she knew she could break his upper arm using the splint as a fulcrum. Grayson silently

184 | A. R. Nicole

blessed the young man who had given her a few Krav Maga
lessons in college. Ultimately, they'd saved her life and she'd
use them against the psychopath in front of her again in a
heartbeat.

"Have they been treating you well?" she asked steadily. Her
voice sounded more confident than she'd thought possible.

Maybe I can actually do this.

Cain wrinkled his nose, offended. "They're monsters. They
don't know how to treat a dog, let alone a human being."

Grayson wracked her brain, trying to come up with an
appropriate response. She was totally out of her element. But
Cain seemed to want overdone theatrics, so she was determined
to at least give it a decent try.

"Forgive them, my love. They don't understand."

"Of course they don't. Animals don't understand anything
sophisticated. Have they finally given you some peace?"

She nodded enthusiastically. "Yes. They don't want to
interfere with me unless they have to."

"Why is that?"

"Because they...they believe that you hurt me. They want to
give me time to heal."

Cain's facial expression revealed his genuine shock at her
statement.

*Seriously? You didn't think putting a knife to my neck would
be an issue?*

"Did I?"

Shit. Of course I can't admit that.

"Of course not. You were protecting me."

He nodded, relief washing over his face.

Is he really buying this? He can't be buying this.

"You understand now, my Beatrice."

"I'm starting to."

Or I'm super confused and really don't want to be in a room with you. You know, six of one, half-dozen of the other. Just keep talking.

Cain leaned back in his chair as far as he could, eyes closed. "You know they're listening to us," he said calmly.

"Does it matter?" she replied.

"No, it doesn't," he said, smiling at her.

Grayson picked at the fuzz on her sweater nervously. "Can I...ask questions?"

"Of course you can," he said, eagerly sitting straight up in his chair and nodding as enthusiastically he could manage through the bandages. "I love it when your curious mind is hard at work."

There was a part of her, one lonely, hidden part, which perked up at his words.

Gabriel hates my questions...

She didn't linger. Grayson steeled herself against the answers she knew were coming and started in. "When did you know that it was me? You know, that I was...am...Beatrice?"

"Over a year ago. You challenged me in the emergency room. You told me that I was wrong. You saved my patient's life. I realized you were looking out for me, protecting me. You bested me. You weren't afraid of me. In that moment, I knew you were perfect. I knew you were destined to be my Beatrice. "

She shivered in her seat.

I remember that patient.

"Why didn't you tell me then?"

"I had to be sure. I watched you for a long time, Beatrice. You never disappointed me."

Oh, that's disgusting. He's been stalking me for a year.

She awkwardly cleared her throat. "Why did you have to take a life?"

Cain smirked at her across the table. "My dear Beatrice, I took nine."

Grayson took a deep breath.

Ninth-grade English and Wikipedia, please don't fail me now.

"Nine bodies. For the nine levels of the Inferno."

"Yes."

"Why not just come to me?" she asked, leaning on her elbows. "We could have just gone away, left together. Nobody needed to die."

"I couldn't do that. Dante must travel through the Inferno in order to ultimately join the Paradiso and see his Beatrice."

Grayson wrinkled her forehead, feigning confusion. She didn't want him to know how much she really knew. Cain caught her expression and was quick to elaborate.

"They were of the Inferno, my Beatrice. Unrepentant sinners. They had to die. So that I could get to you."

"But taking a life is a sin. So did you not sin, Dante, when you killed them?"

Ugh, I hate talking like this. I feel ridiculous. But he's buying it.

"I sinned to protect you, my love. This, God forgives. I am of the Purgatorio, those who repent for their sins and ascend to Heaven."

"And you ascend for me, my Dante?"

"I do everything for you, my Beatrice."

I feel like I'm going to be sick. And I don't know how long I can keep talking like this.

She inched forward on the table, her head resting in her hands.

I have to get him to talk about the people he killed.

"Tell me about them. The sinners."

Cain visibly hesitated.

"They should not concern you," he said evasively.

He glanced over her back shoulder toward the mirror.

No you don't, you bastard. You asked for me. I came all the way down here. You're going to talk to me.

"Please, my beloved," she cooed, reaching across the table to grasp his good hand in hers. "They're torturing you for your crimes. Crimes you committed for me. I must know."

Something in her eyes softened him, and much to the surprise of the two men behind the mirror, Cain started talking. "What would you like to know, my love?"

"Lisa Oakes."

His face fell. "Ah, yes, Lisa. She was unfortunate. Such a sweet girl."

"She was the first."

"I was gentle with her."

You were gentle with her? You fucking killed her!

"Why did she have to die if she was so sweet?"

"She wasn't like us. She wasn't one of us."

"Because she was a DO?"

He nodded.

"She was found in a place of learning, a church of students. I blessed her as I left. She went to Limbo. No pain will come to her."

"But not for the others."

Cain's eyes darkened. His nose curled. Deep wrinkles crossed his forehead. "No. They deserved to die."

"Tell me about them."

He shook his head and sat back away from her. "Your mind should not be tainted by such things."

"But Dante went through Inferno," she cooed softly. "Beatrice herself convinced Virgil to guide him through it. Surely she knew about the horrors he saw?"

"It doesn't matter. They are too much for you to bear."

Cain's tone told her he wasn't going to budge. Desperate for results, Grayson tried another angle.

"I know about Dr. Nelson," she said gently. "He was lustful. He tried to put his hands on me."

Cain nodded. "He put his hands on many others. They were all tainted."

"I know about Dr. Porter, the glutton. And Dr. James and his avarice."

He nodded again.

"I know about Dr. Carrol and his wrath."

"So many times, that viperous snake sought to demean you, to terrorize you. I removed the thing that gave him his power."

She reached across the table and squeezed his good hand, hoping to God she was faking reassurance well, and continued.

"What threat was Priya?"

The dark, black pools of Cain's eyes lifted from the table. Grayson struggled to maintain his gaze and not lose what little she had in her stomach.

"That witch filled your head with lies. She treated her patients with potions, not medicine. She was a nasty little heretic," he spat.

"She loved her patients," she chided.

"She filled their bodies with poison and their minds with false hope. She was dangerous. And her teachings filled your head with lies," he repeated.

Grayson closed her eyes and steadied her breathing. She could feel the tears welling up in the back of her eyes. If she cried, he would know she was faking everything. It would be all over. She forced them back down.

"And Greg Harlan?"

Cain sighed. "So much potential. So much hatred. Gregory abused his wife. And he assaulted you. He tried to kill you. I watched over you in the hospital, my Beatrice. Did you know? I watched over you all night long."

"I know, my Dante. You told me. You kept me safe."

He nodded. Grayson kept up the momentum. "I found Nathan. You know that. I told you."

Cain shook his head in disgust. "A most unfortunate event. You were never supposed to see him."

"But what was his sin?" she asked innocently. "Nathan Alexander never brought any harm to me."

"My poor naïve love," he scolded softly. "A fraudulent sinner is always dangerous. I could not let him near you anymore. You believed his lies. And he gained a life he never should have had by using them."

Grayson took another deep breath and squeezed his hand again in hers. "But who was the ninth, my love?"

Cain grinned and leaned closer to her. "Alexi Gregoriyeva."

Grayson's eyes widened. "Alexi?" she breathed.

Oh God, I really am going to be sick.

"He betrayed you, didn't he? All those years ago. He turned on you after you took him into your confidence. He made you cry. He demeaned you. Your position in the department was forever blemished because of the things he said about you. And then he attacked his own brother. On my service. He put his own brother in a coma over his father's money. Cain and Abel. Ironic, really. A journey that begins and ends with a Cain."

He smiled triumphantly and sat back in his chair, releasing his hand from hers. He continued to stare at her.

Grayson didn't break her gaze from his. "What will you do now?"

"About what?"

"We're separated. You aren't with me," she whispered.

"You left me, my love," he scolded. "You did this to me."

Grayson dropped her head and let her hair fall over her face. *Shit! Shit, shit, shit!*

She had to think of something, and quickly. She let out a shaky breath, trying to buy time. She was so overwhelmed by everything Cain had said to her, she was a razorblade's edge away from breaking down altogether.

Wait, that's it…

Grayson closed her eyes and let her tears start to flow. It caught Cain off guard, and he leaned forward, straining against his handcuffs to touch her.

"Beatrice, my Beatrice…" he whispered. "What's wrong?"

She looked up at him through tear-laden lashes.

"I was so scared," she started, her voice shaking in time with her tears. "I thought they had come to take me away from you. I knew they would be looking for me. I thought you were them. I fought, to get to you. I couldn't let them hurt you. They tried to hurt you. They would have killed you; they would have shot you."

"You were protecting me?" he balked, eyes wide.

"Of course I was protecting you."

"My Beatrice…" he sighed.

She took a deep breath herself. *Keep it up, Gray… he's actually buying it!*

"What are we going to do?" she whispered.

"Don't worry," he said. "We will be together soon. Wait for me, my Beatrice." He tapped his fingers twice on the tabletop and nodded.

The classic Cain "you are dismissed" gesture. How cute.

Grayson nodded back, wiped her eyes, and stood up. He smiled at her as she calmly strode out of the interview room.

Harrison and Captain McCallister met her at the door. She gave them a meek smile as the uniformed officers closed the door to the interrogation room, then darted down the hallway.

Logan took off after her, pausing outside the women's restroom. He could hear her dry heaves from the doorway. McCallister came up behind him, hanging his head.

"Was it worth it?" Logan asked, the regret heavy in his voice.

The older man shook his head.

"To put her through all that? No…I…I don't think so. But at least it's enough for the lawyers." He put a hand on Logan's shoulder. "Don't tell Ryder about this, detective. Not yet. He doesn't need to know."

"Or see that tape."

Logan nodded and leaned against the doorway.

It took over an hour for her stomach to settle enough so she could withstand the trip home. She cried the whole way.

26

GABRIEL SHIFTED UNCOMFORTABLY on the long leather couch. He didn't object to the couch itself but more to the circumstances demanding he occupy it. Trips to the department's psychiatrist never sat well. He understood on principle why it was necessary. It didn't make the appointments any more enjoyable, and he'd had several during his tenure with the department.

Thankfully, this was his first for actually being shot. At his other appointments, he'd been the shooter.

"You look uncomfortable, detective," Dr. Shin remarked from his chair across the room.

Gabriel shrugged and avoided eye contact.

Dr. Shin scribbled something in his notepad.

In his mid-fifties with salt-and-pepper hair, Dr. Matthew Shin had the longest service record with the Denver police department. He had a reputation for not taking any crap from any of his patients, and if you weren't ready to return to duty, he'd be the first to tell both you and your captain. He wasn't universally liked, but he was definitely respected. And if there was ever a difficult case, it went to him without question.

"When am I ever comfortable in your office, Dr. Shin?" Ryder responded after a moment.

"True. Point taken."

He looked up through his wire-frame glasses and regarded the young man in front of him. He liked Gabriel Ryder. He was a good cop, a brilliant detective, and was viciously loyal to the department. He had his issues—the drinking in particular—but no more than anyone else who'd come through his roster.

When his name had popped up on his patient list for Tuesday morning, he hadn't been surprised. Then he'd read that the young detective had been the one shot, not the shooter, and he'd become much more concerned. An officer's first time getting hit was never pleasant, and according to the files that had been sent over ahead of his appointment, he'd needed emergency reconstructive surgery. That usually made the psychological consequences much, much worse.

"How are you doing with your recovery from surgery?"

"Fine, I guess."

"Have you been back to check in with your physician since leaving the hospital?"

Ryder's eyes diverted briefly to the floor. Avoidance. It was a stall tactic Shin was familiar with from the young man.

"Sure."

"Try again, detective."

Gabriel gritted his teeth. "I had supervision when I went home from the hospital. I was checked on then."

"My exact question was, have you seen your surgeon?"

"I just answered you," he spat.

Dr. Shin cocked his head slightly at that. Detective Ryder usually was not confrontational this early in their appointments.

Am I missing something?

"Explain that to me. Your surgeon made a house call?"

That question earned him a smirk from the couch.

"Yes."

"Interesting."

He leafed through a ream of paper on his side table.

"I read the reports from the hospital that were sent over. I know Dr. Allen quite well, as well as McWilliams. We went to medical school together, believe it or not. You were extremely lucky, detective."

"I know that."

"And the reconstruction on your leg seems to have gone better than expected, though Allen was a bit evasive on the phone about the process."

Gabriel chuckled.

"That's funny?"

"He didn't exactly perform the surgery."

"He is the physician of record."

"I know that."

Dr. Shin sat back in his chair and regarded the young man. This was rapidly feeling like they were playing cat and mouse, and Gabriel Ryder was winning.

"All right, detective, clearly I'm missing something. Explain."

Gabriel sat back on the couch and grinned slightly. "Dr. McWilliams took care of my chest wound. My fractured leg was the bigger problem. Dr. Allen was occupied with saving Douglas Cain's arm. Someone else fixed me."

"Who?"

"One of his senior residents."

"Alone?"

"Yes."

"That isn't particularly safe."

He saw Ryder visibly bristle. He'd struck a nerve.

"It was an emergent situation, Dr. Shin."

"I understand that. You're comfortable with being fixed by a student?"

"This student."

"Really?"

He nodded.

"Why is that?"

"I didn't have much choice, did I?"

"That doesn't mean you have to be comfortable with it. Be honest with me here. Doesn't it bother you that Dr. Allen was not really the surgeon who operated on you?"

"No."

The answer was instantaneous and offered without hesitation. That earned Ryder a pair of raised eyebrows and some scribbling in the notebook.

"You know this senior resident?"

"Yes."

"It was the resident on service call that night?"

"No."

"His backup?"

"No. She wasn't on call."

"She?"

"Yes. She."

"Interesting. Give me a name, detective."

Gabriel shifted again and cleared his throat.

"Grayson Carter."

Dr. Shin nearly spat out the sip of water he'd been in the middle of drinking. "Excuse me?"

"My surgeon was Grayson Carter," he said calmly.

"The young woman who was abducted? The one you got shot trying to rescue?"

Ryder nodded.

"Good heavens," Shin mumbled, scribbling furiously.

He drew out the operative report and post-operative notes Dr. Allen had provided for him. He read them once, then twice. Her name was all over them. He'd missed it completely.

"This says your alignment is perfect. The surgery went extremely well. And that's what Allen told me on the phone..."

He trailed off. Gabriel just shrugged.

"This woman was kidnapped, held against her will, escaped, held at knifepoint and gunpoint, and then operated on you the same night? Good God. No wonder she's on my schedule later today."

Gabriel shifted awkwardly on the couch. "I need to speak with you about that, actually."

Dr. Shin peered at him over his glasses. "Because?"

"Because I'm the one who asked Captain McCallister to intervene and get her an appointment with you."

———

"Why would you do that?" Shin asked, scribbling something else onto his notepad.

"Because I'm worried about her."

"She can see one of the victim's services counselors easier than she can see me, detective."

"I'm aware of that. I want her to see you."

"Why?"

"Because I trust you. And because I know she won't be able to fake you out for long."

"What has you so worried?"

Gabriel closed his eyes briefly before replying. This was

going to open up a whole new Pandora's box for Shin to play with.

Oh well. This is more important.

"She won't talk about what happened to her. To anybody. Not to her roommate. Not to her best friend at the hospital. Not to the other detectives. Not to me. She's having nightmares."

"Nightmares?"

He nodded.

"And you know this how?"

"I've seen them."

Recognition glinted across Dr. Shin's eyes. "Your at-home doctor's visits?"

Ryder nodded. "It was a requirement for me to go home as early as I did. She stayed with me for two days."

Dr. Shin paused, the tip of his pen resting against his lower lip. "You're sleeping with her," he stated matter-of-factly.

Gabriel smirked. "Yes, but not in the way you're thinking."

"By that you mean you're not having sex. But you are sleeping together. Interesting."

Gabriel quirked his eyebrow, intrigued by Shin's response. The doctor didn't miss a beat.

"It's not your usual style, detective. You're known around here for…rather brief, purely physical entanglements. Nothing more."

"I'm aware of that."

"So you're what, biding your time until your leg heals? Playing up the sick patient role a bit before you get her properly between the sheets?" he scoffed.

Gabriel shot up from the couch and started to cross to the door. "I don't have to listen to this bullshit," he growled.

"Sit down, Gabriel," Shin chuckled under his breath. "We're not done here."

"*I'm* done here."

"Yes, perhaps *you* are, but *we're* not. And if you ever want to take part in Douglas Cain's prosecution, then you need a clear evaluation from me. I'm not giving it to you if you run out of here. You know from experience that I'm not bluffing. Now, sit down."

Ryder glared at the doctor, his hand firmly twisted around the doorknob. Shin's face didn't change. He reluctantly sat back down on the couch, scowling.

"You care about her, don't you?" Shin asked after a moment, his eyebrows raised.

Gabriel nodded mutely, his forearms resting on his thighs.

"Since when?"

"After I first met her."

"Love at first sight?"

The older man chuckled under his breath. When Gabriel didn't move to correct him, the doctor softened his tone of voice and continued. "When was the last time you broached the subject of her kidnapping?"

"Sunday. I tried to go see her. To check on her. She wouldn't see me. She…she gave me a flimsy excuse. When I told her I was worried about her…state of mind, she said she didn't feel well and hung up. She hasn't taken my calls since."

"Are you worried that something else is going on?"

"Such as?" *Of course I'm worried something else is going on, you idiot.*

Shin shrugged nonchalantly. "Such as…anything. Your line of work and mine both prove that anyone is capable of anything."

"You have something in mind?"

"No. But I feel like you do."

Gabriel twisted his fingers together before giving up and running them through his hair nervously. He tapped his foot rhythmically on the floor. Shin simply waited.

"In your experience," he began somewhat hesitantly, "how long does it take before someone falls victim mentally to their attacker?"

"Fall victim mentally?" Shin parroted. "You mean PTSD?"

Gabriel shook his head, his fingers still solidly gripping his hair.

Shin tried again. "You mean Stockholm Syndrome."

Gabriel nodded.

"Case reports are all over the map, detective, but you know that. Do you really think she is showing signs?"

"You're the psychiatrist."

"And you are very capable of getting inside other people's heads. Something has brought up the idea."

"She's never kept anything from me before."

"That you know of," Shin countered.

Gabriel's eyes shot up from the floor. "She's never refused to see me. Except once, when I did something legitimately horrible. There was something in her voice on the phone on Sunday. She's...she's hiding something from me. I'm worried whatever psychotic bullshit she was subjected to in that basement actually took. That the latency period is over."

"Why don't you let me worry about that?"

Gabriel didn't shift position on the couch. He kept his face in his hands, deathly still.

"Look, she's coming to see me later today, detective. Let me evaluate her properly," Shin said gently.

Ryder nodded.

"You realize that I can't discuss her case with you once I take her on as a patient."

He nodded again. "Just help her, Dr. Shin, and we'll call it more than even."

"All right, detective. That's enough for one day. Schedule your next appointment with Ranita on your way out."

27

GABRIEL STROLLED INTO the bullpen of Major Crimes, feeling only marginally like he'd been run over by a truck. Appointments with Shin were always a mess, but at least he'd been able to spend most of this one talking about Grayson instead of himself.

She really had him worried. After a particularly long day of physical therapy and an even longer Saturday night entertaining Nolan, all he'd wanted to do on Sunday was spend the afternoon with her. But she'd blown him off, rather pitifully. He'd spent the night with a bottle of scotch instead.

Captain McCallister had told her a little white lie to get her to agree to see Dr. Shin, saying that it was standard procedure for all kidnapping victims to meet with him. That wasn't true; they all went through a formal evaluation by Victim Services, not the head psychiatrist in the department. But it had gotten the job done, and she'd agreed on a Tuesday afternoon appointment.

Gabriel glanced over at his partner's desk. It was vacant, a still-steaming cup of coffee sitting to the right side of the stained blotter. He looked over at Logan's desk and found a very similar picture. They could have left in a hurry, but more likely they were called away to look at a piece of evidence somewhere in the office.

Something to do with Cain.

He set off to find them.

He didn't have to look far. He saw his captain's tall frame and silver hair through the conference room's partially shuttered blinds. One of the television monitors was on, the screen casting a blue-tinged glow across his drawn features.

Ryder walked over to the door and pushed it open, stepping in with a smirk on his face.

He intended to surprise them.

He did.

Logan turned at the sound of the opening door. His face instantly fell. Blake wrenched himself around in the chair he was sitting in, and his mouth dropped open. Captain McCallister froze.

"Tell me about them. The sinners."

Gabriel snapped his face up to look at the flat screen mounted on the opposite wall. There was Cain, chained to one of their interrogation tables, smiling unabashedly at the woman seated across from him.

Gabriel's hands started to shake. The color of her hair. The set of her shoulders. The delicacy of her right wrist as it rested softly on the cold metal table. He could've picked her out from across the precinct, without the volume on. But her voice…her voice was unmistakable.

"Grayson?" he whispered to the screen.

"Oh shit," came Nolan's mumbled epithet.

Logan tried to say something, but Ryder shook his head and held out a hand to silence him. His gaze was fixated on the screen. She had her hands draped over Cain's. She was leaning toward him from across the table. And he was staring at her like she was fresh water in the middle of the Saudi desert.

What the fuck is she doing with him?

"They should not concern you."

"Please, my beloved. They're torturing you for your crimes. Crimes you committed for me. I must know."

Her voice was soft and supple. She leaned in even closer to Cain across the table. Gabriel's hands reflexively balled into fists.

She's touching him. HIM.

"What would you like to know, my love?"

Blake looked nervously back and forth between his captain and Logan. All three men were on edge, keeping one eye on the interrogation footage and another on Ryder. They'd agreed to watch the tape, with Nolan present, to bring him up to speed.

No one had remembered Ryder's appointment with Shin. They'd never thought about him setting foot in the department. Now, they were pinned down in between the nauseating footage and a visibly agitated detective.

But Gabriel seemed to be keeping his rage under control. They all were about to breathe a sigh of relief…then the final minute of tape started to play.

"What will you do now?" Her voice had dropped to a low, desperate tone.

"About what?"

"We're separated. You aren't with me."

"You left me, my love," Cain scolded. "You did this to me."

The young woman on camera started to cry softly.

"Beatrice, my Beatrice…What's wrong?"

She looked up at him. "I was so scared. I thought they had come to take me away from you. I knew they would be looking for me. I thought *you* were *them*. I fought, to get to you. I couldn't let them hurt you. They tried to hurt you. They would have killed you; they would have shot you."

"You were protecting me?"

"Of course I was protecting you."

"My Beatrice…"

"What are we going to do?"

"Don't worry. We will be together soon. Wait for me, my Beatrice."

Grayson walked off screen and out the open door at the edge of the shot. Cain leaned back in the cheap metal chair, closed his eyes, and sighed contentedly. "She's mine."

The screen faded to black. The tape ended.

Everyone held their breath.

They didn't have to wait long. A low growl started at the doorway and crescendoed into a savage cry.

Ryder lunged forward and grabbed the first thing he could reach—which happened to be a cup of lukewarm coffee—and hurled it into the wall. It shattered on contact. The liquid sprayed like a Pollock painting across the beige paint.

The raw fire behind Gabriel's jet-black eyes kept everyone else silent. No one dared get near him.

Gabriel stood in the doorway, shaking and panting like a rabid dog. His hands clenched violently into fists at his sides. Blake was certain he'd never seen a human being that acutely tortured by inconsolable rage. Without warning, Ryder spun around and stormed toward the elevator, throwing his coat on around his shoulders.

"Holy shit, what the hell was that?" Nolan asked, rooted to his chair in shock.

Harrison walked over to the glass wall and leaned against it, watching his partner storm into the elevator. "I don't have any fucking idea, man, but that's not going to end well."

28

GRAYSON SAT COMPLETELY rigid, straight-backed, her hands folded in her lap.

Dr. Shin was scribbling notes into a well-worn notepad, occasionally looking up at her over the rim of his glasses. He'd seemed like a nice enough man when she'd walked in, but the idea of having to be in a psychiatrist's office at all was unnerving.

She understood why the department made sure other victims were properly evaluated and given treatment, but she could keep a close eye on herself...couldn't she? Or at the very least, Noah could watch her for any warning signs. She was determined to get in and out of this appointment with a clean bill of mental health.

...even if it's a load of crap.

Dr. Shin cleared his throat. Her eyes snapped up from her lap and focused on the man sitting across the Turkish rug. He was smiling warmly at her, his notepad now casually resting on his thighs. His pen had been discarded on the small side table beside his chair.

"You look nervous, Dr. Carter," he said in a warm, inviting tone.

She shrugged, then nodded. "I can't say this is my favorite way to spend a Tuesday afternoon, Dr. Shin. And please, call me Grayson."

"I don't think anyone truly enjoys coming to my office, to be honest. But it's a necessary evil."

"I can understand that."

"Do you think you need to be here?"

Okay, I guess the small talk is over. "Um, well, no, not really."

"Well, if that's the case, then this should be a short visit for you. Why don't we start with the most recent events and work our way backward?"

"All right."

Shin shifted slightly in his seat. "I understand you spent some time taking care of one of our detectives."

That's a weird place to start.

"I did, yes."

"Who?"

"You must know the answer to that already if you're asking me about it."

"Point taken. I still have to hear you say it."

"Gabriel Ryder."

"From Major Crimes."

She nodded.

"He is one of the detectives involved in the case against Douglas Cain, is he not?"

"Yes, but you know that already, too."

———

Shin smiled to himself. Detective Ryder's assumptions had been correct. She was going to be difficult. She already had her guard up from the look of the small wrinkles forming on her forehead.

"So, tell me about your involvement with him."

It was a loaded question, and Shin knew it. He waited, curious to see how she'd respond.

"I volunteered to look after him to facilitate his early release from the hospital."

"And prior to that? You took care of him in the hospital, I understand."

Grayson nodded. "I assisted in the surgery to repair his broken femur."

Shin gave her a disapproving look over the rim of his glasses.

"Try again."

Grayson hesitated, her mouth half-open. Shin could see the wheels turning. She was going to try to insist that she'd only been the assisting resident on Gabriel's surgery. She was trying to come up with a plausible story to cover her tracks. When she swore under her breath, he couldn't help but grin. She knew she'd been caught.

"All right," she sighed. "Apparently you already know. I did the surgery. I didn't assist."

"Much better," he murmured with a smile. "Now, I understand that you did that the same night that you escaped from Douglas Cain. True?"

She nodded, her eyes shooting to the floor at the mention of her kidnapper's name.

"That must have been hard, to have them force you to do such an invasive procedure under such circumstances."

"No one forced me. I…I volunteered," she stammered.

"Really?"

This is news. Allen didn't say anything when we spoke on the phone. Neither did Ryder. I'd assumed they'd pressured her.

"Of course. The attending on call was trying to save Cain's arm. There was no one else."

Maybe not…

"That doesn't sound like you volunteered. That sounds like you were there and the staff took advantage."

"I'm the one that approached Dr. Allen, Dr. Shin, not the other way around."

"You really thought you were capable of performing under such circumstances?"

The psychiatrist watched the hair on the back of Grayson's neck stand up. He could practically hear her inner monologue.

What? You think I'm not capable? You're a goddamned psychiatrist. What do you know?

"I've nailed a femur under worse," she said sullenly.

"Explain that to me."

"I know what I'm doing. It's harder to do the right thing when you have an attending in the room who doesn't know the steps to the procedure, let alone how to do the steps properly. Sometimes, it's easier to work on your own."

"You're saying Dr. Allen doesn't know what he's doing?"

She glared at him. He could hear her again.

Goddamn it, stop putting words in my mouth.

"Of course not. I'm saying it wasn't my first time flying solo on a gunshot to the femur."

"But on someone you know...someone you know well..."

She waved him off as the tears threatened behind her eyes. "I had to get it right. There was no room for making mistakes."

"Did you make any?"

Grayson's heart rate sped up. The blood drained from her face. Shin took notice.

"No. I...I don't think so. Why?"

He shrugged. "I'm asking, not accusing. Does Detective Ryder know?"

"Know that I operated on him?"

"Yes."

"Does he know you volunteered?"

"No."

She shook her head calmly.

Shin decided to switch gears. Clearly, operating on Gabriel had been difficult, but it wasn't causing the nightmares he'd mentioned. This young woman was a competent surgeon. The surgery wasn't the issue.

"Tell me about the shooting in the basement of St. Joseph's."

Dr. Shin watched as Grayson's face instantly changed. She looked pained, fearful, and sunk back into the couch like it could offer her some protection. She started violently wringing her hands in her lap.

"What…what do you want to know?"

"Anything. What do you remember?"

Dr. Shin waited patiently while she retreated into herself, clearly trying to pick a place to start. Grayson drew her legs up underneath herself on the couch. A protective posture, he noted.

"I remember running. The concrete was cold."

"You were barefoot?"

She nodded. "I didn't want him to hear me leave." Her voice was flat, monotone. Inhuman. It even gave Dr. Shin the chills.

"Okay. Where were you running?"

"Just away. I couldn't stand being in that room anymore. He told me things were going to change. It was the last night."

"The last night for what?"

"The last killing. The ninth circle."

Shin rummaged through some of the notes that Captain McCallister had sent up ahead of her visit. He'd read up on Douglas Cain's apparent obsession with *Inferno*. The close association between the murders and the levels of hell in the book was quite clear. Shin nodded, indicating his understanding and for her to continue.

"I just ran. I didn't really know where I was."

"Then what?"

"He caught me. He pushed me up against a wall. He smiled at me."

Her breathing sped up and became shallow. Shin noticed her pupils were incredibly dilated, a marker of the adrenaline coursing through her bloodstream.

"And then?"

"I smiled back and sliced his face with a knife."

Shin's eyes widened at the coolness with which she said those words. Like she had said any other run-of-the-mill sentence. "I baked him chocolate chip cookies" would have been more appropriate for her tone.

Grayson smiled meekly when she noticed the psychiatrist's shock. "It's not as dramatic as it sounds. It was a plastic knife. I hid it one night. He wrenched it right out of my hand."

Shin nodded for her to continue.

"I cut his other cheek with my nails and he dropped my hand. He was bleeding all over his shirt. Then I heard him."

"Heard who?"

"Gabriel. He told Cain to get away from me."

"Did he comply?"

"No."

"What did you do?"

She looked at her lap, wringing her hands harder and harder. Her fingers were going white under the pressure.

"Grayson?" he urged.

"I...I did...nothing."

"Nothing?"

"I froze. I didn't know what to do. I stood there like a complete idiot and stared at them."

Shin raised his eyes and opened his mouth to reply, but she kept going.

"I know better. How many times do you hear that the first rule is to get away, run away, get out of arm's reach? I *know* better. I *know* to run. And I just stood there."

"Keep going. What happened next?" he prodded gently.

"He grabbed me. Cain. He pulled my arm behind my back and held a dirty knife to my throat."

She was visibly starting to shake. Shin sat back in his chair, listening carefully. He'd struck a nerve. She was clearly reliving the attack behind her glassed-over eyes. It was better to just let her talk.

"He kept pushing it into my neck. There was blood on it. He used it to kill Alexi. I…I thought he was going to kill me. He told them to put their guns down. I saw Gabriel's face. I knew he was going to do it, and I told him not to. I *begged* him not to. He did it anyway. Cain got it and pointed it at my back and told him to back off. He put his hands up and walked backward."

She was crying now. Silent tears dropped relentlessly onto her trembling cheeks.

"He was too fast. He moved the gun and fired twice. Gabriel fell to the floor. He…he…"

Shin let her pause and gather herself. She took a few deep breaths and dried her eyes with the backs of her hands.

When she continued, her voice was steadier. It still shook, but it was definitely steadier. And lower. Almost vicious.

"I…I don't really remember…I know I hit him in the face. Somehow, I got behind him and hit him hard enough to break his arm. He just went down. I wanted to hit him again. I…I think I would've killed him. Logan pulled me off of him. Blake was screaming. Gabriel wasn't moving. There was so much blood. I called the trauma and the active shooter codes. I don't really remember much after that."

"You don't remember being examined by Dr. McWilliams at the hospital?"

She shook her head.

"I…no. Noah told me I had a full exam. They did a rape kit. I don't remember any of it."

Shin scribbled in his notebook. "Did Douglas Cain say anything when he had ahold of you?"

She hesitated, then nodded.

"Tell me what you remember."

"He…he said…he told him that he was hurting me."

Shin wrinkled his forehead. "Who's him?"

"Gabriel. He told Gabriel he was hurting me."

"Was that before he put his gun down and backed away from you?"

She nodded, hiccupping against the tears.

"Do you feel like Detective Ryder abandoned you?"

"I did. Then."

"What about now?"

She hesitated, and Shin jumped at the opportunity.

"In my opinion, he didn't do anything of the kind. If Cain was threatening him with your life, someone he was supposed to be protecting, I'm sure he had a short fuse to comply. There were two other detectives there with guns. Either of them could have taken a quick shot if necessary."

Grayson kept her head down and stayed quiet. He pressed further.

"I know Detective Ryder quite well. Or at least I think I do. I've never known him to back away from a fight when it involved his own life, which…to me…means that he truly believed his proximity was a real threat to you. As odd as it might seem, by putting distance in between the two of you, he believed he was buying time."

"He got shot because of me, Dr. Shin."

"He got shot doing his job, actually. And I doubt he would've had it any other way," he countered.

"I should have moved when I had the chance."

"There's nothing anyone can do about that now. Hindsight is always 20/20. And even if you had, who says that wouldn't have made things dramatically worse? You stood still out of more than just fear for yourself, my dear. You stood still out of fear for him, didn't you? That Cain would snap and charge at him? Or shoot him?"

She nodded slowly. "I...uh...yes. How did you...?"

Shin shrugged and scribbled something in his notebook. "That's what I thought."

Dr. Shin walked over to a side table in his office and poured two glasses of water. He kept one for himself and gave the other to Grayson. She accepted it with shaky hands and took a small drink.

"Do you dream about the shooting?" he asked calmly when she had steadied herself again.

She nodded.

"How often?"

"It's in pieces. I never dream about the whole thing."

"How often?" he asked again, gently.

"A few times every night."

"Does it wake you up?"

"Sometimes yes, mostly no. I just remember it in the morning. Like it's fresh. It's the first thing I think of after I wake up."

"What about your time as Cain's captive? Do you dream about that?"

The young doctor froze beside him. She concentrated on the bottom of her water glass like it contained the essence of life itself. Dr. Shin waited for several minutes, and when she didn't answer him, he decided enough was enough. It was time to push her.

"Grayson, tell me about the night that you were kidnapped. You went to the hospital by yourself. Why?"

"I...I...I can't..."

"We're not leaving this office until we talk about your abduction. You can either tell me now or tell me at two a.m., but either way we are going to discuss this. If you have any doubts about that statement, you're welcome to speak with my secretary. She doesn't go home until I do."

Grayson looked over at the man sitting beside her. From the expression on his face, she realized he definitely wasn't kidding.

She didn't want to talk about it. She didn't want to face whatever monsters she had tucked away inside her head. But she also knew he wasn't going to let her go before she talked.

She took in a few shaky breaths. Her eyes were glazing over. Shin knew the look well. She was hyperventilating. Her head was getting fuzzy. Her vision was blurring at the edges.

A panic response.

"What were you doing at the hospital?" Dr. Shin asked again.

"I was trying to break into Dr. Cain's office."

"Why?"

"Because I wanted to know who the ninth victim was going to be. I...I couldn't sleep. And he kept calling me Beatrice. It didn't make any sense. I even corrected him once and it didn't stop. So, I started looking. And when I realized who he thought I was...it all made sense. I knew there was one left. I thought maybe there would be a clue in his office somewhere."

"Why not talk to someone from the department? Why not call Detective Ryder?"

Grayson stayed quiet for a second, the wheels spinning behind her glassy eyes. "I didn't want anyone but me to get in trouble."

Shin narrowed his eyes at her. There was more to that side of the story.

Let's put a pin in that for now.

"Were you successful? Breaking into his office, I mean."

"No. And the longer I was there, the stupider I felt. I finally just decided to give up and go home. I got down a few flights of stairs before I felt something wrap across my mouth. Everything went black so fast. And I woke up in the gray box."

"The gray box?"

"The room where he had me. It was all gray."

"I see," Shin said, nodding. She had given it a name. The gray box. That wasn't a particularly good sign.

"I woke up in four-point restraints. He eventually came and took me out of them."

"Cain visited you?"

She nodded. It appeared that the young doctor couldn't stop talking about her abduction, now that someone had forced her to open the floodgates.

"Twice every day. He would bring me food and a change of clothes in the morning. Then a new tray of food in the evening. He never stayed long, except for the last time. Saturday night."

"Why did he stay longer then?"

"He wanted to talk to me. He brought a different dinner. He told me things would be different soon. He wouldn't tell me who he was going to kill. I tried to get him to tell me, but he refused. And that's when I got really scared."

"Why?"

"By then, I knew no one was coming for me. I wished and wished, but Gabriel never kicked down the door and took me away from that place. They either didn't know I was missing or had already looked and missed me. I knew no one was coming. And when he said everything was going to be different, I knew I wasn't going to have another chance to get away from him. So, I got out of the restraints, changed into the black clothes he brought me and hid by the door. I folded up blankets and pillows to look like I was still in the bed."

"He had you tied up?" Shin grimaced.

Grayson nodded sharply, pieces of her hair falling loosely around her face.

"After he left the last time, he tied me up. But he put me in the kind of restraints I know how to get out of. One of the ICU nurses showed me once how patients can get themselves out of them if they try hard enough. I tried hard enough. When he came in, I ran out the door."

"Do you dream about the gray box?"

She nodded.

"Does it wake you up?"

"Only when he takes me away," she said, the tears starting to fall again.

"You mean when you don't get away? From Cain?"

She nodded. "Or when he walks away and leaves me."

"Detective Ryder?"

She nodded, sniffling.

"I see."

Shin hesitated a moment before continuing.

This next question might be too much for her.

"Do you have feelings for Douglas Cain?"

Grayson's eyes snapped up from her lap. She slammed her water glass down on the side table and dashed to the corner of the room.

Shin cursed under his breath and stood up. He walked up behind her and gently pulled her hair out of her face as she threw up what little she'd had in her stomach. She was shaking so badly she could barely hold onto the trashcan. His heart went out to the poor girl.

When it was clear she was finished but weakened, he held onto her and guided her back to the couch. He sat down next to her and handed her the water glass. She tried to push it away, but he insistently held it close to her face.

"You need to drink. You're about to pass out. And it will get the taste out of your mouth. Drink. Just a little bit."

She nodded and took a sip of the water. Then two. Then three. When she took the glass into her own hands, he scooted back and looked at her closely. She was shaken up, but not broken. He had more room to go with her yet.

"That provoked quite a reaction."

She looked at him with sarcasm glinting in her eyes. "You think?" She stared into her water glass for several seconds. "I didn't think I'd ever have to even look at him again. Or hear his name. But of course, I was wrong."

"Really?" Shin asked, narrowing his eyes. "What do you mean?"

"Sunday. Sunday was...pretty bad."

Dr. Shin frowned. Douglas Cain was in lockup.

How would she have seen him Sunday?

"What happened?" he asked worriedly.

Grayson looked at him like he should already be in on a big secret. "No one told you? They called me in to interrogate Cain on Sunday."

On the outside, Dr. Shin remained cool and collected. On the inside, his conscious self fell off of the couch. "They did what?"

"He wouldn't talk to anybody, then suddenly Saturday night he said he would talk to me. I came in Sunday. Logan... Detective Harrison...asked me to. I almost didn't."

"What happened?"

She shrugged. "We talked."

Shin narrowed his eyes at her. "Try again."

Grayson sighed heavily. Shin watched patiently as she went to war inside her own head again. Her lips moved, subtly, silently. She was talking to herself inside her own mind. He didn't have to wait long for her reply.

"They had him chained to the table, but I was still scared of him. Just...he...he looks at me, and it makes my skin crawl. Like he can see me even when I have all of my walls up. I don't like it."

"I doubt most people would. So how did you muster the courage to be in the same room with him?"

"I knew I was their only shot. Otherwise, a jury would just call him crazy and be done with it. Give him a pardon or a plea deal or send him to an institution for a few months. Douglas Cain isn't crazy, Dr. Shin. He's a murderer. He doesn't deserve pity. He deserves the electric chair or lethal injection or worse for what he's done."

There was that low, vicious tone again. There was power behind it. Hidden behind fear, but it was definitely there. Shin raised his eyebrows.

She's not weak. She's just scared. She bites back when she needs to.

He smiled. "You often do things at a personal cost to yourself, don't you?"

"If it needs to be done," she replied.

Like fixing Ryder's femur the same night she gained her freedom.

"So Cain just talked to you. No suspicion that anything was going on?"

"I don't think so. Not by the end of it."

"Why not? I'd be suspicious of you if you'd just broken my face and shattered my arm."

She turned her head to look at the older man and cracked a small smile. "I…I kind of… played him."

"Excuse me?" *What did she just say?*

"I…I acted like I cared about him. Like I was scared the police were going to take me away from him. He didn't want to tell me about the murders, but I said I had the right to know what he did for me. I threw in some vague references to Dante that I read on Wikipedia, and he just started talking."

Shin raised his eyebrows over his metal-rimmed glasses, the admiration plain as day on his face. "How long were you in there with him?"

"I don't know. A half hour, maybe? It didn't take long."

"How were you afterward?"

She looked dejectedly toward the trashcan in the corner. "A lot like I was five minutes ago."

"You were physically sick?"

She nodded. "It took me a long time to calm down. Logan… Detective Harrison…took me home. I cried the whole way and for most of the rest of the day. I could hardly get out of bed."

Realization dawned on Shin's face. The flimsy excuses. The refusal to see Ryder on Sunday when he'd wanted to see her.

"Did anyone check on you that day?"

She shook her head. "I didn't let anybody near me. Not even my roommate."

"Did Detective Ryder attempt to contact you?" he pressed.

She wrinkled her forehead at the question. Shin wrinkled his right back at her.

I know I just asked you the same question twice. Answer it anyway.

"He tried. Um, I gave him an excuse about not feeling well."

"Have you seen him since?"

She shook her head. "No. Why?"

"You need to tell him what happened on Sunday."

"Why? It doesn't matter."

"It involves his case, and it involves you. It matters on two counts. He needs to hear what happened. And he needs to hear it from you, not stumble onto it on his own."

What a disaster that would be.

She nodded slowly, clearly not fully agreeing with him.

"Trust me on this one, my dear," he grinned. "Our time is nearly up, but I do have one more question for you, if you don't mind."

"Do I have a choice?"

"Not really," he chuckled, then turned himself on the couch to face her more directly.

"What is Gabriel Ryder to you?"

Shin watched her face as the young doctor formulated her reply. He hadn't meant it as an inflammatory question, something meant to set her off and provoke a hysterical reaction. Deep down, he'd come to be somewhat protective of the young man he'd just asked about, and ethically proper or not, he cared about her response.

"I...I don't really know how to answer that question, Dr. Shin."

When he didn't react, she kept talking.

"Are you asking me if I love him? I don't know. I've never loved anyone before. Not romantically, anyway. I feel safe around him. He makes me laugh. He takes care of me when I'm too stubborn to ask anyone for help. And when he kisses me, I lose track of everything else. That has to be close."

That was the softest and steadiest her voice had been through their entire appointment.

Shin leaned back on the couch and nodded slightly. Inside, he was beaming. He'd been right. She'd fallen for Ryder just as he had for her. They just didn't realize it yet. There were too many things in their way.

Shin stood up from the couch and held out his hand for her. Grayson took it and stood up as well, grabbing her messenger bag.

"If you don't mind, Dr. Carter, I would like to schedule another appointment for a few weeks from now. I'd like to check in with you again."

"All right, Dr. Shin. As long as you stop calling me that."

And with a small smile, she was out the door.

29

IT WAS JUST going on six o'clock when Grayson stepped off the elevator and started down the stark white hallway toward Gabriel's apartment.

She'd come to a compromise with him on Sunday night—truthfully, just to get him off the phone before he became suspicious and showed up at the house unannounced.

Dinner. Tuesday night. His place.

She smiled to herself as she passed the first of several small alcoves, each of which had a glittering silver mirror hung above a stark white lacquered table. Grayson stopped and checked her reflection. Her hair was windblown from walking across the street in the storm and her cheeks were flushed from the cold, but all in all she still looked presentable.

After her appointment with Dr. Shin, she'd felt dirty. Discussing Douglas Cain in any way seemed to do that to her. The slightest thought of him made her skin itch. So she'd showered and changed into something a little classier than jeans and a T-shirt. The dark red silk V-neck combined with her favorite black pencil skirt and kitten heels made her feel like she at least belonged in the building. Marginally. Her life was definitely more jeans-and-polar-fleece-comfortable compared to Gabriel's, but she figured she could at least make a bit of an effort.

Especially after I blew him off on Sunday.

She scolded herself as she closed the distance to Gabriel's front door. After talking to Dr. Shin, she felt even worse about lying to him than she had before. And the psychiatrist had been right. It was his case. Why shouldn't he know? He was going to find out about the interview eventually.

Grayson unbuttoned her coat at the front door and knocked twice. No response. She knocked again and got the same eerie silence.

"Gabriel?" she called, trying the handle.

It turned easily, and the door slid open. She tentatively pushed it wide and took two steps into the apartment, calling his name again.

She shouldn't have bothered. He was only a few feet from the door, pacing like a caged animal with a glass of amber liquid in his right hand. A matching bottle, with a significant amount missing, was sitting on the kitchen countertop.

"Hi," she said quickly, managing the best smile she could.

The curl on her lips immediately vanished under the icy glare he shot back at her. She paused. Her coat was only just off her shoulders, and a small voice in the back of her head told her to put it back on. She obeyed.

Grayson stood still, helpless, unsure of what to do. Gabriel continued to glare at her, then took a long drink of the scotch in his glass and went back to pacing. Grayson waited nervously for him to say something. Anything. She tapped her foot in anticipation against the marble floor. Nothing.

After watching him glare and pace and drink for more than a few painfully silent minutes, she couldn't stand it anymore. She walked the several paces she needed to into the living room and stood in his path. He was so lost in thought, he nearly barreled right through her. She put her hands up to protect herself.

"Gabriel!"

He stopped just inches from her, well within her personal space, breathing hard and fast.

She laid one hand on his chest. "Is something wrong?"

The words were no sooner out of her mouth than he latched onto her wrist with his free hand and wrenched her hand off of him. His fingernails dug into her soft skin. She grimaced but stayed silent.

"Don't insult me by playing stupid," he spat, draining the last of the glass and hurling it against the wall.

Grayson shrank into her coat as the crystal shattered against the wall. She was too afraid to move, even breathe. He released her and pushed past to get to the kitchen.

She spun around but didn't follow him.

There are knives in there, the voice in the back of her head reminded softly. *Wait, what? Why did that thought cross my mind?*

Before she could even attempt to process her inner monologue, Gabriel returned, a fresh and very full glass in his right hand.

He'd gone for a new bottle.

"Wh…what are you talking about?" she squeaked.

"I said don't play stupid," he hissed, passing her into the living room.

He turned to face her from the fireplace and leaned against the mantel. Grayson didn't miss the slight sway in his stance.

"Let me make it easy for you." He leered at her over the top of his glass and took several steps toward her. "Sunday."

The word sounded like pure poison as it left his mouth.

Grayson felt her stomach turn. She slammed her eyes closed.

Oh no, he found out. He found out I talked to Cain behind his back. He's livid. Oh God, how am I going to apologize for this?

She fought to stifle the screaming voice inside her head. By the time she opened her eyes, he was right on top of her. He circled around her like an animal stalking wounded prey. He was smiling, but his eyes betrayed the anger behind his upturned lips.

"I know where you were," he breathed into her ear. "I saw what you did."

"You...you did?" Her voice was shaking and too high-pitched.

"I saw the tape. I heard what you said to him."

She startled slightly at that comment. *Why does it matter what I said to him?*

His voice dropped even lower and he leaned in closer, stepping right up behind her. His breath was hot and warm in her ear. "I heard you tell him you love him."

Grayson's heart dropped to the floor. The room started to spin.

He thinks...no...how can he possibly think that? Oh no. No, no, no, no!

She fought against the screaming in her head again. Gabriel continued stalking her around the living room as her vision blurred. She was struggling to breathe.

"You protected him. You miss him. You aren't together anymore. What are you going to do?" he spat, mimicking her tone from the tape.

Mocking her.

Grayson felt the tears start to form behind her eyes. She fought them back, sniffling in self-defense.

"You vapid tramp. Did you really think I wouldn't find out?"

Gabriel advanced on her again, and she backed up toward the door.

He was drunk. He was angry. And he thought she was in love with Douglas Cain. She opened her mouth to try to say something, anything, to get him to understand what had happened.

Didn't Logan say anything? Or the captain?

Apparently not, the voice in her head replied sarcastically as she stumbled back against the bar.

Gabriel stopped just in front of her and put an arm on either side of her hips, caging her in on all sides. She could see the muscles of his arms flex underneath his shirt. Her heart rate sped up. Her breathing shallowed. Her vision blurred further. His fingers flexed against the marble counter.

Oh God, he's going to hit me.

Grayson closed her eyes against the impending blow. But nothing ever came. Instead, she felt him flex his elbows and lean forward, just beside her left ear.

"Was it fun for you, to play with me like that?" he murmured. "To watch me run myself to the ground for you and know that your ultimate prize was off slaughtering innocent people? For *you*? Stupid girl."

He pulled back from her, smirking. His eyes were too dark, nearly black, and loaded with alcohol.

Grayson didn't see them. She didn't want to see them. Her eyes were still closed. She shivered involuntarily.

"I was right about you the first time, you manipulative little bitch."

Her eyes violently snapped open. Grayson took in the triumphant curl in his lips, the dark, hazy look in his eyes, the way he ran his tongue hungrily across his lower lip. Silent tears ran unchecked down her face. Her hands wouldn't stop shaking.

She couldn't look at him anymore. Grayson tore her gaze away from him.

She felt him square his shoulders and puff out his chest. She felt him sneer at her cowering form. He chuckled triumphantly under his breath and took a drink.

"Pathetic."

One word. That's all it took.

Grayson made a decision.

Without warning, she slapped him across the face as hard as she possibly could.

The crack of her hand against his cheek echoed off the walls and down the hallway.

Gabriel staggered backward, already off balance from the scotch. His eyes saw pure white, then blurred out into blackness.

By the time he steadied himself and regained his sight, Grayson was standing in the open doorway, looking over her shoulder at him.

"Apparently, I was right about you, too, detective. How could I have been so stupid? To think that someone like you could ever see beyond his own goddamned ambition. Hope you had fun slumming, Gabriel. I'm sure easy and uncomplicated won't be too hard to find once I'm gone."

She slammed the door behind her as she left.

It took Ryder a moment to fully register the words that had come out of her mouth. Then he went nuclear.

He grabbed the bottle from the counter and hurled it against the wall above the couch. It shattered. Scotch dripped down the walls like amber bloodstains.

The desperate, feral scream that escaped his lips echoed through the walls and down the hallway after her. It wasn't human.

Grayson prayed for the elevators doors to close around her before whatever had made that noise decided to come after her.

30

LOGAN HAD JUST walked in and waved to the doorman when the sound of someone crying reached his ears. He expected to find a lost child sniffling on the other side of the lobby. Instead, he saw Grayson Carter emerge from the elevator with her head in her hands, moving as fast as she could toward the front door. She looked worse now than she had on Sunday when he'd taken her home.

"Fuck, Ryder," he muttered. "What the hell did you do?"

He moved sideways to intercept her before she got outside. "Grayson?"

He called to her, but she didn't seem to register his voice. She kept barreling forward, trying to wipe the tears out of her eyes long enough to see where she was going.

Logan put his arms out, catching her by the shoulders. The moment he touched her, she started fighting against him. "Grayson! Grayson! Hey, doc, it's me. Look up."

She wildly looked around from side to side, then straight ahead at him. Her eyes were glassy and glazed over. It took a moment for her to fully recognize him. When she did, there was no relief in her face. There was no smile.

"What the hell is going on? What happened?"

She shook her head violently and looked at the floor.

Logan dropped his voice. "What did that fucker do to you?"

She shook her head again and managed to whisper "I can't" before pushing past him and out into the snow. Harrison stood still for a moment, watching her cross the street and get into her car. Once she'd gotten it started and pulled out into traffic, he stalked over to the elevator.

He ground his teeth the whole ride up and all the way down the hallway to a familiar front door. On a hunch, he tried the handle. It was unlocked. He barreled into the apartment and into an unsteady, very surprised former partner.

"Logan, what the fuck?"

Harrison didn't give him a reply. The bastard didn't deserve one. Without even bothering to shut the door, he grabbed Ryder by the front of his shirt, lifted him off of the floor, and shoved him into the nearest wall.

Gabriel's head hit with a loud thud. The drywall cracked.

"What did you do to her?" Logan growled.

"Goddamn it, put me the fuck down!"

Gabriel fought against him. Logan was not only pissed off but stone-cold sober. He easily held the younger man in place.

"Answer me," he yelled, throwing Gabriel back against the wall again.

When he didn't respond, Logan let Gabriel slide down to his feet just long enough to ball up his fist and shove it into his abdomen.

Gabriel hunched forward, grimacing against the pain. Harrison didn't stop. He didn't fucking care anymore.

Logan grabbed his shirt again and flung him onto the glass covered, scotch-soaked couch. He loomed over Ryder as the younger man tried to stop the room from spinning. When Ryder tried to fight back, Logan punched him in the jaw and sent him sprawling backward.

"Stay down, you fucking asshole. I'm done with you."

"Why?" Gabriel spat, still clutching his abdomen where Logan had punched him. "Because some bitch played me for a fool while she was fucking a serial killer? Shit, I'd have thought you'd be on my side on this one."

"What in the fucking hell are you talking about?"

Gabriel glared up at him from the couch. "You saw her. On the tape. You heard what she said to him."

Logan's right eyebrow cocked up. *Is this idiot fucking serious?*

The older man shoved himself away from the couch and shook his head.

"Yeah. What I saw on that tape was a girl scared out of her mind confronting the bastard who'd stalked her, kidnapped her, and had very specific plans to rape her like a fucking animal. And what I also saw was that same girl playing the psychopath like a fucking harp."

A sarcastic laugh escaped from Ryder's lips. "Excuse me?"

"She. Was. Faking it. Are you fucking serious? You thought that shit was real?"

Logan propped himself up against one of the club chairs and shook his head.

"Ryder, she spent an hour sick as a dog at the precinct on Sunday, then cried the whole ride home. It took everything she had to just walk into that room with him."

Despite the scotch coursing through his bloodstream, Gabriel was instantly sober. Logan kept talking.

"Cain made it clear Saturday night he was only going to talk to her. I asked her to come in. She agreed. I didn't tell you because I knew you'd flip your shit. I knew you wouldn't let her. I didn't know she was going to put on an act in there, but it worked. He told us everything we needed. He's gonna fry because of her."

Gabriel curled his hands around his mouth and leaned his forearms onto his thighs.

It was all an act? Oh God, she tried...I didn't listen. I called her...oh God, no...

"She put herself through hell for *you*, you fucking moron."

Gabriel stood up abruptly from the couch and staggered to the window.

Logan shook his head. "She's gone." He softened his voice a bit as he walked over to join Ryder. "I ran into her in the lobby. She's gone."

Logan looked sideways at Ryder, and for the first time since he'd known him, he thought he saw the man's eyes shine with genuine regret.

"Jesus Christ, Ryder, what in the hell did you do?"

"Something unforgivable," he muttered.

Harrison shook his head again, turned, and disappeared into the kitchen. He came back with two glasses and a new bottle of scotch. He opened the bottle on the coffee table, poured two glasses, and handed one over.

"Start in on that. You're not going to want to be sober for a while."

"Logan, what have I done?"

Harrison clicked his glass against his former partner's. "I don't know, buddy. Maybe the bottom of the bottle will have some answers. But don't expect anything more than a hangover."

31

SOMEHOW, SHE GOT home.

When she looked back on that evening, Grayson couldn't actually remember the drive. She didn't remember getting into her car, turning the engine over, or navigating the snow-covered roads. She didn't remember pulling into the back alley or walking through the kitchen door. She didn't even really remember sitting down on the couch.

But she did remember crying. Violently sobbing, curled up into a ball, cold and without any hope of getting warm.

That's how Barbara found her when she walked in the front door at seven o'clock sharp, curled up into the side of the couch and sobbing uncontrollably. She dropped her bags on the entryway floor and tore her coat off as she rushed over to the couch.

"Gray? Grayson! Talk to me. What the hell happened? What's wrong? Sweetie, talk to me. What's wrong?"

Her frantic, high-pitched voice only served to make the crying worse. Grayson wrapped her arms around her roommate as she collapsed even further into the couch.

When the sobs became dry heaves and there were no more tears, Barbara apparently unilaterally decided enough was enough. She used all the force in her upper body to pull Grayson up to a sitting position and rubbed the backs of her hands under her friend's mascara-stained eyes.

"All right, that's enough. You've cried so long you don't have any more tears. Now, tell me what happened. Are you hurt?"

Grayson shook her head.

"I thought you were supposed to be at dinner tonight."

"I was," she said hoarsely. "It didn't go so well."

"You want to talk about it?"

"Not really."

"It went that badly?"

"Gabriel accused me of two-timing him with Douglas Cain."
Barbara's mouth went slack.

Grayson looked up at her. "Wow. You're speechless. It really is that bad, then."

Grayson tried to sound sarcastic. She even tried to nonchalantly shrug her shoulders. It just came off as pathetic. Babs threw her arms around her and hugged her tightly.

"That's it," she said into Grayson's shoulder. "I'm done with all of this horseshit. You haven't been yourself for over two months, and I want my Gray back. We're getting out of here and going on vacation."

"Babs…"

"I'm not kidding. I just got you back after you were kidnapped by that psychopath, and now you're a hysterical mess on our couch. I've never seen you this miserable. I'm sick and tired of seeing you unhappy. Let's just go. You have time off until after January. I have time off. Noah has time. We can just leave and go away to the mountains."

That sounds incredible.

"We're never going to find a place to stay this late in the holiday season. You know that," she argued.

"Just leave that to me. Please, Grayson. Please, let's go and get far away from here. I can't stay cooped up in this house. Let's go away and spoil ourselves and pretend for a week that all this never happened."

Truthfully, it sounded wonderful. She wanted to be as far away from Denver and Douglas Cain and Gabriel Ryder as humanly possible. Hiding away in the mountains sounded perfect. And she was too tired to argue.

"Okay."

"Okay. I'll take care of everything. You go upstairs, change into something warm and fuzzy, and I'll bring you some tea and Advil."

"Just the tea, please."

"Tea and Advil. You're going to have a bad headache from crying so hard."

Grayson stood up and trudged upstairs. By the time she changed into pajamas and crawled into bed, she could feel a splitting headache beginning behind her eyes. She fluffed up her pillows and turned to lie down on her side. Her eyes rested on her night table, on a familiar book. She picked it up and opened to the marked page, immediately registering the handwriting in the margins.

There it was again. The overwhelming combination of his vicious voice and wicked eyes and the feel of him unconsciously wrapping his arms around her in his sleep.

She closed her eyes and tried to remember the blue eyes and playful smirk she was used to, but suddenly it all shifted and Gabriel was circling her like she was an antelope with a broken leg.

She wailed softly, stifling most of it into her pillow, and let the book fall onto the floor.

That's how Babs found her ten minutes later, in the dead sleep of the emotionally exhausted, her arm hanging off the bed, stretching out toward a well-worn copy of *Pride and Prejudice*.

32

GABRIEL RUBBED THE back of his neck and leaned over his desk. Strong coffee and a double dose of painkillers had done nothing to dampen his rip-roaring hangover. The fluorescent lights and incessant ringing of the squad floor phones weren't helping.

He'd spent the night passed out on his living room floor, having consumed the better part of a bottle of scotch. For the first time in a very long time, he hadn't given a shit about dressing for work. He was wearing old jeans and whatever wrinkled excuse for a button-down he'd grabbed out of the back of his closet. His hair was a mess. There were bags under his eyes. He looked like hell. He felt like hell.

And everyone knew well enough to stay the fuck away from him.

Once the first layer of cobwebs had cleared that morning, he'd realized he needed to apologize to her. She might not ever want to see him again or want anything to do with him, but the last words he said to her were not going to be "pathetic, manipulative bitch."

Her cell phone had gone directly to voicemail. It was either dead or she'd shut it off. He doubted she'd answer it anyway, but it had been worth a shot.

He'd tried Mason next, who'd promptly told him to join Greg Harlan in the seventh level of hell and hung up.

Gabriel had had the sense of mind to ask Logan to call Barbara Parker. She had actually picked up, but it didn't take long for her to catch on to what Logan was after. In not-so-subtle terms, she explained that if Gabriel ever came near Grayson again, she'd cut off some very important pieces of his anatomy and feed them to wild dogs while he watched.

The phone call hadn't been a complete waste, however. In the minutes before she'd thrown her walls up, Barbara had slipped, not only mentioning that she was taking Grayson out of town but up to a ski resort about four hours away. It wasn't the name of a town or an address, but it was somewhere to start.

That was where a few old favors had come in handy. It had taken a couple of phone calls and very vague explanations, but Gabriel now had an unofficial BOLO out on Grayson's SUV.

On top of the splitting headache, Ryder had had to endure the scathing looks from both of his partners. Apparently, while he was busy forgetting how to say his own name last night from inside a bottle of scotch, Logan had updated his partner.

Nolan had muttered "fucking asshole" at him across their desks before burying himself underneath a large pile of self-imposed paperwork. Ryder had tried to explain himself. Nolan had told him to shove anything he had to say up his own ass.

That had been at nine a.m. It was going on five o'clock now. That sentiment hadn't changed.

A phone in the department started ringing, and Ryder slammed his hand up to his forehead, eyes clenched shut against the noise.

Whose fucking phone…

"Ryder. It's yours. Answer it, you asshole," came his partner's mumbling voice from across the desk.

Sure enough, the oversized black box on his desk had a red light blinking on and off next to a label that read "line one." He shook his head to try to dampen the headache, which only made things worse, and picked up the handset.

"Ryder."

He stayed quiet, listening to whoever was on the other line. "You're sure? All right. How far out? Yeah, thanks."

He set the handset back in the cradle and stood up.

"You find her?" came Blake's low voice from across the desk.

He nodded. "Highway 82 heading into Aspen. State patrol tailed them into town."

Logan overheard. He quickly walked over and leaned up against Blake's desk. "This is really stupid, Gabe. You're going to get in a lot of trouble for this."

He shrugged. "What the fuck do I care?"

"Yeah, right, you don't care about your career or this partnership, do you? It's always all about you. Well, have fun," Blake spat.

Ryder startled. "You're…you're not coming?"

Blake shook his head. "This is your goddamned problem, Ryder. I'm not losing my job because you fucked up your personal life. And I have my girls this weekend." He looked back down at his desk without saying another word.

Gabriel swore under his breath, grabbed his coat off the back of his chair, and stalked off toward the elevators. Harrison shook his head and lumbered after him, stepping onto the elevator car just as the doors were closing.

"He's right, you know, Ryder."

"Don't fucking remind me, Logan."

"You're putting both of your careers at risk by acting like an asshole."

"Then he can get a new partner who doesn't put his career at risk," he parroted back sarcastically.

"You don't want that and neither does he. Calm down."

"I have other things to worry about right now," he said. The elevator doors opened out onto the basementt level of the parking deck.

"Yeah, I see that."

The two former partners awkwardly stood facing each other for a minute. Gabriel fished out the keys to his car. "I've gotta go."

"You're going alone?"

"Do I have a choice?"

Harrison shrugged and kept his place, his arms crossed across his chest. Ryder opened the door to his car and looked over his shoulder. "You're not thinking of following me up there."

"No, idiot. I'm driving. Your car's sex on wheels, but it's not going to handle six inches of snow over Vail Pass."

"I'm taking my SUV."

"When did you get another fucking car?"

Gabriel rolled his eyes.

"All right. Give me thirty minutes to pack a bag. It's on you to find somewhere for me to sleep that isn't your backseat or somebody's couch."

Without a word, Gabriel got into his car and peeled out of the parking lot.

Logan jogged over to his truck. He wouldn't put it past Ryder to start a stopwatch and leave without him. This was going to be cutting it close.

Thirty-five minutes later, a slate gray Mercedes M-Class pulled into traffic in downtown Denver and headed toward the interstate, west toward the mountains.

33

THURSDAY MORNING IN Aspen dawned clear and crisp. The snowstorm they'd fought driving over the mountain passes had cleared out, leaving several inches of fresh powder on the ski slopes and glittering snow on the evergreen trees.

Grayson curled up on the window bench, a cup of hot coffee held in between her hands, and looked out over the morning calm. Hardly anyone in town was awake, just an elderly couple trying to navigate the new snow on the other side of the street.

Despite her very comfortable surroundings, she hadn't been able to sleep. When five a.m. had rolled around, her biological clock had forced her out of bed for her usual cup of coffee. She had been on cup number two by the time the sky had started to pink up in the east.

Barbara had somehow managed to rent a condo at the Innsbruck, a recently renovated boutique hotel off of Main Street. It was beautiful, the perfect luxurious mountain lodge. They each had their own rooms. The living area was massive and plushly furnished. The kitchen was well-stocked. But by far, her favorite fixture was the window bench. It was the size of a bed, with pillows and blankets piled on all sides, and bordered up against a massive bay window. She could see well into town and far up the mountain.

A soft yawn from the hallway pulled Grayson out of her thoughts. Noah was leaning against the wall, dressed in sweat pants and slippers, hair askew. He'd most definitely just rolled out of bed.

Medicine residents...not the earliest risers...

"Good morning, love," he said, rubbing the sleep out of his eyes.

"Morning."

"You're up early."

"So are you. Coffee's ready." She nodded toward the half-full carafe in the kitchen.

Noah poured himself a cup and sat down opposite her on the window seat. "The storm's gone."

She nodded.

"Did you get any sleep?"

She shook her head. "Not really."

"Gray, are you ever going to tell me what happened on Tuesday?"

She sighed. "I'd rather not."

"Something he can't come back from?"

She shrugged, then nodded.

"That's all I need to know, love." He took a sip of his coffee, He'd told the detective to go to hell on Wednesday morning. Apparently, that had been the right response. "What do you want to do today?"

She shrugged. "I don't care."

"Do you want to go skiing?"

"I don't think I'm quite up for that yet. But you and Babs should go. She loves to ski."

"I need to rent some skis somewhere. Maybe she knows a place."

"Probably."

"Why don't we just walk around town today?" he suggested. "The weather's nice."

Grayson knew that tone. He didn't trust leaving her on

her own, and that's exactly what she wanted. "That'll be boring for you."

"I've never been to Aspen at the holidays. How could it be boring?"

She smirked. "You're just trying to keep an eye on me so I don't put a gun to my head, aren't you?"

"Well, that's maybe a close second to getting skis and shopping." He grinned.

She managed a small smile back.

"There's my Gray," he mumbled into his coffee.

Barbara was up by eight and insisted that they go down the street for breakfast. Bundled up in their coats and warm hats, they walked several blocks down the street to a quaint pink and white cafe. It was busy, and they waited nearly twenty minutes for a table, but Barbara seemed pleased with herself when they finally sat down.

"I take it you've been here before," Grayson said, looking over the menu.

"Once or twice." She winked.

"What's good?" Noah asked.

"Pretty much everything. Sometimes I literally come here and eat chocolate cake for breakfast. They make incredible desserts."

"I'll stick to something with eggs in it, thanks," he replied.

Grayson leaned over toward Babs and tapped her shoulder. "So, exactly how did you get us into that condo?"

Babs smiled. "It's a secret."

"Babs…."

Grayson's breath hitched in her throat.

Oh dear God, please don't tell me he had something to do with this…

Completely unaware she'd caused her friend's heart rate to skyrocket well above panic level, Barbara put her menu down. "Okay, fine, I'll spill. My company rents out a block of condos every holiday. There's a drawing every year to see who gets them."

"You got one?"

"No. But I promised my coworker that I would pick up his work in February if I could take it, and he agreed. Besides, he already had plans to go back to the East Coast with his family to visit his in-laws. It worked out."

"Oh." *Thank God.*

"Yup. Easy."

"Thank you," Grayson said quietly.

"Hey, we all needed a bit of a vacation. And I loved this town the last time I came here in the winter. Must be something to it."

"Um, ladies…" Noah's voice drifted over the table.

They looked up to see their waitress waiting on them, pen raised to her order pad.

"Oh, sorry. Could we have a few minutes?"

"Sure," the redhead replied sweetly. "Can I bring you something to drink while you're looking over the menu?"

"Three coffees," Noah said.

"Coming up."

She disappeared to go after their drinks.

"So, Noah needs skis. There's a rental place up by where we get our ski passes. Gray, are you sure you don't want to come skiing?"

She nodded. "I just don't quite feel up to it right now. I can always get a day's rental if I change my mind."

"Good point. We can just spend the day walking around town then. Taking it easy. And we can go out tonight!"

Grayson sighed and sank down in her chair.

"Why don't we just hit a bar tonight, Babs?" Noah countered. "Besides, Friday would be better for really going out."

"True...oh! I know a great place. I went the last time I was here a few years ago. I'll call and see if we can get in tomorrow." She whipped out her cell phone and dialed.

Grayson looked across the table to Noah and mouthed "thank you" when Barbara wasn't looking. He winked at her.

"Shit. They don't open until four. I'll have to call back later." Barbara shut her phone as the coffee arrived.

Breakfast was uneventful and delicious. Noah paid their check, and both he and Grayson followed Barbara into town. She led them toward the base of the ski mountain, first to the Ski Company to get Noah's ski pass and then down the street to an outfitter. The girls spent a good thirty-five minutes just trying to get him to commit to a ski boot.

When he had everything he needed, they sent him back to the hotel with his equipment while they started walking along the cobblestone streets.

Babs linked her arm in Grayson's and turned her down one of the busier pedestrian streets. The quaint two- and three-story brick buildings were still glittering with the overnight snow. It was cold enough that none of it would melt. The bright blue skies and gleaming sun were almost blinding against the white background.

Grayson sighed heavily. It felt so good to just be outside.

"So," Babs pressed, "what do you want to go shopping for?"

"I don't have anything particular in mind," she shrugged.

"I need a new polar fleece jacket. There's a North Face store down the street. We can start there."

"Okay."

She browsed through the store on autopilot. Barbara found

two armfuls worth of clothes to try on, all of which fit her perfectly. Grayson wandered through the carousels while she waited for Barbara to pay.

"You didn't find anything?"

"No," she said, shaking her head. "Nothing I need."

"But maybe something you want?"

She shook her head.

Babs handed over her purchase to the woman behind the counter, who started ringing things up into the register. "Are you okay?" she asked.

"Not really," Grayson replied truthfully. There was no sense in trying to deny it. She knew she felt like hell and likely looked like it, too. Why put energy into trying to hide the obvious?

"Anything I can do?"

"Just hang around with me and don't let me mope too much."

"I can handle that."

Barbara paid the woman and grabbed her bags, then herded Grayson out the door.

"C'mon. I doubt Noah's even made it back to the room yet. Let's go this way."

She pulled her further down the street and into a small women's boutique. It was packed from floor to ceiling with clothing, and a circular glass case full of jewelry in the center of the room glittered in the overhead light. It took a second for Grayson to adjust her eyes to the light.

"What are we doing in here?" she asked.

Babs rolled her eyes and walked over to speak to the salesgirl.

Grayson started walking around the store, occasionally pulling out pieces of clothing from the racks to look at them more closely. Every single piece was intricate, delicate, and ridiculously expensive. She nearly had a heart attack when she pulled a two-hundred-and-fifty-dollar blouse off the hanger. It quickly went back on the rack.

"Can I help you find anything?" A thin, blonde woman in a black suit walked up to her, smiling.

"Oh, no. Thanks. I'm just looking around."

"No, she's not!" came the call from further back in the store. Barbara came bounding up behind the woman with a grin on her face. "She needs something to wear out tomorrow."

Grayson's face went white. "Oh no...Babs, I can't do this again..."

Barbara scowled, immediately recognizing the fear in her friend's eyes. She politely asked the salesgirl to excuse them for a second and lowered her voice.

"Hey, this is from me, okay? There's no secret bank account this time. We're going out tomorrow night. I want us to go to a nice place. I know you didn't pack anything special. So, pick something out. It's an early Christmas gift."

"Babs..."

"Oh, just humor me. Pick out something you like. And stop looking at price tags. My bonus this year was killer!" She batted Grayson's hand away from the dangling white strip of paper and sauntered back deeper into the store.

On cue, the salesgirl came back around.

"Miss Parker asked me to help you find something for tomorrow. Can I be of some help?"

Grayson looked helplessly at the clothes in front of her.

"Um, I...I'm not quite sure what I should be looking for. I don't know where we're going."

The salesgirl smiled warmly. "I'm afraid I've been asked to keep that a secret, but I can guide you in the right direction. Tell me a little bit about what you usually like to wear."

34

GABRIEL KICKED UP the collar of his overcoat and tucked his hands into his pockets as he barreled out the front door of the hotel. Logan was right on his heels.

Both the valet and the doorman, dressed in black wool trench coats and black cowboy hats, parted like the waters of the Red Sea and held the doors open for them. The pair stormed out beyond them onto the front sidewalk. Harrison nodded at them in thanks; Gabriel kept his eyes on the concrete.

They silently crossed the intersection when the light turned and started up Mill Street. It was only a short walk from the Hotel Jerome into the epicenter of town.

They'd arrived last night after ten o'clock, exhausted and looking for somewhere to lay their heads down. When Gabriel had pulled up outside the upscale hotel, Logan had assumed he was stopping for directions.

When Ryder had handed over his car keys to the valet and walked around the back to get his bag, he'd cocked an amused eyebrow.

"Get out of the car, Logan."

The older man had followed his former partner into the lobby and waited patiently, leaning against a marble pillar, while he'd checked them in. Ten minutes later, they were heading upstairs.

"Figures you'd check us into the snootiest hotel in the whole ski town," he'd joked.

"You can sleep in the car if you'd prefer."

"I'll pass."

They had two suites on the top floor: pricey, unnecessary, and exceptionally comfortable. After an exhausted sleep, they'd bundled up in heavy coats and scarves and headed out into the crisp Thursday air.

"So, you wanna tell me how you managed two rooms in that place? And what exactly is this going to cost me?" Logan asked as they walked up Mill Street.

"Don't worry about it."

"I'm not worried. I'm curious."

He sighed. "I've stayed there before. The manager's an old family friend."

"You hate your family, Gabe."

"So does he."

Logan let out a laugh and slapped him on the back. "So where are we going?"

"I need coffee."

"Thank God. You're thinking straight again."

Ten minutes later, they were sitting at the counter in a small bakery. Logan was eagerly digging into an incredibly large muffin. Gabriel sat staring out the window at the street, silent and brooding over a cardboard cup of dark roast. The place was crowded, but not uncomfortably so. It was loud enough that they could talk without being overheard.

"So, you got a plan now that we're here?"

"No. Not really."

"You're just going to sit here and wait for her to walk by the window?"

"It's a thought."

"Jesus Christ…" Logan shook his head. "You're pathetic."

"Yeah. Right." He swirled his coffee in the cardboard cup.

Logan took a bite of his muffin. "You figured out how much of an asshole you were to her?"

You have no idea. "Getting worse by the minute."

"What are you going to say to her?"

"I don't have any idea." *Absolutely no idea.*

"Are you kidding me? You hauled me all the way up here and you have no plan?"

"You got any brilliant fucking ideas, genius?" Ryder asked sarcastically.

"That's all on you. I'm just here to drive if you get shitfaced again."

"Not for a long time," he groaned, rubbing his forehead.

"You're losing your edge," Logan replied, chuckling. "You never used to get a hangover like this when you worked narcotics."

They finished their breakfast and stepped back out onto the street. Hour by hour, more people were waking up and filtering into town. There were skiers, snowboarders, sheik's wives, Hollywood starlets, and hippy locals. Everyone melted together, basking in the winter sun.

Ryder turned down one of the side streets and shoved his hands back into his pockets. Logan followed beside him.

"So, we really are just going to walk around aimlessly, aren't we?"

"No. We're going to check the hotels first, then fan out from there. Just like we would to find anyone else."

"She's not a suspect, Gabe."

"I know that," he hissed.

"So, stop treating her like a target. She's not a fucking animal. You've made that mistake twice now. Don't start again. We're here so you can lick your wounds and try to convince her you know you're an asshole before you slink off into the shadows with a new bottle of scotch. Got it?"

Gabriel sighed heavily. "Just make sure I don't lose it today, okay?"

"Ten-four, buddy. But you're picking up the bar tab after we're done with this shit."

They spent several hours running around downtown Aspen, checking off hotels and condominium complexes that rented out during the winter months. Nothing. No sign of her or Mason or Barbara. By three in the afternoon, the skiers were starting to come off of the mountain, and they were no closer to finding her.

"Goddamn it," Logan swore, sitting down abruptly on a bench along one of the cobblestone pedestrian streets. He leaned back and kicked his heels out. "Sit down, Gabe. I need to get off of my feet for a minute."

The younger detective scowled but complied, sitting down on the other side of the bench and dropping his forearms onto his knees.

"Did you expect to just luck out and find her in a few hours?"

"It would've been nice, yeah."

Logan chuckled and laced his fingers behind his head. He scanned the street, taking in the families with small children mixing in with the full-length fur coats and cowboy hats. Several couples were already a little tipsy on après-ski cocktails.

Goddamned tourists don't know how to handle their booze at altitude.

He leaned his head back and shut his eyes. The afternoon sun felt good on his face. The pain in his feet had faded into a dull hum when he heard a familiar voice among the crowd. He smirked against the warm air.

Oh, come on, there's no way...

He turned his head toward the sound, and a satisfied smile spread across his face. He turned back and relaxed.

Gabriel's leg was rapidly tapping up and down on the cobblestone street. He was getting agitated. He never could sit still for long. "Ready?" he asked, seeing Logan relax further into the bench beside him.

"I think we should stay right here."

Ryder pushed off his legs to stand and glared at him. "Logan, I don't have time to..."

"Sit the fuck down, Ryder, and relax."

"Goddamn it..."

"Gabe, sit down before you do something else stupid."

The tone in Logan's voice made Gabriel stop mid-rise. He sat back down and focused on the concrete in front of his feet. "What is it?"

"Do your best to be subtle, Wonder Boy. Three o'clock."

Gabriel popped the collar of his overcoat as he looked down the length of the pedestrian street. Logan kept one eye on him in his peripheral vision. It took Ryder a minute to scan through so many people, but when he spotted her, he locked on and didn't lose her. The change on his face was priceless.

"Grayson...?" he whispered.

Logan smiled again and leaned back further on the bench to give his partner a better line of sight.

There she was, wrapped up in dark jeans and a red and gray ski jacket. She had a shopping bag dangling in one hand. The opposite arm was linked with Noah Mason's. She was leaning into him a bit, and he was supporting her weight, smiling and laughing. Barbara was on her other side, her own hands loaded down with shopping bags, her face alight and happy. They were weaving through the crowd, steadily avoiding skis to the head and poles to the legs.

As they got closer, Gabriel dropped his head down and twisted his body in line with the flow of human traffic. It shielded him as much as possible from their line of sight. Logan did the same. As the trio passed, he caught a snippet of their conversation.

"...hope it isn't too fancy."

"It's not. You'll be overdressed after you change."

"If you say so."

"It's just around the corner..."

The group passed without taking any notice of the two men and blended back in with the crowd. Gabriel raised his head up and looked at Logan, who was grinning from ear to ear.

"You are the luckiest son of a bitch, Gabe. I swear to God."

Logan stood up and gestured with his head, indicating they should follow.

Gabriel nodded and fell into step beside him, pursuing the trio at a reasonably safe distance. They rounded a corner and Barbara's arm extended out, pointing at a small orange brick building on the corner of the street.

Gabriel took note of the location and the name.

Logan leaned over. "I'll go have a word with the bartender."

Gabriel nodded as his former partner peeled off and headed

into the establishment while he kept up pace behind the trio. It took another fifteen minutes, but finally they turned into a small hotel off of Main Street.

"The Innsbrook." He read the front sign aloud.

His cell phone vibrated in his pocket. A text from Logan was waiting.

They have reservations at 7. So do we.

They're in the dining room.

We're at the bar.

Gabriel snapped his phone closed and turned back around toward the Jerome. That gave him enough time to get back and pull himself together.

She'd looked good. Happy. Face flushed, wide smile, glinting eyes. They were taking care of her, Mason and Parker, in a way he couldn't. Goddamn it, in the way he should be and couldn't be because of his fucking overactive brain.

He rubbed his hand over his face.

And because of your jealousy, mumbled the little voice in the back of his head. *Why else would it matter so much that you thought she was involved with Cain? It didn't matter who he was or what he was. It mattered that he was competition. And you actually care about who wins for a change.*

He crossed the street when the hotel came into view.

Shit.

Maybe he should just leave well enough alone. Let her be happy. Stay happy. Not interfere.

No.

He had to see her. Actually see her. Just one last time.

Then he'd let her go.

35

THE JUSTICE SNOW was a bar and restaurant in the middle of Aspen, attached to the old Wheeler Opera House. A combination of rustic speakeasy and ski town eatery, it offered great food, a unique atmosphere, and an incredibly knowledgeable bar staff.

A long wooden bar with metal-on-wood bar chairs took up the majority of the main room with tables for two and three lined up against the windows overlooking the street. At the end of the room, down a few stairs, was a smaller, more intimate dining room with upholstered booths, a large chandelier, and old photos staggered across the walls.

Barbara had only been to the place once, but she had had a wonderful time. She was nearly skipping with glee as Noah opened the door at the top of the icy steps. She shoved Grayson into the warm vestibule.

The place was already busy. The bar was packed and lively. Most of the tables in the front room were full. The girls slid out of their coats and gloves almost instantly after walking through the door. The warmth from the fireplace was incredible.

"Can I help you?" A well-dressed hostess approached them, her bleached smile on full display.

"Yeah. We have a reservation for three. Parker."

The young girl looked at her list. "Oh, yes, here we go." She grabbed a few menus from the stand as the trio handed their coats over to the coat check. "Follow me." She led them around a maze of people to a table by the far end of the bar. "Is this okay?" she asked, setting the menus down.

Babs nodded and pulled out one of the chairs.

"Okay, enjoy your dinner."

Noah grabbed another chair and pulled it out for Grayson. "You don't need to do that," she said quietly.

"No, I don't, but I can," he murmured.

Babs grabbed the bar menu that was standing straight up in the middle of the table.

"They have the best cocktails here. Seriously. Everybody has to try something different."

"What do you suggest?" Grayson asked.

"Everything I had last time was great. Just pick something, Gray," she said.

They fell silent scanning the drink list. Noah ended up choosing a small-blend scotch. Babs opted for a variation on a cosmopolitan.

Grayson chewed the bottom of her lip between her teeth, completely overwhelmed. A new presence in her peripheral vision nearly startled her off of her chair.

"Having a little problem picking one?"

She looked up at a rather handsome young man, dressed in black pants and a black button-down, his dirty blond hair just uneven enough to look rugged.

"Um, kind of."

"First time here?"

She nodded.

"Our bar menu can be a little overwhelming. I'm Mike, one of the bartenders." He shook her hand. "What are you in the mood for?"

"Um, something I've never had before, but there's the problem. I don't know what I'd like."

"Well, let's start with a base. What's your liquor of choice?"

"Tequila," Babs answered for her, smiling brightly.

The young man quirked an eyebrow. When he got a nod from Grayson, Mike continued.

"Okay, tequila it is. Sweet? Smooth? Sharp? Spicy?"

"Something sweet, but not too much. Maybe with a little bite to it?"

Mike smiled. "I can do that. Anything you don't like?"

"Anchovies. That's about it."

"No anchovies. Got it." He winked at her and strode calmly back behind the bar. Grayson turned back to the table and glared directly at a scheming Barbara Parker.

"Well, he's adorable."

"Babs…" she groaned, rolling her eyes.

"He is!"

"So you go after him then."

"He wasn't making googly eyes at me. Or a special drink *for me*, by the way."

"He's a bartender in a tourist town. He has to be good. For business."

"Yeah. Right." Babs rolled her eyes and took a sip of water.

A few minutes later, Mike was back with their drinks. He stayed beside the table until Grayson gave him her overwhelming approval for his concoction. He slipped a piece of paper underneath her glass.

"A souvenir," he said, winking at her again.

She pulled it out and read it.

"And just what is that?" Noah asked.

"Not what you think," she said, handing the paper over.

Noah read it, then passed it to Babs. "What is this?" she asked.

"It's a recipe, Babs. For the drink," she said, rolling her eyes. "Every piece of paper isn't always a phone number."

"Cheers to that," Noah said, raising his glass.

Grayson and Babs followed suit, and they fell into an easy conversation, just as they always did. Eventually, they ordered dinner, which was delicious, and another round of drinks. During the second round, Noah's cell phone went off and he grinned, excusing himself from the table to take the call.

"Probably Kyle," Grayson grinned.

"He's smitten," Babs nodded.

"Must be nice," she replied.

"Gray, stop. It's not worth thinking about now."

"I know, I know."

"Drink up, sweetie. The next round's on me."

They'd been at the bar for less than twenty minutes.

Logan was already two drinks in and thoroughly enjoying chatting up one of the bartenders. He was doing a great job laying on the charm. She was fawning all over him, leaning over the glossy wood and pushing her arms together to enhance her assets oh-so-perfectly.

They'd chosen a vantage point at the end of the bar closest to the main door. From there, they could see the entire main room and into most of the smaller dining room. The few tables that were out of view only had room for two people and were already occupied.

When he heard her voice float over the low din, Ryder's eyes snapped up from the glass in his hand. His head cocked to the right just enough to be able to see her. He saw hints of her hair glistening in the dimmed light and silk laying across her shoulders. He didn't get a good look until she followed Barbara and the hostess across the restaurant floor to their table.

By the grace of God, Noah placed her in the chair facing the long end of the bar. It put her on profile. He could easily see her through the crowd.

There wasn't any way for her to see him.

She looked wonderful. Her hair was down and blown out straight. Her cheeks were flushed, probably from walking in the cold. A pair of tight, dark jeans and knee-high boots were topped off by a black silk shirt that was...

Holy hell.

...completely open in the back. The edges came together when she sat up straight, but when she leaned forward they fell open, exposing her beautiful skin. He could just see the curve of her back, and even from his vantage point across the room, he could tell she wasn't wearing anything underneath. It was just subtle enough to be one of the sexiest things he'd ever seen.

Gabriel watched her greedily. The hair on the back of his neck stood on edge when one of the bartenders sidled up to her side of the table. He balled his fists together when the man smiled at her. He nearly had a stroke when she smiled back at him.

The bartender winked at her. Gabriel hissed under his breath and pushed up from the bar.

"Easy, killer." Logan laid a hand on his shoulder, well aware of the tension escalating next to him.

Ryder watched the man pour their drinks and take them back to the table, hanging around until Grayson smiled at him again. Then he slipped her a piece of paper.

Gabriel nearly lost it, pushing himself back from the bar again.

"Stop it," Logan hissed. "He's happily married with two kids. And Parker looks disappointed. He didn't give her his phone number."

Gabriel gave his former partner a sideways look.

Logan shrugged. "I learned more this afternoon than when their reservation was. Had a drink or two. Sue me."

Gabriel nodded casually and settled back down. He stared into his scotch, dejected and desperate.

"She looks good, buddy."

"Yes, she does."

"Are you planning to talk to her?"

"No." He shook his head. "I'm not ruining her dinner."

"You came up here to talk to her. Remember?"

"I came up here to apologize to her," he corrected, mumbling into his drink. "This isn't the place."

"So why are we at this bar then?"

"I…fuck if I know. I had to see her."

They each went back to their respective pastimes, Logan chatting up the bartenders and Gabriel concentrating on the woman across the room.

Most of the time, she was smiling. But when Noah and Barbara were talking amongst themselves, he noticed the look that fell across her face.

He noticed the loss of the smile.

It's fake. She's putting on a show for them.

Around nine-thirty, Grayson starting to fidget, her hands wringing together fiercely in her lap. It wasn't too long before she stood up from the table, said something to the both of her dinner companions that kept them sitting down, and started toward the door.

Gabriel ducked his head. Grayson quickly donned her coat and gloves, then pushed out into the night air.

"Get going," Logan smiled, kicking Ryder off of his barstool.

"Logan..." he started apologizing hastily.

"I'll be fine," he said, nodding toward the same bartender he'd been chatting up all night and grinning wickedly. "I've got your card for the tab."

Gabriel rolled his eyes.

"Have fun."

The cold night air struck him hard in the face. His eyes worked quickly to adjust to the dim light along the nighttime streets. He looked left, then right, and found her halfway down the block, no doubt headed back to her hotel. Gabriel waited a few moments, then turned up the collar of his coat and began to follow her.

They let her walk back alone?

He knew she wasn't drunk. She'd only had two drinks, and those had been spaced out around dinner. Her gait was steady and straight. But she wasn't fully sober, and she was alone in a strange town.

She shouldn't be alone.

———

Grayson kept her gloved hands in the pockets of her coat and burrowed down as much as she could into the scarf wrapped around her neck. There wasn't any wind tonight, but the stillness in the air brought its own chill.

She was cold, and all she could think about was getting back to the hotel and turning on the fireplace. Maybe that would work out the permanent chill that had settled deep down in her bones.

There weren't many people out on the streets. It was that odd time in the night in between the end of dinnertime and the beginning of the usual Aspen nightlife. People were either already at home in bed, hunkered down in their bar of choice, or still putting on mascara and picking an outfit. That third option was going to be her night tomorrow night, if Barbara had her way. But tonight she was going to go rest.

Noah and Babs were going out to another bar several streets down when they finished at Justice Snow. She just didn't feel like it. All she wanted was to be warm again.

Grayson was only a block away from the restaurant when she got the strange feeling that someone was following her. She stopped underneath a street lamp and looked around. An already-drunk couple was stumbling toward the center of town on the other side of the street. Another man was attempting to ride his bicycle up the street and not slip on the ice. She didn't see anyone else. Not a single other person.

She shook her head and started walking again.

Halfway down the next block, she got the same feeling and stopped again. The street was deserted. Grayson shook her head, muttered something to herself about being overly paranoid, and turned down Main Street. The feeling came back a third time, but the longer she felt it, the more she realized that it didn't feel dangerous. That thought in itself was strange. Whatever or whoever was following her didn't seem to mean her any harm.

Grayson arrived safely at the Innsbruck and stripped out of her clothes, throwing on a comfortable pair of sweat pants and a long-sleeved T-shirt. She grabbed a book off of her nightstand and headed out toward the main room, flipping the switch on the wall to turn on the gas fireplace. She tucked herself into the window bench, a blanket thrown across her lap.

Gabriel stood outside in the snow and looked up into the living room of the trio's condo.

Grayson came into view and curled herself up onto the window seat, leaning up against the cold glass with an open book in her lap. It was only a quick flash, but he recognized the cover.

She brought that with her? Why?

He stood in the shadow of one of the large evergreen trees, watching her read and occasionally stare out toward the dark mountainside looming in front of her. Every now and again, she reached up and wiped her eyes.

He yearned to wrap her up in his arms, feel her lean back into him, and read to her like he had before.

Goddamn it.

The tightness reared up inside his chest, making up his mind for him. He quickly spun away from the tree and started walking back into town.

A flash of movement in her peripheral vision caught Grayson's eye, and she looked up from her book. The winter landscape was calm, but she stared out at it for a long while, hoping to see something—anything—move in the silent winter night.

36

THE NEXT MORNING, Grayson found herself curled up on the same window bench that she had occupied the night before, sipping a cup of coffee and looking out over another inch of fresh snow.

She waved to Noah and Barbara from the window as they walked into town, skis and poles slung over their shoulders. They'd decided to spend the day on the ski slopes. She had gracefully declined, promising instead to meet them on top of Aspen Mountain for lunch.

She spent a lazy hour gazing out the window and poring over her book, then got dressed. She bundled up in her black polar fleece jacket and gray hat and headed out into the sunshine. It was much busier in town today than it had been yesterday.

Friday tourist surge, she reminded herself.

Grayson wove in and out of groups of skiers heading to the mountains and late-risers heading out to breakfast. She stopped into a small coffee shop, picked up a hot chocolate, and sipped on it leisurely as she wandered in and out of the shops.

Babs had been so hell-bent on visiting a particular set of boutiques yesterday that she'd missed a few places on her own list. Grayson rolled her eyes inwardly. When Barbara Parker got into a shopping mood, there really wasn't any force on earth that could stop her.

Despite the large crowds and the warmth shooting down from the sun overhead, Grayson shivered.

There's that feeling again.

Someone was following her. She stepped into the nearest store and walked around, spending a little too much time looking out the shop's front windows. The human traffic flow didn't stop. No one was loitering around on the cobblestone street outside. She shook her head at herself and eventually walked back outside.

This paranoia has to stop. Nobody is following you. Cain's in jail.

She was out in broad daylight in the middle of a swarm of people. There was no danger here.

It's all over. Stupid girl.

Just after noon, Grayson made her way to the gondola in the center of town. The Silver Queen went straight to the top of Aspen Mountain and dropped off next to the Sundeck, one of the on-mountain restaurants. She waited patiently to buy a day pass, then herded herself through the line.

She shuffled into one of the pods along with seven other people, sitting down quickly as it took off at a steep incline. She'd expected to feel out of place dressed in street clothes instead of ski gear, but no one seemed to notice. With a sigh of relief, she focused on the scenery as the pod ascended toward the summit.

At the top of the mountain, the skiers disembarked first, scrambling to grab their skis out of the outside storage racks. Grayson lagged behind, carefully making her way across the snow-packed slope to the restaurant. She checked her watch as she walked up the stairs leading to the outside deck. It was just going on a quarter to one. She was fifteen minutes early.

"Well, a little sun never hurt anyone," she mumbled.

She found a good spot by the western railing. The view was incredible. She had a clear view of Aspen Highlands, and beyond that, Snowmass Mountain. A little further north, she could just see the Maroon Bells. Everything was white and shimmering in the afternoon sunshine. Despite the heavy lunchtime buzz around her, it was peaceful. Grayson closed her eyes, turned her face up, and sighed.

Finally, I'm warm.

She heard someone step up beside her. She dropped her face back down, figuring Noah and Babs had decided to come in for lunch early. She put a smile on her face and opened her eyes.

But it wasn't her friends standing by her side.

It was Gabriel.

The smile dropped off of her face, instantly replaced by a combination of shock and fear. Her eyes widened. Her breath caught in her throat. Grayson grabbed onto the railing to steady herself, pressing herself back against it as forcefully as she could.

Ryder was staring at her intently, his eyes sharp, his face completely unreadable. She took a shaky step away from him. Her vision was starting to blur and the scenery was tilting sideways. She stumbled.

Grayson barely registered the strong arm that wrapped around her waist or the low voice that guided her over to a table at the far corner of the deck. She sat down without actually telling her body to do so.

A strong hand guided her head down to rest in her hands. "Breathe," she heard him say, and on command she sucked in a deep breath.

The scenery was still spinning. She tried again. The same arm that had led her to the table kept her steady in her chair. Another deep breath. She opened her eyes. The floor had stopped moving. She willed her heart to stop racing, and slowly but surely, she felt the hard thumping in her chest fade away.

She was acutely aware of him leaning over her, rubbing slow circles on her back.

"Grayson?" His voice was low and calm, heavy with concern.

The shock of seeing him hadn't dissipated, but she couldn't stall any longer. Grayson slowly lifted her head out of her hands and licked her dry lips, trying her best to keep her breathing slow and steady. His face was tense and his eyes were worried. She startled at that. Of all things, she hadn't expected to see concern for her when she saw him again. Hatred, malice, disgust, disappointment...yes. Concern for her? Definitely not.

Gabriel was looking over every inch of her, tilting his head slightly one way, then the other, checking her over for injury.

What on earth?

She brushed a piece of hair out of her face and sat up straight, forcing him to remove his hand from her back. Grayson stared at Gabriel across the small table, dumbstruck.

"Are...are you...all right?" His voice was soft. He ran his hand through his hair, his fingers noticeably shaking.

He's nervous?

"I'm fine," she murmured, diverting her eyes away from his.

Grayson started chewing on her lower lip, harder and harder. It was a desperate attempt to distract herself from the pull she felt to him.

She gasped at the sudden feel of his fingers on her lips. She dropped her lower lip from her teeth and lifted her eyes to his.

Gabriel quickly withdrew his hand and ran it through his hair again. "I, uh...don't do that. You'll make yourself bleed."

She stared at his hand as he placed it on the table. Just like the first time she'd met him, his touch was still electric. She shook the thought away.

"Wh...what are you doing here?" she asked, her voice noticeably shaking.

He took in a long breath. "I had to see you."

She shook her head. "I don't have anything to say to you."

Her voice was sharper than she'd intended it to be. The fear that she'd felt on Tuesday night was still fresh. So was the anger. But when she looked at him, there was no trace of the animal that had stalked her around the apartment that night. The two versions of Gabriel swam together behind her eyes. She couldn't separate them. It was still too soon.

I can't do this.

She moved to stand up, but his right hand reached out to grab her before she got far.

"All I'm asking for is five minutes," he said quietly.

She barely heard him. His eyes were glued to the decking beneath their feet. He was talking to the floor, not to her.

More curious than reluctant, Grayson sat back down. "Okay. Five minutes."

She turned to face him in her chair and waited. He took his hand off of hers, but he didn't look up. He didn't say anything. She waited longer. Still nothing.

"If this is a joke, Gabriel, it isn't funny," Grayson said, suddenly irritated at having to sit in silence while he figured himself out.

Ryder looked up and stared straight at her across the table. "This isn't a joke."

"Then talk," she said. "Get this over with. What are you doing here?"

"I'm here to apologize," he replied.

That wasn't at all what she'd expected to hear. She narrowed her eyes at him.

What the hell is his game here?

"Apologize?"

He nodded.

"What makes you think I want to hear anything you have to say?"

"You probably don't." He chuckled weakly. "In fact, I'm probably the last person you want to see right now. But I couldn't let what I said to you at the apartment be the last thing you heard me say."

Her face softened when she saw the guilt on his face. The remorse. Then she remembered his words.

Screw this.

"Gabriel, what you said to me…what you accused me of doing…with Cain…"

"I know, I know…" He held up a hand to silence her. "I don't expect you to forgive me for how I acted, and I'm not asking you to. I'm not asking you to have anything to do with me. I was a fucking animal. I couldn't stop for one minute and just listen to you. You tried to tell me. And I lost it. I…I don't believe anything I said to you that night. What you did for the department by getting him to talk…"

He tentatively reached across the table and took her hand in his again.

"All I want is to apologize to you. You don't have to accept it. You don't have to forgive me. You shouldn't forgive me. But I'm sorry, Grayson. Christ, I am so fucking sorry."

He rubbed his free hand over his forehead, as if trying to stave off an impending headache.

Grayson looked down at their hands together on the tabletop. Her eyes narrowed, her forehead wrinkled. And just as quickly, the tension released. Her eyes softened. She remembered how he'd looked at her when he'd woken up in the hospital. She remembered the feel of his palm encircling her hip in bed, inching her just a little bit closer. She remembered…

"Pathetic."

Just as quickly, her walls went back up as she withdrew her hand from his. He closed his eyes and nodded in defeat. She refused to look at him. She didn't trust herself.

Gabriel stood up from the table silently and took several steps away from her. Then, thinking better of it, he turned back.

Grayson had only had time for one deep, shaky breath before he was back at her side. She looked up at him, startled. The look in his eyes was heartbreaking. They were cold, defeated. Empty.

He didn't say a word as he withdrew a small box from inside his coat pocket and placed it in front of her. She eyed him warily.

"It's not what you think. I'm not trying to buy my way back into your life. These…these are yours. They have been for a long time. I just…never got the chance to…" He smiled wearily as she ran her fingers over the box. "They're going to light up your eyes," he whispered.

With that, he turned from her and was gone. He didn't look back.

Grayson waited until he was off the deck before she tore her eyes away from him and focused on the small box in front of her. She nervously opened it and lost her breath when she saw what was inside. A pair of teardrop emerald earrings glinted back at her in the winter sunshine. She ran her fingers over them, just to convince herself that they were real.

Oh my God…how did he…when did he…?

Her heart was pounding in her chest. She looked around wildly, trying to find him, all at once desperate to go after him. There were too many people around. He was lost in the crowd.

She stood up from the table to get a better look, and only succeeded in noticing Barbara and Noah step off of the gondola and head toward the restaurant. She immediately sat back down and shoved the box into her coat pocket. She ran her fingers over it as they waved to her and stepped up onto the deck.

She smiled back as best she could, but her heart was still racing.

Gabriel was in Aspen. He'd tracked her down, apologized, and then left her without another word. She closed her eyes and turned her face up toward the sun. Remembering the last look on his face made her bite her lower lip.

She knew he didn't deserve another chance to get back into her life, but she couldn't deny the feeling she'd had when his hand had dropped to hers. She ran her fingers over the box hidden in her pocket.

By the time Noah sat down in the recently-vacated seat opposite her, she was no closer to slowing down her racing heart.

37

GRAYSON WIPED THE steam off of the bathroom mirror and sighed at her reflection. Despite lunch in the sun and an afternoon nap, she looked pale and tired. She shook her head in shame and wrapped her wet hair up into a towel. Her mind was on anything but getting ready to go out.

She was half-tempted to tell Babs that she wasn't interested in going, but the other half of her brain immediately scolded her for having such a thought.

You promised, and you called it an early night last night. Just go. You'll have fun.

Besides, her friend was beside herself with excitement.

It's important to her.

Grayson sighed and went back to drying her hair. The least she could do was go and have a bit of glamorous fun. She'd been nothing but a wet blanket since they'd arrived for their holiday. She was even starting to get on her own nerves. She was in the middle of pinning her hair up in curlers when Babs knocked gently on the door.

"Gray? Can I come in?"

Grayson looked around frantically for a particular small box and hid it in the top drawer of her nightstand. She hadn't figured out exactly what to do with them yet. "C'mon in," she said, retreating toward the steamy warmth of the bathroom.

Barbara followed her and took up a perch on the toilet seat. "So, are you excited about tonight?" she asked.

"I guess so. I don't have any idea where we're going," she replied, fighting with a bobby pin.

"The Caribou Club. It'll be fun. I promise."

"I trust you." She nodded.

Babs sighed, then took over putting her friend's hair up. "Are you doing okay?"

"Sure. Why wouldn't I be?" she replied, attempting to sound cheerful.

"You know damned well why. You've just been off by yourself a lot. You were on another planet at lunch. I'm worried."

"I'm fine, Babs. I wouldn't be going out tonight if I wasn't okay."

"You'd tell me if something was wrong, right? Or Noah? One of us?"

"Of course."

Barbara visibly relaxed. "Phew. That's a relief."

"Why?"

She shrugged. "You looked really pale when we showed up at the Sundeck. Like you'd seen a ghost."

"Just too much time in my own head."

"No more time in your head then," she scolded.

"Don't you have to get yourself ready?" Grayson replied, rolling her eyes.

"I can handle myself." Barbara turned her friend around and forced her to sit down on the small bathroom stool. "All right, now what're we going to do with those eyes tonight?"

"Please, just something subtle."

"Are you sure? That dress kinda demands something dramatic."

Grayson warily eyed the closet door. "I don't know if I really feel comfortable wearing that."

"Gray, you have to! It looks so good!"

"I'm going to be overdressed. I'll look silly."

"No, you won't. To both of those statements."

"Really, Babs. Just something soft. Please."

"Oh, all right." She rolled her eyes. "Just this once."

Thirty minutes later, she had moved most of the contents of her own bathroom into Grayson's and was alternating between finishing her own face and putting Grayson's hair up properly.

"One of these days, I'm going to do this myself," Grayson pouted as Barbara reached for another bobby pin.

"Oh hush. You look fabulous. And I can see the back of your hair better. It's just easier for me to do it. Go get dressed."

She hopped off of the countertop and opened up her closet. There was the offending garment, staring directly at her from the middle of the rack. "Are you sure this is a good idea?" she called out, fingering the fabric.

"Just put it on!" came the frustrated reply.

Grayson stepped out of her robe and hastily put on the lingerie that she'd been forced to accept in addition to the dress. Thin, lace boy shorts, matching garter belt, and black thigh-high stockings with a solitary seam line running up the backs of her legs teamed up with a backless, lace-detailed basque. Truthfully, she felt ridiculously overdone in just the undergarments.

She hazarded a glance at herself in the mirror. It might have been over the top, but she had to admit, it did something for her figure.

She heard Babs rummaging around loudly in the bathroom, and she hastily grabbed the dress off of the hanger. She'd just finished zipping herself up when her roommate emerged from the bathroom, her makeup perfect and hair pulled up off of her face.

Babs giddily clapped her hands together and opened the bedroom door. "Noah! C'mere!" she called down the hallway.

He came scampering in, already dressed in a slim-cut navy suit and light blue shirt.

"Holy hell, Gray," he stood in the doorway and took her in. "You look freaking amazing." He walked over and took her hand, twirling her around in her bare feet. "And you were worried about this dress," he admonished playfully.

"I know, right?" Babs winked as she walked out of the room to go dress.

"Are you okay?" Noah asked once she was out of earshot.

"Of course. Why do you both keep asking me that?" she asked.

"You seem like you're on another planet. You have all day, love."

"I'm fine."

"All right. If you say so." He looked her over again. "You really do look great."

"Thanks." She blushed.

Eventually, the trio piled into a warm, waiting town car and headed into town. Babs had insisted on calling one, declaring that she'd never make it to the club alive if she had to walk that distance in heels.

Grayson fidgeted in the back seat, playing with the hem of her dress. When they turned off the main street, her fingers moved to her hair. She pulled a section around her neck and twirled the ends around in her fingers. When that didn't calm her down, she started chewing on her lower lip.

That didn't help either.

38

THE CARIBOU CLUB was Aspen's oldest members-only club. It transformed from a private dining room to an elite after-hours club when the clock struck ten.

The space oozed high mountain luxury. Elk antler chandeliers were suspended from the ceiling in every room. The upholstery alternated between worn-in leather and rugged, dark fabrics.

Logan sat next to Gabriel at the bar, drink clutched in his hand.

When he'd strolled into the lobby of the Jerome that afternoon, Logan had immediately known something was wrong. He'd found Gabriel hunched over the end of the hotel bar, looking miserable, and it didn't take long for him to spill his guts. He'd confronted Grayson, and from the sound of it, things hadn't gone as he'd hoped. That wasn't really a shock, but Harrison knew his former partner had still been holding onto a shred of hope.

After a silent and uncomfortable dinner, Logan had forced Gabriel out into the nighttime mountain air. They'd wandered aimlessly along the cobblestone streets for more than an hour. Eventually, they'd ended up at the Caribou Club. A badge and wide smile were the only two things Logan had needed to get them in the door.

The older man waved the bartender over. Gabriel muttered his thanks when the fresh glass magically appeared in front of his face.

"C'mon, Gabe, you knew this was going to go down like this," he said.

"Yeah. I know. I still don't have to like it," he muttered, swirling the amber liquid inside his glass.

"There's a ton of available women here..." he started.

"Don't finish that sentence," Ryder hissed.

"It was just an observation. Relax." Logan shrugged and spun around on his barstool, leaning back on his elbows and taking in the surroundings. It was going on eleven, and the bar was crowded. Overly made-up women and the men who bankrolled their shopping habits were mingling with Hollywood starlets and playboy billionaires.

Logan shook his head. The sports bar down the street was much more his speed.

He happened to shoot a glance by the front door. Recognition flashed across his face. A smirk spread across his lips. He elbowed his partner in the ribs.

"Son of a bitch, Logan," Gabriel hissed, grabbing his left side.

"Ah shit, sorry. I keep forgetting you're on the injured list."

"What the hell was that for?"

"I wanted to get your attention."

"Use my fucking name next time."

"Turn around, jackass."

"What the fuck for?" he grimaced, rubbing his side underneath his suit jacket.

"Humor me."

Reluctantly, Gabriel turned around and followed Logan's line of sight. He nearly fell off his chair.

There she was, looking shy, vulnerable, and like she wanted to be anywhere else. Grayson was waiting patiently at the top of the stairs while the other two members of her group checked their coats. As usual, Parker and Mason flanked her and guided her up to the bar. The closer she got, the stronger the tightness in his chest became.

Her dress was incredibly conservative compared to the rest of the crowd. Long, white sleeves and a high boatneck tapered into a thin band at her waist, then dropped down into a long column of white wool to the floor. The slit up her right thigh revealed sheer black stockings, and she was a few inches taller, thanks to a pair of patent leather heels. Her hair was down, soft curls hanging around her neck and over her shoulders. She turned her back to him as she placed her drink order.

Gabriel clenched his fists and dug his fingernails into his palms.

The smooth skin of her back was open to the air, completely exposed by the backless dress. Two small wisps of fabric ran down the edges of her torso, then came together at a bow at the base of her spine. Following their tracks only drew attention to her behind as she swayed back and forth unconsciously to the music.

Gabriel took a long drink out of his glass. It didn't help to steady his nerves. He bared his teeth, itching to drape his jacket over her to cover her up. He watched her lift her glass and take a sip of something dark pink.

Grayson tipped her head back and laughed at something Noah whispered in her ear. She unconsciously pushed her hair behind her right ear.

Gabriel saw a glimmer in the dim light and squinted to get a better look. His eyes widened when he realized what had given off the shine.

The emerald earrings.

———

Logan watched his friend's reaction and mentally prepared himself to spend another night at the bar by himself. He didn't mind. He was happy for the kid. Besides, he had a prospect or two lined up and waiting. He smiled into his glass and took a drink, relishing the burn it left behind.

He'd never admit it, but the decision to drag Gabriel down here hadn't been his.

It had been hers.

He took his phone out of his pocket and read over the text messages again. The first was from him, around dinnertime.

Are you holding up okay?

I suppose so. Why do you ask?

Because I'm sitting at a hotel bar with an extremely depressed partner. I figured you two talked.

We did. I don't know what to think, Logan.

For what it's worth, I've never seen him like this. Whatever you said today, it broke him.

It had taken over an hour for her to send a response.

The Caribou Club. 11 p.m. Bring Gabriel.

39

GRAYSON SPENT THE better part of an hour making her way through the various rooms of the Caribou Club.

Babs had been right. It was definitely a popular place and getting more and more crowded by the minute. Of course, she'd also been right about not being overdressed. Compared to some of the other women in the club, Grayson looked like a nun, but she still felt over-exposed.

Barbara was fluttering around like a social butterfly, ooh-ing and ahh-ing at the celebrities in the crowd. All Grayson wanted to do was fade into the nearest wall and stay there. It was after midnight. She'd subtly scoured every inch of the bar and each secluded corner they'd passed.

He wasn't there. He hadn't come.

Eventually, Barbara coaxed Noah out onto the dance floor with her. Grayson was able to attach herself to the side of the bar. She quickly touched up her lipstick and, thankfully, she didn't have to wait long to get the bartender's attention.

"Another of the same?" the young man asked over the din of conversation around them.

She nodded.

"Comin' up."

She shifted from one foot to another as she waited, keeping her eyes on the bar. She didn't notice the tall man walk up next to her.

"Hi there," he said in a southern, slightly slurred accent.

Grayson turned to find a well-dressed, middle-aged man leering at her. He reeked of too much cologne mixed with cigar smoke and hard liquor. The preppy pretty-boy trifecta.

Ugh, not this again.

She nodded at him, then turned her focus back to the bar directly in front of her.

The man moved in closer. "My name's Ian. Can I buy you a drink?"

She shook her head and looked sideways at him. "Thanks, but no. I have one coming."

He didn't take the hint. "Aw, c'mon. Pretty little girl like you should have somebody buying her drinks. I promise you a good time." He tried to wink at her. All it did was magnify how intoxicated he really was.

"Then go find one. I'm not interested."

The bartender set her drink down in front of her and Grayson grabbed it, intending to walk off to another corner of the club. She was three feet away from the bar when she felt a hand clamp down on her free wrist.

"Now, nice girls don't act like that," he slurred, tugging her back toward him. "Just where do you think you're going?"

Grayson set the drink back down before she stained her dress and turned around to face the man, glaring. "Get your hand off of me," she hissed.

"Most women like it a little rough," he smirked, tugging again.

She started to pitch forward, but a strong arm wrapped around her waist and pulled her back against a tensed, rock hard torso.

"Drop her." The voice was low, threatening, and one she instantly recognized.

Gabriel pulled Grayson back against him, glaring at the drunken playboy over her shoulder. The man didn't take the hint. If anything, it got him agitated. He stepped forward, away from the bar, attempting to smile.

"C'mon, honey. I can do better than this schmuck. I'll give ya the time of your life."

Oh God, this is like some sickening form of déjà vu.

Grayson pressed herself back into Gabriel's chest. She was shaking again. She closed her eyes to keep the nightmares from rearing their ugly heads in the middle of the club. Her breathing dangerously shallowed.

Gabriel recognized her fear. The drunk still had ahold of her wrist.

She's going to have a flashback if I don't get this asshole off of her.

His fingers flexed against her abdomen.

She whimpered.

Gabriel growled. "Last time, asshole. Drop her. Move on."

"Mind your own fucking business," Ian shot back, clamping down harder.

Before she knew what was happening, Gabriel had slid out from behind her and grabbed the man's free arm, twisting it backward. Ian hissed in pain, immediately dropping her wrist.

Grayson staggered back several feet out of the way, reflexively rubbing the skin where he'd held onto her.

Gabriel glared at the man. "She's out of your league. Get the fuck out of here."

He forcefully shoved the man backward. Ian smacked back hard against the bar, both hands clutching onto the counter to steady himself. Gabriel turned back to Grayson, concern immediately replacing the anger in his eyes.

———

Grayson's face shifted from relief to fear as she saw Ian throw himself off the bar, launching himself at Gabriel. He registered the change.

"Gabriel, look out!"

No sooner had she said the words than the man reached him. Gabriel dodged out of the way, but Ian drunkenly plowed forward, sending Grayson stumbling backward into the group of partygoers directly behind her. Ian didn't have the coordination to keep himself upright, and he toppled over on top of her.

Ryder instantly yanked the man off her and threw him toward the other side of the room.

Thankfully, one of the partygoers had seen Grayson coming and managed to grab her before she'd hit the floor. She stammered out some semblance of an apology to the older gentleman.

"Don't worry about it, hon," he replied from underneath his Stetson. "Happens all the time. But you might want to get them to break it up."

Grayson looked over to find Gabriel locked in a down-and-dirty, knock-down-drag-out bar fight. It was impossible to tell who was winning. Ian got a good hit in at Gabriel's left side, directly over his healing ribs. Ryder doubled over in pain.

The drunk leered down at him and started to bring his knee up toward his head.

"Gabriel!" Grayson cried out in panic.

Ryder brought his head up at her voice and dodged the attack. Ian pitched forward. Gabriel grabbed him by the collar of his shirt, reared back, and slammed his fist into his face. That was all it took. One hit, the sickening crack of broken bones, and Ian went down, knocked out and slumped against the bottom of the bar.

By now, half of the club had turned their attention from their cocktails to the fight, and security was pushing through the crowd.

Gabriel pulled his badge out from his suit coat and flashed it as one of the men started toward him. The hulking six-foot-five bouncer immediately backed off and focused his attention on the man slumped on the floor.

Gabriel wiped the edge of his lip and raised his eyebrows in surprise when he saw blood on the back of his hand. Apparently, the drunk bastard had gotten in more than one good hit. He turned away from the scene at the bar and sought out Grayson on the spot she'd occupied only a moment before.

She wasn't there waiting for him. Instead, he laid eyes on the rich hardwood where she should have been.

He panicked and pushed his way away from the bar, just in time to see her force her way out the front door. He swore under his breath and took off after her.

40

AS QUICKLY AS she could, Grayson ran out of the Caribou Club, up the stairs, and into the cold winter air. She didn't have her coat and knew she would succumb to the freezing cold within minutes. The mountain winter air was unforgiving.

It didn't matter. She couldn't breathe downstairs.

Gabriel had knocked her would-be suitor out cold, and in a split second, the club had become too small, too warm, and too crowded. Her claustrophobia had gone into overdrive, and the only possible cure had been the icy cold of the winter night.

She sucked in a deep breath as the cold air smacked her in the face, then she bolted left down the arched walkway without thinking twice. She wrapped her arms around her waist and rubbed her already-cold fingers against her sides. She registered the sideways glances from the few partygoers traversing the alleyway, but she didn't pay them any attention. If she kept walking, she would get further away from the club and would stay at least a little bit warmer.

Grayson was so wrapped up in her own thoughts that she didn't hear the footsteps quickly gaining on her or register the deep voice calling out her name. It took the weight of her coat being draped over her shoulders to force her to stop in her tracks and raise her eyes up from the cobblestone street. She fingered the ivory wool like it was completely foreign to her, but she pulled the material tighter around her body all the same.

Gabriel slowly circled in front of her, careful not to startle her, and held up her scarf. He laid it across her shoulders, then reached back to release her hair and drape the curls over the soft cashmere. She managed a small smile when his fingers lingered longer than necessary on her skin.

"Hi," he said, his voice low and steady. He managed to grin, albeit briefly. His eyes betrayed his worry.

"Um, hi," Grayson murmured, trying to pull her coat even tighter around her shoulders.

"You want to put that on?" he asked, gesturing to the coat.

Grayson nodded, her eyes once again focused on the cobblestones. Gabriel circled around behind her, holding the coat out so she could place her arms properly through the sleeves. As she buttoned it, he dug into his own coat pocket and withdrew her leather gloves. He came back around to face her and handed them to her. She readily accepted them and pulled them over her numb fingers.

Gabriel tucked her scarf up around her neck and pulled several wild strands of hair out of the way. His warm fingers felt so good on her cold skin. She closed her eyes and sighed softly.

When she opened them again, he was very close to her and his hand was cupping her cheek. The light from the street lamps reflected off of his eyes. They were curious and full of fire, like when she'd first met him.

"Are you all right?"

She shook her head. "No, I'm definitely not all right."

"What's...what's wrong?" he stammered hastily, grasping her by the shoulders and holding her out at arm's length to look her over.

"No, I'm not hurt, I..." She shook her head in frustration. *How am I supposed to explain something I can't even...?*

Gabriel moved Grayson out of the flow of pedestrian traffic and over to one of the brick archways. He tipped her chin up so she would look at him.

"What are you doing here?" she asked hesitantly.

"You left without your coat. I came to give it back to you," he smiled softly, his hand still on her cheek.

"You know that's not what I meant."

"You mean what was I doing at the Caribou Club?"

She nodded.

"Logan decided I needed a drink, or three, after our meeting at lunch. He got bored at the Jerome, so we came here."

Her eyes trailed back down to the stone beneath her shoes.

Gabriel scowled at her downcast eyes. "Was that the wrong answer?" he asked.

She shook her head. "No, that's what I thought you'd say," she murmured, twisting her fingers together.

When he didn't push her further, she let out a soft sob and sagged backward against the wall. Grayson tipped her head up against the brick, hoping the tears that were threatening at the corners of her eyes wouldn't fall.

"That's what you were supposed to think. I asked him to... to..." She couldn't finish the sentence. Her head was swimming. She was completely and utterly overwhelmed.

"You asked who to what?" Gabriel leaned on one hand against the wall by her shoulder, shielding her from prying stares as her eyes shimmered.

"Logan. I texted him. I asked him to bring you," she choked out.

Gabriel's eyebrows raised slightly and his mouth turned upward. "Why did you do that?" he asked softly.

She didn't open her eyes. "I wanted to see you again," she confessed.

He pushed the hair on the right side of her face behind her ear, trailing his fingers down to play with the emeralds that dangled there. "Is that why you wore these?"

She nodded.

"To tell me to come to you?"

She nodded again.

"I was right. They do bring out your eyes."

"How did you...I mean, when did you..."

You picked out the earrings I tried on that Saturday with Babs...

Gabriel waved her silent. "Don't worry about it. I'll tell you later."

Grayson took a shaky breath. "You're hurt," she whispered.

"What?"

Grayson ran a shaky, gloved finger over the cut on his lip. "I got you hurt. Again. He fought you, and you got hurt. That's what happens around me. People get hurt..."

Gabriel watched the first tear run down her cheek and quickly wiped it away with the pad of his thumb. "I'm not hurt, Grayson."

She shook her head, eyes clenched tight. "That's not true. You're bleeding. Your lip. Your ribs. He...he hit you..."

She hiccupped against the sob threatening to escape.

"Hey, stop it." He ran his fingers across her cheek and tilted her head to look at him. "Grayson, look at me."

It took a few minutes, but she finally opened her eyes. She tried to pull away, but he caught her chin and forced it level with his.

"I. Am. Fine," he insisted. "No one hurt me, least of all you."

Tentatively, she reached up and ran her fingers across his left cheek. There was a bruise already starting to form underneath his eye. "Then what's this?"

"A scratch," he shrugged, catching her leather-clad fingers and holding them in his.

"That's not a scratch," she argued back.

"It is to me."

She shook her head, defeated. "Why did you come up here?"

"After you?"

She nodded.

"Because I wanted to. It's instinct to protect you, remember?" He smiled warmly at her. "Do you want to go back inside? I'm sure Barbara and Noah will be looking for you."

"No." She vehemently shook her head.

"What do you want to do?"

Grayson shivered, and instinctively Gabriel reached out to rub his hands up and down her arms to warm her. She stepped in closer to him.

"You're not wearing any gloves," she whispered.

"I'll survive."

Gabriel glanced beyond her shoulders, looking up and down the passage. Sparkling white Christmas lights glittered to the right, past the entrance to the club.

"Would you like to go for a walk with me?"

"A walk? Now?" *Seriously?*

"Unless you're too cold. I can take you back to the Innsbruck."

She vehemently shook her head a second time. "I don't want to go back there right now."

"Okay. Then go for a walk with me."

Gabriel pushed back from the wall and wrapped Grayson's arm into his. He steered them toward the twinkling lights, and she readily fell into step next to him. They walked in silence along the quiet street, underneath trees dripping with white and yellow Christmas lights. Grayson clung to his arm, carefully placing each step on the ice-covered cobblestone streets.

Gabriel took his time, easily supporting her weight on his arm. Grayson could feel his eyes on her. She intermittently glanced at him in kind. But he didn't speak. He was waiting for her. She held out as long as she could.

"Thank you," she finally whispered.

"For what?"

"For getting that guy off of me."

He kissed the top of her head. "You're welcome."

"You were fast enough this time." She smiled softly up at him.

Gabriel chuckled into her hair. "Yes, you're right. Finally." He frowned. "I wish he hadn't touched you." He absently fingered the skin of her wrist underneath her glove. "Does it hurt?"

She shook her head. "No."

"Good."

They continued walking, ultimately finding themselves in the middle of one of the deserted pedestrian cobblestone streets. Christmas lights were strung up in between the buildings, hanging low over the street. The trees were covered in snow and even more glittering white lights. The scene was magical. Grayson paused to look up past the lights and into the stars sparkling in the night sky.

Gabriel stood back and looked at her.

When she dropped her head back down to street level, her eyes were bright and sparkling in the light. She smiled at him, like a child. She looked happy. Genuinely happy. Like the last few months hadn't happened. He hadn't seen that look in quite a long time. In fact, he hadn't seen it since they'd been caught in a snowstorm together.

Gabriel stepped up to her and wrapped an arm around her waist. "Tell me something," he said. "Why tell Logan to take me to that place?"

She rested a hand lightly on his chest, on top of his overcoat. "I told you. I wanted to see you."

"Why?"

"Would you believe me if I said I wanted to talk to you?"

"I might."

She blushed. "You got to apologize to me this afternoon. I never got to apologize to you."

"To me?" he asked, surprised. "What do you have to apologize for?"

"I should have told you about Sunday. About the interview. With Cain." Grayson hung her head and shook it slowly from side to side. "I was so convinced that you would keep me away from there, and I wanted to help. So, so badly. I didn't want him to get away with it. He can't get away with it. And afterward, I was so shaken up I couldn't get out of bed. I barely made it home. When you called, I…I knew you'd figure it out. I knew you'd be angry with me. I…I just thought I needed time, to be able to explain it right…"

She was shaking again, lost inside the memory of that weekend. Gabriel pulled her close and gently ran his fingers through her hair. "It wasn't your fault."

"It wasn't entirely yours, either."

"I never should have reacted like I did, Grayson. There's no excuse."

"I still should have told you. Shin told me to tell you. I just never got the chance."

He chuckled into her hair, leaning closer.

Speaking of Shin, he's going to have a field day with this one.

"It goes without saying, but you're forgiven."

She buried her face into his chest.

He kissed the top of her hair. "You're getting cold," he murmured.

She nodded.

"You need to get inside. Somewhere warm."

Grayson looked up at him, pretending to scowl behind her eyelashes. "Why are you always so concerned about me?"

"As I understand it, I'm supposed to be concerned about the woman I love."

His voice was deep. Soft. Calm and steady. He didn't hesitate.

It took Grayson a moment to really register the words. But when she did, she pressed herself even closer to him and dug her fingers into the back of his coat. Gabriel tightened his grip around her waist and murmured to her, softly.

Eventually, she pulled back enough to look up at him. She was smiling, her bottom lip trapped in between her teeth.

"Did you hear me?" he asked calmly.

She nodded.

"And what did I say?"

"You said...you said you love me," she replied, equally as calm.

"And?"

He raised his left eyebrow at her in question.

"And...."

A quick flash of mischief darted across her face. Before he could react, Grayson pushed herself up onto her tip-toes and gently pressed her lips to his.

Gabriel reacted immediately, grabbing the back of her head to steady her lips against his and tightening his hold on her waist. His tongue slipped into her mouth and she moaned against him, relaxing into the strength of his arms.

By the time he pulled away from her, she was lightheaded, out of breath, and her eyes were shining at him.

"…and, I think we need to get out of the street," she whispered, breathless.

41

GRAYSON FELT HER heart jump into her throat as Gabriel guided her across the street toward the Hotel Jerome.

She knew the hotel's reputation, and when he pressed his hand into the small of her back to guide her through the front door, she finally got to witness the luxury firsthand. Dark woods mingled with expensive upholstery and a live piano player at the bar. She couldn't contain her laughter as he steered her through the lobby, toward the elevator.

He pressed the button, then leaned down beside her. "What's so funny?" he whispered hotly in her ear.

She shivered at the feel of his warm breath on her neck. "Only you would book a room at a place like this on short notice," she giggled nervously.

He draped an arm around her waist and tugged her back against him. "Are you complaining?"

"Of course not," she breathed, leaning against him. "Are you?"

He kissed her neck. "No."

The elevator doors opened, and Gabriel guided her into it. She tried to pause in the center of the small box as the doors closed behind them, but Gabriel spun her around and backed her up into the wall.

Grayson gave in and leaned back against the cold marble, letting him run his hands down her arms and around her waist. Her muscles tensed as his fingers skillfully undid the buttons on her coat. The elevator jerked to life, and he thrust his arms on either side of her to steady her as she tilted to one side.

"Careful, sweetheart."

She looked up at him through heavy lashes and grabbed her lip between her teeth.

Gabriel advanced on her and pressed her even harder against the wall, bringing his lips down on hers. She tried to bring her arms up around his neck, but he pinned them against her side and pushed his thigh in between her legs.

Grayson threw her head back and moaned softly.

Oh, dear God…

Gabriel smirked and nipped at her neck as the elevator car slowed down. He clearly knew what he was doing. He'd probably spent years perfecting this particular skill set.

Her breathing was ragged and her face was flushed when he pulled away from her. He rested his forehead against hers, running his fingers along her already damp skin.

"Breathe," he whispered as the doors opened.

Gabriel took her hand and pulled her out of the elevator car, leading her down an empty hallway. He slid his keycard into the door lock and pushed it open.

Grayson hesitated at the threshold, only for a second, then walked into the darkened room ahead of him. She was about to feel around for a light switch when she noticed the twinkling lights from the window.

She maneuvered her way around the dark outlines of the hotel room furniture, shedding her coat as she moved, and gazed out the bedroom windows into the Aspen nighttime skyline. There wasn't a cloud in the sky. The moon was full and climbing over the top of the mountain.

"Oh, wow," she breathed.

Gabriel leaned against the wall, watching her. Her body was highlighted against the moonlight. He itched to touch her. He couldn't wait to get his hands on her. If she let him, that is. His fingers flexed and extended rhythmically in preparation.

She leaned forward against the glass, and Gabriel hissed under his breath. The moonlight dripped down the valley along her spine to the edge of her dress.

When he couldn't stand it any longer, he quietly walked up behind her. He swept her hair aside and kissed the base of her neck. She leaned back and shivered against him.

"Mmmm," she breathed. "You're good at that."

"Am I?" he chuckled.

She nodded slightly as he kissed her again.

"Should I stop?"

She lolled her head further back against him, eyes closed. She expected to feel his lips latch back on to the skin at the base of her neck. Instead, she felt him tense behind her, his fingertips digging into her hips.

"Grayson?" his voice dropped. "I'm not kidding. Answer me."

She turned and slipped her arms around him underneath his suit jacket. "You want to stop?" she asked, her voice soft and hesitant against his chest.

"Of course not." Gabriel held her at arm's length and stared at her. He had to bend down to lock eyes with her. "But I also just forced you out of my life by being a self-involved, arrogant asshole. And it's not the first time. I'm not keen on that happening twice in one week."

Grayson's eyes softened in the dim light. She placed both of her palms gently on his chest, leaned forward, and kissed him.

Gabriel ran his hands up the bare skin of her back and laced his fingers behind her neck, not pulling her forward but holding her steadily in place.

When she broke the kiss and opened her eyes, he was staring at her so fiercely she couldn't breathe. Those eyes, the ones that had the fire back in them, were just barely under control.

"You're not getting an easy bid with me," he warned, still hesitating.

Grayson reached up and ran her fingers through his hair, letting them glide around his ear and down his neck. Gabriel tipped his head into her touch, never breaking eye contact.

She smiled.

He hasn't done that since he was in the hospital.

She let him drop his face into her hand, relishing the feel of the weight pressing against her palm.

"Gabriel," she whispered, "I don't want easy. I want someone to love me. Every part of me. Desperately. And if that means baggage, then fine. I don't care."

"You might not think that in the morning."

"As long as you're still *here* in the morning, there isn't a damned thing that could change my mind."

He pressed his palms into her hips, his fingers digging into the material and her skin underneath. Every muscle in his body was tensed and on the verge of collapse. He was forcing air into his lungs by sheer will.

"Are you sure?"

"You're really starting to take the fun out of this," she mocked.

"Am I?" His mouth quirked. He brushed her hair behind her ear and ran the pads of his fingers over her earring. "I should stop that."

"Yes, you should," she breathed.

Gabriel circled back behind her and pushed her hair to one side of her neck, putting her bare shoulders on full display. He traced his fingers languidly down the curve of her neck, across her shoulder blades, and ever so slowly down to the point where the fabric of her dress met the small of her back. He pressed up behind her, kissing the sensitive spot behind her ear, flicking his tongue against the skin and applying persistent pressure.

Grayson's eyes rolled back into her head. Her eyelids slid closed.

Where in the hell did he learn to do that, and how do I get him to do it again?

Grayson tipped her head forward, giving him better access to her neck, and Gabriel readily took advantage of the exposed skin. He kissed and licked his way up her neck, and then back down. When he softly bit into the flesh where her neck and shoulder met, Grayson gasped. An arm wrapped around her opposite shoulder. Strong fingers ran along the front edge of her collarbone. Gabriel forced her back against his hips, his finger splaying out firmly across her abdomen.

When she couldn't take the darkness any longer, Grayson opened her eyes. She could still see the twinkling lights of Aspen stretched out in front of her, but they faded into the background as she focused on their reflection in the window.

The way Gabriel was wrapped possessively around her, the gentle force of his hands pressing down on her, and the look on her face as he bit down again on her neck made her entire body flush with pleasure.

He had absolute and utter control over her, and she was silently begging him for more. They were a portrait of hedonistic, primal consumption, and all she could do was surrender herself into his waiting arms.

Gabriel's right hand strayed away from her abdomen, his long fingers easily grazing over the slit in her dress before fanning out over her stocking-clad thigh. He trailed down to her knee, then back up, the pads of his fingers trailing along the back seam of her stocking. He paused at the lace border, fingering the fabric, and Grayson felt him smile wickedly into her neck. The feel of his breath against her nerve endings sent a wave of pleasure crashing through her.

When his fingers trailed higher and ran into the clasps of her garter belt, she felt his strong intake of breath against her skin. She relished the tentative touch of his fingers against the satin straps and the shakiness of his breath as he let it go.

"Jesus, Grayson," he breathed into the crook of her neck, eyes closed, enveloped in the heat of her body and the smell of her perfume. "You're going to kill me."

Gabriel looked up at her reflection in the window, and what he saw in her reflection was pure, unashamed lust. She was staring directly at him from underneath her long eyelashes, her eyes dark and full of fire. There was just the slightest hint of a smile at the corners of her mouth. She had him reeling. She knew it. And she was loving every moment of it.

He let go of the garter strap and wrapped his fingers around the edge of the dress, gradually pulling it up higher and higher until the top of her stocking and then the strap of the garter belt was exposed in their reflection.

Grayson ran her tongue along her lower lip as she watched, her inner heat slick and warm from watching Gabriel expose her to the night air. She reached back and snaked an arm around his neck, her fingers running up into his hair.

"Mmmm," he groaned contentedly as she raked her fingers through the strands. "What are you doing to me?" he whispered.

She giggled softly and bit her bottom lip. Gabriel dropped the fabric of her skirt, and it fell back down over her leg. His hand remained where it was, languidly tracing circles along her inner thigh down to the clasp that held her stocking up. He swiftly released it.

When she felt the spring of the satin against the back of her leg, Grayson snapped her eyes open. She wriggled in his arms and turned around to face him, her fingers still laced through his hair. His eyes bored into hers, concern evident in his face at the sudden movement.

"What's wrong?" he asked quietly.

She suddenly looked embarrassed, flushed and staring at the floor. His hand reflexively came up to cup her cheek while the other rested on the curve of her back.

"Grayson?" he prompted.

She swallowed, and her swollen pink lips parted just enough for her breath to escape from them. "You shouldn't do that," she whispered huskily.

"Why not?"

"You'll like it better if you leave them on."

Holy shit. Did I just say that?

What in the fucking hell did she just say?

Gabriel's eyes narrowed for a beat, then recognition and mischief glinted across them in a flash. When she saw it, she smiled at him and bit her lip again. He grabbed the small of her back and brought her lips to his, forcing her bottom lip from between her teeth and sucking it into his mouth.

"What will I like better?" he asked when he released her.

Grayson answered him by reaching behind her and guiding his hand to the zipper concealed at the small of her back. She pressed down to start the separation of the first few teeth, then pulled his lips to hers as he finished the job. He didn't have far to go, and when the zipper bottomed out, she immediately stepped forward, intent on guiding him to the bed.

Gabriel growled against her skin and shook his head.

Oh no, you don't. You wanted to play this game, but we're going to play my way.

He spun around and backed up against the leather armchair tucked next to the fireplace. He sank down into the chair, releasing her. Grayson stood in between his legs, her arms crossed against her chest, holding her dress in place. Her swore he could hear her heart pounding inside of her chest.

Gabriel registered the nervous look that flashed across her face and sat forward, one arm resting on his thigh and the other extended. His fingers possessively wrapped around the back of her thigh underneath her skirt. He tugged her forward.

"You have something to show me, sweetheart?" he asked huskily.

He watched as Grayson steeled herself against every modest instinct he knew she possessed and let her hands drop away from her chest. Without the support, the dress slipped easily from her shoulders, fell past her hips, and pooled at her feet. She stepped forward and discreetly toed it toward the side of the chair.

Gabriel sat rooted to the chair, fascinated by the creature in front of him. He started to rake his eyes over her but stopped almost instantly. Grayson was nervously tapping her foot against the floor and wringing her fingers together. He couldn't concentrate with her moving like that. He wanted, no... *needed*...her to be still.

His hands shot out and gripped her around her hips, his fingers pressing desperately into the lace fabric. Grayson stopped moving. He stared for much longer than necessary at the small strip of bare skin that peeked out in between the boning of the basque and the upper edge of her panties. It was so smooth, so perfect. And all he wanted to do was run his tongue along it, feel her muscles clench underneath his touch. He ran his fingers along it instead, back and forth, then bent forward and placed a soft kiss at the top edge of the lace. He felt her shake underneath his lips. He kissed the same spot again. She moaned softly into the quiet room.

Gabriel let his fingers fall over her hips, tracing the straps of her garter belt down to the tops of her stockings. Abruptly, he released her completely and leaned back in the chair. He still saw the nervousness in her trembling fingers, but he saw the lust and the raw confidence simmering just beneath the surface in her eyes. Now, he just had to bring that out.

"Turn around."

Grayson's eyes widened but she obeyed, gracefully turning in place on the tiptoes of her stiletto heels. He twirled his finger around in a circle in the air, indicating for her to do it again. She turned halfway around, then stopped with her backside facing him and looked back over her shoulder.

"Like something you see, detective?" she asked.

Gabriel braced himself against the armrests, completely undone by the confidence he heard in her voice. She leaned back a little further, letting her hair fall down her nearly-exposed back, shaking her hips slowly from side to side. When she righted herself, she twisted around to look at him over her right shoulder. For fun, she winked at him.

Fuck.

Gabriel launched himself at her, twisting her around and pulling her down on top of him. She squealed, her knees landing on either side of his hips. Grayson caught herself on the back of the chair as Gabriel's arms came around her. She hovered over him, her legs spread over his hips, his hands gripping her backside and forcefully pressing himself into her. His fingers traced the edge of her boy shorts where the lace met the curve of her bare flesh.

Grayson moaned and threw her head back. It took every miniscule ounce of focus he had left to keep from doing the same. The feel of his fingers on her skin was like electricity, and he couldn't get enough of her. Her hair fell down her back, and Gabriel reached for it. He grabbed the ends in his fist and pulled just hard enough to hold her neck extended back.

Exposed. To him.

His free hand ran along her lace-covered abdomen as his lips continued their assault on the skin of her neck. He ran his lips across its length, from ear to shoulder and back again, then his tongue, then his teeth, until she was begging him to let her move. He relaxed his grip on her hair and snaked his hand to the back of her neck, gently pushing her head forward to look at him.

Grayson immediately brought her right hand up to his face and ran her fingers along his jawline, guiding his mouth to hers. She kissed him, long and hard and desperately. Gabriel didn't move. When she tried to back away from him, he pressed gently at the back of her neck, keeping her close as he opened his eyes and looked into hers.

"You're going to be the death of me, woman," he groaned hoarsely.

His free hand slid around to rest on the back of her thigh and stroked the top of her stocking.

"At least you'll die happy," she replied, without skipping a beat.

Gabriel opened his mouth to reply, but he was too stunned by the confidence in her voice to say anything. She beat him to it anyway, bringing her lips to his and sucking his lower lip into her mouth. He closed his eyes. Grayson dropped her hands to his chest. She snaked her palms underneath his suit jacket and over his shoulders, then gently pushed.

Gabriel sat up and wrenched his hands away from Grayson's hips long enough to rip the jacket off. He dropped it unceremoniously onto the floor. She smiled against his mouth, then ran her tongue along his teeth as her fingers started to free the buttons on his shirt. She got most of them, then scowled in frustration when she couldn't get to the last ones. Gabriel chuckled and pulled the tails of his shirt out from his pants. When he tried to finish them off, she put her palms on his shoulders and shoved him back into the chair, shaking her head. He put his hands back on her hips and let her finish, watching her fingers make quick work of the small buttons.

Once she had the shirt unbuttoned, she impatiently yanked it off of his shoulders and tossed it to join the suit coat. The moment her attention turned back to him, she froze. Gabriel couldn't help the smirk that crept across his face. He was naked from the waist up, flanked by well-worn leather.

Grayson was unconsciously licking her lips at the sight of him, and he chuckled at the unashamed sexual attraction that was pouring off of her in waves. She quirked her head at him, questioning his reaction.

"Like something you see, love?" he asked, repeating her own words back to her.

Grayson bit her lower lip and nodded, never taking her eyes off the honed muscles of his chest. Without saying a word, she bent down and kissed the far edge of his collarbone. Slowly, gently, she worked her way across to the far tip on the other side, dipping her tongue along the inner ridge, forcing him to throw his head back against the chair. She left his shoulders and brought her mouth down on the midline of his neck, kissing her way down over his Adam's apple and into the hollow just above his sternum.

Gabriel tried to wrap his arms around her, but the soft pressure of her fingers skimming their way along his biceps forced him to keep his arms still. He was draped out over the leather armchair, pinned down by her arms, her lips, and the slow slide of her hips over the tops of his thighs. He was completely at her mercy and loving every minute of it. He swallowed and took in a shaking breath.

Control. Keep control. Keep...fucking...control...

Her lips continued down his chest to his abdomen, her tongue darting out to moisten the skin. When she dipped her tongue just inside the rim of his belly button and grazed her teeth along the sensitive skin underneath it, he bucked against her. Gabriel felt the pressure on his biceps increase as Grayson pinned him against the armrests, then slowly dissipate as she gracefully slid down to the floor.

When he recovered enough to open his eyes, Gabriel found her flushed and panting in between his legs. There was no mistaking what her eyes were fixated on as her hands ran up the length of his thighs, stopping just short of their intended target. He saw her hesitate, then look up at him with a current of fear behind her eyes.

Gabriel knew that look, and there was no way in hell he was pressing pause on current events to have a discussion about the non-necessity of that particular maneuver during their first time together.

Fuck it. I couldn't handle her mouth on me anyway.

Without hesitating, he pushed himself up from the chair and hauled Grayson to her feet. He pressed himself against her, threaded his hands into her hair, and used the momentum to guide her across the room and into the far wall. He managed to toe off his shoes and socks as he stumbled forward and still had the wherewithal to put his arm out and break the force of their impact as they smacked back against the drywall.

Grayson threw her arms around his neck as he leaned down and kissed her fiercely. His free arm grabbed her leg and hauled it up around his waist. She willingly hooked her ankle around his hip as he trailed his fingers along the rim of her stockings. She rocked her pelvis against him gently, only once, and he threw his head back and called out her name.

"Stop playing dirty," he hissed, his breath hot in her ear.

"I wish you would start," she countered, squeezing her leg around him.

Gabriel's eyes shot open. His breath hitched at the skin of her neck.

"Be careful, Grayson," he whispered hoarsely, resting his forehead against hers.

She pushed up onto her tiptoes and gently brought her soft lips to rest against his. When she pulled away, he hungrily drank in her eyes. They were black, dilated, and starving.

For him.

The smallest hint of a smile crossed her lips.

"Play with me, Gabriel."

42

THE DARK LOOK that overtook his features was almost too much for Grayson to bear. The fire was back behind the deep blue of his eyes, raging and ready for her. The growl that snaked from his lips was the sexiest thing she'd ever heard. The Gabriel of the high-end suits and Italian fairy tales was gone.

This Gabriel was pure power, pure sex, and every inch of him was intently focused on the flush deepening across her chest.

Holy shit.

Grayson saw his biceps twitch. The muscles rippled underneath his skin, and then he was on her, his body pressed up against and into hers. Her legs were spread across his thigh, her heat radiating through the fabric and onto his skin.

Gabriel sunk his teeth into the side of her neck, biting hard enough to elicit a response but not enough to leave a lasting mark. Grayson arched away from the wall and threw her head back, hands pressed against the hard surface for support. She rocked her hips into him again, mewling. The move earned her a ragged curse as he sucked on her earlobe, the fingers of his left hand actively working on the ties at the back of the basque. Grayson felt the lace material loosen around her waist. He reached up between her breasts and violently tore it off of her. The expensive fabric landed somewhere on the floor, and Grayson couldn't have cared less where.

Gabriel pressed himself even further into her, the heat radiating off of his chest and onto hers. A faint sheen of sweat was starting to show on his skin.

Grayson bit her lip at the thought of licking the salt off of him. She ran her fingers up his chest and gripped his shoulders to steady herself. The feel of his restraint, the tremor in his arms and legs as he held back and kissed her softly, was exquisite.

She raked her fingers possessively through his hair and wiped the first drop of sweat away from his forehead with her thumb. He was desperately trying to keep himself under control. She could feel it; she could see it. As much as he wanted her, Gabriel was still afraid of hurting her. She ran her fingers over his temple, gently around the lines that had formed at the sides of his eyes.

"You're not going to hurt me," she assured him softly, her kisses light on his lips.

When he didn't respond, she let her hand drift down to his belt. She had the hook undone and the leather halfway pulled off of him before he caught her hand.

"Don't," he growled, taking her lower lip in his and pushing her palms back flat against the wall.

His fingers trailed up her abdomen and he took one breast into his hand, leaning his other forearm against the wall for support. He ran his fingers around the flesh, twisting her nipple just hard enough to elicit a soft mewling noise from her lips. Grayson tossed her head back and closed her eyes, focusing on the feel of his lips as they worked down her neck, across her shoulder, and down her chest. She tightened her leg around his waist when he took her into his mouth and sucked greedily. She could feel his erection straining through his pants and rocked her hips languidly against him.

Fuck!

Gabriel hissed her name against her neck.

Grayson's senses were overloaded. She didn't notice his fingers gliding lower and lower down her abdomen until they grazed over the lace of her boy shorts. He began to tease her through the fabric, stroking the already-sensitive nerves with precision. Spread out and exposed, Grayson melted back against the wall.

Gabriel kept one arm wrapped around her waist, holding her up. She could feel his fingers were becoming slick and wet through the lace. Her muscles began to tense without her permission.

It wouldn't be long.

Gabriel seemed to sense she was close. He picked up his pace, pressing Grayson back into the wall with each pass across her slick heat, grinding his hips against her in time with his fingers. Her voice became airy, weak, overpowered by the feeling of his fingers gliding over her.

She moaned as he took a particularly slow pass, then cried out as he slipped two fingers inside of her. Once, twice, the feel of his thumb gliding over her clit, and she came, head thrown back and her fingers gripping forcefully into his hair. Gabriel growled possessively against her neck as she swore into the moonlight.

Grayson relaxed her entire body into his, temporarily sated. Gabriel nipped at her collarbone, suckling the sensitive skin, then bent down and gathered her up in his arms. Three long strides, and his shins grazed against the edge of the bed. He laid her down gently on top of the sumptuous comforter.

Grayson felt like she was being lowered onto a cloud, but the sudden loss of Gabriel's skin on hers made her shiver from the cold.

"Stay," a disembodied voice echoed from the shadows.

She didn't stay cold for long. A small, disembodied click drifted across the bed from the wall. The gas fireplace sparked to life near the leather armchair. Gabriel stood next to it, his back to her, tensed and barefoot.

Grayson propped herself up on her elbows to get a better look at him.

Goddamn, I could get used to the view.

His hair was a wild mess, but she hardly noticed. She bit her lip at the sight of his shoulders and back, the muscles rippling underneath his sweat-tinged skin. His jeans hung low on his hips, and even from behind she could see the cut of his abs against the firelight. The mere thought of him climbing on top of her made her wet all over again. When he turned to face her, he stayed rooted to the floor, silhouetted by the fire burning behind him. She held out her hand and crooked her index finger into her palm, beckoning him forward.

He obeyed, but not quickly, taking his time coming back to the bed, circling around the furniture at all too slow a pace. Grayson felt a delicious shiver run up her spine. His eyes never left her body, particularly the half still covered in stockings and a garter belt. Gabriel stretched out next to her, wordlessly, propping himself onto his side and running a hand up and down her leg.

Grayson raised an eyebrow when his fingers lingered around the inside of her ankle, then widened her eyes in surprise at the hum that traveled up the inside of her leg.

What the hell was that?

He did it again, and she dropped back on the bed. She tried to wrestle her leg away from him, but he held her firmly in place with one hand. The other lazily worked on the clasps holding up her stockings.

"Gabriel," she whispered, relishing the feeling of his fingers playing with the exposed skin of her upper thigh.

He smiled against her skin and kissed her through the stocking, then slowly, meticulously, began rolling it down her leg, trailing kisses down the long path from her thigh to her kneecap, along the ridge of her shin to the top of her foot. Her stiletto hit the floor, followed by the soft sigh of the discarded stocking. He did the same on the other side, taking his time and smiling at the very vocal response he provoked.

The heat from the fireplace was trickling over to the bed, warm fingers extending out over the lovers and heating the comforter on which they lay. Grayson threw her hands above her head, gripping onto a pillow for dear life. Gabriel was just out of reach, and if she didn't hold onto something, she was sure she would fly right off the bed.

Gabriel kissed the inside of her ankle, his tongue darting out across the thready pulse that fluttered just behind the bone. Her thoughts blurred. It was all she could do to remember how to breathe. Grayson felt her heart rate speed up as his fingers climbed back up her legs and up to her garter belt, which he unclipped and tossed aside without taking his mouth off of her. He hooked his fingers over the top edge of her panties. Her abdomen trembled as he slid the fabric down her body and discarded them onto the floor.

Grayson closed her eyes and kept her hands fisted into the pillow tightly. She sensed Gabriel rear up onto his heels, his body suddenly blocking much of the light from the fireplace.

"Grayson," he called softly to her, in the dark.

She opened her eyes when she felt his fingers run along her cheek and down her neck. He was hovering over her, his eyes wide and wild and completely focused on her. He smiled reassuringly as she stared up at him, then reached up above her head, gently loosening her hold on the pillow. She ran one hand through his hair and he leaned into her, closing his eyes briefly as his forehead met hers. When he opened them, he rushed to kiss her, desperately running a hand over her hip bone as he did so. She moaned softly and deepened the kiss, her tongue tangling with his.

"Mine," he whispered, squeezing the flesh in his hand to make his point. "You're mine."

Grayson ran her hands across his shoulders and down his back, stopping abruptly when she ran into the top of his pants. She pulled away from his kiss and scrunched her eyebrows together, staring down at the offending fabric.

Gabriel eyed her warily, her sudden change in expression unexpected and worrisome. When he felt her tug at his belt loops playfully, he relaxed and released the breath he hadn't realized he'd been holding.

"You have too many clothes on," she pouted.

"What would you suggest I do about that?" he asked, trailing kisses along her forehead and down the front of her ear.

"Get rid of them. Before I cut them off of you," she threatened, tugging harder.

"Now there's an interesting idea," he murmured against her skin.

"Gabriel…" she pleaded.

The strain in her voice was all he needed to hear. He chuckled softly as he stood up from the bed, unzipping his pants and discarding them along with the remainder of his clothes. Grayson licked her lips hungrily at the sight of him, the hard muscle of his abdomen finally exposed in all its glory. She hazarded a quick glance lower, and her bottom lip shot in between her teeth.

He was long, rock-hard, and perfect. The thoughts of what she could do to him, with him, were wickedly delicious, and Gabriel watched each of them flash across her face as she drank him in. He smirked at her as he advanced toward the edge of the bed.

"You still want me to play dirty, sweetheart?" he asked huskily.

She nodded, her mouth suddenly too dry and her brain too overloaded to form a coherent sentence. He climbed back into bed beside her. He ran his index finger down her chest and in between her breasts, smirking as her breath caught in her throat.

"Then let's play dirty."

Gabriel pushed up on his hands and loomed above her, his eyes raking over her bare chest and quivering abdomen. He slid in between her legs, which opened to accept him without resistance. He drew his tongue along her skin, sucking the salt away and breathing in the scent of her arousal mixed with her perfume. He could feel himself harden even more as his fingers traced along the lines of her skin, his lips following along behind them, dipping lower and lower.

Grayson writhed beneath him, moaning in pleasure and whispering his name as her head tossed from side to side. He ran his fingers up the inside of her thigh, then dipped them into her heat. She bucked against him, crying out, then gave herself over to the rhythm he set, grinding her hips into his hand.

When Gabriel felt the beginnings of her release, he slowed down and brought his face up from its place licking and sucking across her abdomen. Her lust-heavy eyes opened slightly and she managed a small smile through her shallow breathing. Gabriel grabbed her wrists and pulled her arms over her head. He wrapped one hand around both of her wrists and pushed them into the mattress. He looked down at her hungrily, pinned, restrained, and at his mercy…and he froze.

Restraints…oh fuck.

He immediately released her and pulled back like she'd burned him.

Grayson startled beneath him, unable to hide the shock or the disappointment from her face. He knew what she was thinking. He was sure of it. And he was sure she was going to leave. He pushed back from her, putting an arm's length between her naked body and his. She followed him.

"Gabriel, wait."

She reached up and rested her hands on his shoulders. Gabriel shook beneath her soft touch, forcing himself back under control. She held still, like she knew he needed time. Before long, he raised his eyes to hers, worried about what he would find.

"I…I'm sorry. I didn't think…" he began.

Shit, why the fuck didn't I think about her being tied up? Good job, asshole, she's probably going to have a flashback courtesy of your fucking libido.

"Shut up," she whispered softly.

Grayson pulled him down to her and kissed him, gently then more and more forcefully. When she pulled away, she was gasping for air.

Gabriel stayed stock still, every muscle in his body tensed and rigid. His brain refused to register that Grayson hadn't bolted from him.

She's going to stop this. She's going to tell me she can't do this...

The woman draped across his chest seemed to have other plans. "I trust you," she whispered into his ear.

A low moan escaped Gabriel's throat.

She can't be fucking serious.

She repeated it. "I trust you."

Gabriel swallowed hard and gave in.

He grabbed her hands off of his shoulders and laid her wrists across each other over her head again.

"Stay put," he growled, biting her neck as he shifted his hips.

———

Grayson sharply sucked in a trembling breath when she felt the head of his throbbing erection graze lightly over her entrance. Gently but steadily, Gabriel pushed forward. Her lips parted as he entered her, her slick heat screaming in pleasure at the feel of him. He tried to steady his breathing. Too much, too fast, and this was going to be over for him.

Grayson tried to steady her own breathing, but just the feel of Gabriel inside her was almost enough to bring her over the edge again. She gently rocked her hips against him, taking him further. Gabriel moaned her name. He lowered his mouth to her neck as he started to move, his tongue darting out along her flesh in time with his thrusts.

She desperately wanted to touch him, to rake her fingers down his back and press him in closer to her, but her wrists were still locked above her head. Instead, she wrapped her legs around his, then steadily slid them up to wrap around his waist. The pressure forced him to change his angle, and the shift caused her vision to flash white. She was so close...

Gabriel bit down on her neck and whispered hotly in her ear. "Hold on to me." Gabriel's fingers disappeared from her wrists.

Grayson's hands flew to his shoulders, greedily running her fingers down his sweat-slicked back. Oh God, he was tense and throbbing. She wildly moaned his name at the feel of his skin underneath her hands. Gabriel unlocked her ankles from behind his back and threw her right leg up to his shoulder. Grayson could feel him slide even deeper inside of her, his throbbing erection pounding hard against nerve endings she wasn't aware she even had. When he rocked harder against her pelvis, she arched up off of the bed and dug her nails into his back. He smirked against her shoulder, humming in satisfaction.

Over and over, Gabriel sank fully into her. Grayson licked her lips, mewling and thrashing her head from side to side. Gabriel didn't take long to build up the pace, relentlessly and steadily sliding in and out of her, her muscles quivering in pleasure against the assault.

He shifted his weight and pushed in deeply, bringing his mouth down to her ear. His voice was low, thick, and heavy with his own need. He spoke two words, but they were all she needed.

"Come, baby."

Grayson's eyes shot open and locked with his. She called out incoherently, clinging to him wildly as every muscle in her body contracted. The sweat from his body dripped down onto hers. Gabriel thrust forward, the feel of her quivering around him all he needed to find his own release.

Oh fuck.

He called out her name then stilled against her, gently rocking his hips against hers as he rode out the waves of pleasure coursing through him. As Grayson felt the last of his pulses subside, he shuddered, then collapsed against her. He seemed to still have enough sense about him to pitch his weight to one side, but they both came down on the mattress still tangled up together.

Gabriel recovered before she did, pushing himself up on his forearm long enough to grab a blanket from the edge of the bed and spread it out over their sweat-covered bodies.

Grayson purred at the feel of the soft fabric against her skin, and without opening her eyes, she turned and nuzzled into his chest.

He had never particularly enjoyed the moments after sex, usually preferring another glass of scotch and the view of his companion leaving his apartment to any additional physical contact. But to look down at Grayson, her hair wild and tangled, cheeks flushed, eyes closed, softly resting her head on his chest…

He kissed her forehead and gently pushed sweat-soaked strands of hair away from her face. He wrapped one arm over her waist and the other slipped underneath her neck and around to her back. Grayson tangled her legs up in his, keeping their most intimate connection intact, and walked her fingers up and down along his back.

He kissed the salty skin by her cheek and sighed contentedly. "Happy, sweetheart?" he asked, kissing her forehead again.

She nodded. "Can we do that again?" she mumbled against his chest.

Gabriel chuckled and pulled her closer. "Now?"

She shook her head. "I'll go crazy. Maybe tomorrow." She opened her eyes, glancing up at Gabriel shyly as he traced patterns along her hipbone. "I...I should get cleaned up."

He leaned over her and kissed her gently. "Bathroom's on the right. Use the robe hooked on the back of the door."

He nipped at her collarbone as she sat up, holding the edge of the blanket against her chest. She swung her legs over the edge of the bed. Gabriel held fast to his side of the blanket. Grayson glanced back at him over her shoulder, feigning a scowl. He grinned mischievously at her, then blatantly raked his eyes over her exposed backside. She gave the blanket a slight tug, and he relented, smiling as she wrapped herself loosely in the fabric before sauntering gracefully toward the bathroom.

Gabriel leaned back and hooked his hands underneath his head, breathing steadily. He felt himself twitch and harden at the thought of her spread out and screaming underneath him.

Holy shit. I didn't know she had that in her.

He turned his head and looked at the floor, eyeing the knocked-over stiletto heels, stockings, and lace lingerie.

I'm going to have to take her shopping.

The sound of flowing water from the bathroom faucet met his ears. He pushed himself off of the bed. He grabbed the handset by the leather chair and made a quick phone call, replacing it in the cradle as the bathroom door clicked open.

Grayson padded out of the bathroom, wrapped up in a long black silk robe. Her eyes rapidly readjusted from the light of the washroom to the flickering firelight of the bedroom. She immediately sought him out.

He was easy to find, standing silhouetted in front of the window. She licked her lips and leaned against the wall, admiring his broad shoulders and the rippling muscles of his legs and back. The view of his backside wasn't bad either.

She cleared her throat softly, and Gabriel glanced over his shoulder. She wrapped her arms around her waist and slid in next to him in front of the window, relaxing into his side. He draped his arm over her hip and pulled her into him.

"Feel better?"

"Mmm-hmm," she nodded. "It's all yours, if you need it."

"Fine. Answer the door."

Huh?

He kissed her forehead and headed to the bathroom. Grayson was about to ask him why on earth she should answer the door when it was well after one in the morning, but a sharp knock beat her to it. She hurried over and tentatively cracked it open.

"Yes?" she asked.

"Room service, miss," a young man chimed, a silver tray balanced on his right hand.

"Oh, um, did we…"

"Mr. Ryder did, miss. I was told you might be answering the door."

"Oh, okay."

She stepped aside and held the door open for the young man. He stepped dutifully into the room and placed the tray on the coffee table by the leather chair. Grayson blushed when she noticed Gabriel's clothes and her lingerie strewn haphazardly around the room. The young man had enough grace to pretend he didn't see them. He pulled the lid off of the tray and turned around to face her.

"Will there be anything else?" he asked.

The rough sound of someone clearing his throat had both the hotel steward and Grayson jumping in place.

Gabriel was leaning against the wall, dressed in dark pajama pants and nothing else, his arms crossed rigidly over his chest. "We're fine."

The young man nodded and hastily made his way toward the door. Gabriel signed for the order and palmed the kid his tip, never taking his eyes off of her. When the door clicked shut, he pushed off the wall and strode deliberately toward her. The fire hadn't gone from his eyes. It was still there, smoldering beneath the surface.

Grayson took in a sharp breath and held it.

She took a better look at him as he reached past her and grabbed something off of the tray. The pajama pants hung tantalizingly off of his hips. She wanted to run her lips along the strip of skin above the drawstring. And she definitely wanted to get her hands on what was underneath them, too. Repeatedly. And soon. She flexed her fingers to keep them under control.

"Up here, love," he chuckled softly, popping the cork on a bottle of champagne.

Grayson raised her eyebrows in surprise as he poured the sparkling liquid into two stemless glasses and handed one to her. He winked as he clinked his glass against hers.

"What's the occasion?" she asked, sipping the liquid. It was light and sweet and absolutely wonderful.

"You." He shrugged.

He sat down in the leather chair and kicked his feet up on the ottoman. She curled up on one of the arms of the chair.

Gabriel reached up and fingered the sash of her robe. "I like this on you."

"Matching set?" she laughed, pointing toward his pants.

"What? No," he replied, sipping at his champagne. "Not unless Araks has combined with La Perla without my knowledge."

Grayson rolled her eyes at him. She hadn't the slightest clue what Araks was, but La Perla rang a bell. "Do I even want to know how much this robe cost?"

"Probably not."

"Why do you have it here?"

"Always with the questions, darling," he scolded softly, topping off her glass.

"My last one of the night. I promise."

He leaned in sideways and kissed the tip of her shoulder. "Fine. I bought it after you were attacked. The first time."

Grayson winced at the memory. Gabriel pulled her off of the armrest and into his lap. She curled her legs up and rested her head on his shoulder.

"I kept it in the car, but never seemed to find the right moment to give it to you. Just like these," he said, reaching up and running his thumb and index finger around one of the emerald earrings she still wore.

He could see the faint lines emerging on her forehead. She was thinking, probably lining up a new string of questions. Gabriel steeled himself against them. They never came. Her face suddenly relaxed, and she rested against him.

"Okay." She sighed.

"Okay?" he asked, surprised.

She nodded. Gabriel relaxed back in the chair, rubbing her back with one hand and sipping his champagne with the other. It wasn't long before he felt her breathing even out and her body fully relax into him. He set his glass aside, then rescued hers from its precarious position resting on her thigh. She was fast asleep.

He sat with her for a long time, his hand resting on her hip and his fingers running absently through her hair. He whispered her name to calm her down whenever a nightmare started to take hold.

As the moon dipped toward the western edge of the mountains, he pulled a blanket over her shoulders. She stirred softly and sighed his name into the night air as she relaxed into the crook of his neck.

Gabriel tipped his own head back and closed his eyes.

So this is love, huh?

43

THE SKY WAS still black when Grayson's eyes fluttered open. Her surroundings weren't familiar, and her blood pressure instantly spiked through the haze of sleep. Unfamiliar places now brought a whole host of issues roaring to the surface that she was desperate to keep pushed aside. She quickly relaxed when she recognized the view out the window and the blazer draped over the back of a very familiar leather armchair.

She was warm, almost too warm. She tried to raise her arm to push the overly-fluffy comforter away from her shoulders, but there were strong fingers wrapped protectively around her wrist. They clamped down in protest at her movement.

Grayson registered the muscular leg thrown over hers and the twitching bicep muscle underneath her neck. And then she became very, very aware of something hard poking her in the back. She grinned, stifling a giggle. Somehow, she had woken up next to a very handsome, very aroused detective, and the entire thing struck her as completely ridiculous.

All the memories from the previous night came flooding back, and she closed her eyes. The longer she thought about the feel of Gabriel pushing her up against the wall, the feel of his hands on her and inside her, the feel of *him* inside of her, the harder she breathed and the more sensitive her skin became in the morning air.

In the back of her mind, Grayson registered that she was completely naked and didn't remember actually making it into the bed last night. She filed the thought away for later. Her skin was tingling all over, aching for his touch, and that was much more important. Grayson arched her back and craned her neck to look back over her shoulder.

Gabriel was asleep, eyes closed, face relaxed, his breathing slow and steady. He looked younger, more carefree. It upset Grayson to think of how much stress his job put on him, and how much additional stress he loaded onto himself seemingly just for the fun of it. It showed at the end of the day. But not now. Now he looked happy. At peace.

It's almost a shame to think about waking him up.

Grayson smiled mischievously as an idea popped into her head.

Maybe there is one good way to wake him up...

Ever so slowly, she turned in his arms.

He was still fast asleep, dead to the outside world. She began running the pads of her fingers up and down his chest, along his collarbone, and over his shoulders. He stirred at her touch but didn't wake up.

Grayson bit her lip and hesitated, once again momentarily conflicted. Gabriel needed his sleep. She knew that, and here she was deliberately trying to wake him. The sight of him naked in the early morning light and the growing fire within her belly overruled any doubts she had.

She lightly ran her fingers through his bed-mussed hair, then leaned up and kissed him. She kept her fingers in his hair, stroking the strands and pushing them away from his eyes. She kissed him harder, pulling his lower lip into her mouth. Her inner muscles clenched in excitement.

Gabriel registered the pressure on his lips and something soft teasing his ear. He responded without thinking, pressing back against the soft lips that were attempting to control his. That earned him a disembodied mewling and a firm pressure on his shoulders. He groaned quietly into the morning air. He willingly fell onto his back, eyes still closed, pulling whatever warm and wonderful creature was in bed with him on top of him.

He heard soft laughter and felt something warm and soft settle lightly on top of him. He blinked rapidly, waking, expecting to find himself in an empty room. It wouldn't have been the first time in the past few months that his mind had played the same cruel joke.

Instead, he woke up to find Grayson straddling him, completely naked, in the early morning light. Her hair was an absolute mess. Her face was flushed. And she had an innocent smile on her face that made his heart melt. Gabriel rested his hands on her hips for a moment, then began running his palms up and down the sides of her abdomen while she drank him in.

"Good morning," she giggled, leaning down to kiss him.

He threaded his fingers through her wild hair and pulled her down to him, opening her mouth with his tongue. He felt her surrender in his arms, her soft body yielding to his demands. The caveman inside of him beat his chest in triumph.

Mine.

Eventually, he released Grayson enough to let her breathe. He watched her struggle to lift her eyelids through the haze of pleasure coursing through her. Her blue eyes were bright and sparkling against her flushed cheeks, and they were both focused excitedly on him.

"Good morning," he replied, running his hands up and down her back.

She shivered excitedly at his touch, which Gabriel misinterpreted as a chill from the cold. He reached down and grabbed the comforter, draping it over her shoulders. He pulled Grayson down to him, wrapping his arms around her possessively.

She rested her cheek against his chest, inwardly grumbling about her thwarted morning plans.

"You're cold," he said.

"I'm fine," she sulked.

He kissed the top of her hair gently. "You're up early."

"I usually don't sleep late."

"You weren't having a nightmare, were you?"

The concern was obvious in his voice, even though he was trying to hide it. She smiled and shook her head. "No. I didn't have any last night."

"Good." *That's not true, but at least you don't remember any of them.*

Gabriel wrapped his arm around her as she slid off to his side and snuggled up next to him. He threw a hand behind his head and stared up at the ceiling. Grayson traced patterns on his chest absentmindedly.

"So, exactly how did I end up naked in bed with you?" she asked.

Gabriel wrinkled his forehead, chuckling. "I'm not quite sure how to answer that, sweetheart. How far back do you need me to go?"

She rolled her eyes at him. "I mean, the last I remember, I was wearing a silk robe and sitting over by the fireplace."

"You fell asleep in my lap. I carried you over here and put you to bed."

"And somehow the robe just walked itself back onto the hook in the bathroom?"

"No. I did that," he grinned, kissing her forehead. "And it's over on the desk chair."

Grayson pushed herself up on her forearm long enough to catch the glint of the fabric on the back of the high-backed chair across the room. She shook her head and laid back down against him.

"Well, if we're up, I suppose we should have breakfast," he mused into her hair.

Grayson twisted around to look at the bedside alarm clock. "Gabriel, it's five in the morning. Nothing's open."

"Something might be."

"It's too cold out to go looking," she pouted.

"I'll wear a coat."

"And that keeps me warm how?"

"I'll bring you back something warm for breakfast."

She propped herself up on her elbow. "Can't we just stay here?"

"If you wish," he shrugged.

She grinned at him, and he couldn't resist the impulse to reach a hand up to her face and draw her down to him. The feel of her lips on his was incredibly addicting. The soft pressure soon turned more intense, and it didn't take long for him to push up and roll her over onto her back.

"I know something else that will keep you warm," he whispered as he trailed his tongue along the edge of her ear.

Gabriel rocked his hips against her, his already-thick erection twitching against her stomach. Below him, Grayson licked her lips and kissed the salt off of the skin on his neck.

Gabriel startled at the feel of her lips insistently trailing along his skin. He ran his hands along her breasts, her stomach, her hips, her thighs, soaking in her soft whimpering. Her body yielded to his possessive touch, quivering and shaking in clenched anticipation. When he brought his hand in between her thighs, he found her slick and wanting.

Shit, she's so wet.

His cock twitched at the thought. Gabriel had to fight the impulse to rear back and bury himself inside of her without warning. It took every ounce of control he had to keep still. He growled, low and harsh, against her throat.

Grayson sucked in a sharp breath and swallowed, running her nails against the skin of his back. She ran them down the length of his spine, pressing hard, forcing him to breathe through gritted teeth. Ten bolts of delicious electricity rippled across his skin. She let up, soothing the tracks with her fingertips, working back toward his shoulders. Gabriel leaned over her, his breathing shallow and ragged. He gingerly kissed the side of her neck.

Grayson was getting impatient. She was warm and gasping and ready for him. He was treating her like she was made of glass, something delicate and fragile, and for once, she hated it. When Gabriel dropped his lips to her neck, she curled her nails into his back again, pressing harder, running them down the full length of his spine and sinking them into the muscles of his upper thighs.

"Fuck, woman," he hissed, biting down on her neck.

Grayson arched up against him, pulling her instep up along his leg to rest at his hip. He reached behind him and wrenched her hands away, pinning them down at her sides. She wriggled against him in protest, but he stayed steady above her. He rolled his hips into her wet heat, and she bucked up off the bed at the feel of him pulsing against her entrance. She ached for him, burned for him, and he seemed hell-bent on driving her crazy.

"Gabriel," she whimpered.

"Shhh," he soothed, dropping his forehead to hers.

He released her, but when she tried to wrap her arms around him, he pinned them back down.

"Don't move," he commanded, parting her legs with his thigh.

Grayson twisted her fingers in the sheets, her skin on fire where Gabriel had touched her. He ran his hands along her collarbone, over her breasts, and down her stomach. She trembled underneath him, completely overwhelmed by the pads of his fingers running over her sweat slicked skin. She gently whispered his name again. He kissed her in reply, sucking her lower lip into his mouth as his hands settled on her hips.

With one swift motion, he was inside her, buried completely. She immediately clenched tightly around him, spasming at the feel of him pressing insistently against her womb. Grayson struggled to keep still, her knuckles white against the sheets, her fingers desperate to feel his skin.

Gabriel started to move, rocking his hips in and out in time with his breathing, slowly but surely building the pace inside her. A sheen of sweat glistened off his pecs. She watched the muscles in his arms strained as he kept himself hovering above her. He nipped, bit, and sucked at her skin, clearly relishing the feel of her quivering muscles around his cock when he hit a sensitive spot.

Grayson was overwhelmed, completely and utterly consumed by the feel of him inside of her. She could feel him twitch and pulse as she clenched around him. He grew heavier, thicker, harder as he thrust into her. When she was certain she could take no more, she felt Gabriel start to lose control. His breathing became ragged, his thrusts harder, his pace frantic and desperate. Grayson whimpered, feeling all of him and needing more of him. He dropped his face into her neck, and she shuddered as his hot breath trickled down along her sensitive skin.

Gabriel sucked her earlobe into his mouth, tracing his tongue along the edge, and she detonated. Her spine arched up off the bed, her lips gasping for air and screaming his name. He powered forward, harder, faster, sweat dripping off his forehead. In the throes of her orgasm, Grayson dropped the sheets from her fists and grabbed his ass, pushing him further into her as she spasmed and rippled around him. He lost it, plowing hard and long into her as she desperately clung to him, his cock pulsing as he emptied into her.

Grayson felt Gabriel ride out the waves of his release, rocking gently into her as she came down from her own high. He dropped his mouth to hers, kissing her again and again, pleading with each shaking breath for her to open her eyes.

Grayson let her hands wander up to his shoulders, gently tracing the tensed muscles as she relished the feel of his lips gliding over hers. She opened her eyes and found him shaking above her, the raw emotion behind his blue eyes painful to behold. Grayson ran her fingers through his sweat-soaked hair, pushing the wild strands away from his eyes.

His shaking increased and Grayson gently pulled him down beside her, letting him rest his head against her chest.

Gabriel immediately wrapped his arms around her and his legs over hers, trapping her beneath his body. She tried to move underneath him, but his hold on her only tightened. It was aggressive, possessive, almost desperate.

Grayson startled at the pressure, but just as quickly relaxed, running her fingers back and forth through his hair.

"Hey," she soothed, "what's this? What's wrong?"

Gabriel stayed quiet for several minutes, his eyes closed and his brow furrowed. Grayson waited patiently for him to come back. His ear was resting close to her heart, and the longer she watched him, the more she became convinced that he was memorizing the sound of it beating beneath her ribcage. His breathing was evening out in time with hers.

It's like he's trying to…to…memorize me.

Finally, she couldn't take the silence anymore. "Gabriel?" she whispered softly.

He stirred against her, just barely. "You're mine," he finally mumbled against her skin. "You belong to me."

Grayson smiled. "I know," she replied.

44

GRAYSON TIPPED HER head back, closed her eyes, and sighed. She was warm, finally warm, and it felt incredible. She was sitting alone outside a small coffee shop along one of Aspen's side streets. Gabriel was inside.

The mid-afternoon sun felt wonderful on her skin. After several hours tangled up in each other's arms, they'd separated. Just long enough to shower and make themselves look present-able to the outside world, of course. True to his word, Gabriel ordered breakfast for them in the suite. By the time Grayson had emerged from the bathroom with a head full of wet hair and her robe securely tied around her waist, a new silver tray full of coffee, croissants, and fruit had been laid out by the window.

All morning, Grayson had been mentally preparing herself for a walk of shame in her dress from the night before. During breakfast, a soft tap on the door had heralded the arrival of two large shopping bags. She'd shot Gabriel a look as the hotel manager himself handed them over to her, but he'd made a point of blatantly ignoring her. Inside the bags, she'd found crisp black pants, suede boots, and a deep blue cashmere sweater, all in her size. The outfit, of course, came complete with matching bra and panties, both in a similar shade of blue.

Grayson had blushed at the thought of the phone call Gabriel had to have made to request them, but from the look he'd given her once she'd dressed, he clearly considered the end result well worth the effort.

They'd spent what was left of the morning walking around town together. It was easy and comforting to have her arm linked in his and feel him guide her effortlessly through the sea of human traffic. When the main lunch rush had passed, he'd deposited her outside the cafe and told her to stay put.

The buzz of her cell phone in her pocket snapped her head back down out of the sunlight. It was a text from Babs. Grayson didn't bother to read it; she just hit the button to call her cell.

Her roommate answered on the second ring, completely irritated. "Gray, I swear to God, you'd better be dead or getting laid."

She blushed. "Um, hi to you, too."

"Where the hell are you?"

"In Aspen."

"No shit. Where? I'm coming to smack some sense into you."

"What for?" she asked, surprised at the vehemence behind her roommate's tone of voice.

"Noah said he saw *him* last night. He's the whole reason you had a goddamned breakdown a few days ago. If that son of a bitch is stalking you, I swear to God…"

"Babs, relax."

"Gray…"

"Look, I'm fine. Stop worrying. Where are you?"

"We're up skiing. Just stopped for lunch. I was going crazy waiting for you at the condo. Noah couldn't take my craziness anymore."

"Okay, well, keep skiing. I'll catch up with you and Noah later."

"Grayson…"

"I've gotta run. Bye!"

She ended the call just as Gabriel pushed the cafe door open, carrying two cups of coffee and a small paper-lined basket. He set them down on the table next to her and eyed the phone in her hand. Gabriel didn't bother trying to hide his scowl. "Is everything all right?"

Grayson nodded, putting the phone back into her pocket. "Just Babs."

"Oh." He sat down next to her, his eyes narrowed underneath his sunglasses. "She's not happy, is she?"

Grayson bit her lip and shook her head. "No. It sounds like Noah spotted you last night and told her. I think she's out for your blood."

She sighed.

Gabriel leaned over and kissed her cheek. "I'll take care of it."

"No, you don't need to…"

He waved her off dismissively. "Whatever she thinks of me, and whatever I think of her, it doesn't change the fact that she's important to you. So the two of us at least have to be civil. She can glare at me as much as she wants. It's not going to make me keep my hands off you."

Gabriel emphasized the point by tugging on her hand and planting a light kiss on her lips. Grayson blushed and tried to refocus her attention on the food in the basket before she jumped him in a public place.

When the hell had her libido gotten so out of control?

Oh right, last night. And this morning. Twice.

"What is this?" she asked.

"Grilled cheese." He shrugged.

"That is not a slice of Kraft singles in there."

"No, it's not. It's brie, gorgonzola, and goat cheese with slices of grilled pear. Try it. You'll like it."

"I usually do when you pick out the food." She smiled, grabbing a precut triangle for herself.

———————

Gabriel sipped on his coffee for several moments, then reached out to grab a piece for himself. The moment his fingers touched the warm bread, his cell phone rang.

"Damn it," he cursed under his breath.

Grayson raised an eye at him as he pulled the black box from his coat pocket and checked the screen.

Nolan. Why the hell would he be calling in the middle of the day?

He slid his finger across the screen and answered it. "Ryder."

"Well, don't you sound as happy as a clam," came the voice in his ear. "You get laid yet?"

Gabriel's eyes darted quickly over toward Grayson, just to ensure she hadn't heard. She was watching the people pass on the street, blissfully unaware and munching on her half of the sandwich.

"None of your damned business," he hissed quietly.

"Well, you sound better."

"I'd be even better if I wasn't on the phone," he spat.

"Am I interrupting the birth of your first-born son?"

Gabriel held his tongue. "No."

"All right then. Shut up. Sorry to be the bearer of bad news, but you're being called back down to Denver. Effective immediately."

Gabriel's blood began to boil. "What the hell for? You and I both are off. For a while."

"From new cases, yeah, you're right. Not from cases we already have open."

Gabriel felt the hair on the back of his neck stand up. "What happened?"

There was a pause on the other end of the line, then some shuffling of papers and the click of a door lock.

"Blake?"

"Yeah?"

"Where are you?"

"Back interrogation room. Look, I don't know how to tell you this, but Cain's gone."

Gabriel closed his eyes and willed his breathing to stay steady. He didn't need to lose it in the middle of a public place, much less frighten Grayson.

"Say that again."

His partner took a big breath on the other end of the line. "Cain's out. He got loose. They were in the middle of a prison transfer and he overpowered his handlers. Cut their throats with a shiv and took off in a squad car. They found it ditched a couple of miles down the road. Then nothing. He's in the wind, Gabe."

Fuck.

"Fuck."

"Yeah. The brass wants you recalled to track him down." Blake lowered his voice, the sympathy heavy in his tone. "I'm sorry, man, I really am. McCallister went to bat to keep you out of it. Well, both of us. They didn't give him any choice. It's a media disaster. People are already calling for blood. They threatened his badge. And yours."

"Do you have any idea where he'd be headed?"

"Not from what I have here. The prison sent over everything from his cell that they had, but it's not much. Just a bunch of ramblings about three bells and the same doodle over and over again. It looks like nonsense to me. If it's supposed to be bells, Cain needs to take a drawing class or two before we catch him."

"Can you send me a picture of the drawing?"

"Sure, uh, hold on…let me try to do this and not cut you off…"

There was static and fumbling on the other end of the line, then a ding on Gabriel's phone to indicate a message had come through. Gabriel pulled the phone away from his face long enough to look at it, then abruptly stood up and walked several feet away from the table.

"That's a sketch of the Maroon Bells," he said hastily into the receiver. "It's a mountain group just outside of Aspen. He knows where she is. Shit."

"What? What are you talking about?"

"Grayson. He must know she's in Aspen. God-fucking-damnit, he's coming for her."

"How in the hell would he know where she is, Ryder?"

"I…I don't know. But those mountains are literally an hour's hike out of town. Fuck! How did he find her?"

"You're the expert on this psycho, Gabe, not me."

Gabriel was pacing frantically in the middle of the sidewalk, dodging oncoming pedestrian traffic as much as he was able to. To be fair, most of the oncoming pedestrians were making sure to stay out of his way anyway.

"Go back through the interrogation tape. See if she mentioned anything the day she came down to the precinct. I…I never watched the whole thing."

I should have.

"Talk to the surgical department at the hospital, the secretaries, the other residents. Anyone that would have known how to get in touch with her for emergencies while she was on leave."

"Already in the works. But Ryder, you've got to get back here. He's loose. They're out for your blood. You've gotta come back to Denver."

"I can't do that."

"Gabe, they're not giving you a choice."

Gabriel glanced up toward the table. Grayson was sitting up straight, her back completely rigid, the grilled cheese and coffee long forgotten.

He turned his back to her. He had to think straight for the next few minutes, and he couldn't do that with her staring at him. "Is McCallister in his office?"

"Yeah, I think so. Why?"

"Get him on the phone. I need a favor."

45

GRAYSON SAT NERVOUSLY in the leather armchair, curled up underneath the fluffy comforter. Gabriel had ripped it off the bed and wrapped it around her the moment they'd burst through the door to his hotel room. Then he'd started pacing. He was still pacing, up and down the short length of the room behind her.

Something was wrong. Something was absolutely and incredibly wrong. The fireplace was on full blast beside her.

She was still cold.

Gabriel had hauled her up from her chair at the café in a panic. They'd sprinted back to the Jerome with hardly a word spoken between them. At a crosswalk, she'd hesitantly tried to ask him what was going on, and the look on his face had screamed not now.

She'd put her head down and followed him diligently back to the hotel, curling up on the chair as instructed, sealing her lips shut against the hundred questions she'd wanted to ask. That had been forty-five minutes ago. He still hadn't said anything to her, and his pacing was becoming more frantic.

A sharp rap at the door shocked Grayson out of her head. Her heart shot into her throat.

Gabriel shot a glance in her direction, the concern and fear plain as day on his face, then strode purposefully to answer it.

Grayson's mouth went dry.

Oh God, oh God...

Her heart stuttered back to normal when she saw who it was.

"This had better be good, Gabe," Logan said, walking into the room in a rumpled white undershirt and loose-fitting jeans.

He looked like he'd enjoyed the night, and most of the current day, in bed. He wore the smirk to prove it. When he saw the look on Ryder's face and registered the young woman huddled underneath the bed comforter at the end of the room, alarm bells instantly started going off.

"All right, what the fuck is going on here?" he asked, looking between them.

Grayson shook her head and shrugged. "You know as much as I do."

Logan plopped down on the side of the unmade bed. "All right, Ryder. You've got your girl looking like a deer in head-lights, and I'm not liking the rate of your fucking pacing. What the hell?"

Gabriel rubbed his hand along the back of his neck. He was stalling, but not because of Logan. He kept glancing backwards in her direction. He was worried about her reaction to what he was about to say.

"Nolan called. I'm being recalled to Denver. Now. I'm…I'm leaving in about an hour."

"Great icebreaker," Harrison said sarcastically, throwing his arms across his chest.

Gabriel glanced sideways at her again. It was obvious he did-n't want to say what was coming next.

"Douglas Cain escaped from prison six hours ago."

It took a moment for the words to truly register, but when they did, the tumbled rush of emotion was overwhelming. Shock gave way to fear, fear gave way to despair…then anger.

Overwhelming, all-consuming anger. Not at the news that Cain had escaped, but at Gabriel.

Grayson's eyes narrowed, and she glared at him from underneath the comforter. It was suddenly too warm in a room that minutes ago had been achingly cold. She jumped to her feet and pointed a finger right at him.

"What the hell, Gabriel? You've had me cooped up in here for the better part of an hour and you couldn't say, what, eight goddamned words to me?"

"Considering the reaction…." he started.

"Shut up!" she fired back.

Grayson turned away from him, staring out the window with her arms crossed over her chest.

———

Gabriel made a move to go to her.

Logan grabbed his arm, shook his head, and held him back. "So, they're calling you back to go after him? Track him?" he asked, steering the conversation.

Gabriel nodded, never taking his eyes off of the woman scowling beside the window.

"Please tell me you have a plan for her," Logan said softly, nodding his head in Grayson's direction.

Much to both men's relief, Grayson was too lost in the angry maelstrom swirling in her own head to hear them.

"I called the captain," he replied steadily. "He's agreed to hand over use of the safe house. It's not far from here, but it's outside of the main part of town."

"You're sending her there alone?" Logan balked.

"No. At this point, I don't think Barbara Parker or Noah Mason are unreasonable targets for Cain. They're going as well."

"Have you told them?"

"No. I thought it best to tell Grayson first."

"Good thought. Try for better execution next time, buddy." Logan slapped Gabriel across the back.

"Thanks," Ryder shook his head and took a quick glance at the window.

She hadn't moved.

"But I need a cop to stay with them. I don't trust anybody up here, Logan. I don't know how long I'll be gone and I don't know how long it's going to take me to catch this sick fucker. "

Gabriel dug into his pocket and fished out his phone. He handed it over to Logan with the screen lit.

"What's this?"

"Nolan sent it over. It's a scrap of paper Cain had in his cell. The drawing is of Maroon Bells, a mountain group not too far outside of Aspen. He kept talking about the three bells to the other inmates and how he was going to take some woman there. He somehow found out she's up here."

"Could be coincidence," the older detective shrugged, handing the phone back. "Maybe it's all part of his sick little plan. There are three of those goddamned books, right?"

"Yeah. *Inferno, Purgatorio,* and *Paradiso.* So?"

"So…I don't know. Maybe the whole 'there are three books and here are three mountains' thing is significant to him?"

Gabriel took a minute to think, all the while keeping Grayson in his peripheral vision. She still hadn't moved. And Logan might've had a point.

"It's possible. If it's coincidental, that'll at least buy me some more time." He ran a hand through his hair and again stared at Grayson. "I'm not taking chances on this one. For…obvious reasons."

Logan smirked and rubbed the back of his neck wearily. "Wouldn't it be safer to move her out of the state completely? Like to Utah? Or Canada?"

"I don't have that kind of time, Logan. It takes days to arrange transfers like that. You know that."

He nodded, leaning his head down to stare at the floor. "Yeah, yeah, I know."

"I'm asking a lot, I know. I wouldn't…"

Logan held up his hand to cut him off. "Don't worry about it."

The lines on Gabriel's face instantly softened. "I owe you one."

Logan shrugged. "Catch this sick piece of shit and buy me a decent drink when this is all over. We'll call it even." He pushed to his feet. "I'll be packed in twenty." Logan left the room without another word.

Gabriel waited until the door closed behind him before turning his attention back to the very pissed-off surgeon standing at the window. He walked up behind her, keeping a fair distance, his hands stuffed into his pockets.

Grayson was attempting to ignore him as long as she could, repeatedly eyeing his hazy reflection in the glass. Gabriel kept his distance, and he kept silent. The minutes ticked by slowly, one by one, but in the end, she sighed and turned to face him.

"What in the hell am I going to do with you, Gabriel?" she asked calmly.

He startled. That was not the response he had been expecting.

"Excuse me?" He looked down at her and was floored to find Grayson actually smiling at him.

"You heard me," she said calmly. "You've got to stop treating me like I'm going to shatter at the slightest bit of bad news."

"This is worse than a little bit of bad news, Grayson."

"Well, yeah, sure, but keeping it from me didn't help, did it?"

He shook his head. She patted the side of the leather chair, and Ryder slumped down into it. She made a move to perch on the armrest, but he had other plans. He quickly wrapped an arm around her waist and pulled her down into his lap. She laughed and scooted around to reposition herself on top of him.

Gabriel pressed her to him, burying his face against her neck. She ran her fingers through his hair and stroked his shoulder with her free hand.

"So, you're leaving," she said after a moment.

"I don't want to. I don't have a choice," he replied dejectedly.

"I know that."

"You do?" *This is news.*

"Of course."

She pulled him away from her far enough so she could see his face and he could see hers.

"What guy wants to walk out on a sure thing?"

Gabriel's mouth dropped open. Grayson winked at him before bursting out into a fit of giggles. He shook his head and smiled, chuckling under his breath.

"I know you don't want to go, Gabriel. I understand why you have to." She leaned against him. "I still don't have to like it," she whispered.

Oh, thank God…

He hugged her tightly. "Thank God for you," he mumbled into her hair, kissing along her hairline, down her neck, and across to the tip of her shoulder. He sighed and sunk his entire weight into the back of the chair.

"So, what happens now? I stay here?" Grayson asked after several quiet minutes.

He shook his head.

"You're going to a safe house not far from here. Logan's going to stay and keep an eye on you."

"He's going to babysit me, you mean," she replied, wrinkling her nose.

"No, I mean he's going to watch over you with a loaded gun and a short fuse to pull the trigger."

"What about Noah? And Babs? Can I at least tell them what's happened?"

He nodded. "They're going with you."

"What? Why?"

"They're close to you. And you told me once that Cain threatened to harm them. He doesn't have anything left to lose here, Grayson. He'd use them as bait to get to you, no question."

"Oh no…"

The blood drained from her face. Gabriel fished his cell phone out of his pocket and handed it to her. "Call them. Maybe start with Noah."

She nodded, opened the phone, and dialed a cell phone number she knew by heart. It took two rings for him to answer.

"Ryder, you asshole, what have you done with our Gray? We're worried sick!" came the heated voice across the phone.

Grayson pressed a reassuring kiss into Gabriel's cheek when he flinched. "Noah, it's me."

"Oy, Gray! Where are you? What happened? Did he hurt you?"

"I'm fine." She rolled her eyes. "Listen, where are you? Are you with Barbara?"

"Of course. We're just in the door from skiing. Why?"

"I need you to sit down with her and put me on speaker-phone. We need to talk. Something's happened."

46

TO DESCRIBE THE safe house as a quaint cottage tucked back in the mountains would have been an understatement.

A massive understatement.

In fact, it was a five-bedroom chalet built into the northern side of a secluded mountain. It had once belonged to an up-and-coming recording artist. After she'd blown her meager savings on cocaine, the property had been confiscated as part of the raid that had put her in jail. Thanks to a few private donors, the house had been bought at auction and placed into a law enforcement trust.

It looked like any other upscale vacation rental in the Roaring Fork Valley. It was even showcased on a resort rental property website, to keep up appearances. Officially, it was used to house important witnesses before trial and as a way-station for the witness protection program. The somewhat remote location made it less than ideal for Denver-based cases, but the department had hung onto it for five years.

Gabriel was silently thankful for that fact as he followed the winding switchbacks toward the property, his blanched knuckles gripping the steering wheel.

He glanced over at the young woman sitting in his passenger seat. Grayson hadn't said two words since they'd picked up Noah and Barbara at the Innsbruck. She'd just been staring out the window, watching the white snow whip by.

He looked into his rearview mirror. Logan was right behind him, navigating Grayson's 4Runner up the same winding road with her friends in the backseat. He had insisted his partner do the driving, and surprisingly neither Noah nor Babs had argued.

He slowed the car to a stop at a T-junction, then swung to the right and continued on. The silence was doing a number on his nerves. Gabriel knew he had to leave her. He knew why. He knew that Grayson knew why. But he didn't like it. And the fact that she was so quiet wasn't helping. The laughter and sparkle she'd had in her eyes at the hotel only an hour ago were gone, but they hadn't been replaced by anything. No anger. No fight. Not even fear. There was just…nothing.

He tightened his grip on the steering wheel.

Grayson kept her eyes on the landscape as Gabriel drove. She didn't know what to think. She was too numb to think. A few hours ago, she had been blissfully happy, and now he was driving her to a safe house because her serial murdering stalker had escaped from prison.

I can't believe this is happening.

Cain was coming for her. Noah and Babs were possible targets. And Gabriel was leaving her here. Stranded in the mountains. Alone.

She desperately wanted to be strong, and for a while, she'd managed to keep a smile on her face. But the more she'd thought about it, the colder and colder she'd become. She couldn't shake the desperation creeping under her skin, the feeling that this wasn't going to stop. This was going to be her new life, running from Cain. People were going to keep getting hurt, because of her. The thought made her sick. The thought made her want to run.

Grayson sighed and stole a quick glance at her driver. Gabriel was oozing tension in waves. His knuckles were white against the black leather steering wheel. She knew he was upset. She wished he was relaxed and smiling at her, like he had been earlier that morning.

She reached over the middle console and rested her hand on his arm. He tensed but didn't pull away. She leaned over to him and dropped her head lightly on his shoulder. It wasn't the most comfortable position, but the physical contact was reassuring. She wouldn't be able to touch him for who knows how long, and she wanted all she could get.

"We're almost there," he said, glancing down at the top of her head.

"Okay."

Her anxiety immediately skyrocketed. Her breathing sped up. So did her heart rate. She couldn't help it. She started shaking. Gabriel swore under his breath beside her.

"I'm sorry, Grayson."

She kept her eyes on the floorboards. "For what?"

"For this. For leaving."

"You don't have to apologize for that. I understand."

"Grayson…"

"No, I get it," she said calmly. "You don't have a choice. I know you'd stay if you could. You can't. Logan will take care of us if anything happens."

Get it together, girl. Quick!

Gabriel eased the car off of the road and down a meandering driveway, parking outside the front door. He shut the engine off and twisted in the driver's seat. Grayson didn't waste any time. The moment the engine shut off, she opened the passenger door and hopped down from her seat. Logan pulled her SUV in behind them.

Gabriel slammed his eyes shut and pinched the bridge of his nose, fighting back the nagging pain of an impending headache, then followed her around to the trunk.

Man the fuck up, you asshole. You're leaving in less than an hour.

She started to take her luggage from the car, but Ryder rounded the back of the SUV, ripped the bags from her hand, and carried them into the house without a word. Logan followed with Barbara's bags thrown over his shoulder. Babs gave her friend a questioning look. Grayson just looped her arm into hers and sighed.

"Well, let's go check out the new digs, Gray," she said cheerily.

Noah followed behind them, silent, his own bags in hand.

The entryway was beautiful. The towering ceiling boasted a chandelier full of candles suspended over a large polished wooden table and a vase full of white orchids. It opened up onto a large great room with floor-to-ceiling windows that looked out over a massive wooden deck and, beyond that, a spectacular view of Snowmass Village.

A large semicircular sectional couch faced a magnificent fireplace set into stone in between the windows. A chef's kitchen sat off to the right. One hallway wound around beyond the kitchen, another to the left by the fireplace. The entire home was decorated in warm brown leather and honey oak wood. Under different circumstances, Grayson could have seen herself wrapping up in a blanket on the end of the couch and spending a whole day there, just reading and admiring the scenery.

Logan spoke first.

"All right, um, Noah and Barbara, you both are down this hall with me. Doc, you're down that way." He pointed to the left hallway. "C'mon, let's get you settled in," he said, guiding Noah and Barbara away with him and throwing his head off toward the left hallway with a wink at Grayson.

Grayson shoved her hands in her pockets and followed a rather long hallway back to a set of double doors. They were already cracked open. She leaned her weight into one of them and it groaned, falling away under the pressure.

She found herself standing in the middle of an exceptionally large master suite. Her suitcases were peeking out from behind the closet door, but she didn't pay any attention to them.

Gabriel was standing by the window, his hands behind his back, his shoulders thrown back and tense. She walked up behind him and waited.

"I have to go."

"I know," she said, sliding closer and resting her head on his shoulder.

Jesus, he's tense. What's wrong? What isn't he telling me?

"I need you to promise me something, Grayson."

"Okay."

Gabriel wrapped an arm around her waist and kissed the top of her head softly. "I need you to promise me that you'll do whatever Logan tells you to."

"I think I can handle that." She grinned.

"I'm not kidding," he replied, his voice severe. "Even if it means someone else is in harm's way."

"Um, all right…" she hesitated.

He turned her to face him and placed his hands on the side of her face, tipping her eyes up to look at him.

"Gabriel, what is it? What's wrong?"

She could see the worry in his face and the fear in his eyes. He wasn't trying to hide it anymore, and the intensity was staggering.

Something is wrong. What aren't you telling me? Talk to me.

"Just promise me."

"I just did."

"Now promise me you'll do whatever I tell you."

"Okay, Gabriel, I promise, but what's…"

He cut her off. "Whatever I tell you, Grayson. Even if means my life."

Whatever words were going to come out of her mouth were instantly forgotten.

What? What the hell does that mean?

She pushed his hands off of her face and backed up.

"What the hell do you mean 'if it means your life'?"

Gabriel didn't turn from her, but he didn't answer her either. She crossed her arms in front of her chest. "Gabriel, answer me. What is going on? What aren't you telling me?"

They stood in front of one another, squared off and silent.

Gabriel slammed his eyes closed against the pain throbbing across his forehead. Seeing the pain in his face, Grayson couldn't help but give in. She unfurled her arms with a soft sigh and placed a hand on his upper arm to get his attention.

Gabriel looked up from the floor. Grayson saw the pain in his eyes, and it was heartbreaking. He wrapped an arm around her waist and pulled her into him.

Grayson let her head rest gently on his shoulder. Her free hand lightly ran up and down his spine, its rhythm simple and soothing.

"I'll promise whatever you want me to, Gabriel. Just tell me what's going on," she said calmly.

"I don't know what to expect from him, Grayson. Cain's desperate, and he has nothing to lose. If it comes down to a decision between getting in the middle or running away, I want you to run. Fast."

"But…"

"I can't keep you safe, keep Logan out of trouble, keep Noah and Barbara breathing, and take out Cain at the same time. Neither can Logan. If he tells you to do something, do it. If I tell you to do something, do it. Otherwise someone will suffer for it."

Please, please understand, Grayson. Run. Just run.

She nodded into his chest. She knew he was right. If anything happened, she needed to run. Against every instinct, she needed to run. His attention would be split, between Cain and her.

Just like last time.

She swallowed hard as a flash of Gabriel bleeding out on a concrete floor pushed forward into her consciousness. The blood drained from her face instantly. Her heart jumped into her throat. Grayson struggled to breathe.

I need to run.

"Okay. I promise. I'll run."

Grayson felt Gabriel relax. It was only for a moment, and it was gone before she could take a breath, but she knew she'd felt the relief crash over him at those five simple words.

Gabriel kissed the top of her hair, then reached a hand underneath her chin and tipped her face up to his. He leaned down and kissed her again, hard.

Wait, hang on. Why does it feel like he's doing more than kissing me goodbye?

Before she could react, Gabriel pulled away and stormed out of the room. She stood rooted to the floor, staring at the open door and the shadows beyond it. She heard the front door open and close, the sound of a car engine firing to life, and the distinct grinding of snow tires on gravel.

Grayson wrapped her arms tightly around her waist and shivered against the cold. If she looked hard enough, she thought she saw the slightest hint of a Mercedes SUV winding down the switchbacks toward the main street, and then it was gone.

Silence descended around her. She fought back the tears that threatened behind her eyes.

Stop being an idiot, Gray.

A few minutes later, there was a soft knock at the still-open bedroom door.

"Yeah?" she said shakily.

Logan slid in between the doors and shut them behind him. He stood sheepishly beside them, his hands awkwardly shoved into his pockets. "Hey, the other two are getting antsy. Thought I'd come see if you needed help."

"No, I'm good," she replied, trying to control her voice.

Logan sat down on the side of the bed and shook his head. "You think I believe that?" he grinned.

Grayson ran her hand quickly over her arms, up and down, trying to warm up. "Really, I'm fine." *Please, Logan, drop it.*

Logan cleared his throat. She knew he saw right through her. She didn't care.

"He's gone?"

She nodded.

"I figured he wouldn't stay long. He say anything?"

"I'm supposed to do what you tell me to," she said wistfully.

"Probably good advice when guns are involved."

Grayson's eyes flickered in his direction. "You think it'll be like that? That he'll really find me up here?"

"I hope not. But we're holed up in a safe house, aren't we? You know better than anybody how psycho this Cain guy is.

And apparently he bought your little act at the precinct hook, line, and sinker."

"Yeah, no kidding."

Now I really wish I hadn't done that. She moved her hands faster up and down her body. Why is it so cold in here?

Logan pushed off the doorframe and came over to stand by her at the window. "You must've put on quite a show, you know? To get him to leave."

Grayson's eyes widened. The older detective smirked. He'd bluffed, but he'd been right.

"How did you know?" she asked.

"I didn't really. Just a hunch." He shrugged. "It worked. But why do it?"

Grayson rested her head in her hands. "Do you honestly think he would have left me here if he knew how fucking petrified I am?"

Logan chuckled. "Of course not. That's my point."

Grayson eyed Logan over her fingertips. "Mine, too. He has to go back to Denver. They'll take his badge or worse if he doesn't. He's not losing his job over me. I can't let that happen."

Logan snorted. "They won't take his badge. It's an empty threat."

"I won't risk it," she replied defiantly.

"Even if they do, the captain will tell the Chief of Detectives to shove it up his ass. They'll be begging for him to come back."

Grayson nodded and turned to look out the window again. She was trembling. Harrison playfully bumped into her right side.

"Don't worry. I'll look after ya."

"I know. Don't tell him, Logan."

"Tell him what?"

"That it was all an act. That I'm not really holding it together like he thinks I am."

"I'll do my best," he said, putting a comforting hand on her shoulder. "I think Mason's making dinner. You coming out?"

She shook her head. "I'm not hungry."

"Okay. Just let me know if you need anything. I'm the first door down the other hall."

She nodded absently. He flipped the wall switch for the fireplace and shut the door behind him.

Grayson stood looking out the window until the sun had fully set behind the mountains. Then she grabbed a blanket from the bed, wrapped herself in it, and collapsed by the fireplace, silent tears rolling down her face.

47

GABRIEL HAD AN iron grip on the steering wheel as he ascended Vail Pass at breakneck speed. It had started snowing again. Combine the fluffy downfall with the minimal ambient light, and it was getting difficult to navigate the stream of tourist traffic heading back into the city. He swore under his breath as a minivan pulled out in front of him, going twenty miles an hour under the speed limit, and he slammed on the brakes.

He felt the back of the SUV fishtail. It was starting to get icy. *Shit.*

That's all he needed. Black ice. He got the machine back under control and distanced himself from the offending minivan, anticipating another stupid maneuver from the driver. The slowed pace gave him time to think. He'd called Nolan to let him know he was on his way the second he'd cleared the safe house driveway. It kept him from turning around. His partner had had some news.

A second sweep of Cain's prison cell had unearthed a hiding place in the wall behind one of the bunk beds. The small space was only big enough for a few scraps of paper, but they'd found a list of names hidden there. Grayson's was at the top. The others were of his nine victims. There was also a long line of numbers, which forensics thought was probably a bank account somewhere in Europe. The forensic accountant was on his way in.

Cain's passport had been flagged, as had all of his domestic bank accounts, but they'd been almost fully liquidated in the days before he'd been arrested. The money was gone. Two unmarked units were still sitting on his apartment. They'd missed him, according to the doorman. He'd left with a suitcase over his shoulder and little else.

The poor doorman hadn't known about Cain's arrest and was apparently beside himself that he'd let a serial murderer saunter out the door with a smile and a wave.

Cain was still a few steps ahead of them, and Nolan didn't have any idea of how to catch up.

Blake had asked about her. Of course he had. His partner was the type to care about other people more than himself. Gabriel had been as evasive as possible without running off the road. One thing his partner had asked kept playing over and over again in his head.

Are you sure she's okay?

He couldn't answer that. When he'd left her, hours ago, he'd thought so. But now, driving through a snowstorm in the middle of the night in the opposite direction, he wasn't so sure.

Gabriel stepped on the gas.

If Cain was truly outsmarting them, if he could sneak around the city while it was swarming with cops all hell-bent on finding him, there was no telling where he was now. The drawings they'd found in his cell and the ramblings about the bells could mean anything. Whether Cain actually knew she was in Aspen or just meant to take her there after he'd gotten his hands on her again…Gabriel swore at the thought.

An image of Cain standing over Grayson, tears in her eyes and a gun in his hand, came out of nowhere.

Goddamn it, what the fuck am I doing?

He glanced over his shoulder and crossed three lanes of traffic, barely making the exit ramp. He tore across the bridge and floored the gas pedal as he turned onto the onramp, heading back toward Aspen.

He hit a few buttons on the steering wheel and waited. He heard the click of the line picking up.

"Let me guess, Ryder…" came Nolan's voice over the speaker system.

"Tell McCallister I'm not coming in, Blake. I'm turning around."

There was laughter on the other end of the line.

"Something funny?"

"Gabe, I told him that forty-five minutes ago. No shit you're turning around. I'm surprised it's taken you this long."

"Nolan…"

"Look, I've already covered for you. They're not going to take your badge. The captain's been on the phone with the chief of detectives for the past hour."

"Don't get in trouble with the brass over me."

"I'm not. And I happen to agree with you. I don't think this jackass is in the city anymore. Or he won't be for long. The guys sitting outside Grayson's house just checked in. A blacked-out sedan made a couple of passes about twenty minutes ago, then took off. They lost him after a few blocks. I think Cain is looking for her."

"Did they get a plate?"

"It didn't have any. My guess is, the bastard's going to throw something on it once he gets out of town so we're not looking for an untagged car."

Gabriel nodded silently. It was smart and planned. Cain had had help. "Anyone look good for helping him get out?"

Nolan sighed. "Yeah, that's being taken care of. Mr. Charmer got under the skin of one of the new nurses at the prison. When she heard what happened, and found out who Cain really is, she immediately went to her supervisor. The girl's scared out of her mind. Thinks we're going to crucify her."

"Try to work your magic on her, Blake."

"Yeah, right. She's due here in about fifteen. I'll let you know if I get anything useful out of her."

"Ask her about what he promised her."

"Huh?"

"Cain did more than tell her she was pretty. He must have talked about what they'd do together once he got out. Ask her about specifics. He probably gave her details about where he wants to take Grayson once he gets to her again…just made her believe she was the lucky lady instead."

"Oh. Good point. Yeah, hang on, I'm gonna write that down." Gabriel heard scribbling and shuffling in the background. "You got any other pearls of wisdom for me, buddy?"

"You can put the interrogation on speaker…"

There was a snort on the other end of the line. "Oh, hell no. You need to drive. I'm not going to be responsible for you wrecking that pretty sports car of yours."

"I didn't take the car."

"So…you're saying it's sitting in the garage. Keys are on the counter?" his partner joked.

"Blake, don't touch the fucking car."

"One of these days you're gonna let me drive that thing."

"Don't count on it."

Nolan sighed into the receiver and switched topics. "Listen, there's one thing I can't sell to McCallister, and it's how this freak would know she's up in Aspen. I mean, yeah, the whole bells thing, but that could just be him with the Dante's Inferno shit. Especially if he made a pass or two at her house. It sounds like he doesn't know where she is."

"I don't give a shit. I'm not taking any chances with this son of a bitch. End of discussion."

"All right. I'll pass the word along. Don't kill yourself getting back up there. I'll call if anything useful turns up."

"Thanks, Blake."

Gabriel moved to end the call.

Nolan stopped him. "Oh, wait, one more thing. I called the captain up there. You should be getting a nice care package from the Aspen PD delivered to the house."

"Of what?"

"Service pistols, hollow-points, Kevlar, two turtle doves, and a partridge in a pear tree. Merry Christmas."

The line went dead.

Gabriel smirked, shook his head, and stepped on the gas.

48

IT WAS WELL after ten o'clock when his tires sank down into the gravel driveway. The lights in the house were on, but low. He could hear muffled voices behind the front door. And music. Rather beautiful music.

He put his key in the door lock and pushed the front door open. His ears immediately registered the click of a gun's safety. Automatically, Gabriel raised his hands out away from his sides and dropped his bag. He heard the sound again, off to his left, and a low chuckle.

"Ryder, you fucking idiot," Logan said, walking out into view from the side hallway. "I could've put a bullet in your head." He put his gun back into the holster slung over his shoulder. "What the hell are you doing back here?"

"Change of plans," he replied evasively, picking his bag up off of the floor.

"Why didn't you call to tell me you were headed back? Would've saved me trying to shoot you."

"Didn't think to."

"You want something to eat?"

He shook his head. "I ate on the way," he lied. Gabriel could see the TV on in the main room. Noah and Barbara were spaced out on the couch, completely oblivious to his arrival.

"Babysitting's easier with the TV on." Harrison shrugged, pointing in their direction. Gabriel ignored him.

"Where is she?"

"Bedroom," he motioned with his head.

"She's asleep?"

"Dunno. She hasn't left since you did. Didn't come out for dinner."

Gabriel nodded. "I think we're in the clear tonight, Logan. Have a drink."

Without another word, Ryder turned on his heels and made his way down the hallway toward a familiar set of double doors. He knocked softly, and when he didn't get an answer, he burst through them.

The only light in the room was coming from the fireplace. Shadows danced effortlessly across the walls. Last night, with Grayson splayed out across his bed, they had been welcome. Beautiful, even. Now, they were menacing. They were hiding something.

Gabriel's eyes adjusted quickly, and he scanned the room. She wasn't in bed. The lights to the bathroom were off and the door was closed. The love seat at the window was empty. He closed the door and took several more steps into the room, then stopped dead in his tracks.

A small, huddled mass was curled up at the base of the fireplace, hidden underneath a blanket.

And it wasn't moving.

Gabriel immediately dropped his bag in the doorway and went to her, kneeling down at her side. He pulled the blanket away from her face. She was asleep, eyes clenched shut and whimpering against a nightmare. She'd been there for a while. The pattern of the carpet was imprinted on her left cheek.

"Grayson?" he called softly.

She didn't stir. Gabriel passed his fingers along her cheek and called to her again. She stayed within the clutches of her dream, whimpering and pleading against the dark. He stood up and scanned the room briefly, then settled on an idea. He crossed to the bathroom and shut the door behind him.

Several minutes later, he emerged, his sleeves rolled up at the elbows. Gabriel knelt back down next to her and gently called her name. She stirred, calling his name from the depths of sleep. He gathered her up in his arms, blanket and all, and pushed up to his feet.

———

The sudden movement registered deep in her dream, and Grayson felt something warm envelop her. Something warm and strong and suddenly the monsters were gone. Cain was gone. The gray room was gone. She could hear the sound of running water far, far off in the distance.

Wait, running water?

She woke slowly, fighting back against the nightmare of the gray room, and looked right into Gabriel's burning blue eyes.

"Hi, sweetheart," he said softly, kissing the top of her head.

From the fog of sleep, Grayson didn't register that he was real, instead mistaking him for a very vivid dream. She didn't mind. Whatever this new dream was, he was in it and she wasn't in the gray room anymore and that was enough.

Her arms were bundled up into a very soft blanket, so she did the only thing she could: nuzzle into dream-Gabriel's chest and stop thinking.

Gabriel kissed her again and then set her down on the bathroom countertop. The granite was ice-cold even through the fluffy blanket. She shivered, but the bathroom itself was full of steam and getting steadily warmer.

Grayson rubbed her eyes and blinked, the haze slowly but surely fading away. She registered the soft candlelight and the warm water running into an oversized bathtub.

Gabriel was standing in front of her, his hands gripping the countertop on either side of her hips, watching her. When her eyes finally focused on him, really and truly focused on him, he brought a hand up to her face. He was warm. And more importantly, he was real.

"Grayson, look at me," he commanded gently, tilting her chin up.

"Gabriel?"

She was acting drugged, but he knew better. He could see the dried-up tear tracks on her cheeks, even in the dim light. She'd cried herself to sleep. She was too tired and too dehydrated to think clearly.

Why in the hell did I leave her? I knew something was wrong.

"That's right," he said.

"You left," she mumbled, shaking her head.

Gabriel thumbed the worry lines across her forehead. "I did. I'm sorry."

"You need to go," she pouted.

"No, I need to be here with you. Come on." He motioned toward the bathtub. "We need to get you warm again."

"I'm not cold."

"You're shaking. And arguing." He smiled. "It's adorable, but you're still cold. Come on. Arms up."

It was like taking care of a child. Grayson stared off over Gabriel's shoulder as he undressed her. He kept the blanket wrapped around her until the last possible moment, then threw it back onto the countertop as he lowered her into the water.

He watched Grayson close her eyes and slide completely under the surface, letting the warm water wash over her face and through her hair. For a moment, she looked peaceful, like the warm water had actually managed to wash away the remnants of whatever monsters she had been fighting in her dreams. But as the seconds started to tick by, Gabriel felt the hair start to stand up on the back of his neck. She was still under the water, and she was showing no intention of coming up for a breath of air.

Fuck!

He panicked. In one swoop, he dunked his arms into the water, hooking them underneath her shoulders, bringing her to the surface. "Grayson! Goddamn it," he hissed as water splashed loudly over the edge of the tub.

She sputtered and opened her eyes wide.

"Look at me, damn it!" he demanded.

She turned her head on command. Gabriel still had his arms underneath her. He was furious, and he refused to let go of her. And right then, in that moment and for whatever reason, he watched her come back to herself.

Gabriel saw the last haze clear from her eyes and the recognition wash across her face. When he felt her shift to support her own weight, he raised a hand to her face, desperately pulled her in to him, and kissed her. Her arms lifted out of the warm water and wrapped around his neck. Small, warm streams ran down the back of his shirt. He didn't pay them any attention.

When he pulled back, Gabriel kept his hands on her face and stroked her temples with his fingers until she opened her eyes.

"You're really here," she said quietly. "You…you came back."

Her voice was so soft, so weak, it didn't seem real. Gabriel nodded.

"Why? Why come back?"

"I never should have left in the first place," he replied, dropping his forehead to rest on hers. "I'm sorry."

"I got you all wet," she murmured, stealing a glance at his damp shirt and running her fingers through the ends of his hair.

"I'll live, sweetheart," he said, standing up. She shot him a questioning look when he started unbuttoning his shirt. "I'm already wet," he shrugged, winking at her as he tossed the shirt aside.

Grayson leaned back against the edge of the tub and watched him shed his clothes, her bottom lip finding its way in between her teeth.

Gabriel caught the fire in her eyes and smirked as he turned back to face her, completely naked.

"Easy, love," he said. "Scoot forward."

She readily complied, and Gabriel sank down into the water behind her. His legs wound around on the outside of hers, hooking her ankles. Grayson settled back into him as he leaned back against the edge of the tub. He turned a silver knob, and a stream of warm water gently flowed out from the faucet.

"Mmmmm," Grayson purred, running her fingers up and down his left thigh.

Gabriel worked his fingers into the muscles around her neck and shoulders. It didn't take long for her breathing to slow down and for her head to loll back onto his chest.

"Feel better?" he whispered into her ear.

She nodded. "I do better when you're around, apparently."

Gabriel smirked and kissed the top of her head. "So do I."

They spent several quiet minutes together, just listening to the warm water trickle into the tub. It didn't take long for Gabriel to notice Grayson start to fidget in his arms. She had questions. So did he.

Grayson twisted around slightly, a half-hearted attempt to face him. "Why did you decide to come back? Won't they fire you?"

Gabriel shook his head slightly, then pulled her back down against his chest. He was suddenly overwhelmingly possessive. "I'll be fine. My captain's taking care of it. Besides, I never should have left. I knew something wasn't right. You were hiding from me, weren't you?"

Grayson hesitated, her face red from the shame that he'd seen right through her, then nodded.

"Why did you do that?" he scolded.

"You…I…I knew you wouldn't have left if you'd known."

"Of course I wouldn't have," he hissed.

"You can't lose your job over me, Gabriel."

"I won't. Relax."

Gabriel ran his fingers along her collarbone. She nuzzled back down against him.

"Gabriel?"

"Hm?"

"Don't leave again."

"I'm not planning on it, sweetheart," he replied.

He stayed with her until the water began to cool and her breathing indicated she was just at the edge of sleep.

"Hey," he whispered, bringing her back into consciousness. "Let's get you into bed."

She nodded but made no move to get up.

Gabriel waited a minute, then tried to stand. Grayson

frowned and murmured, shaking her head against his chest. He chuckled.

"You're going to have to let go for a minute," he said, guiding her away from his chest.

She frowned, clearly already in the throes of sleep, and shook her head again.

He chuckled in response and stood, quickly drying himself off with the nearest towel. He wrapped the material around his waist, then helped Grayson up and out of the water. She stepped out onto the cold stone floor and he wrapped her in a large towel, running the soft cotton over her skin. She accepted a second, smaller towel for her hair, which she twisted and fluffed through the fabric until it was only slightly damp and curling around her face.

Gabriel grabbed the towel from her hands, discarding it. He wound her hair around his fingers, tipping her head back so he had full, unobstructed access. He kissed her steadily, then trailed his lips down her neck and across to her shoulder. Grayson sagged into his arms and sighed.

"Time for bed," he whispered.

In one fluid motion, he bent down and swept Grayson off of her feet, carrying her out of the bathroom and into the warmth of the bedroom. The fireplace was still on, and the king-size bed was more than marginally inviting to both of them. He was exhausted, and clearly so was she, but Grayson was his first priority. He wasn't going to sleep until she was taken care of.

Gabriel held her in one arm as he tossed the comforter and sheets aside, lowering her underneath them gently. Grayson turned on her side and buried her face into the pillows. Gabriel tucked the comforter around her. She was asleep within minutes.

He set his bag up on a chest of drawers and unzipped the main compartment, intending to find a pair of sweat pants and join Logan for a drink in the main room. The sound of soft, tortured moaning caught his attention before he ever made it to the door.

He quietly stepped up to the side of the bed and found Grayson tossing and turning, clearly in the midst of a nightmare. He reached out and ran his hand over her forehead. She calmed instantly, lacing her fingers with his.

Well, so much for that drink.

Gabriel pulled his hand from Grayson's. He locked the bedroom door, turned the fireplace off, and drew the curtains, plunging the room into complete darkness. He navigated his way to the bed and slid in next to her, attempting to find the warmth of her body in the cool sheets. Grayson searched him out in her sleep, tossing and turning until he pulled her safely into his side.

Gabriel quieted her by talking to her. The low, steady tone of his voice was able to soothe away whatever nightmare had been trying to take hold. He ran his hand up and down her back, finally resting his hand on her hip and folding the other behind his head.

Her breathing was slow and measured. She was peacefully sound asleep. The nightmare was gone.

Gabriel stayed awake for hours, listening to her talk in her sleep. Occasionally, he'd murmur to her in Italian and she would press herself against him earnestly, drawn to the deep baritone of his voice.

He willed his body to keep still, ignoring every instinct he had to climb on top of her and drive himself into her. She needed him to comfort her and keep her safe, not fuck her like an animal. The thought brought all kinds of inappropriate ideas to mind. He filed them away for later, and eventually fell asleep with his fingers laced in her hair.

49

GRAYSON WOKE UP warm and enveloped in soft, naked skin. She whimpered happily and reached up, running her fingers through a mess of dark hair.

He's still here.

Gabriel's legs were tangled with hers. Her head was safely tucked in against his chest. She purred against him and stretched up to kiss his neck. Her lips had barely touched skin when she felt a hand reach up and clutch the back of her head. She wiggled happily and pressed her lips harder against him, trailing up the skin to his ear where she took his earlobe into her mouth and sucked.

Gabriel bucked underneath her, moaning in his sleep and pulling her on top of him. Grayson perched a leg on either side of his hips, running her hands down his abdomen. She felt the muscles flex at her touch and did it again. It was too dark to see that he'd opened his eyes, but she could feel them on her. When two hands settled onto her hips, pressing firmly into the flesh, her inner muscles clenched in anticipation.

"What are you doing?" came his low, sleep-heavy voice out of the darkness.

Grayson's hips moved on their own, seduced by the sound of his voice. Gabriel's palms clamped down harder into her flesh. She could feel him tense underneath her. His cock was already hard and pressing into her stomach. She bent down, her hair falling over her face, and began trailing kisses from his sternum southward.

Gabriel quivered underneath her, rocking his hips into her without his conscious consent. "Grayson, stop," he hissed.

"Why?" she whispered sweetly, trailing her tongue down the middle of his six-pack.

"I…I won't stop," he said, his hands flying off of her skin to fist in the bed sheets.

Grayson reached her hands out and trailed her fingers up his forearms to his biceps and around his shoulders. She ran them back down the same path, her lips gliding along the ridges of his abdomen. Gabriel moaned, his hips bucking involuntarily off of the bed. Grayson smiled against his skin; he could feel her teeth against him.

Gabriel grabbed her around the waist and pushed, sending her sprawling onto her back and spreading her legs around him. He braced his weight on his hands and ground his hips against her. Grayson arched her back off the bed at the feel of him. She raked her nails down the length of his back, earning her another pass of Gabriel's hips against hers and his teeth against her neck. She felt him trail his tongue up her neck to her ear, his fingers curling in her hair.

"Just what is running through that head of yours, darling?" he breathed, hot and heavy in her ear.

He pushed her legs up higher with his knees and pulled down on her hair, exposing her neck. Grayson quivered, shaking at the feel of being pinned down and completely vulnerable. She felt him grin as he ran a hand up the inside of her thigh. She convulsed at the feel of his fingers on her, so close to her. Gabriel ground his hips into her heat. She could feel how ready he was for her, how hard and how thick, how desperate he was to be inside of her. He towered over her, panting and heaving with lust. All directed at her.

"Well?" he breathed, reaching out and running his fingers between her breasts, down her stomach, and along her aching heat.

———

She whispered his name as he slid her fingers into her, marveling at the yielding, ready wetness he found there.

He stroked her slowly, closing his eyes to better hear her respond to him and feel her muscles quiver around him.

Good God, she's so ready...

Gabriel passed his thumb over her clit and she shot up off of the bed, throwing her arms around his neck. He whipped an arm around her, clutching her to his sweaty chest. He dropped his mouth to her ear.

"Tell me, Grayson," he growled against her neck. "Tell me what you want."

She mewled against him and tipped her head back, hanging onto him for dear life.

Gabriel worked his fingers inside of her, taking her right to the edge of release and slowing back to a low hum. A sheen of perspiration was building on Grayson's skin, her hair damp and clinging to her neck. It was all she could do to keep breathing. He kept murmuring to her, telling her how good she felt, how wet she was, how much he wanted her. Her eyes rolled back into her head and she arched backward, her hair just grazing the pillow tops.

Gabriel lowered her down onto the mattress, his bicep screaming in protest, as he kept thrusting his fingers inside of her. She was panting, whispering his name over and over again, desperate for the release he was denying her. He dropped his gaze from her face to her chest. Her breasts were trembling in time with her shallow breaths, and he couldn't resist them.

Gabriel brought his mouth down onto her, sucking and running his tongue greedily over the swollen mound. She arched her back off the bed, crying out as Gabriel's firm hands pressed her hips back into the mattress. She fought against him, and against the orgasm threatening to crash over her, pulling herself up against him. She brought her lips down roughly on his, sucking on his tongue and biting his lower lip until they both screamed for air. She ripped herself away from him, suddenly. Gabriel forced himself to freeze, his eyes blazing at her in the dim light.

"Against the wall. Now," she demanded.

Fuck. Me.

Gabriel growled against her neck, biting down into the tender skin. He hauled himself off of the bed with Grayson clinging to him. He threw the twisted sheets aside and stalked to the far wall. He slammed his free hand against the wall for leverage.

Grayson snaked an arm around his neck, her legs wrapped tightly around his hips. Her other hand fell in between their bodies, guiding him to her as quickly and smoothly as she could. He jerked at her touch, the soft caress of her fingertips on his cock was enough, sending a shockwave crashing through him. He moaned into the curtain of her hair as he felt her slick, wet entrance envelop him.

"Now," she whispered.

He obeyed, slamming into her with all the force he had. Grayson hung her arms around his neck and lolled forward as he thrust into her, his hips desperately pushing her up against the wall and hands furiously gripping into her backside. He called her name, over and over in time with each thrust. He was steadily losing control, and so was she. Her legs tightened around his waist; her muscles quivered around him.

He wasn't going to last much longer. He reared back and took her ear lobe into his mouth, gently tracing his tongue along the edge.

"Come for me, Grayson," he whispered.

He didn't have to ask twice.

50

GABRIEL AND LOGAN had left early in the morning to scout the perimeter of the property and investigate a security camera that was malfunctioning.

Once they were out the door, Noah had unilaterally decided to get both women out of the house. They couldn't leave the grounds or be seen in town, but at least he could get them to stop moping, huddled together in the main room. He'd shooed both women out onto the deck and quickly followed with a pitcher of Bloody Marys.

Now, hours later, the girls were spread out lounging in a pair of Adirondack rocking chairs with Noah between them, completely relaxed.

"What a beautiful day," Grayson sighed, turning her face up toward the gleaming sun.

"It's even better with a cocktail," Barbara smiled back, tipping her glass up to her lips.

She usually wasn't one for Bloody Marys, but the way Noah had made them was different. He hadn't revealed his secret recipe, but Grayson had a hunch it came from a certain Denver-based bartender.

The three friends sat out in the sunshine and talked, about everything but work. Noah and Barbara kept the topics of conversation light, occasionally shooting each other looks over their respective shoulders. It was good to see Grayson actually smiling again, especially considering the circumstances.

Neither of them had missed the look on her face when she'd come out of her room that morning, followed not more than a minute later by Gabriel. He hadn't taken his eyes off of her all morning, and the glint behind them was unmistakable.

"All right, Gray, spill it," Babs said, nearly through her third Bloody Mary.

Grayson gave her a look as she drained her own glass. She was already feeling the buzz of the alcohol.

"What now?"

"I wanna know about DDH," she said, wiggling her glass at Noah for another refill.

"Why are you calling him that?" Grayson giggled.

"Because it's appropriate."

"What does that even mean?"

Babs threw back her head and laughed. "It means Dark and Devastatingly Handsome, silly."

Grayson laughed along with her, a little too loudly. "You keep changing it. How long have you been calling him that?"

Babs shrugged and tossed back a good third of her newest drink. "What? I told you. It's appropriate," she shrugged.

"Barbara, that's awful. And you hated him less than twenty-four hours ago," Grayson scolded.

"It's true!" she squealed, jumping out of her chair. "Noah, isn't it true? He's a pain, but he's gorgeous." Barbara Parker was clearly feeling the effects of the alcohol and the altitude.

"I'm not getting involved here," he said, stirring up the second pitcher. "I've got my own burly barman waiting back in Denver. No need to muddy the waters by checking out another bloke."

"Shouldn't I be the one giving him a nickname?"

Grayson giggled again, pulling her feet up underneath her on the rocking chair.

"And just what name would you give me, darling?"

Grayson jumped and turned around in her chair.

Gabriel was leaning against the outside wall, his arms folded across his chest and a playful smirk on his face. Her face flushed crimson. She looked up at him through long, guilty lashes.

Gabriel pushed off the wall and stepped toward her. She skittered out of the chair and looked around hastily for the stairs. The alcohol was coursing quickly through her system, thanks to the adrenaline, and it was making everything just a bit hazy. She was closer to them than Gabriel was. She had a chance...

Gabriel stepped toward her again, playing with her. He saw her eyes dart to the edge of the deck and tensed. Grayson launched herself down the stairs, taking them two at a time. Gabriel went after her. Noah rolled his eyes, throwing a glance at Babs, who motioned for another Bloody Mary to watch the show.

Grayson ran as quickly as she could through the snow. She could hear Gabriel right behind her, gaining on her.

What the hell has gotten into me? Oh right, two Bloody Marys on an empty stomach.

The cold air burned her lungs, but she kept running, kicking up a fine mist of snow behind her. She was almost to the tree line when she felt a gloved hand clamp down over her left wrist. She squealed and pulled up. Gabriel's arm wrapped around her waist. He lifted her off of the ground and spun her around. A little too vigorously.

His strength combined with her blood-alcohol level forced them both down into the snow. Gabriel turned enough to take the majority of the impact with Grayson landing on top of him. She instantly rolled off of him and threw snow in his face, hoping to get away, but he grabbed her through the mist of white flakes and pulled her back on top of him.

"Gabriel! Stop!" She laughed.

"Come here," he growled.

She pressed her hands onto his chest and sat up, straddling him in the snow, her hair a wild and slightly damp mess. Gabriel reached up and pulled it out of her face, pushed up on his elbows, and kissed her. When he sat back, she smiled at him. He smiled back, then grabbed a handful of snow and brought it down right on top of her head.

Grayson's face froze in shock when the cold snow hit her scalp. She sat stunned, unable to speak, as the heat of her skin melted the snow and sent cold rivulets of ice water down her neck. She cocked her head to one side and looked down at him.

He was still propped up on his elbows, staring at her with a very self-satisfied smirk on his face.

Ass.

"Well?" he asked.

"Well what?" she fired back.

"Are you giving me a nickname or not?"

"After you just doused me with snow like a complete lunatic?"

"Now's as good a time as any."

"How about inconsiderate jackass?"

"Logan has that one covered. Try again."

"Sex god comes to mind."

"Really?" he asked, eyebrows raised.

She shrugged nonchalantly, then kissed him, hard and long enough to leave him breathless.

"I'm flattered, darling, but it doesn't seem appropriate for everyday use," he gasped as she pulled away.

"I assume pookie is out?" she joked sarcastically.

"Unless you want another round of snow on your head," he said, wrinkling his nose is disgust.

"Fine, fine," she rolled her eyes. "What would you suggest?"

"It's up to you, darling."

"Oh hell, I haven't any idea. Everything I think of just comes back to sex."

"Something on your mind?" he chuckled.

"This week? Um, maybe..."

"Rocked your world, did I?" He raised his hips underneath her.

She playfully hit him on the chest. "Idiot."

"Nolan has that one covered. Try again."

"Well, I give up," she said, throwing her hands up in the air and raining snow down on the both of them. "You're going to have to settle for stud muffin."

"Let's keep trying..." he said, leaning up to kiss her again.

A whoop from the balcony had both of them pulling away from one another and looking back toward the house. Logan was leaning against the railing, beer in hand, with Barbara and Noah carrying on in the background.

"Hey, you two want to get arrested for public indecency?" he called.

Grayson raised her eyebrows at Gabriel.

"I did bring my handcuffs," he joked.

"Really?"

The mischievous look that shot across her face had Gabriel rooted to the ground. Grayson bit down on her bottom lip. She leaned down close to his ear.

"Last one to the deck wears them, detective."

She jumped to her feet and tried to take off running, but Gabriel grabbed her around the waist and pulled her back into the snow, launching himself off in the direction of the house.

This was one race he was absolutely going to win.

The group spent the night on the couch, eating popcorn and watching a string of action movies that Logan had picked up from the village's mom-and-pop video-mart. The girls took up one end of the couch, and the men took up the other, draining the better part of a good bottle of scotch between the three of them.

Gabriel kept one eye on his glass and one eye on Grayson. She was smiling, draped under a blanket with Barbara and glued to the television. Her face was flushed from a glass of wine, and her eyes were sparkling in the heat of the fireplace.

Logan elbowed him in the ribs, a toothy grin on his face. Gabriel shrugged and took a drink from his glass. No use denying it anymore. He was a done deal.

A shrill ring sounded from the kitchen.

Grayson rolled her eyes and pushed herself up from the couch. "It's probably one of my residents," she said, absently picking the phone up from the countertop and placing it to her ear without looking at the screen.

"Hello?"

"Hello, my Beatrice."

51

"H...HELLO DANTE."

Saying his name made her physically sick to her stomach. Grayson closed her eyes against the bile rising in her throat and clutched the edge of the kitchen countertop. Her heart raced inside her chest, threatening to give out. She forgot how to breathe. Her grip on the handset was white-knuckled and frighteningly tight.

The sound of the movie and the conversations going on behind her faded into a low din. She could hear every breath he took on the other end of the line. She could almost picture him smiling at the sound of her voice.

That smile...

The feel of a warm hand on her hip made her jump. She snapped her eyes open.

Gabriel stood behind her and was giving her a questioning look. He pressed his palm into her hip. The pressure was incredibly reassuring, but it didn't dampen her trembling.

Grayson almost started talking to him, her mouth open and poised. At the very last second, she remembered she had the phone pressed up to her ear. Shaking, she started writing on the kitchen counter with the tip of her finger, one letter at a time.

D. A. N. T. E.

She kept her eyes on his face. With each letter, she watched the dark clouds roll over his eyes. They turned black and unbearably sharp. Every hint of warmth faded from his face.

He was ice-cold, hard, and unyielding. He was everything she didn't need him to be in that moment.

Grayson turned and walked to the nearest window, desperate to be away from him. Cain was talking again.

Shit!

She needed to pay attention. When she didn't answer him, because she had no idea what he'd asked her, he repeated himself.

"Beatrice...I asked you a question. Have they hurt you?"

She shook her head, then remembered her voice. *He can't see you shaking your head, you idiot.*

"N...no. No, they haven't."

A long sigh filtered across the line. "That's good. They should be wary of hurting something so precious to me."

Grayson felt the bile rise in her throat again. The edges of her vision started to blur.

Oh dear God, not now...don't faint now...

She pushed a hand out to support herself on the window, her palm flat against the cold, frosted glass.

Slow down your breathing. Focus.

"They've been taking good care of me," she said truthfully.

"I take care of you. *They* keep me away from you," he hissed.

"I know. I'm sorry," she said softly, trying her best to soothe him without it sounding forced.

It had little effect.

Cain started to rant about the incompetence of the police department and the depravity of their actions. As he continued rambling on, Grayson suddenly felt the same warm hand wrap around her waist. Strong fingers darted out to skim the soft skin in between the bottom hem of her shirt and the top line of her jeans.

She looked up into the dark glass and saw Gabriel reflected in it. His eyes were calm. The blackness was gone. He wasn't cold. He was warm and strong and worried. He kissed the hair on the top of her head and she sank back against him, finally unwilling to keep herself upright without help. He caught her, supporting her weight with one arm. The hand on the other arm lifted a scrap piece of paper up to eye level in front of her.

Keep him talking. Find out where he is.

Grayson shot him a look into the glass and mouthed *how* over her shoulder. Gabriel released her and quickly scribbled another line, holding the paper out for her to read.

Be Beatrice again.

The repulsion must have registered on her face because he immediately turned her around and tipped her face up to look at him.

"Like before," he mouthed.

She took in a deep breath and nodded.

Okay, here goes nothing.

"They're keeping you from me, my love," Cain hissed. "You should be with me."

Grayson laced her voice with overdone affection in a desperate attempt to mask her fear. "But, how can I? They're keeping you in prison. I can't reach you."

"No longer, my Beatrice. Those walls are far behind me. They could not hold me."

"They let you go?" She feigned surprise, as best she could.

"I left. Let us leave it at that for now."

"How?"

"You do not have to know such things."

She took another breath.

Try to sound excited. "Then I can come to you? We can be together?"

"Soon, my angel. Very soon."

"Where are you? How can I find you?" Grayson was trying for desperate. It came off rather well.

"It's dangerous, my love. They are watching you, aren't they? They have you captive."

She nodded and managed a small sob into the microphone. "They're always watching me. They don't let me outside. I'm scared."

"Do not be afraid. I will find you. Do you know where they are keeping you?"

Grayson frantically grabbed the pen from Gabriel's hand and scribbled onto the paper.

He wants to know where I am!

Gabriel frowned, then mouthed "mountains."

"There are mountains. I saw them from the car. They keep the blinds drawn. I can't see outside."

"Then they did take you from the city. I went to your home. You were not there."

He was at my house.

Grayson shivered. "They took me away so quickly."

"What else did you see?"

She scribbled *details?* onto the scrap of paper.

Gabriel took the pen and wrote three lines, handing the paper back to her.

Grayson walked over to the kitchen counter and sat down on one of the barstools, not trusting her legs to keep her upright.

"There's snow. Lots of snow. I could see it forever. There were trees, big and green and full of snow. And there was a sign. A red leaf on a gray background."

She paused at the last line and pointed, her eyebrows raised. Gabriel nodded coolly.

"What else, my Beatrice?"

"And a red barn. A big red barn."

"Hmm." A hum over the line. "Did you see the lights? The kind from a town?"

She scribbled *'lights? town?'*

Gabriel nodded, glancing down at his watch.

"Yes. Yes, I saw lights."

"Very good, my love. Keep your phone close. Hide it from them. I will come for you. Be ready."

The line went dead. Grayson dropped the phone like it had burned her. It slid across the granite countertop, clattering to the floor.

She abruptly stood up from the barstool and walked back to the window, clutching her arms around her waist and rocking back and forth from her heels to her toes and back again. Gabriel followed her, gently resting his hands on her shoulders.

"Well done, sweetheart," he said softly, leaning into her side to kiss her temple.

She let out a strangled moan. "Please, please don't make me do that again," she begged, hanging her shoulders and staring at the floor.

"You should sit down," he said calmly.

"I need a drink," she countered.

"All right," he agreed. "I'll bring it to you. Sit down."

Grayson robotically walked back over to the main room, where three pairs of eyes were trained on her. The movie was already on mute. She sat down next to Logan, who tossed a blanket around her shoulders, and stared blankly at the floor until Gabriel sat on her other side and pressed a warm cup into her hands.

"Drink up, darling," he said softly.

She raised the cup to her lips and tasted chocolate, Bailey's and vanilla. She sagged back into the couch, and Gabriel pulled her sideways to lay against his shoulder.

"Um, anybody want to tell me what the hell that was?" Babs asked from the opposite end of the couch.

"Cain," Gabriel replied, drawing the blanket higher up Grayson's shoulders.

"What? How did that fucker get her phone number?" she shrieked, jumping up from the cushions.

"My guess is he's had it for quite a while, just never used it," he said, tucking the blanket edges around her.

"What did you do, Gabe?" Logan asked. *Please tell me you didn't do anything stupid, Wonder Boy.*

"He asked where she was. We…well, she…fed him a bland description from a Christmas card. She hinted at the Aspen SkiCo logo, to get him in the ballpark. He bought it, didn't he?" he asked, looking down at the top of her head.

Grayson nodded, taking another sip.

"It bought us time. He's trying to find her. Before we give him our location, I want a plan in place."

"She wasn't on for too long?"

"I kept her under ten minutes. He shouldn't be able to do much with that."

"What's with the ten minutes?" Noah asked.

"Timing," Logan shrugged. "There's more than one way to track a cell phone, and most of them are kept under lock and key at the Pentagon. A few black-market programs can track a phone without the owner being aware, but it takes at least ten minutes of continuous signal to give any decent GPS location; longer if the service is scattered like here."

"Isn't there an app for that?" Babs asked sarcastically.

"Sure, if you get the app installed on the phone. Then it doesn't even matter if the thing's powered off. If it has a signal, it can be tracked."

"He's tracking my phone? He knows where we are?" Grayson shrieked.

"Shh, calm down," Gabriel soothed. "I checked your phone yesterday. It's clean. Besides, Cain prides himself on his intelligence. He won't use one. He wants to figure it out on his own. It means he's smarter than we are. "

Grayson burrowed into Gabriel's chest. He tightened the arm he had around her abdomen and ran his thumb gently against her lower ribs.

"So, what did he want?" Babs asked, sitting forward on the couch.

"He wants me," she sighed. "He called to tell me he'd escaped from prison."

"Tell me this is all a bad dream," the blonde moaned, dropping her head into her hands.

"So what do we do? Move again? A different safe house?" Noah asked.

"No," Gabriel replied coolly. "We stay here. And catch him."

"What?"

"He's not going to stop. He's made that exceptionally clear by murdering two maximum security prison guards."

"And now calling me," Grayson added softly.

"Don't worry, Grayson," Gabriel soothed. "He's not going to get anywhere near you."

"I hope you've got a fucking plan, Ryder," Logan muttered.

"I might," he smirked. "What she told Cain wasn't much, but he'll start tracking property outside of Denver. If he gets lucky, he'll make the connection with the SkiCo logo. He'll narrow his search to the Roaring Fork Valley."

"We just wait for him to knock on the bloody door then?" Noah scowled.

"Not quite. Tomorrow, she'll call in a panic, claiming she escaped from us. We'll give him a location and ambush him."

"That sounds ridiculously simple, Ryder," Logan said, shaking his head and taking a long drink of scotch.

"We just have to get him to believe it's real," he said, turning his head to try to catch Grayson's eyes.

She purposefully avoided him.

"Grayson," he prompted. "Can you do this?"

"He's going to take me away again," she whispered.

Gabriel scowled and hauled her onto his lap. "No, he won't. You're not going to be anywhere near him."

She narrowed her eyes and looked up at him. "Are you kidding? He'll never buy it unless I'm standing around waiting for him."

"Technically, you're going to be hiding from us, sweetheart. You'll have a good reason to not be standing around in the open."

The wrinkles in her forehead deepened. "I don't like this, Gabriel." She shook her head.

"I'm open to suggestions, if you have any."

Gabriel cocked his head and stared at her, a slight smile tugging on his lips. He was trying to make her smile.

Grayson took it as mockery. She set her cup down on the coffee table and stood up abruptly, throwing the blanket off into his lap and stalking off toward the master bedroom.

Gabriel sighed and stood up to follow her.

"G'night, lover boy," Logan called after him as he disappeared down the hall.

52

GABRIEL QUIETLY OPENED the door and stepped into the bedroom. The fireplace was lit. Grayson was curled up in the love seat, her knees held tightly against her chest. He took several steps forward, steeling himself for a fight.

Instead, he startled at the sound of hushed tears.

Wait, she's crying? What the hell?

He silently knelt down in front of her and waited. Grayson visibly tensed when she noticed him at her feet and curled deeper into herself. She did everything she could to keep her eyes from meeting his.

Gabriel shook his head and pulled her face up out of her hands.

"Grayson, what's wrong?" he asked, running his fingers over her tear-stained cheeks.

She shook her head violently, hair whipping from side to side, and buried her face back in her hands.

"Stop it," he scolded. "Talk to me."

She lifted her head only slightly, her eyes shining with tears.

Gabriel's eyes shifted in confusion.

What the hell is going on?

She didn't give him a chance to ask. She launched herself out of the chair and wrapped her arms around his neck. He stumbled back onto his heels, but it only took a moment to regain his footing. He wrapped both arms around her and stood up from the floor, taking her with him.

Grayson let her body go along with his, her weight falling into his arms. Her sobbing became uncontrollable as she buried her face in his neck.

"Grayson, come on, talk to me. What's wrong?" he murmured gently, running his fingers through her hair.

She sniffled, trying in vain to get herself under control, and said something he couldn't hear into the crook of his neck.

"What?"

"He's going to kill you, Gabriel. Because of me."

"Grayson," he murmured in her ear, gently shaking his head. "Stop. No one's killing anyone."

"You're going out there, aren't you? To catch him."

"Of course."

"You can't!" she fired back, pushing away from him.

She stumbled into the fireplace mantel, wincing as the wood made contact with her shoulder blades.

"You said he won't stop."

"He won't stop until he gets to *you*," he corrected, "and I'm not going to let that happen. You'll be safe here. Logan and I will take care of everything. You don't have to go near him."

"I'm not worried about me. Goddamn it!" she huffed, throwing her hands up in the air.

Okay, I am, but that's not why I'm upset.

"Then what…"

"*You*, you idiot. I'm worried about you." She wiped the tears from her eyes.

Gabriel hesitated. He could see the fear in her eyes. His heart ached inside his chest. She was upset and suffering because she was worried about him. Grayson hiccupped against the tears that threatened to flow again.

She's so worried about me she's going to make herself sick.

"You're going to go in with some master plan and the second something goes wrong…" she said, trying to hide the hitch in her voice.

"You have such little faith in me, sweetheart?" he asked softly.

It was almost playful. Grayson whirled around to scold him, a new onslaught of tears threatening to unleash themselves from behind her eyes.

Gabriel scooped her up in his arms and carried her over to the bed.

Enough of this.

"Gabriel!" she squealed as he dropped her down on the mattress and climbed in on all fours beside her. He kissed her forehead and sat back against the headboard, pulling her up beside him.

"Gabriel…" she whispered.

"Grayson, enough," he said, wrapping an arm around her and resting his hand on her hip. "I'm sick and tired of seeing you upset. This ends now. And I'm not letting you anywhere near the son of a bitch."

"I don't want…"

He held up a hand to silence her. "Trust me. And do what I tell you. Don't get in the middle."

She nestled up against his side and rested her head on his stomach. Gabriel absently ran his fingers through her hair as she continued to quietly sob against him.

"I don't want you to go," she whispered.

"You know I have to, sweetheart."

"I don't like it."

"I've gathered that," he chuckled.

"At least take Logan with you."

"No."

"Gabriel..." Her voice dropped.

"Absolutely not. Someone needs to stay here with you."

"I already have Babs and Noah breathing down my neck."

"They don't have the expertise to..."

"Gabriel, please," she begged, pushing up onto her forearms. "You've asked me not to get in the middle. You've asked me to do what you tell me to. I've agreed. Now I get to ask for this. Don't go by yourself. Take Logan."

They stared each other down for several moments, the hush of the room interrupted only by the crackling from the fireplace. The desperation behind her eyes finally did him in.

"You're going to come after me if I don't, aren't you?"

Grayson nodded. It wasn't worth hiding the truth.

"All right," he sighed. "If you insist."

53

IT WAS WELL into the afternoon when Gabriel walked into the main living room, pulling a black sweater over his head. Logan was at the kitchen counter, leaning back on one of the barstools, also dressed in black, rhythmically loading hollow-point bullets into a spare clip.

Barbara and Noah were out on the deck, keeping Grayson calm. Gabriel glanced out the double doors leading outside and saw her leaning against the deck railing, eyes closed and face turned up into the sun.

He slid into the seat next to Harrison and picked up an empty clip. They had to make the phone call soon.

"It's almost time, buddy."

"Yeah," he replied. "I know."

"Think she can handle it?"

"She'll do fine," he nodded.

"You really think he's going to buy it? Seems too good to be true."

Gabriel shrugged. "She escaped from him once, technically. He has a rather high opinion of himself and a very low opinion of us. He knows she's capable."

"He thinks we're incompetent. So we put smart girl plus stupid cops and…"

"…and she gets out since she's desperate to see him," he finished, nodding.

Logan shoved the now-full clip into the 9mm and engaged the safety, then grabbed another empty one from the table.

"I hate this cloak-and-dagger shit, Ryder."

"I know."

"Just kill the fucker. Put two in his chest and be done with it. Maybe one in his head for good measure."

"I'm seriously considering it," he replied, chambering a bullet into his own .45mm Beretta. "You know we have to take him alive, Logan."

"I don't have to tell you to finish this quickly. Don't let Cain get the upper hand here."

"I won't."

Gabriel slung his holster over his shoulders and placed the gun underneath his left arm. He crossed the room, walked outside, and leaned against the side of the house.

Thank God, she's finally stopped crying.

Last night had been difficult. Grayson's nightmares had returned with a vengeance. She'd tossed and turned and called out his name over and over in her sleep.

Gabriel had tried to comfort her, every single way he'd known how to, but nothing had worked. As a last-ditch effort, he'd carried her over to the fireplace. The overwhelming warmth and the feel of his arms protectively cradling her against his chest had quieted her screaming. The nightmares hadn't gone away, but she'd fought less against the demons inside her head.

"Gray, you've got a visitor."

Noah's voice jerked Grayson back into the present as her face dropped down from the warm sun. She blinked, adjusting her eyes to the light, and focused on the man leaning against the weathered siding.

"It's time?" she asked.

He nodded.

Oh shit.

Her heart jumped up into her throat. At first, the sight of Gabriel dressed in black, gun holstered on his left side and blue eyes focused on her had been intoxicating. Then the reason he was dressed that way had firmly smacked her back into reality. She nodded and wrapped her arms around her waist as she passed by him and walked into the house.

Logan smiled at her reassuringly from the kitchen table. It didn't help steady her nerves.

"Are you ready?" Gabriel asked, walking up and resting his hands on her shoulders.

"As I'll ever be," she nodded.

"You remember what to say?"

"Yes."

He stepped in front of her and looked closely at her face.

"Grayson, you're going to be fine. Just breathe."

"Okay."

She didn't believe him. Grayson grabbed her cell phone from the countertop. She scrolled through her recent calls, found the number she wanted, and dialed. He picked up on the second ring.

"Beatrice? Beatrice, is that you?"

His voice was strained and muffled, overly eager. It was more than a little off-putting. Grayson turned her back on the two detectives and walked into the corner of the kitchen.

I can't do this with them staring at me.

"Yes, yes it's me," she whispered into the receiver.

"What's happened? What's wrong? Have they hurt you?"

"No, I…I got out. I ran away."

She closed her eyes, remembering the panic she felt in the basement of the hospital. If she had called Gabriel, what would she have said to him? She swallowed hard.

Fake it, Grayson. You have to make this work.

"You got away from them?" Cain couldn't hide the excitement in his voice.

"I couldn't stand it any longer. I had to get out of there. But they're coming. You have to find me." Her voice shook. She forced it to.

"Where are you?"

"In the trees. I can hide here for a while."

"Tell me more, my precious," he pressed. "Describe where you are."

"There's a long road. And a red barn. The sign says Shadow Crown Ranch."

There was shuffling over the receiver. Cain's breathing was becoming more and more tense. "Stay hidden. I'm coming for you. Stay in the trees."

"Hurry. I'm scared."

"Stay hidden. I will be there soon."

The line went dead. Grayson dropped the phone.

Gabriel appeared out of nowhere, wrapping his arms around her waist and kissing her hair. "Did he buy it?"

She nodded. "He said he'd be here soon. He told me to stay hidden."

Gabriel nodded. "Good. Stay here."

His arms tightened one last time around her, and then they were gone. Grayson whipped around and silently watched him gather his things. Logan was already waiting at the door, his rucksack slung over his shoulder and a black skullcap pulled over his head.

"Let's go, Ryder. Time's ticking."

Logan disappeared out the door and into the already dimming afternoon light. The younger man nodded and moved to follow him.

"Gabriel, wait," she called, grabbing the sleeve of his coat.

He stopped short of the door and faced her.

Grayson panicked. She wanted to tell him to be careful. To not go. To stay with her and call someone else to take care of it.

Something.

Anything.

Instead, she pushed up onto her tiptoes and kissed him. Her lips were trembling. Their pressure was light and timid. If she pressed harder, she knew she wouldn't let him out the door. It would feel like saying goodbye. She still had a rock in the pit of her stomach that she couldn't shake. Something was going to go wrong. She could just feel it.

Gabriel stood still, letting her have what she needed. She knew he could see the tension in her shoulders and feel the fear in her lips. She really was worried about him. When she started to pull away, he wrapped an arm around her waist and pulled her back into him.

Grayson mewled against his lips and closed her eyes.

"Gabriel," she whispered.

"Stay here," he whispered into her ear. "I'll be back soon."

"Please be careful." Her voice was shaky.

"Don't worry. I'll be fine. Stay here. I mean it."

He kissed her forehead and winked playfully, and then he was gone. She waited at the door until she could no longer hear the sound of the SUV's tires echoing off of the gravel road.

54

THE SHADOW CROWN Ranch was a vast, sprawling property on the backside of Snowmass Village, tucked in between the ski resort and the unmarred wilderness of the Rocky Mountains. Rolling fields backed up onto undisturbed wilderness during the summertime, and dozens of horses were free to roam among the wild grass. Those same horses—and their owners—wintered in warmer climates, so now the snow-covered fields were pristine, untouched, save for the tracks of wildlife that wound sporadically across them. One lone dirt road meandered in between the fields like a wild stream, eventually passing by a weathered red barn and disappearing back through the woods.

From their vantage point at the edge of the tree line, Logan and Gabriel had a clear line of sight to both the road and the barn. They were close enough to be within running distance of the barn door, but far enough away to be easily hidden from the road.

Gabriel pulled his gun from the holster underneath his arm and checked the magazine, for the fourth time in an hour.

"Nervous, Wonder Boy?" Logan chuckled under his breath, several trees away.

"He's late," came the reply.

"He'll be here. Be patient."

"I fucking hate waiting."

"Especially when you have something to go back to, huh?"

Ryder shot a look over his shoulder, but just as quickly refocused his attention.

"What? Even I'm human, Ryder," Logan grinned, turning back to the road.

The low rumble of car tires on gravel echoed over the quiet fields, and soon the faint kick-up of dust started creeping over the far hill.

"Get a grip, man. Here he comes."

Logan drew his sidearm and released the safety.

Gabriel slid the magazine back into his gun and chambered a bullet.

They waited silently.

A dark sedan with tinted windows worked its way steadily up the road. It was traveling too slowly, even for the dirt road, and veering off toward the edge quite often. The driver wasn't paying attention to what was in front of him.

Gabriel concentrated on the driver's side window, his fingers clenched steadily around his pistol. His breathing was slow and quiet. Measured. Deliberate.

Come on, Cain. Show yourself.

Eventually, the car slowed to a stop, thirty feet shy of the barn's far side. It idled for several minutes, the tail pipe exhaust curling up in a cloud of white smoke. Gabriel gritted his teeth against the cold.

Come on, asshole. She's too scared to come out. She doesn't know it's you. Come out and get her. Come save her.

On cue, the car's engine died down and the driver's door opened.

Douglas Cain gracefully extracted himself from the driver's seat and stepped out onto the icy dirt road. Everything was quiet. The snow on the fields was untouched. He could see well around the property.

She was here, he could feel it. He smiled to himself. Beatrice, his angel, would come to him in the virgin snow. It was perfect. He shielded his eyes from the ever-diminishing sunlight streaming over the fields from the western mountains.

She must be hiding in the trees. Just like I told her to. Good girl.

He started walking toward the northern edge of the tree line, scanning from side to side, looking for her. He made his way through the long, slender shadows of the barren aspen trees and stopped at the edge of the woods.

"Beatrice?" he called. "It's all right. I'm here. You can come out now."

When his call was met by silence, he walked on, his eyes searching in between the trees to catch a glimpse of her.

"Beatrice?" he tried again.

Still, no answer. Cain kept walking, his senses so intent on catching the smallest motion directly beside him that he failed to notice the two detectives emerge from behind the western tree line.

The sun was at their backs. He couldn't see them.

Gabriel smirked. *Perfect.* When he was within striking distance, Ryder raised his weapon.

"Cain!" His voice cracked through the frigid air, echoing across the fields.

Cain stopped in his tracks, startled, whipping around toward the source of the call. He brought his hand up to shield his eyes against the dying sunlight. He wouldn't have to hold it there for long. The sun was nearly behind the distant mountains.

"Hands on your head and down on the ground! Now!" Gabriel called, motioning toward the snow with the muzzle of his gun.

Logan advanced behind him, his own gun raised. Cain remained stationary. His arms both relaxed down at his sides. He smiled in recognition. He knew these two.

The detectives from the hospital.

They were the ones.

The ones who took her away from me.

He'd known they would follow her. It didn't bother him. His heart rate remained steady.

Oh well. It won't change anything.

Logan advanced several feet, his gun squarely leveled at Cain's chest.

"Second warning, Cain. Hands up, face in the dirt," he boomed.

The man stayed silent, unmoving, the same cold smile plastered on his lips.

Logan pulled up mid-step. Gabriel registered his partner's hesitation and advanced forward just as the last ray of sunshine dipped down below the western mountains. Something was off, and too late, he realized exactly what it was.

No more glare.

Without warning, Cain's hand flew to his side. He pulled a gun from underneath his jacket, leveling it at Logan. Ryder opened his mouth in warning, but the echoing concussion of the gunshot overpowered his call.

Logan stumbled back, gripping his right shoulder. Blood trickled down between his clenched fingers.

Cain's mouth turned up into a satisfied sneer as he advanced toward them, bringing his hand down to fire another shot.

Gabriel shoved Logan to the side and fired two shots, one grazing Cain's scalp and the other his ribcage.

"Drop the fucking gun on the ground. Now." *Why did I say I wouldn't kill this motherfucker?* Gabriel's voice was low and cold. He trained his gun straight on the man's chest. "I said now, asshole."

Cain shook his head, working through the daze and the pain and the ringing in his right ear. When he registered Ryder training down on him, the gun now aimed to kill, not stun, the malice drained from his face. All that remained was fear. He turned, bolting back across the field toward his waiting car. Gabriel turned away and reached out to help stop the bleeding on Logan's arm.

"You idiot, fucking shoot him," his partner hissed, shoving his hand away and raising his 9mm to take his own shot.

Gabriel whipped around, leveling his gun at Cain. He was nearly to the car.

Damn it, he's quick.

Logan's shot went wide, the slug burying into a fencepost. Gabriel fired twice, intentionally shattering the driver's window and windshield of the car. The sound of the splintering wood and shattering glass sent Cain careening toward the barn. He slammed his shoulder into the door and disappeared inside.

"Shit." Gabriel swore and sprinted forward ahead of Logan. They were nearly at the door when shots rang out from the barn.

He ducked for cover behind the blown-out car. Logan veered off around the opposite side of the barn, forcing his back up against the wall.

"What the fuck, Ryder? Where is he?"

Two more shots rang out, and the barn went silent. Carefully, Gabriel extracted himself from the side of the car and made his way to the barn door.

"I thought you said this was going to be easy," Logan hissed, lurching in from the other side.

"I lied." Gabriel smirked. He nodded toward his partner's bloodstained coat. "You gonna live?"

"I'll survive. Move it."

They entered the barn, one behind the other, guns drawn. There was no sign of Cain.

The interior was cool and dark. What light was left from the setting sun filtered in through several windows, casting blue and black shadows across the floor. The back two corrals were occupied by a pair of restless Clydesdale mares, who were stomping the ground and blowing hot steam out of their nostrils.

Gabriel motioned to his left and Logan peeled off, narrowly avoiding the bullet that embedded itself in the wooden support beam next to his head.

"Goddamn it, duck! The fucker's still armed," Harrison yelled, tossing Gabriel a full clip before diving off behind one of the workbenches.

Gabriel fired two shots in the direction of the gunfire. The sound of boots running over wood floors echoed against the walls, then silence. He waited, tucked behind a support beam, his breath curling up around him in the cold air.

And waited. And waited.

The sickening crack of metal hitting bone and a large body hitting the floor ripped through the silence.

Gabriel hastily worked his way around to the far side of the barn, all the while keeping watch for Cain among the shadows. He found Logan face down on the floor, blood oozing from the side of his head and mixing with the scattered bits of hay. A metal crowbar was just out of reach.

God-fucking-damn it!

Ryder crouched down beside him, pushing into his side with all his weight to get him on his back.

Logan groaned as he turned over, opening his eyes to the pain. He reached up and held the back of his head with one hand, then pulled it back to look at the blood across his fingers.

"Son of a bitch," he groaned, shutting his eyes.

"Where is he?" Gabriel growled.

"Fuck if I know."

The sound of wooden boards creaking under too much weight traveled around the stalls. Logan pointed toward the ceiling where sawdust was seeping through the boards.

"Stairs. To the loft," he whispered.

Gabriel nodded, made sure Logan's gun was within reach, then silently worked his way back toward the stairs that wound up toward the loft. The air was quiet and still. Unnaturally so. Someone was holding their breath.

Gabriel moved into the room, gun held at his side. He fished a flashlight out of the back waistband of his pants and turned it on. He raised it in his left hand, his right hand at a ninety-degree angle above it, gripping his gun. He advanced and started systematically sweeping the room.

The beam from the flashlight was making its way back to the center of the room when the crack of the floorboards signaled him to turn around.

There, behind him, flanked by the open blackness of the open end of the loft, was Cain. And he had a gun raised, aimed directly at Gabriel's head. The evil in his face was unmistakable. It oozed out of his eyes like oil. He licked his lips into a sneer as he took a step forward into the light of the flashlight.

"Drop the gun, detective," he hissed.

Gabriel started to raise his gun higher, but a flash of something across Cain's face stopped him.

"Now, now, I wouldn't do that if I were you," he said, turning slightly to look down off of the ledge. "I have a pretty good shot at your little friend down there. It looks like I didn't hit him hard enough with the crowbar. I'd hate to ruin that pretty face with a bullet."

"You don't have the aim for that," Gabriel spat.

"Are you sure about that?" Cain sneered back.

"I'd put two in your head before you even got a shot off."

"Are you really willing to take that chance?"

"You're going to kill both of us anyway, right? Why don't we just get it over with?"

The two men stared each other down, each unmoving and confident. When Cain turned over his shoulder to keep track of Harrison, Gabriel saw his chance.

He threw the flashlight aside and raised his gun, firing twice. The movement gave him away, and Cain threw himself up against a stack of hay bales, his own gun firing blindly into the darkness. His lips curled upward when he heard the cry and muffled curse after his second shot.

Cain peeked out from behind the bales, his eyes now adjusted to the dimmer light, and grinned. He stood to his full height and strode to the opposite side of the loft, picking up the discarded flashlight as he did so. He set the light down on top of another stack of hay and trained it down on the middle of the room.

Gabriel slammed his eyes shut against the blinding light. The pain had forced him to his knees. His right arm was killing him. Searing pain rocketed up through his elbow and into his shoulder. He shielded his eyes with his left hand and opened his eyes.

There was a bullet wound in the center of his right arm, blood trickling onto the wood floor. It still looked straight. He tried to rotate it and swore as the pain returned with a vengeance. It hurt, but everything was moving like it should. No broken bones.

Nothing else for her to fix this time, he thought sarcastically.

Gabriel wrapped his fingers around the hilt of his gun and made a fist. Instantly, the pain returned, and he hissed through his teeth.

Fuck. Okay, not trying that again...

Chuckling from the front of the room caught his attention, and he raised his eyes up into blinding light. Cain was standing over him, his gun trained down on Gabriel's forehead, his eyes alive with triumph.

"Now, let's try this again, shall we?" he mocked. "Your gun belongs to me now. Hand it over."

Gabriel glared at him, flexing his fingers again in an attempt to bring the muzzle off the floor. The searing pain returned, and he doubled over.

"Well, then," Cain's voice carried across the air, "If you just can't lift it, slide it along the floor. You have some experience with that."

Cain smirked as the young man before him cringed at the memory. "I guess that will just have to do."

Gabriel hissed as he pushed his weight into the weapon and sent it sliding across the floor, into a hay bale and out of Cain's reach.

"Pathetic."

Cain kept the gun trained on Gabriel's head as he advanced forward. "You have no idea how long I've waited for this moment. You took her away from me. Twice. There will not be a third time."

"What makes you think she wants anything to do with you, Cain?" Gabriel bit out, fighting against the pain in his arm.

"The sound of her voice. The words she says to me. She calls me her Dante." He grinned. "My Beatrice knows her true love. She is mine."

"She doesn't want you."

"Nonsense." He smiled. "She called me to come and rescue her. She got away from you, didn't she? How delightful. She's out there." He motioned out the lone window in the loft toward the far trees. "She's out there waiting for me. Once I'm done with you, and your pathetic friend, we'll go away together. You won't come between us again."

Gabriel stared directly into the barrel of the gun trained on him. He smiled. "Cain, you're a fool."

That comment earned Gabriel a flash of doubt across his attacker's face and a small but noticeable drop in the gun's trajectory.

Push again.

"She's not out there," he stated, shaking his head.

"Of course she is. She told me herself. I know my beloved's voice."

Gabriel grinned. "Yeah, I'm sure you do. And it was her voice. But she lied to you. She got you to come right where we wanted you to. She did what I told her to." Gabriel smiled wider. "She wants nothing to do with you, you idiot."

Cain snarled and advanced on Gabriel, shoving the gun into his face. "You lie."

Gabriel shrugged in reply. He could see the panic and hatred in Cain's eyes, see the wheels turning over and over inside his head. They were spinning at a furious pace, his anxiety climbing and climbing with each passing moment.

And then, abruptly and unexpectedly, the anxiety disappeared. A sickening calm spread across Cain's face as he refocused on his prey.

"I see it now," he sneered in triumph. "You want her for yourself. You want my Beatrice."

Gabriel's eyes widened. It was only for a split second, but it was a sure signal to Cain that he was right. The doctor leaned closer and lowered his voice.

"She's too good for you. You're a lowly cop. No upbringing. No means. No class. No strength. What would such a woman want with the likes of you?"

Gabriel diverted his eyes to the floor.

Cain continued. "It's going to be wonderful, you know, when my Beatrice and I are finally together. I can't wait to see her, stretched out and begging for me."

Gabriel's face snapped upward, his eyes narrowed and jet black. Dangerous. Cain was too busy talking. He didn't notice.

"How beautiful, her soft skin and pink lips open, all for me. But even more, I can't wait to feel her..."

Gabriel's lips gathered into a vicious snarl. Both hands clenched into fists. The pain in his right arm was completely forgotten, nothing more than a dull hum. He was shaking with rage. Cain was still too distracted to notice him cock up onto the balls of his feet.

"...the feel of taking her for the first time..."

Cain closed his eyes and shivered in anticipation. When he opened them, they were hazy and filled with the lust from his own fantasy. He smirked at Gabriel, who was to him still helpless and cowering on the floor.

"I can't wait to tie her down and hear her beg me to stop."

The barn fell silent. The faint stirrings of the two horses below echoed over the creaking of the floorboards.

All hell broke loose.

Gabriel launched himself off of the floor, catching Cain completely off guard. His shoulder collided with the other man's torso, sending him stumbling backward. The gun went off, but the bullet ricocheted off the floorboards and out into the night air.

Cain fought wildly to get Gabriel off of him but didn't watch his footing. He pitched backward off of the edge of the loft with Gabriel locked onto him, his long arms flailing wildly against the open air.

They smacked into the concrete on the ground floor, one on top of the other. Cain managed to push Ryder off of him and crawl several feet to the wall. He pulled himself up, gripping onto the support beam for dear life. He turned around, gun in hand.

Gabriel swiftly punched him in the face, sending him careening back into a workbench in the corner. The rusted blade of an old scythe sliced across Cain's forehead, sending a bright river of blood into his eyes. He swore under his breath and grabbed the wound, fighting to wipe the sticky liquid from his eyes.

Gabriel lunged again, aiming to take control of the gun. He missed, and Cain's right arm flailed wildly to keep it out of reach. Gabriel's shoulder slammed into Cain's abdomen. He howled in pain, doubling over and coughing up blood. Gabriel struck again, full force, sending them both through the front door of the barn into the night air, into the snow.

Cain kept enough of his wits about him to sucker punch Gabriel in the ribs as they fell. The younger man sprawled out on the gravel, stunned, the wind knocked completely from his lungs.

Gabriel slammed his eyes shut against the pain rocketing around inside his body. Vaguely, he heard Cain clawing and scratching around beside him, desperate to get back on his feet on the icy gravel. But just as suddenly as the scratching had started, it stopped. He waited for Cain to attack, to kick him, to shoot and finish the fight, but nothing came.

He opened his eyes. His gaze settled first on Cain, who was propped up on his elbows twenty feet away, frozen stiff. It wasn't hard to figure out why he wasn't moving. He was staring directly into the twin barrels of a loaded shotgun.

Gabriel's eyes wandered up the glinting barrel. When he realized who was wielding it, his heart stopped inside his chest.

Grayson was standing in front of Douglas Cain, her finger on the trigger.

55

GRAYSON FIXATED ON the cowering figure in front of her. It felt good to be holding a gun again. It felt particularly good to be aiming it at Cain. She steadied her finger on the trigger and sucked in a deep breath.

Her uncle's voice kept repeating over and over in her head.

Deep breath. Shoot with both eyes open. Exhale and fire. Remember the kick.

Technically, she'd learned to shoot with a hunting rifle and not a shotgun, but…close enough.

"Maybe you didn't understand me," she said, her voice calm and collected. "I said, put your hands on your head and your face in the cement. Now!"

"I'd do as she says, you bastard. I'm not wasting my night cleaning your fucking brains off the pavement." Blake Nolan appeared on her left side, his own gun drawn and leveled at Cain's chest.

For his part, Cain sat completely still. Unmoving. Shocked, as if all he knew in the world to be true had suddenly vanished. Angels had turned to demons.

Nolan snuck a sideways glance at Grayson and smirked.

Yup. A look like that on a woman with a loaded gun will do that to you, buddy.

He gestured with his left hand, and two uniformed state troopers, dressed for the winter cold, stepped forward out of the dark. Grayson and Blake kept their guns leveled until Cain's hands were locked in handcuffs and he was on his feet, being led toward the back off a waiting SUV.

He tried to look back at her, even opened his mouth to say something, but the feel of a billy club pressed to the back of his neck was enough to force him into the back seat without a word.

Grayson breathed a sigh of relief and pulled the shells out of the rifle. She glanced over her shoulder and watched Nolan take control of the scene, directing troopers and crime scene techs, as if everything had been well planned.

In reality, he'd shown up at the safe house less than an hour ago, still munching on a hamburger and covered in French fry grease. It hadn't taken long for him to explain. Logan had called him that morning, asking for backup.

Where was Logan, where was Gabe, what the hell was going on, and where was the extra ammunition?

Grayson smiled to herself. Blake had sputtered and stuttered at her when she'd followed him out to his Subaru and run her fingers over the barrel of the shotgun he kept in the backseat. He'd nearly had a stroke when she'd asked to carry it and volunteered to accompany him.

That was something Gabriel still didn't know about her: six cousins, all good ol' farm boys. Her uncle had insisted she learn how drive a stick shift, field-dress a deer, and shoot when she was a teenager, just so she could keep up with them.

Gabriel. Shit, where's Gabriel?

The thought instantly shocked Grayson out of her head. She turned around, searching for him, the rifle crooked over her arm. The patch of snow where he had been was vacant, and there was blood staining the ice-covered stone.

Oh no...

She was just about to yell for Blake to call for another ambulance when she heard a throat clear behind her. She whipped around and found Gabriel staring at her, arms crossed over his chest, his eyes cold and trained straight at her. She held her place, afraid of the outburst she knew was coming, until she saw the blood on his hands and the dark stains on his shirt.

"Oh my God, Gabriel," she whispered as her eyes went wide.

She handed the rifle off to a passing trooper and darted over to him, immediately putting her hands on his arm.

His jaw stiffened at the touch. "What are you doing here?" he ground out.

"Sightseeing," she replied sarcastically, rolling her eyes without missing a beat. "Now shut up and let me see."

"Grayson…" he hissed.

"You can yell at me all you want later, okay? Just give me your arm."

"Better listen to her, buddy," Nolan said, slapping his partner on the back.

Gabriel narrowed his eyes. "Why the fuck are you here?"

"Happy you're alive, too, partner." Blake leaned in and dropped his voice. "Better do as she says. Apparently, she actually knows how to shoot that fucking thing. Who knew?"

Nolan winked and headed toward the entrance to the barn, two troopers and crime scene techs on his heels. Gabriel turned back to Grayson and relinquished his arm.

She instantly took to examining him. "Gabriel, you've been shot!" She pushed his sleeve up over his elbow.

The cold air stung against the open wound. "I'm fine."

She rolled her eyes again and pointed across the street. "Ambulance. Now."

He shook his head. "I'm not going to the hospital."

"You'll go if I tell you to," she said, pulling on his uninjured arm. "You're going to let me have a look at that arm, and if I say you're going, then you're going."

Gabriel opened his mouth to argue with her but thought better of it. He dutifully followed her across the street. The entire stretch was lit up by the flashing red and blue lights of the police cruisers.

He begrudgingly hauled himself up into the back of a lit-up ambulance. The EMTs eyed them suspiciously, but once Grayson explained who she was and what was happening, they were more than happy to help.

Gabriel sat on the gurney and let her work, moving his wrist and fingers when she told him to, keeping still when she told him to. It hurt like hell, but he refused the morphine one of the techs drew up. He took two Tylenol just to keep Grayson from scowling at him.

Thirty minutes later, he was washed out, stitched up, and chock full of antibiotics. She'd dressed his wound with a soft bandage, Nolan had thrown him a new shirt from the trunk of his car, and then they'd both disappeared.

The bullet had clipped a few muscles, but it was really a glorified flesh wound. Soft tissue damage only. No nerve damage. And by the look of the wounds, he'd barely have scars.

Just like my leg.

He absently reached down and rubbed his knee.

He looked out from his new perch on the back step of the ambulance. The threesome ambling precariously toward him was unmistakable. Logan was in the middle, a blanket draped across his shoulders, with Nolan and Grayson flanking him on either side.

Gabriel smirked. At least he wasn't the only one being read the medical riot act tonight. Blake was the first to come within earshot.

"…being an idiot," he finished.

"I'm fine. Thanks, Mom."

"Stop being a stubborn asshole and listen to her, Harrison."

"You'd like that, wouldn't you?" Logan asked, glaring to his left at Grayson.

"Very much so," she nodded, "But since you're going to be just as stubborn as he's been, sit down and let me look at the back of your head."

She nodded toward Gabriel as she spoke, then climbed up into the ambulance with Blake right behind her.

"You're not stitching me up, you animal," Logan griped, plopping down beside Gabriel and glaring at Nolan.

"Shut your mouth and let me learn something," he fired back.

Grayson rolled her eyes. "If you two don't stop fighting, I'm going to turn this car right around and we're not going to Disneyland," she joked.

Logan burst out laughing as she took a seat behind him and started patching up the nasty wound Cain had made with the crowbar.

"You're sure you won't let them do a quick CT scan of your head?" she asked. "You took a bad hit."

"If I start talking funny or suddenly keel over, scan away. Until then, I'm staying away from hospitals. And doctors. No offense."

"Have it your way," she shrugged, grabbing a suture from the laceration tray.

Ten minutes later, Logan was sufficiently stitched back together. He winced as he brought his hand up to the dressing wrapped around the back of his head.

"Don't suppose you can give me something for the pain, huh, doc?" he smiled.

"There aren't any pharmacies open at this hour. How about a glass full of thirty-year-old scotch?" She winked.

"That'll do," he smiled.

"With a head wound?" one of the EMTs balked. "I don't think that's such a good idea, miss."

Grayson shrugged and tapped the back of Logan's head. "He'll keep it to one, boys. Don't worry." She shoved Logan's shoulders. "Go get your interview with the troopers over with, and I'll drive you back to the house. There's a bottle waiting."

Logan smirked and stood up, dropping the blanket off of his shoulders.

"Well, I guess I should do as the doctor ordered," he smiled and grinned mischievously back at his former partner. "You know, Gabe, if she's willing to ply me with scotch when I'm a good boy, who knows what she'll do to you if you behave."

"Oookaaaayyy!" Blake exclaimed, plowing over Gabriel as he jumped out of the back of the ambulance. His cheeks were flaming red. "We're going to go do that statement now. See you two in a bit."

He hauled Logan off toward a waiting blue and white squad car as fast as he could, swearing at the older man and pointing a finger in his face.

Grayson smiled, shook her head, and started tidying up the mess in the back of the ambulance.

Gabriel turned sideways and silently watched her until she was finished. She stepped out of the back of the bus and stood in front of him, hands crossed in front of her.

"All right, let's have it," she said calmly.

Gabriel cocked his head to one side and looked at her, confused. "Excuse me?"

"I told you that you could yell at me later. It's later. So, let's hear it."

"Why would I do that?"

"Oh, well, let's see. You told me to stay at the safe house. I didn't. I promised I would do what you told me to do. I did the exact opposite. But maybe more importantly, I got within five feet of a murdering, delusional psychopath who's been intent on kidnapping me for his own sick fantasies. Oh, and he was diving for a gun at the time." Grayson looked right at Gabriel, a mix of humor and genuine concern in her eyes.

She was trying to keep things light, he could tell, but underneath the façade, she was genuinely nervous. She didn't know what to expect from him, and in her mind, uncontrolled rage was a very real possibility.

The thought made him sick.

She shouldn't be afraid of me.

Grayson danced from one foot to the other, trying to hide her anxiety under the pretense of being cold.

Why isn't he saying anything?

"So…let's start with that and see if we can get anywhere," she joked.

Gabriel held out his left hand and she grabbed it. He pulled her to him. "You're right," he said sternly. "You shouldn't be here."

She dropped her eyes to the pavement, waiting for the hammer to drop.

Gabriel waited a beat, then continued. "It was foolish. Reckless. You could have gotten yourself killed or abducted or worse."

As he spoke, she was constantly nodding, agreeing with him.

"You lied to me, Grayson. You promised me you would stay out of harm's way."

She nodded again and opened her mouth to say something.

Gabriel put a finger on her lips and forced her chin up. She was scared to look at him. His face was cool and measured for a moment. Then his eyes softened and his lips curved into a soft smile.

"And I have never been more proud of someone in my entire life."

Her eyes narrowed, obviously confused at both his words and the lack of anger associated with them.

"Grayson," he soothed, pulling her closer, "as much as seeing you standing in front of Cain scared the hell out of me..." he paused, grinning, "...you should have seen the look on his face. And yours. You shattered his world into a million pieces."

She relaxed into him, and he wrapped his arms around her waist.

"You still shouldn't have come out here," he scolded.

Grayson smiled and reached out, running her fingers around his ear and back through his hair. They both startled when Blake skidded to a stop in the gravel beside them.

"Now, don't you dare start yelling at her, Ryder," he huffed, clearly out of breath. "She came out here because I let her. Grayson, don't let him get away with any bullshit..."

He trailed off when he registered his partner's quirked eyebrows and the young doctor's fingers halfway through his hair.

"...or...I could just get Logan back to the house..." he said, grabbing his coat off of the back of the ambulance and whistling as he walked away.

"Apparently, you're supposed to be nice to me, detective," she smiled.

"Apparently," he nodded. "I'm still curious as to where you got ahold of that rifle."

"Secrets are secrets for a reason."

"Grayson," he scolded.

"Oh, all right," she sighed. "Nolan had it in the back of his car. I grabbed it before he could say anything."

"You know those things kick, right?"

"I shot my first one when I was fourteen."

Gabriel coughed. "Really?"

"You don't believe me?"

"You don't strike me as the type that knows how to shoot a gun, sweetheart," he replied steadily.

She made a face. He chuckled and wrapped his arms tightly around her hips.

"Prove me wrong tomorrow," he said. "Just don't be upset with me tonight."

"Fair enough," she said. She ran her fingers through his hair again, smiling. "You need to stop getting shot, you know."

"I'll work on it."

"Do you have to talk to somebody about what happened? Give a statement like Logan?"

He nodded. "In the morning. I don't feel like it now."

Grayson nodded and pulled back.

Gabriel tightened his arms around her, panicking. Where the hell is she going?

"They need to take the ambulance," she explained softly, nodding toward the front of the bus where the EMTs were answering a call over the radio.

He nodded and stood, pushing away from the vehicle and trying to pull her with him. Grayson twisted out of his arms and shut the back doors, banging twice on the back window when they were closed.

"Clear!" she called.

The ambulance peeled off onto the dark dirt road, sirens kicking on when it was just out of sight over the hill. She stepped back a few feet, directly into waiting, outstretched arms. She startled momentarily, then settled back underneath the warm forearms and an even warmer flannel blanket.

Gabriel backed them up across the street and against the property's weathered wooden fence line. She lazily ran her fingers over his uninjured arm.

"Where's the car?" he asked.

Grayson looked around, then shrugged. "Looks like Blake took it. Must've taken Logan back to the safe house."

"He'll be back," Gabriel replied.

"Okay."

They stood together, warding off the cold in the sea of blue and red flashing lights. Grayson let her head fall back onto Gabriel's shoulder.

"Please tell me this is all over now," she whispered.

"It's over," he whispered back, kissing her temple.

"Do you have to go back to Denver?"

"No. Not right now, anyway."

"Can we stay here?"

"On the fence?" he chuckled.

"No. In the mountains. For Christmas."

He shrugged. "I don't see why not."

"I didn't get you anything, you know."

"Grayson…" He kissed the top of her head and pulled her closer to him underneath the blanket. "I have you. That's all I need for Christmas."

"That's quite a line, detective."

He chuckled again. "Did it work?"

"Yes," she giggled. "It worked."

THE END

Glossary of Medical Terms
(listed alphabetically)

16s: A measurement of IV gauge or size

ABCs: From the ATLS protocol, abbreviation for Airway, Breathing, and Circulation, the first steps in the algorithm

ACL: Abbreviation for Anterior Cruciate Ligament

Amiodarone: An antiarrhythmic cardiac medication

Antecubs: A description of an IV placed in the elbow crease, or antecubital fossa

AP Pelvis: A front-to-back x-ray view of the pelvis

APC-III Pelvis: A severe injury to the pelvic ring resulting in instability

Art line: Arterial line

Articular: As in articular reduction, at the level of the joint

ASIS: Abbreviation for Anterior Superior Iliac Spine, a bony landmark of the pelvis

ATLS protocol: Abbreviation for Advanced Trauma Life Support protocol; the algorithm followed for acute management of life-threatening trauma injuries

Benzodiazepines: A class of medication used for its sedating effect

Bilateral: Both sides, left and right

Borderline hypotension: Blood pressure that is nearly too low

Bounding pulses: Easily palpable, strong pulses

Catheter: A flexible tube inserted to drain fluid, often in the bladder

Chronically: Opposite of acute; for a long period of time

Cirrhosis: A chronic liver disease marked by degeneration of the cells and inflammation, usually caused by alcohol use or hepatitis

CK: Creatine kinase, a muscle protein released during rhabdomyolysis, that contributes to kidney failure

Clavicle: The collarbone

Comminuted fracture: A break in the bone that is in multiple pieces

Compartment syndrome: An increase to intra-compartment pressures within muscular compartments which causes cessation of blood flow and muscle death

DIC: Abbreviation for Diffuse Intravascular Coagulation, a life-threatening change in the ability of the body to stop bleeding

Dilaudid: A strong narcotic pain medication

Displaced: Not properly aligned, as in fracture ends that no longer align with one another

Distal radius: The end portion of one of the forearm bones at the level of the wrist

Divert: To change course

Dressings: Surgical bandages

Dysphagia: Trouble swallowing

ED: Abbreviation for Emergency Department

Electrolytes: Ions, often measured in the blood

Embolization: The process of obstructing a blood vessel with a mass, whether naturally or artificially

Epi: Short for epinephrine

Etomidate: A short acting anesthetic used for induction

Ex-fix/external fixator: A combination of pins and bars outside of the skin that temporarily stabilizes a fractured extremity until definitive fixation can be performed

Exsanguination: A severe and rapid loss of blood

Fasciotomy: Operative release of the fascia tissue surrounding the muscle compartments of an extremity, performed to release pressure within the compartment and prevent tissue death

FAST exam: Acronym for an ultrasound examination looking at four particular intra-abdominal recesses for blood

Femoral nails: A metal rod that is placed inside the femur for fracture reduction and fixation

Femoral neck: A particular anatomic portion of the proximal femur; part of the hip joint complex

Fentanyl: A strong narcotic pain medication

FFP: Abbreviation for Fresh Frozen Plasma, a blood bank component used during trauma resuscitation

Four part intraarticular proximal humerus fracture: A fracture involving with shoulder joint with four separate fracture fragments

GCS 5: Glasgow coma scale score of 5, a sign of significant injury and neurologic impairment in a trauma patient

GI: Abbreviation for Gastrointestinal; pertaining to the gastrointestinal tract

H&P: Abbreviation for History and Physical paperwork, the initial paperwork performed for an admission to the hospital

Hemi: Short for hemiarthroplasty, a partial joint replacement, a common treatment for the hip following fracture of the femoral neck

Hemodynamically unstable: The combination of an abnormal blood pressure, heart rate, oxygenation, and respiratory rate indicating physiologic instability

Hemoglobin: A protein responsible for transporting oxygen in the blood

Hyoid bone: A bone in the anterior neck, often fractured when a person has been strangled

Hypertensive: High blood pressure

Hypotensive: A descriptor indicating low blood pressure

ICU: Abbreviation for Intensive Care Unit

IV PPI's: Abbreviation for Intravenous Proton Pump Inhibitors, medications used to prevent gastric ulcers

Intensivist: A subspecialty physician who works exclusively in the ICU

Interventional radiology: A subspecialty of radiology which specializes in invasive procedures, including embolization

Intra-abdominal injury: An injury to the organs and structures on the inside of the abdomen

Intra-operative fluoroscopy: Use of mobile x-ray during a surgical procedure, common in orthopaedic surgery

Ivy-League gunner: A tongue-in-cheek description of an ambitious, type A college student intent on a particular career goal

Lag screw/neutralization plate: A type of construct used to fix fractures utilizing a particular screw and plate combination

McBurney's point: A location on the right lower abdomen, pain at which may be related to appendicitis

ME: Abbreviation for Medical Examiner; a subspecialty trained pathologist dedicated to the examination of a deceased person in order to determine cause of death

Mercury Cyanide: An extremely toxic salt composed of mercury and hydrocyanic acid

Midline: In the middle; central

M&M: Abbreviation for Morbidity and Mortality Conference; a medical conference examining the patient cases involving death or suboptimal outcome

MVC: Abbreviation for Motor Vehicle Crash

Narcan: A medication used to reverse an overdose of narcotics

Nasogastric tube: A tube inserted through the nose, down the esophagus, and into the stomach, used to introduce or remove fluid from the stomach

Nephrology: A subspecialty dedicated to the kidneys

Neurology: A subspecialty dedicated to the brain

New-onset arrhythmia: Newly diagnosed abnormal heart rhythm

PACU: Acronym for Post-Anesthesia Care Unit; the location where patients are transferred after surgery to recover prior to returning to their assigned hospital room

Palliative: Relieving pain without directing addressing the root cause of the problem, as in palliative care consult for a terminally ill patient

Palliative care fellow: A doctor who is undertaking additional training in the care of the terminally ill and actively dying patient

Pathologic fracture: A break in the bone secondary to abnormally weak bone, commonly due to cancer and metastatic disease

Pelvic binder: A device used to decrease intra-pelvic volume following fracture of the pelvic ring

Pelvic ex-fix: An external fixator applied to the pelvis; see ex-fix

Pelvic packing: A technique used to help decrease bleeding secondary to pelvic fractures which involves placing sterile towels along the pelvic rim inside the body

PGY2's/3's: Abbreviation for Post-Graduate Year; a particular year in residency training

Plate it: To place a plate and screw construct to stabilize a fracture

Platelets: Small, a-nuclear cells involved with blood clotting

Pneumo: See pneumothorax

Pneumothorax: A condition where air becomes trapped outside of the lung but inside the ribcage, causing collapse of the lung

Poly-extremity: Involving multiple limbs

Pressors: See vasopressors

Proximal humerus: The most cephalad portion of the upper arm bone, part of the shoulder complex

PT: Abbreviation for Physical Therapy

Pull traction: Use manual force to pull longitudinal traction on an extremity in order to lengthen and reduce a fracture or dislocation

Renal failure: Damage to the kidneys resulting in a lack of cell function and buildup of toxins in the bloodstream; kidney failure

Rhabdomyolysis: A serious syndrome resulting from muscle cell death and release of damaging proteins into the bloodstream, which can possibly lead to kidney failure

Rodding (as in a femur): Placement of a femoral nail

Sat's: Short for Saturation; intending to describe the level of oxygen in the blood

Sepsis: A state characterized by abnormal vital signs in the setting of infection

Septicemia: See sepsis

Stage-3 shock: A descriptor of vital signs and clinical findings describing a severe level of hemodynamic instability

STEMI: Acronym for ST-Elevation Myocardial Infarction, a type of heart attack

Stitch: Surgical suture

Stress steroids: A particular dosing protocol of intravenous steroid medication

Subclavian vein: A large vein underneath the collarbone that returns blood to the heart

Subspecialty: A particularly specific area of medicine, e.g. cardiology, neurosurgery, orthopaedic surgery

Succinylcholine: A synthetic compound used in anesthesia to induce paralysis for intubation

Syndesmosis: A ligamentous complex at the level of the ankle joint

Syphilis: An infectious disorder caused by a spirochete bacteria

T-waves: A marker on an EKG, or electrocardiogram, which can be normal or abnormal depending on its morphology

Tachycardia: An abnormally fast heart rate

TEG: Acronym for Thromboelastogram; an intricate method for analyzing blood clotting mechanisms in the bloodstream

Tibia: The shin bone, the larger of the two lower leg bones

Tibial plateau: The proximal portion of the tibia; part of the knee joint

Tubed and lined: A descriptor indicating that a patient has been intubated and has had central and peripheral IV access established

Turf it: Patient transfer to another service

Type-1 diabetic: Also called juvenile diabetes; an inability to produce insulin or a defect in the body's ability to use insulin to regulate blood sugar levels

V-fib: Abbreviation for Ventricular Fibrillation; a very dangerous heart rhythm

Vasopressors: Medications given to maintain appropriate blood pressure

VDRF: Abbreviation for Ventilator Dependent Respiratory Failure; a condition in which a patient has been unable to wean off of a mechanical ventilator machine because he/she cannot breathe well enough to maintain enough oxygen in the bloodstream on his/her own

Ventilator: A mechanical breathing machine

Versed: A strong benzodiazepine used for sedation

Weber B Bimal equivalent: A type of ankle fracture often requiring operative repair

Wide mediastinum: A description of the area in the chest containing the heart, bronchus, esophagus, and great vessels; a widened mediastinum can indicate severe injury

Widened pubic symphysis and gapping of the right posterior SI joint: A description of an particular injury pattern to the pelvic ring, including injury to the front and the back of the pelvic ring, indicating instability

About the Author

A. R. Nicole is a North American writer with a background in medicine and a fascination with the written word. Many lazy afternoons are spent either devouring the latest novel, her loyal pup sleeping beside the chair, or writing a new one.

Follow her at:
www.ARNicole.com

Continue on with Grayson and Gabriel in
A.R.Nicole's newest series, *Aftershock*

*It had been over a year. Seventeen months since things
had changed. Seventeen long months for
the fire to smolder below the surface.
There were things almost lost. Almost forgotten.
Almost…*

AFTERSHOCK

BOOK ONE

PROLOGUE

"MARTIN, HOLD DOWN the fort, will ya? I'm gonna go throw some of this shit away before it stinks up the place."

The pale-faced newbie behind the oiled mahogany bar threw his hand up to his face and saluted.

Wrong hand, and wrong salute, kid. But hey, I give you credit for trying.

I slap my hand up to my forehead, the right way, and sauntered out the back exit with a bag of garbage thrown over my shoulder. I hate this menial labor bullshit, but if I leave it until tomorrow night, the hotel manager's going to be giving me shit like you wouldn't believe. The guy's a prick, living off of Daddy's money and Mommy's unwavering alcoholic support. The staff unanimously hate his guts. The only problem is that if I ever tell him that to his face, I'm out of a job and he'll likely get a fucking promotion.

Martin's only been behind the bar a few weeks. He's the newest hire, an attempt by the management to appeal to the metrosexual clientele that comes in here. He's young, poor, inexperienced, and likely to push any rich, bored housewife's buttons. He's perfect … for that. He's just not my kind of guy. Spends too much time thinking about the new *Star Wars* movie and less time thinking about how to get laid. But who am I to judge? I'm an ex-Marine that got slapped with one DUI after Afghanistan. PTSD will do that to ya. The only job I can land now is as a late-shift hotel barman, and I only got it by calling in one hell of a favor.

Don't get me wrong. The job pays well for what it is. And by hotel, I don't mean the Holiday Inn. I mean The Fairtile, one of the most exclusive boutique hotels in Manhattan. Nobody checks into this place under their real name, and it's not because there's a hooker waiting in the room upstairs. It's because too many paparazzi would be waiting outside to sneak a scandalous shot. But listening to the problems of overpaid sports stars and celebrities who are famous for being famous is really starting to get under my skin, you know? I really don't give a shit if the Lamborghini dealership didn't have the car you wanted in chrome. I haven't had a good night's sleep in over three years because of my fucking PTSD and I'm eking out a living in New York City on a little more than minimum wage. Which one of us has the bigger problem list here?

Oh well. Back to the garbage.

I pop the back door and step out into the sticky, humid air of early morning Manhattan. I can feel my cheap white button-down start to stick to my chest as I leave the safety of modern air conditioning. The atmosphere is heavy, thick, full with the promise of summer thunderstorms and the putrid fumes that follow. Everybody says that the rain washes away the filth of the city. No, it doesn't. It just washes it down to the depths where only we, the underpaid and underappreciated servants of the uber-rich, can smell it. Summer rains bring the worst things into the city. I hate them.

The moist concrete clicks against my black patent dress shoes as I make my way over to the dumpster. It's green, like all the others, and already brimming with flies and garbage. I slap my hand over my mouth as I take in my first whiff.

Fucking hell, they need to get this shit out of here more than once a week. Afghanistan wasn't this bad.

Budget cuts, you see. Trash is only removed from local businesses once a week. The elite get it twice a week so the stench doesn't ruin their delicate sensibilities. Most of them don't even know it. They have "people" to take care of such things. The entire thing makes the tattoos on my forearms crawl.

I toss the bag into the pile, ducking and diving to dodge the swarm of flies that shoots up from the shadows. The smell instantly gets worse, and I hold back the bile in my throat.

Goddamnit, what the hell did they toss this week?

And it's only then that I realize that the smell that has me reeling isn't coming from inside the dumpster. It's coming from beside it.

I let the black lid slam down hard on the rusted green metal and force air through the fingers held against my lips. I'm expecting a dead dog, or a big rat ... something rotten and putrid and fucking horrible. What I get is even worse.

I'm not a religious man. I fell out of love with the church after I quit being an altar boy. Even after my tours overseas, all the carnage and the bloodshed and messed-up shit that I've seen, I never found a reason to believe in God. But for the first time since I was six years old, I can't fight it. I hit my knees.

"Jesus, Mary Mother of Christ..."

THE INFERNO TRILOGY
FROM A. R. NICOLE